To: Abby,

PARABELLUM

When you live in Peace; prepare for War

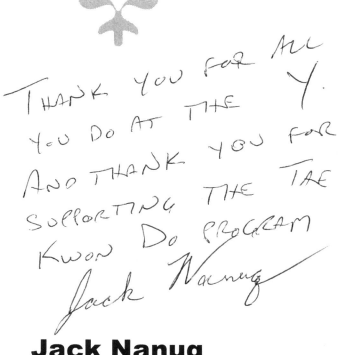

THANK YOU FOR ALL
YOU DO AT THE Y.
AND THANK YOU FOR
SUPPORTING THE TAE
KWON DO PROGRAM
Jack Nanuq

Jack Nanuq

PARABELLUM: When you live in Peace, prepare for War
Jack Nanuq

ISBN: 9781793247988

Jack Nanuq

P O BOX 172
Gallupville, NY, 12073

Ordering Information:
Quantity sales. Special discounts are available on quantity
purchases by corporations, associations, and others. For
details, contact the publisher at the address above.
Orders by U.S. trade bookstores and wholesalers.

Printed in the United States of America.

First Printing, 2019

Front Cover art by Brooke Battista

PARABELLUM: When you live in Peace, prepare for War
                                                    Jack Nanuq

Dedicated to Madelyn Marie Mullins, April 22, 1940 to April 5, 2016. You left a fingerprint on everyone you touched.

PARABELLUM
When you live in Peace prepare for War

BY: Jack Nanuq

CHAPTER 1
December 1, 2000
Albany, NY

Carson Nowak navigated the minefield that was his great-grandmother's attic; careful to step where the random boards were nailed to the joists. The dry-rotted flooring had the structural integrity of toilet paper. No need to crash through the ceiling; that would really set her off. Moldy boxes, piles of clothes and garish Christmas decorations, all covered in layers of dust and pigeon shit, further complicated the task.

He glanced at the map, drawn on the back of a piece of junk mail. The queen of recycling, Nana never threw anything away without finding at least a second use for it. He spotted the old tarp. The steamer trunk should be under that mess. Carson sighed, "Any farther away and it would have been in the neighbor's house."

What the hell am I doing? he thought. Carson had tried to talk her out of this fool's errand, but she insisted it be brought downstairs. When he showed reluctance, she screamed at him in the four languages she knew best. Then in the one she knew the least; English.

"You lazy sunz-a-bitch!"

It stung, even though he knew Nana didn't mean it. Since her last stroke she was quick to anger. "You know better," he responded.

"Go," she pointed a gnarled finger upward.

I guess if I live to be 100, I'll be crotchety too. Probably pissed off because God doesn't want her, he thought.

From the attic he could hear her yelling at the day nurse. Not so much yelling at the girl, as at the television. Curses poured forth. Most in Czech, some in Manx. When she stopped to take a breath Carson could hear CNN commentators discussing the recent election. The US Supreme Court was looking into the count, but it appeared the younger Bush would be the next president.

Nana ranted and raved. She thought him unfit for the job and kept saying "You know what a Bush iz? Iz lady part. Should call him President Puzzy."

The nurse, Haitian by birth, was trying desperately to calm the old woman. Carson knew this because she was speaking French. A language both women shared. He didn't understand the words, but they were melodic. That might just calm the older one.

What has got into her? he thought. "Iris change the channel to QVC! That might help!" he shouted.

When I'm done here, I'm taking Nana for a hot fudge sundae. Her doctor would suggest an anti-anxiety pill, but he knew ice cream worked better than drugs.

He pulled the tarp aside and grabbed the handles of the trunk. *Jesus, what's in here… gold?* He hadn't expected it to be heavy. He summoned his strength and grunted. *Newton's First Law of Motion; a body at rest will remain at rest until acted upon… or something like that.*

The old woman was yelling again, the nurse now crying. Different languages ricocheting around the house like a car crash in front of the UN.

He thought about leaving the trunk there and rescuing the nurse. She didn't deserve this but he suspected he'd have to come back later. *Get it together Carson, man up and soldier on.*

Ten minutes later he lumbered into the kitchen. The trunk banging against his shins. A sweat soaked shirt plastered to his chest. The room smelled of chicory and chicken soup. The old woman shut up immediately and beamed. Her doughy features brightened. The skin usually the color and texture of a white coral beach was now rose-tinted.

The younger woman smiled, "I get you a beer." Her skin was cinnamon and satin.

"Thank you," he said and smiled back.

"Nana, you have to be nicer to Iris. She doesn't need this grief and doesn't know your ways."

"You good boy, tank you," she said staring at the trunk.

"Now apologize to Iris."

5

"Vaat?"

"Apologize right now or I'll take this back upstairs."

Iris brought him a Genesee Cream Ale. "It okay," she whispered.

"No, it's not," and he sat on the trunk.

"You move." Nana tried to push him away.

"No, apologize!"

"Ok...I sorry." It was half-hearted. He knew that was the best they could hope for.

He cupped the woman's face in his hands, "You know I love you, and am only stern with you because it is for your own good." Parroting the words, she had used on him for four decades.

The old woman patted his cheeks and moved to a kitchen drawer. She came away with a ring of keys and a twenty-dollar bill.

She handed the money to Iris and again said "I sorry." This time the apology was genuine. The old woman fumbled with a brass skeleton key and handed it too Carson.

"You open."

The trunk was packed full of ledgers and notebooks. On top was a lumpy leather bundle.

Nana pointed to the oddity and said "Table." She then took a seat in an old wooden chair.

He picked up the package. It was heavy and metallic. *A wrench maybe,* he thought as he set the bundle down on the kitchen table.

She unwrapped the mystery package. It contained a C-96 Mauser broom-handle pistol and a silver cigarette case. She slid the gun toward Carson. "Careful, iz loaded." She said it with the nonchalance of a counter guy at McDonalds.

Nana then picked up the other item. With trembling hands, she popped it open. Inside was a black and white photo of a German soldier, in front of a sidecar motorcycle. She handed the photo to Carson. Except for the eye patch, the man in uniform could have been Carson's twin.

PARABELLUM: When you live in Peace, prepare for War
                                                    Jack Nanuq

CHAPTER 2
Isle of Man
April 1, 1915

The 15-year old newcomer struggled out of her bed and stepped onto the stone floor. The surface was cold but not unbearable. She would leave in a few minutes and there was no reason to light the coal stove. No need to waste a precious resource for a few minutes of comfort. She crouched next to the bed and retrieved her diary and pencil.

1ˢᵗ April 1915 - Today is my birthday and I have been a widow for seven days. I have yet to tell his parents. What should I say? I know what I want to say? But what words should I use? Should I tell them he was a weakling? A sniveling whiner unfit for adulthood or responsibility. He got a blister his first day of real work and it got infected. Who dies from a blister? Should I say I hate him, even in death I hate him. I hate the entire family! If it hadn't been for him and his father I'd be home right now! I'd be safe and warm, not in this foreign land.

This is what I want to say. But, how can I? The censors would never let it get to the Motherland. They would think me deranged and evil. How could she talk ill of the dead, they would ask? Would they think I'm mad? They might lock me up and life will be even harder. No, I must hide my true feelings. I will not lie to them, but I will not be entirely honest either. Tonight, I will write the in-laws and tell them of his departure. Let them grieve for him for I will not.

A kangaroo kicked inside her abdomen and reminded her of the upcoming arrival, one more month. She prayed for a girl. Maybe after the War her daughter could be a dancer? *Will this war ever end? Will we ever see peace?*

She looked outside. The sky over the Irish Sea was multi-shades of blue and charcoal. Fluffy clouds with pastel tinges enhanced the image. Gulls and songbirds celebrated the approaching day. A distant bugle from Camp Knockaloe signaled reveille. The Camp was home to over twenty thousand POWs.

She patted the bump of her midsection and returned to the journal.

My dearest little one;
One day I will tell you all. I will tell you how you came to be born in captivity. I will tell you of your grandfather the cobbler, your grandmother the gymnast. You will know of my family, the good ones.

The widow examined the book. Written in her own version of shorthand, confident only she could decipher the code. Strange cursive tracks that more closely resembled those made by worms in fresh dirt, than any known language. She closed the book, slid it under her nightstand and moved to the wash basin.

She slipped out of her nightgown and cleaned the areas that needed to be refreshed. Then she dressed in her work clothes. Before leaving the room, she threw a black shawl over shoulders.

She walked the lane to the Church of St. Maughold. Sunrise service would start in a few minutes. She made it a point to attend Mass daily. Cows were drifting across green pastures, changing grass into milk; their pungent aroma reminiscent of her original home. A light spring rain, more fog than precipitation, put dampness in the and enhanced the aroma. She pulled the shawl over her head as a black clad figure entered her peripheral vision.

Fr. Fagan, announced his arrival with *"Moghrey mie."*

She recognized the Manx greeting but hadn't yet mastered the dialect, so she responded in broken English. *"Guden* morning to you too Father."

He switched to English.

"It won't be long, will it, Maria?" glancing briefly at her swollen middle.

"About four weeks, the mid-wife tell me."

9

"We be all praying for you. Especially since it is so soon after ye loss." The priest made the sign of the cross.

"My people have saying… 'The dead stay with the dead and those alive stay with those alive.' I am much sorry. It not well translate."

"I understand. Ye be doing well then?"

"Dah, yes, tank you."

They reached the Church and he held the door for her. She shook the water from her shawl and stepped inside. Three nuns and three parishioners were kneeling in the front pew. Sister Veronique's rosary beads were tapping ever so slightly against the woodwork. They echoed inside the almost empty building.

You do that to draw attention to your devotion. Good for you. May you never learn that everyone knows that's what you're doing, the young woman thought.

After their morning Service, Maria and the three nuns walked to the rectory. The air was bright and full of life. The rain gone, the dampness chased away by warm spring breezes.

The group moved at Sister Veronique's pace. She shuffled in her sandals, a blackthorn cane steadying her crooked frame. She scanned the hills. A petrified mole, with two wild hairs set squarely on her chin.

"If only Palestine had been this green I'd have stayed. It might be the land of our Lord's birth, but it was as brown as a sunbaked turd." Her English had a Normand accent.

Maria thought about her brief visit to the Levant. She would always remember it as the place she was taken into custody and where she got pregnant, but not in that order. Her father-in-law had insisted they visit the Holy Land, and other places, before Gregor started his studies.

∞

At noon the women of the rectory heard a pony cart on the cobblestone lane. Maria peaked out a window. Three men stood in front of the small animal. The cart was approximately 4 feet wide and 6 feet long. A large bundle took up half the cargo space.

10

A British soldier wearing a starched khaki uniform with chevrons, and a large holster knocked on the door. The two men with him wore threadbare uniforms of the Kaiser. These men, not much older than Maria, had the look of heeled dogs. Not beaten but respectful and wary. Neither carried any extra weight and their clothes hung loosely like ill-fitted sacks.

The Brit was about a head taller and two stone heavier than his charges. The shorter men were heavy boned but only shells of their former selves. Given the desire they might have been able to overpower the guard, but it was doubtful such desire existed.

But where was there to run to, this is an island? Maria thought. *I think about running also.*

These men with their high cheekbones, flat noses and round blue eyes beamed when they saw her.

"Good afternoon, how may I help you?" the nun asked.

"Would yee be Sister Clarice?" the Brit asked of the youngest nun.

"I would."

"Corporal Miles Davis, at your service. We are from the Camp. These two gentlemen are guests of King George. We've just come from the docks and brought you a gift."

He pulled aside a tarp that covered a large Grey Seal. Water dripped from the animal. "Mr. Cavendish, of the trawler *Newcastle* caught this by mistake. He told me to bring it to you. Says you're from Norway and would know how to prepare the beast. Folks here on the Island don't eat seal and he didn't want to see it go to the dogs."

"That be true, have the boys take it over to that tree and I'll show them how to butcher it."

"I'm afraid they can take it over there, but we cannot be staying to help."

"What do you mean you can't help? That animal must weigh 200 kilos."

"I'm sorry. Sister the lads are expected back at the Camp this afternoon. If we don't get back soon the Commander will think they've escaped. We wouldn't want to cause an incident now, would we?"

The Camp had an agreement with the Islanders. Scores of prisoners went out on work details, with an escort. They filled a need since most able-bodied men were serving in the trenches.

"If I could get word to the Camp, that your services are required, would that suffice?"

"I don't know about that."

"Let me put it too you this way. We are Sisters of Mercy and Charity. If you agree to stay and help, my second act of charity would be to ensure you and the boys have a good meal."

"Ye say that would be your second act of charity. What might ye first act of charity be?"

"My first act of charity would be to share a glass of Jameson, with you."

"Aye, that'd be good. Who am I to stand in the way of charity? The lads could use a good meal, all they get is fish and boiled spuds. I'm just lookin out for their best interests, understood?"

"Understood," the well-traveled nun said. She turned toward the rectory.

"Maria."

"Dah, yes sister," she said as she walked toward the group.

"Would you please take a note to the Camp Commandant?"

"Yes, sister."

"And take a basket. Pick some wild greens on your way back. we'll have them with supper."

"Yes, sister."

Two hours later an exhausted Maria returned to the rectory, her basket full of fresh shoots and leaves. The walk had not been hard but the constant bending to pick the bounty had put a strain on her back. The hoped-for dancer was now bouncing around like a rugby player.

12

When she returned to the rectory it had a festive mood. An outdoor table had been set for a party. The air ripe with the scent of frying meats and boiling vegetables. A light breeze kept bugs at bay, and songbirds were extra vocal. Chickens clucked happily as they scratched and pecked at tidbits under the butchering tree.

The two prisoners hummed and moved about lively. Happy to have performed honest work and anticipating a well-earned meal. Both had shed their tunics and were down to their shirt sleeves. Their gaunt frames clearly visible. Ribs and arm bones wrapped in sinew. Suspenders held their trousers in place; almost five inches of unused waist showed clearly. Neither had the distended stomach of malnourishment but also absent was any hint of extra substance. The sun had started to ripen their pasty complexions. Both men smiled at her but neither spoke. Maria nodded and walked into the kitchen.

"Maria, you are just in time," said Sister Clarice. "As soon as the greens are cooked, we'll be ready to eat. Here, let me take that, you sit down."

"No, I'm fine."

"Now don't be silly, and if you keep that up you will need to go to confession for lying to a nun," Sister Clarice grinned.

"Take a break, while I clean these. What have we got here? Dandelions, chickweed, lambs quarter; wonderful mix. I'll sauté them with bacon." She said as she handled the greens.

"Sister, can I ask you a question?"

"Certainly, what is it child?"

"Why do the prisoners not talk?"

"They're not allowed to, neither speaks English. They are under orders not to speak German. People fear they might be planning an escape or something of that nature. I'm sure they're not the evil devils everyone portrays them to be, but who am I to go against the Crown?"

"But they not German."

"What do you mean they're not German?"

"I from Prague. They be Slovak."

13

PARABELLUM: When you live in Peace, prepare for War
Jack Nanuq

CHAPTER 3
December 1, 2000
Albany, NY

Carson's eyes bounced from the photo to the gun, to the photo, to the gun. Both items fought for his attention. The trigger guard stared at him like a metallic eye; just as the man in the grainy image did. Curiosity pushed his hand to the butt of the pistol. The gun had clearly seen some use. The grips were mismatched. One being hard rubber and the other hand carved wood. Not carved as in decorative manner but in a crude functional manner. There was a gouge in the steel frame at the edge of this grip. As if a bullet or shrapnel had hit the weapon, possibly destroying the original rubber grip.

This type of weapon had seen service in almost every theatre of war, during the past century. Almost two million, including unlicensed copies, were manufactured; testifying to its serviceability.

"Nana, where the hell did you get that gun?"

"Iz nudding," she waved a hand casually. She stared at the man with the eye patch.

What do you mean it's nothing, it is something, a very big something! Carson's brain screamed silently.

This train of thought was derailed when his alpha pager buzzed. He covered the gun with his left hand while he grabbed the gadget with the other. The message read "Ice Cream at 4 PM." He would barely have time to make the appointment.

"Shit," he mumbled. "Nana, I gotta go. I'm taking this with me." He bent over and kissed her on the top of the head. Taking firm possession of the Mauser.

She was staring at the photo and barely acknowledged him. She dismissed him with a waved hand.

"I love you too," he said, as he exited the room.

Before he left the house, he went into the basement. There, he cycled the action of the gun six times until it locked open on an empty magazine. A half dozen brass cartridges bounced off the concrete floor. The necked cartridges resembled miniature Coke bottles. The casings were green with corrosion, clearly not safe for action. He used a thumb to rub away some of the debris at the base of a cartridge. The markings were illegible, but he knew it should read 7.63x25mm. The bullet diameter was 7.63 mm (30 cal.) and the brass casing was 25 mm long. When the primer was struck, the powder would propel the 85-grain bullet at around 1400 feet per second. Many said this was the most powerful handgun until the advent of the .357 magnum. He stuffed the gun and ammo into a garbage bag and then inside his jacket.

∞

His Subaru Forester bounced westward down Central Avenue. Snow was falling and his wipers squeegeed pavement piss from the windshield. Central Avenue became State Street at the Albany/Schenectady city line. It was clear when he crossed into Schenectady. Department of Public Works was letting traffic keep the road open. No sense in getting out the equipment when the public was doing their part to plow the roadway.

Carson thought about the message on his pager and its secret meaning. Four PM really meant 40 minutes and ice cream meant the normal meeting spot. They rarely met more than once a month and they had just met three days ago. He wondered what was up.

The meeting spot was a small Mexican restaurant that had good food, no cameras and most importantly; a back door. As he pulled in the lot, he took note of the two mini-vans. To the uninitiated they looked like the kind driven by a soccer mom. He knew there was a small arsenal and high-tech communications gear in each. The windows were tinted but he could see the silhouette of someone in the back seat. The occupants would guard the contents until the drivers returned, after the meeting.

He parked his car and made a point of kicking loose the gray and black snow turds that had accumulated behind each wheel. The car had a logo that matched his jacket; Hawkeye Property Management.

The cold and dampness was working its voodoo on his hip. The pins that held his femur together felt alive and hungry. He looked at the restaurant and thought maybe he should just spend another night with Lena. Let the sexmorphins chase away the pain.

He scanned the area for anything out of place and walked inside. Just like the mini-vans, the couple sitting in the rear, were not what they appeared. The short blonde woman, Maggie Post, was 53 but looked a decade younger. She spoke three languages, was a master of Mixed Martial Arts and the Boss of Operations. Equal parts smart and tough, illustrated by the fact she had her back to the wall.

Her companion was a scruffy looking white male who wore a sun-bleached Carhartt jacket, frayed at the cuffs and collar. Although dressed like a janitor he was their number two. He sat to the right of the woman and had a visual command of the room.

Carson took a seat across the table, careful not to block the other man's view. He pulled the package from his jacket and slid it toward the man.

"Fred, I brought you a research project. I want it back and want to know if it has a history."

The man hefted the plastic wrapped package and recognition flashed across his face. As he slid it inside his own jacket, he said "I'm not gonna shoot my balls off, am I?"

"Not likely…. you'd probably miss from that range."

"Oh, aren't we the comedian today. Here check out today's specials," as he handed a menu to the younger man.

"That's okay. I know what I want, same as last time."

"Oh Jesus, why can't you eat regular Mexican food like the rest of us. You know, a greasy burrito with orange stuff that runs down your arm."

"If I wanted that, I'd go to Taco Bob's."

The woman spoke for the first time. "Carson, just take a look at the menu. You can order what you want, but just look at the menu."

17

"Got it," he said with deference and respect. He opened the menu and found a buff colored envelope. The item flew inside his jacket with a sleight of hand that would make a card shark envious.

She continued. "We bought you a cabin in Willsboro, on Lake Champlain. It will be used as a safe house. We need you to furnish it and give it a lived-in look. Keys and money are in the envelope."

He nodded in acknowledgement.

They stopped talking as the waitress approached the table. She had the legs and body of a volleyball player. Her blouse was embroidered with the letters L-E-N-A.

"Senor Carson, you are back," she said teasingly. "Can I get you something to drink?"

"I think we're ready to order. Maggie, am I right?"

"I'll have a bowl of pozole and coffee," the blonde woman responded.

"Bueno," said the waitress as she turned toward Fred.

"I'll have a gordita and coffee."

"Bueno," said the waitress as she slowly turned toward Carson.

"Pulpitos Guisados," Carson responded, as he stared pointedly at Fred.

The other man grimaced and scrunched his face as Carson added "Mucho caliente, por favor."

"Bueno, muy bueno. Coffee?"

"Yes, gracias."

When the waitress departed Maggie continued the conversation. "We need a place to debrief some Bosnians. It's remote, but with good access. You've got a week to have it ready."

Lena arrived with their coffees and the conversation ceased again. As she served everyone she added "Lunch ready soon."

As she walked away Fred changed the subject. He looked at Carson and said, "So…you and her?"

"A couple of times, nothing serious. It's awkward, my Spanish is worse than her English."

As if she knew they were talking about her, Lena returned with their meals. She served Carson first and smiled at his order. She gave him a look that said, "Not many gringos order that."

Carson stirred his stew with a fork and then speared a small cephalopod. He waved it playfully at Fred. He put it back in the bowl and cut a tentacle into bite size morsels.

Fred looked at him and sternly said "There's a reason why the Latin name for that is *Octopus Vulgaris*. Note the word vulgaris. Need I go on?"

Maggie interrupted and admonished Carson for playing with his food. "You guys are worse than my kids. You'd think after ten years you'd be nicer to each other," she said with a smile.

Both men stopped the banter and dug into their meal.

Five minutes later the boss's phone rang. Her side of the conversation was clipped and terse. She snapped the phone closed, stood and said, "Fred, we gotta go."

A single step and the back door was within reach. She turned and barked, "Call when the house is ready." She emphasized this with a thumb and pinky to her face.

Carson stayed and finished his meal. He thought about his relationship with the older man. Fred was the closest thing he had to a brother and they shared a bond as if it was genetic. They each had a deep-seated need to put the other in their place not due to insecurity, but due to love. The love of one who's life had been saved.

Carson laid a hundred-dollar bill on the table. With a Sharpie he wrote CALL ME. He left through the back door.

PARABELLUM: When you live in Peace, prepare for War

Jack Nanuq

CHAPTER 4
December 1, 2000
Albany, NY

As the damp air hit his face, he planned his next assignment. The metal work in his leg barked and immediately put him in a foul mood. Someone was about to feel his wrath. Climbing into the car he spoke to his cellphone. "Call Office."

"Hawkeye Management," the voice answered.

"Stephanie it's me, I need you to make some calls for me."

"Sure."

"First, call the Zoo." He was referring to a local biker bar. "Have the boys meet me at the Clinton Avenue property. I'll be there in half an hour. Number two, call James and have him bring a moving van. Number next, call around and find another five or six people for a cleanout. I'll pay OT and buy dinner."

"Ah boss...you're not gonna evict someone this close to the holidays, are you?"

"Let's call it an intervention."

"If you say so. I'll take care of it." Stephanie said as she ended the conversation.

Carson then dialed 555-1212.

"Directory Assistance. City and State." an automated voice answered.

"Ticonderoga, NY"

"Business or Residence?"

"Business. Temp Agency"

He was given a number for a listing and told "Please dial or say One to place your call."

"One," he shouted.

After some clicks and beeps a live voice came on the line.

"Thank you for calling Temp-Staff. This is Amber. How can I help you?"

He introduced himself as Robert Lake and explained he would need three or four lumpers to unload a moving van. He'd also need the same number of women to help set up the cabin.

She assured him she could do that.

"Thank you Amber. The van will be there tomorrow morning, at 9:00. Hang on and I'll give you an address." He tore the envelope open with his teeth and shook the contents onto the passenger seat. A bundle of hundreds, a set of keys and a handwritten note fell free. He read her the address and then gave her a credit card number belonging to the fictitious Mr. Lake. The transaction complete, he hung up the phone.

He then placed a call to Iris.

"How's Nana doing?

"She napping now. Something wrong, is wrong. She take the photo to the couch and cry herself to sleep."

"Let her rest. I've got to work late tonight. Is there any chance you can stay over?"

"I stay only to midnight, no later. I have to watch nieces tomorrow."

"Perfect, I should be done around 10 o'clock. I'll stop by briefly around five and bring dinner. How's Chinese sound?"

"How you say? … Deal."

"Thanks."

He hung up the phone, grabbed the bundle of bills and turned onto Clinton Ave. A black GMC crew cab pick-up truck was parked near Livingston St., in front of a nondescript brick rowhouse. He pulled in behind the truck. Three of the largest men in the Capital Region emerged from the vehicle. Somewhere a football team was missing its defensive line. The truck seemed to groan in appreciation as the men got out.

Carson nodded to Panther, Rhino and Wookie. "Thanks for coming, this shouldn't take long, just follow my lead."

The men strode to the front door of the rowhouse. Toys and other crap was scattered around the yard. It would take a lot more snow to hide the trash from view. Carson's anger increased as he closed in on the structure.

A kid, about ten years of age, bolted out the front door as the group hit the porch. Panther grabbed him and said, "Your old man home?"

"He aint my old man. I'm just making a delivery. Asshole's in the kitchen."

The four walked inside, without knocking. Carson led the way. Through the living room and straight to the kitchen. Two people were in the living room, sitting on the couch and watching Sponge Bob. A woman who looked forty but was really only twenty. She'd been ridden hard and put away wet, too many times. The second was her son, about seven years old. The residents froze in place as the men moved to the rear of the house.

Carson saw the meth-head doing a line on the kitchen table. He grabbed a handful of hair and slammed the face into the Formica top. The prey flailed about like a snake trapped by an experienced handler. The bottom half of its body twisting and turning without effect, the head pinned to a single spot.

Sounds seemed to emanate from the table. Something like "I'll ookin kill you. Led go a me. Beech." The voice more fear than venom.

Carson nodded to Wookie and Rhino. Each grabbed an arm and the creature ceased squirming.

"I'm here for the rent," Carson said, as he let go of the scumbag's greasy head.

"You didn't get my check?" the druggie said, with false astonishment.

"If, and I repeat if, there ever was a check, you just snorted it up your nose. You've been here six months and I've had to chase you, for the rent, every one of them. I've grown tired of this game. You're leaving today."

"You can't do this. I'll sue you."

The three big men burst out laughing and stomped their feet. Carson elected not to respond. The house shook, and plaster fell from the walls. When the behemoths regained their composure, Carson continued. "The boys here are gonna put you on a bus, to your momma in South Carolina."

"What about my family, you gonna put them out too?"

"That's funny! You give a shit about them. Probably got the girlfriend turning tricks to support your habit. She and the kid will be going also. You got 10 minutes to clear out, bus leaves in 60."

"What about my stuff?" Snot and blood trickled onto his upper lip.

"It stays. I'll put it toward the money you owe me."

"I don't know about the bus. I get car sick."

"Jesus, you're a piece of work. Good thing I was a Boy Scout." He pulled out two packets of Dramamine. "Here take these." Four tablets were deposited on the table.

"Take them all." This wasn't Carson's first rodeo.

"Can I have something to drink?" He appeared resigned to his fate. His mood brightened when a beer was fished from the fridge.

Twenty minutes later the family trouped out of the house for the last time. The doper was a zombie now. The heavy dose of **Dimenhydrinate had worked its magic.**

Panther climbed into the driver's seat. He glanced at the druggie menacingly. "He better not get sick in my ride." The others pushed the man into the back seat.

As the girlfriend tried to climb in Carson put hand on her arm. "You and the kid will ride with me." The color drained from her face. "Don't worry, you'll be safe." Carson added. "I'll be back in a minute," he said, as the moving van pulled up. He pointed to his Subaru and said, "That's mine."

The van driver climbed out. "Jamie, you know the drill, everything goes," Carson directed. "Have Tina box up all the non-perishables. We'll load them into my car when I get back. Dirty laundry and bedding to Mrs. Cho's. Everything else in the truck. I'll be back in a couple of hours."

He marched to his car. He noted the woman and child standing on the passenger side. As Carson climbed into his car, he heard the boy say, "I'm supposed to be in a booster seat."

24

"I don't have a booster seat. We'll pretend you're a big boy. Climb in."

"Okay," said the little voice.

Carson then turned to the woman. "Sharon, have you and the kid eaten?"

She shook her head. He hadn't thought so.

"McDonald's okay?"

She nodded. "Are they gonna hurt him?" She pointed to the black truck as it pulled away.

"Do you want them to?"

"I don't know." She said as she opened the front passenger door.

"That's fair... no they won't hurt him unless he refuses to get on the bus."

"Where are we going?"

"McDonald's, I thought you guys might be hungry." Carson said as he pulled away from the curb.

"No... after that." She had the vacant look of an earthquake survivor repeatedly tortured by aftershocks. He felt sorry for the woman. She was guilty of making poor life choices. *But who among us was innocent of that offense. Her decisions just had harsher consequences than others,* Carson thought.

"I can put you on the bus, with him, unless you want to go somewhere else? Where's your people?"

"My mom's in Buffalo and my sister's in Jacksonville."

"How about Florida then... get you out of the cold?"

"Okay, but I got no money."

"It's on me. Ever been on a train?" He handed her $1,000 and added "Merry Christmas."

They were stopped at a traffic light and the stereo in the neighboring truck, blared MOLLY HATCHET'S "Flirtin With Disaster." Carson nodded at the driver and thought *how appropriate.*

PARABELLUM: When you live in Peace, prepare for War

Jack Nanuq

CHAPTER 5
Isle of Man
May 8, 1915

Maria took a seat at her writing desk about one hour before sunset. Sister Veronique had let her retire early because the day had been a busy one. She opened her journal and began her entry.

8th May 1915 - My beautiful baby boy is now a week old. I had been so certain he would be a girl, but I could not be happier. He is named for the greatest man I've ever known.

Oh Tata; how I miss you. I have asked God to give you the job of Janos' Guardian Angel. Please help him be the person you were, not the petty thug his father was, and definitely not the gangster his other grandfather is.

There is so much I want to tell you about Janos. He is beautiful, but he has already given me fits of panic. When he was born, he was 7 lbs., with wisps of blonde hair and the most brilliant blue eyes. The next day he was jaundice. That lasted three days. With the Dr's help it cleared up. At the same time, he was losing weight. I was out of my mind with fear. Everyone told me this was normal, but I didn't believe them. When he got to 6 lbs. 3 oz he started to gain again. He is now 6 lbs. 6 oz. Can you believe it, an ounce a day, at this rate he'll be 30 lbs. by the end of the year?

I wish he could know you personally. If only you had not been taken from us. I miss you so much, your strong arms, your sing-song voice, the smell of your pipe as you toiled in your shop. Now I need your wisdom.

Within the next day or so I must complete the Birth Certificate. Sister Veronique says I must show Gregor as the father. If I don't Janos will be considered a bastard. I can't do that too him, but I don't want him to know about his father or have his name.

Life here is getting better. I am still homesick, but I am resigned to not seeing Momma until the end of the war. The nuns here are good to me. They are teaching me English and more importantly, at least to them, how to cook. They all shake their

27

head when I tell them I spent more time in your shop than momma's kitchen. Sister Clarice calls me a Tomboy.

Maria had been a single child, a rarity in a Catholic community. She and her father shared a special bond. She was both daughter and son to him. Always at his side, her brain a sponge to everything he said. Soaking up every lesson he shared with her.

He had been a skilled harness and shoemaker. He had taught her the intricacies of leather. How steer hide was stronger than cow hide, the suppleness of goat leather, the texture of pigskin.

He died at an early age and at the hands of another. His death set off a complex chain of events that no one could have foreseen, least of all the murderer. Depending upon how you looked at it, one might say the murderer had even brought about the death of his own son. It was cliché, but God does not like ugly. That is a story for another time.

Maria paged through the journal. This brief entry had been the first she had been able to make in the past eight days. She had been surrounded by others since shortly after her water broke.

The entries over the past month had been full of all sorts of details, especially when the men from Camp Knockaloe visited. Father Fagan had spoken with the Commandant and made it known there was much work to do at the Church and Rectory. Roof repairs, gardening projects, fence building, etc. The prisoners came once a week and were paid 14 pence for their labor. They always worked hard at these times and were rewarded with a big meal.

One entry read … *Today I learned they are Petr and Andrej, and both are from small farming towns. At lunch I kept catching Petr smiling at me. He's handsome with turquoise eyes and blonde hair…*

Many of the pages had large boxes drawn on them. These boxes held recipes. She did this so that it would be easier to find them in the future. There were recipes for: Liver with

Onions, Rabbit with Polenta, and even the national dish of Kippers and Potatoes.

She was sliding the journal back into its hiding spot when suddenly a storm blew out of the South and rainwater splashed through the screens. *Where did that come from?* She thought, as she moved to close the windows.

Maria grimaced as things were stiff and sore down below. Plus she was still getting used to wearing a nappy. By the time she got the windows closed her night dress was soaked to the elbows and the floor was slippery. The room was now dark, damp and cold. She lit a candle and then put tinder and kindling into the coal stove. She applied the candle flame to the pile and stepped back to watch it take on a life of its own. When its survival was certain she heaped a shovel full of coal on top of the burning wood and closed the door of the stove. Maria then changed into dry clothes, climbed into bed and blew out the candle.

She was almost asleep when a loose shutter banged against the house. It sounded like a cannon shot and she crab-walked to Janos' crib; certain he would be frightened. Instead she found him awake, wide-eyed and listening intently to Nature's fury. He seemed to be fascinated by the symphony of rain and wind. Thunder boomed, and he smiled. Maybe *Tata* was here, and Janos knew he was safe.

She cradled him in her arms and the room took on the scent of saddle soap and lanolin. Janos cooed softly, and she thought briefly of giving him a teat. But she couldn't disturb the scene, it was love personified.

Tata look at your grandson, your Vnuk, she thought.

A soft knock at the door alerted her to a visitor.

"Come in."

The door opened slowly, and Sister Veronique stuck her head inside. She was carrying an oil lamp and a thermos bottle. "I just wanted to see how you were doing."

"We're fine."

"I brought you some coffee, it's not real coffee, of course. Those devils have torpedoed another freighter. Oh, I'm sorry! I shouldn't speak of your people that way."

The tempest that roiled forth did so with the intensity of the storm that had just blasted off the Irish Sea.

"I nod German! Juzz because I have German name, does nod me German make! I be Czech! Always will be! I hade Germans! Day are why I here. I should be home...home with mama. They are cause of diz. Those devils, az you say, are da cause of all dis. They taken every ting from me. And taken every ting from her. She haz nudding because of dem. No huzban, no daughter, no bizniss, no land. She iz down to one old milk cow. She live on yogurt and brown bread. Imagine, just yogurt and brown bread? Dat pig's ration. I hate Germans, I hate dem, I know I should not but I can nod help diz. Vie diz happen to me, vie?"

All the pain and indignities she had suffered through this past year boiled to the surface; the death of her father, the loss of her virginity, the stifling heat of the Middle East, and the trip across the seas on the prison ship. She sobbed uncontrollably. Her fear and pain were contagious. Janos began to wail.

The nun took the baby from the girl and settled him against her soft habit.

"Hush, little baby, don't say a word,
Mama's gonna buy you a mockingbird..."

As the Janos calmed down, so did Maria. Sister Veronique carried the child to the crib. She then took the Maria in her arms and rocked her gently.

"Oh Sister, I should not say such things. I should not hate, but I do. And I do not want you think I am ungrateful. For, for... for everything the Order has done for me. You have all been good to me. It's just that, it's just that........" She couldn't finish.

"It's okay... can I tell you a story?"

"Yes," she whimpered. It sounded like it took all her strength just to say this simple word.

30

"Twenty years ago, I was working at a mission in Rhodesia. One night some men in the village got drunk and broke into the convent. They did things to us, evil things. I had many of the same thoughts you do. I hated the men, but I knew it was wrong, but I hated them, nonetheless. And I questioned everything, I questioned my calling, my devotion, all my decisions prior to that night, I even questioned the Church." She paused. "In its infinite wisdom they disbanded our Order and dispersed us to other postings, as if we had done something wrong... They cast us to the winds of fate, like so much chaff. I was in turmoil and sought answers anywhere I could."

"About a year later I read a quote, by a philosopher named Nietzsche. He wrote "What doesn't kill you makes you stronger." Suddenly I got an epiphany. Do you know what I learned from that quote?"

"What?"

"I learned it's all horseshit."

"What?"

"It's all crap, all of it. We are sometimes dealt a bad hand and that is the way it is."

"Look at the men coming back from the war. Shell shocked, gassed, missing limbs, walking skeletons some of them are. They are not stronger for the experience." The nun let that sink in. "Maybe these challenges aren't supposed to make us stronger, maybe they are supposed to make us different?"

PARABELLUM: When you live in Peace, prepare for War

Jack Nanuq

CHAPTER 6
December 2, 2000
Albany, NY

Carson woke and without looking at the clock knew it was 4 a.m. He always woke at the same time, without an alarm, regardless of location or time zone. Soft gray light filtered into the room, from outdoors, the light artificial. Dawn was still three hours away. The diffused light fell on a print on the opposite wall and he contemplated the plight of women.

For centuries, philosophers had argued whether Man was basically good or evil. He couldn't answer that question, but he believed women were basically good and Eve got a raw deal. Women were God's greatest creation.

The image on his wall was that of a woman's torso; neck to belt buckle. She was tall, tan and fit. She was wearing a bright white tank top that was two sizes too small; breasts and nipples clearly defined. Her right arm at an angle across her chest; fist balled and forearm muscles rigid. A length of chain was wrapped around the appendage. The end links were stretched and broken. The chain had the cutting edges of a tool used to fell trees. The image was equal parts Sensuality, Strength and Self-confidence. It had been part of a series called "Women Are Stronger Than Steel."

He rose from bed, showered and dressed. He briefly contemplated taking a gun but opted to forgo this. Nothing about today should put him in harm's way. He did slide a lock-blade knife into a pants pocket. After all he had been a Boy Scout.

He drove to the warehouse where the crew had left the moving van. As he punched in the pass code, for the security gate, he saw two beady eyes, near a storage trailer at the back of the yard. He'd heard Newton got a dog and that it was the ugliest thing. Best not disturb it.

Too late; the animal raced forward and charged the car. The beast stood firmly in its path challenging the Subaru to come forward. A growl, like a gear missing a tooth, emanated from the creature. It was had a squat broad body like a spaniel on steroids, the bristly bottle brush hair of an Airedale and pointed ears like a Doberman. With its lips curled and teeth showing it looked more like a space alien than man's best friend.

A flashlight beam came out from behind the trailer and the light's owner yelled something. The dog retreated but refused to turn its back on the vehicle. A lanky Black man, wearing a Navy pea coat, walked into view. The unofficial security guard yelled "Mr. Carson, that you?"

"Yes, it is. Is it safe?"

"Oh sure, he's more bark than bite."

"If you say so. What is it?"

"That's a Spocker Spaniel." Making a satirical reference to the number 2 guy on the starship Enterprise; it did look like a reject from the planet Vulcan.

Carson laughed at the joke. "Does it have a name?"

"Demon" responded Newton.

"If the shoe fits" Carson replied and added "Here I brought you something."

"You didn't have to do that. sir," as he opened a bag of Fig Newtons. His love for this treat was how he got his nickname.

Newton helped Carson secure the Subaru to a tow dolly, behind the moving truck. A short time later Carson turned north onto I-87, known locally, as the Northway. Why it was called the Northway he didn't know, since it traveled in both directions.

Thirty minutes later he stopped at the Glens Falls rest area. He checked the load. When he was sure he wasn't being watched he removed the magnetic signs, for Hawkeye Management, from his car. The signs and his work jacket went into the back seat. He carried a small backpack into the men's room.

When he exited the lavatory, he was almost unrecognizable. He was wearing a baggy pair of khaki pants. The legs were too long, and the cuffs had already been walked into oblivion. A bulky sweatshirt with the number 914, the area code for downstate, and a quilted vest covered his upper half. Inside the vest was a wallet and driver's license belonging to Bryan Sparks. The photo of Mr. Sparks closely resembled Mr. Robert Lake, AKA Mr. Carson Nowak.

After climbing into the cab of the truck he then applied styling gel and gave his hair a greasy unclean look. A black ball cap with a gaudy silver dollar sign completed the ensemble. He was now white trash meets ghetto.

He then slid in a set of dentures with a prominent gold canine tooth. He immediately regretted his actions. His fingers were covered with hair goo and now so were his lips. His mouth felt like he'd licked the underside of a tire on a hot summer day. *Yuck,* his brain screamed. He should have put the teeth in before he did his hair. *The things they don't teach you at Langley.*

∞

Three hours later he pulled into the circular drive of the safe house. The cabin, locally referred to as a camp, was set off the road about 100 yards. It was over 50 years old and covered with Adirondack slab wood siding. Three cars and six people were waiting for him. He climbed out of the truck and moved in a stiff and exaggerated manner. He made a production of rubbing his lower back.

He introduced himself as Bryan, "but my friends call me Buddy," Sparks. He then told them the stuff in the truck belonged to a cousin who was getting away from her asshole husband. He had agreed to drive the truck and supervise because he was "currently between jobs". "Got a bad back. I'll do what I can and if you're not sure where something goes just ax me." He had to work hard to mispronounce the word ask.

Eight hours later the cabin was filled with the personal belongings of the recently evicted tenants. He dismissed the workers with a $60 tip. Not too large that it would be talked about and not too small to be talked about either.

He walked through the cabin. He couldn't have the place looking too neat in case someone searched it. The place needed to look lived-in. Canned goods were moved around

35

randomly, some of the kid's clothes were pulled from drawers and tossed on the floor. The bedding was ruffled, and skin mags were thrown under the couch.

He booted up his computer and sent Maggie Post an encrypted email. The message read "Your breakfast is ready."

After leaving the cabin he again pulled onto I-87. Instead of turning south, toward home, he went in the opposite direction. At 9:00 PM, long after all the workers had gone home, he parked the truck and dolly in the lot of the rental agency's Plattsburgh franchisee. Keys and paperwork were left in the drop box.

He drove his car to an old roadside motel that gladly accepted cash. For all they knew his name was Benjamin Franklin because that was the only identification he presented. Time to get some sleep; four o'clock would be here soon.

PARABELLUM: When you live in Peace, prepare for War
Jack Nanuq

CHAPTER 7
December 3, 2000
Albany, NY

George "Newton" Carver exited his trailer and approached the back door of Hawkeye Management. His body trembled with anxiety.

The business was set in a large metal Quonset hut located in an industrial area of Albany. The building ran east-west three hundred feet long and fifty feet wide. The rear door was set in the middle of the south side. The front entrance to the building was directly across. From the air the building looked like a large soup can lying on its side; with a bulge in the middle. The two entrances corresponded with the bulge.

Newton's nervousness increased as he got closer to the building. He whispered, "You can do this, you can do this, only twenty paces and you're to the other side. You can do this."

"Good mornin, Miss Stephanie" he said as he stepped inside. His voice trembled slightly. He forced a smile.

She looked up from her desk and shouted "Damn! You get more and more handsome every day. Any chance you could teach my husband to dress like that. I swear that crease in your slacks look sharp enough to shave with. Once a Marine always a Marine, am I right?"

He was hair over six feet tall, weighed 182 pounds and stood gun barrel straight. His hair was buzzcut and although only 37 most of his dark head was gray. He was wearing dress shoes, pressed Dockers, an oxford shirt, with tie, and a London Fog overcoat.

"Actually, I was in the Navy, but I served with the Marines."

"That's right, you were a medic, right?"

"Corpsman"

"Is today your day to spend with Nana?"

"Yes ma'am."

"Do you need me to call you a cab?"

"Would it be any trouble?"

"No, not at all. Let me get you a cup of coffee first though. Have you had breakfast?"

His anxiousness got the best of him and pushed him through the reception area. He would later admonish himself for not answering her.

He moved to the glass front door, the proximity of an escape route helped keep his fear at a manageable level. He looked at a banner that read "HAWKEYE PROPERTY MANAGEMENT: CELEBRATING 50 YEARS IN THE CAPITAL REGION." His eyes then darted around the room. The walls of the reception area were decorated with photos of Nana throughout the years. Nana at ribbon cutting ceremonies; Nana with politicians. Nana at Ronald Mc Donald House, with her arms around a set of bald big-eyed children.

"I'll take the coffee to go, if you don't mind. I don't need anything to eat. By the end of the day I'll be stuffed like a Christmas goose." His speech was rapid.

Stephanie carried his cup to the front door and added "Let me grab my phone and I'll wait outside with you."

"You don't have to do that, I'll be fine."

"Nonsense, it's a nice morning and I need to get off my butt already. I'm fighting the secretary spread, if you know what I mean. Does this chair make my ass look fat?" She snickered.

"You look fine to me."

"Now I know I need to get you outside, where there are witnesses. If we stay indoors, I might just do something I'll regret. Let's go."

His nervousness decreased the moment they stepped outdoors.

"Yes ma'am. I sure appreciate your being so understanding. I just get a little claustrophobic. Please don't take offense."

"None taken; black?" she said as she handed him the coffee.

"Yes I am. Thank you for noticing." They both laughed at the joke.

"Seriously though; how are you doing?"

"I'm getting better. It's been 17 years since that day in Beirut. The anniversary was a couple of months ago and it's always rough at that time of the year. It's also tough to be inside a concrete building, the bigger the building the more my anxiety. If I know I have to be inside, like the VA, I load up on Zoloft."

In 1983 a suicide truck bomber crashed into his barracks and brought tons of concrete raining down around him. For three days he was trapped in a dark hell, brick and mortar confining him like a clamshell.

"If it weren't for Nana's help, I think I would have lost my mind years ago. She's pretty special, that one is," he said

Stephanie changed the subject. "You warm enough in your trailer? Winter's here, you need anything, more blankets, space heaters, anything?"

"I'm good. I figure if an Eskimo can live in an igloo, I can get by in an RV. I don't much spend time inside anyway."

"How come you don't have Demon with you today? You afraid he might scare Nana."

"I'm afraid he might end up in a stew pot. She told me once they had to eat dog during the War; the second World War that is."

Twenty minutes later a taxi delivered Newton to Nana's house on Manning Blvd. He walked to the rear and found the old woman and the night nurse on the back porch. The porch was an elaborate glassed-in structure that resembled a greenhouse. He liked it there, nothing between him and the elements except polycarbonate.

The night nurse, Daniel, was a Philippine who spoke broken English and did a horrible job of trying to hide his sexual orientation.

"How you today suh?" he said as Newton walked in.

"Good. And how are we today?" He walked over to Nana and gave her a hug.

40

Daniel said "We good; I good, she good. She eat drugs and food. Coffee no good though; not real, iz chicory, much bad taste. I drink tea, tea good."

Nana loved chicory coffee, with just a touch of cream. It was bitter, earthy and an acquired taste.

She beamed at Daniel's discomfort and said, "Dr. Newton, let me get you something."

"No, that's fine, you finish your breakfast, I'll help myself." He scanned the table. A pill dispenser that had three boxes for each day sat next to a half empty glass of orange juice. The little box marked AM was empty.

Nana nibbled on a half piece of raisin toast. The crust for the other half was sitting on a plate. The plate was decorated with yolk.

He then turned to Daniel and asked, "One egg or two?"

The nurse held up two fingers. "Doctor say she need more protein. I make you some."

"Don't bother."

"Danny" Nana shouted and pointed a finger toward the kitchen. "Doctor you sit, we do stuff today, you need your strength."

She handed him a list and it read:
Christmas Cards
Post Office
Museum
Greek Food

Newton then noticed she was wearing her "dancing" shoes; supple leather with thick comfortable soles. *She can walk all day in those*, he thought. He also took note she was wearing a new dress under her house frock.

"You wanna do all this?" he asked.

"Yes. You eat, then we go."

Newton pointed to a stack of Christmas card and asked, "How many this year?"

"Two thousand, one hundred and fourteen...no wait. Two thousand, one hundred and thirteen, we just sent a family pacing"

41

"You mean packing?"

"Dah, packing, what I say?"

He deflected her question with his own. "How do you keep track of all your tenants?"

"I don't, I just know number. There was a time I knew them all, but no longer."

Danny came back to the porch, with a plate of eggs and toast. "You good now? I go."

"Thanks, … yeah I got this."

As Danny walked out the back door, they both saw him grab his phone, as it rang. They clearly heard him say "Yeah, yeah, I be home soon Joseph; keep your pants on, or don't."

Nana shook her head as Newton picked up a blood pressure cuff. Nana barked again. "You eat. We do that later."

Newton dug into his meal. They sat in silence as Nana slid gift cards for the Catskill Game Farm into the envelopes. A new noise outside made them both turn. A squirrel scampered through leaves at the bottom of an oak tree.

Nana stopped what she was doing and ambled over to the door. The squirrel eyed her cautiously. It bolted a short distance when she threw a piece of crust at it. "You eat too."

As if the animal understood, he ran to the morsel, grabbed it with his front paws and quickly nibbled it into bite-size pieces.

Newton thought; *she knows just what everyone needs.* For a second time today he thought, *she's pretty special, that one is.*

Nana sat at her table and thought back to a similar day almost 85 years earlier…

PARABELLUM: When you live in Peace, prepare for War
Jack Nanuq

CHAPTER 8
December 21, 1915
Isle of Man

Maria was sitting in the gazebo at the back of the rectory yard. This was a rare pleasant day, especially for the first day of winter. Unusually dry and sunny; almost felt like the first day of Spring. She looked at the sky and three lumpy white clouds reminded her of *pirohi,* the stuffed dumplings her mother used to make.

Janos was lying on his back, on a blanket nearby. He was contently chewing on his toes. Now that he had four teeth, and more coming, he chewed on everything. Maria had made him a small leather horse to play with and he had gnawed it to look like something Napoleon had left at Waterloo.

Maria was sewing a pair of fur lined mittens. The leather was seal skin and she had worked it since April. Today might be warm but harsher weather was around the corner. A movement caught her eye and she spotted the small creature.

A squirrel stood on the step to the gazebo and eyed Janos' actions. It then let out a sharp chatter as if saying "you're in my space."

I guess we are. W*hat's the fee for trespassing*? Maria thought. She dug a cracker from her bag. *Will this do? A*nd broke off a corner. She threw the nugget, but it had so little mass it fell short. It didn't matter as the animal bolted the minute Maria moved her arm. *When you're small and on everybody's menu you cannot afford to be brave*, she mused.

"Maria you have a visitor," called Sister Veronique.

"Da… just a moment," she responded as she wrapped Janos in the blanket and picked him up.

When Maria entered the kitchen, the air was rich with the smell of sage and a roasting goose. She set Janos into a bassinette. He cooed contently and went back to chewing on his toes.

Sister Veronique sat at a table with a dour looking woman. Two cups of tea, real tea, sat in front of the women's places. Where it had come from was anyone's guess, as so few trade goods made it to the island.

"Have a seat, Maria" said the nun. She then poured a cup of tea for the new mother. The other woman showed a look of disdain. The face clearly said, "This girl should be pouring the tea and luxury goods should not be wasted on a foreigner."

"This is Mrs. Fletcher and she has come to ask a favor of you."

The visitor wrung her hands anxiously and paused before speaking. She reeked of xenophobia.

"I understand you repair shoes, am I correct?"

"Dah, I do."

The woman then reached into a bag and pulled out a pair of shoes. The soles had separated from the main body. "Can you fix these?"

Maria carefully examined the footwear. Where the leather uppers met the sole, the seam had torn loose. They could be repaired but not with stitching. A concoction of pine tar and cedar ashes would bind the two surfaces together. Maria knew the repair would take less than an hour and about one day for the glue to set. She took her time running her hands over all surfaces of the shoes. They were a plain style, mass-produced in some factory. Half the women in the United Kingdom owned a similar pair.

Maria asked, "Are they dear to you?"

"Of course, they're dear to me, everything is dear, your people make everything dear, they bomb our cities, they sink our ships and they kill our boys, so yes, they are dear to me!"

Maria took this in calmly, at least she appeared calm. She wished her English was better and could give the woman a tongue lashing. But she was afraid she may come across as a simpleton. "I can fix." She tried to make her voice emotionless but didn't pull it off. Her tone insinuated, "You can go barefoot for all I care."

Sister Veronique smiled and came to her rescue. "I think what Maria means, is if this is your last pair, she can fix them. But they may not be worth the effort."

"Of course, it's worth the effort! What would be the cost of said repair?"

"Maria, what do you think is fair?" The nun asked.

"One shilling"

"A shilling! In the name of all that's Holy, how can you ask such a fee? That's outrageous! I can buy a new pair for two shilling!"

"That's a fair wage" interrupted the nun.

"A fair wage... maybe... maybe for a working man, someone with a family and expenses...But she has no cares, no expenses. You provide her with a roof and the Crown covers her food and lodging. The King has been gracious enough to take her into our bosom even though her people savagely declared war on this great land. His Majesty is quite charitable; and now she wants to steal my money. What a way to return his generosity!"

The nun, clearly angry, responded with. "If you think the King is so generous, feel free to take your shoes to Buckingham Palace and ask him to fix them for you. You came here with a need and Maria has said she can perform the task, but I'll not have you cheat her. She has quoted you a fair price and you are free to make your decision. What will it be?"

Maria's English skills did not allow her to follow the conversation, but she understood the exchange, nonetheless. She sat there and enjoyed the fencing match. Sister Veronique was clearly in control.

Mrs. Fletcher sat for a moment. "She'll return them cleaned and shined?"

"She'll return them cleaned and oiled, but polish will cost more."

"Cleaned and oiled it is then. When I can I expect them back?"

Sister Veronique turned to Maria. "How long?"

"One week."

The woman nodded her head in agreement.

"There we are then, you'll have the shoes for the New Year's Dance," said Sister Veronique.

46

Mrs. Fletcher stood and before turning to the door picked up the small fruit jar that held the imported tea. "I guess she can afford to buy her own tea from now on. Good day." She left and pulled the kitchen door closed. A loud bang telegraphed through the house.

Maria's breathing was ragged and a vein in her neck pulsed violently. Her face was as crimson as a boiled beet. Sister Veronique put a hand on the young girl's arm.

"You did well child. That price was a little high, but she had it coming." Veronique stood up and stretched her arms. "And it'd be best you not give too many bargains. If the islanders think they can take advantage of you, they will suck you dry like a pond full of leeches. And they'll do it with no malice. Now help me with this goose and then finish that those mittens for Petr."

PARABELLUM: When you live in Peace, prepare for War

Jack Nanuq

CHAPTER 9
December 3, 2000
Schenectady, NY

The "Cube" was a non-descript concrete building, located near the intersection of State Street and Michigan Avenue. Carson sat in his car, while it idled in a Popeye's parking lot. He scanned the building, the traffic and the surrounding area; on the look-out for any watchers.

Urban planners would call this a mixed-use area; clearly a low-rent district. Derelict two-family homes were interspersed with gaudy stores advertising discount phone cards, interspersed with anonymous industrial structures. Enough old buildings, both vacant and occupied, dotted the landscape to camouflage the structure across the street. The building was so plain as to be almost invisible. Just the way the Agency wanted it. It's only distinguishing feature, if you could call it that, was an absence of any windows. Fifty or sixty years ago, there were windows but they'd since been bricked in.

Carson would not enter the Cube until he could be reasonably certain no one was watching the building. First, he looked for vans, especially any idling vans. The newest generation of surveillance artist seemed to be a wimpy breed and did not cotton to sitting in a cold vehicle.

He then examined the parking lot of a nearby pharmacy, one of those national chains that sold everything from cigarettes to flip flops with drugs and personal care products as an afterthought. Cars seemed to come and go with the appropriate randomness of true shoppers. The cars that did not leave were unoccupied and he recognized them as regular fixtures, most likely employees. Satisfied no one on the street was watching the building he hit the remote and the security gate opened. He then pulled into the lot without delay. As he walked across the parking lot, he continued to scan the street. He couldn't tell if someone was watching from indoors, but he had to take some chances.

PARABELLUM: When you live in Peace, prepare for War

Jack Nanuq

He held a magnetic ID card, belonging to Robert Lake, next to a badge reader and heard the lock click open. Entering a coat room, he pulled the door closed behind him. Had anyone been able to see in this far, their view would have been one of walls lined with rain slickers, safety vests and hardhats. But he was actually in a sally port. The next door would not open until the main entrance was closed. He punched four digits into a key pad and the door in front of him slid open.

The interior of the building was everything the exterior was not; clean and modern. Two dozen glassed-in offices lined the outer walls. Each office furnished with high-end furniture, computers and electronic gear. Five floors above him and three below were outfitted in a similar manner. There were four floors below him, but the lowest level housed the armory and gun range.

He took the stairs to the sixth floor. There was a freight elevator, but everyone was discouraged from using it. By the time he reached Maggie Post's office there was a slight hitch in his giddy-up; the hip throbbed.

She was on the phone and silently waved him in. "Yeah, I'll send him down soon; I wish you had given us some advance notice."

By the time she hung up, Carson was standing with his weight on his right leg and was rotating his left ankle. His body swayed slightly as he maintained his balance.

She said, "You okay, you look like a kid that needs to pee?"

"I'm fine," he said as he drew his left knee toward his chest.

"I need you to clear your morning. When you're done with your yoga exercises; go down to three and meet with USELESS."

This was a bastardization of the acronym for United States Investigation Services (USIS). It was a private company that had an exclusive contract with the US Government to do all background checks and security clearance investigations. Prior to 1994 most of their staff were employed by spook

50

agencies such as the CIA, DOD, and NSA. During the Clinton Administration they came to work on a certain Monday and found they no longer had jobs with the government. In one night over a thousand people got the ax. USIS had been formed over the course of the previous weekend and all terminated employees were given the opportunity to apply for a position with this new organization. Their salaries would remain the same, but they would be responsible for all other benefits. Uncle Bill did this in the name of downsizing. Monica wasn't the only one to get the shaft.

Carson had to meet with these people about every four or five years. It was a pain in the ass but necessary, as they had the power to revoke a security clearance. Without which he'd be screwed. He wouldn't be allowed in the building let alone perform any tasks as Mr. Robert Lake.

As he was walking to the conference room on the third floor, he made a quick call to Hawkeye. No one at Hawkeye, well maybe one, knew he had a second job.

"Steph, I'll be out of cell range for most of the morning. I'll check in about noon." He used this line frequently as he was always travelling for one reason or another.

"Sure thing, boss." She replied unquestioningly. He hung up the phone and wondered what excuse he would need to come up with as they built more cell towers. He stopped at the door to the conference room and knocked.

"Enter."

He found a woman in her mid-40s sitting at the table with a pile of paperwork in front of her. Her back was to him but he could tell she was small. Maybe five-foot-tall; with heels. Arms that were so thin they looked like kite ribs.

She stood and put out a hand; fingers like matchsticks. "Liza Carbon, thanks for making time for me." She looked at him inquisitively. She had a full and very attractive face.

He took her hand and was pleasantly surprised by her firm grip. "Robert Lake; glad to meet you."

She had a plate of cookies and a coffee carafe in front of her. It was gonna be a long morning.

51

He walked to the pot and poured a coffee, using the time to size up this woman. He offered her a cup. "How do you take it?"

"Two creams, no sugar, thank you."

"Can I ask a question... before we get started?" he said as he handed the cup to her. He poured himself a cup and held it to his nose. A mix of Christmas spices filled his sinuses, as someone had brewed a pot of "Holiday Magic."

"Sure"

"Why Carbon?" guessing this was a work alias.

"Interesting question, I guess that's fair since I know so much about you. I chose it because of these." She held her arms out and flapped them like wings. "Look at me. I'm so skinny they look like they're made from carbon fibers. Always been that way too."

Maybe she was born a preemie? Carson thought.

She continued with "Now you. Why Lake?"

"It's so plain most people forget it. If they do need to recall it, they always seem to come up with something similar but incorrect such as Waters. It works for me."

"I like your reasoning. So, is Carson Nowak your real name?"

"Yes, but everyone uses their work name, when in the building. Please stay with Lake or Robert if you don't mind."

"No problem. I'm sure you've done this before, but I want to lay out why I' m here, just so that we're on the same page." She picked up a cookie and waited until she was sure she had his attention. "I'm here to learn your secrets. The powers-that-be have learned, that people who are trying to hide things are vulnerable to extortion and exploitation. For obvious reasons we can't have that. It would be nice if people were not susceptible to temptations but we're all human. We all do things we wish we hadn't. So, if I know your secrets, then the government knows your secrets; and the opposition cannot use that against you. So, my job here is to protect you, from yourself. I am not here to jam you up, unless and I repeat, unless you lie to me. I've been doing this a lot of years and have seen most everything. If you're worried about taking home office supplies or that your bookie is on speed dial just put that that out of your mind. I'm not concerned about that unless you feel the need to hide it from me. From this point forward, honesty is the word of the day. Understood?"

"Understood," he replied. He respected her directness, but it still felt as if he was being dragged to the confessional. She had him by the gonads and it was for his own good. *Damnit to hell*, he thought.

As he answered she slid a disclosure form for him to sign. The disclaimer on the bottom, said something to the effect he had to tell the truth, the whole truth and nothing but the truth. Not exactly those words but with the same message. He signed Robert Lake on the designated line.

"Tell me about your day job, with Hawkeye Property Management. And then we'll talk about what you do for the Agency."

"I'm listed as the CFO, Chief Financial Officer, but I'm more like the CCBW."

"What's a CCBW?"

"Chief Cook and Bottle Washer; kind of Jack of all Trades. Hawkeye is a family owned company that manages and develops real estate in the area. We do property management, construction; equipment leasing and financing. The company was founded by my great-grandmother, shortly after WWII. Everyone calls her Nana."

He grabbed a cookie as she asked, "What's your salary?"

"Last year I paid tax on $195,000. But I also got some bonuses, so I'm not sure what I really earned. The agency gave me another 80K and that's in an off-shore account."

"Do you pay tax on that?"

"Robert Lake pays tax on that."

"Okay, go on."

"Hawkeye manages or owns almost 2,200 units and has 90 employees. I grew up in the business. I was groomed to take the reins but wanted to do my own thing. After high school I went into the Army, light infantry. Trained for desert warfare and in 1990 I was assigned to MFO in the Sinai." He paused so that she could absorb the full picture. "That's where I met Fred Hutchinson, our number two man. Number two man in this building."

"Wait," she emphasized this with a hand in the air. "What's MFO?"

"Multi-National Force Operations; basically peace-keeping."

"Was it? Peace-keeping I mean?"

"It was then, but the place has turned to shit since. Bunch of radicals rule the desert now. Anyway, in '91 Fred and I were deployed to Kuwait for Desert Storm. We did a lot of recon together. After Desert Storm we go our separate ways. I went to air cav and he went to counter-intel. A few years later I climb into a Chinook, you know the twin rotor jobs." He emphasized the comment by twirling both index fingers in the air. "Who's sitting there but Hutchinson? About two klicks off-base something went to shit, and we crashed. My hip and femur shattered. I'm leaking pretty badly, there's blood everywhere. We had a medic on board, but he had a head wound and was out of it. Fred grabs the doc's bag, gave me something for pain and wrapped me up. He and a couple of other guys kept pressure on my leg until I'm evac'ed out. I owe that son-of-a-bitch my life." He took a sip of coffee.

Carbon interrupted, "Hang on a minute." She rummaged through the stack of files. She opened a file "The after-action report has it classified as a hard landing."

"Hard landing my ass, the fuckin thing crashed. The Army likes to downplay negative aspects of operations. Part of that bird is still in my leg."

"Then what?" she asked.

"While I'm in rehab, Fred looks me up. We both knew my career was over. He talked me into returning home and getting back into the business. Said I should use my GI benefits, chase some coeds, drink beer and be part of the real world. I

54

knew what he said made sense. I came back to Albany, got a degree in Finance and began running things at Hawkeye."

"During that time the guys in this building rented some properties from us. Fred put me on the books as a contractor and kept my security clearance valid. I've helped him with a few things over the years. With my leg the way it is, I'm about 90% of what I was. No heavy lifting but Fred and Maggie have Seals and Special Ops people for that kind of thing. Most time I'm a glorified housekeeper, chauffeur, and babysitter; you know CCBW."

"Any other family members work as contractors?"

"I don't have any other family"

"None?"

"None; except Nana. I'm an only child and both my parents were only children. My parents are deceased, so I'm kind of an orphan."

"Sorry to hear that."

"It's okay."

"Let's go back to your leg injury. An injury like that, sounds painful, what do you take for it?" Her tone was neutral.

Carson looked at her and couldn't tell if she thought he abused drugs or if she was concerned about his disability. "Do I have to answer that?"

"You know you do," she said sternly. "Wait, that came out wrong. Let's start with street drugs. Use any?"

"No, mostly Tylenol. I've got some Percocet and Flexeril that I take about 2-3 times/year. I've got a prescription for those."

"Okay, how about debts."

"None"

"None? No car payment, lease, etc."

"None, as in zero, I don't borrow money, and neither does Hawkeye. It's a family tradition, we don't borrow money. I have some credit cards, but everything is paid off at the end of the month and Hawkeye works the same."

"Hmm, I wish more people did that, it would make my job a lot easier." She said this as she checked some boxes on her sheet. "How about gambling? Horses, football, lottery tickets. What's your pleasure?"

"My pleasure is keeping the money I've worked hard to earn. A couple times a week I buy some scratch-off tickets. That's more for entertainment than anything else. I might have 3 or 4 in my bedroom trash."

"Okay, speaking of bedrooms, where do you spend your nights? And with whom?"

"Most nights I'm home. I have a few women I see occasionally, but nothing serious. I don't play the field, because I'm not into casual sex. I don't think there is anything casual about sex."

More than two hours later they wrapped up the interview. During that time the woman was inquisitive, jovial, engaged and even stern, especially when Carson made light of certain questions. In short, she was interesting, and he was sorry their time together was over. She assured him there didn't seem to be any issues, but she had one last request.

In a firm and professional voice, she told him "I want to see your collection of lottery tickets." Before he could reply she added "Tonight, at nine, I've got the address."

PARABELLUM: When you live in Peace, prepare for War
Jack Nanuq

CHAPTER 10
February 2, 1916
St. Maughold Convent
Isle of Man

The day was cold and sleety. Rain and ice pellets shot horizontally against the structure. Wind twisted around the nunnery and sounds of liquid gravel carried to the interior. The kitchen was crowded with women. The cook stove going, and the room smelled of burning peat and fresh scones.

The men from the Camp were expected today but Maria was doubtful they would travel in this weather. This troubled her as she looked forward to Petr's visits. They were the highlight of her week. When he wasn't around, she found herself thinking of him at the oddest times. This was a totally new experience for her as she never felt this way with Gregor.

She was lost in thought as Sister Veronique reminisced about her days in Palestine. "Thank God we never had days like this. All we had to burn was camel dung."

A knock on the door interrupted the group. Corporal Davis was smiling through the window, water streaming off his hat. He was wearing a heavy wool coat and grinning like the cat that ate the canary. Petr and Andrej were standing behind him in hooded rain slickers; both had their heads down.

Maria ran for the door and as she opened it there was a chorus of "Come in, come in." The three men ambled into the room and stood by the door as water dripped from their clothes. Maria was happy to see Andrej was wearing the seal muff she made him and Petr was wearing the seal mittens she finished just before Christmas.

Her expression changed and there were gasps from the group when Petr looked up. He had two black eyes, a crooked nose and split lip. The color of his skin was various shades of black, gray and green. His face resembled the camouflage netting on the coastal guns.

"Jesus, Mary and Joseph, what happened to you? Corporal did you do this?" accused Sister Veronique.

"No ma'am." He paused to let this sink in. "He got in a fight with The Ox; the folks at the Camp are now calling him Petr the Giant Killer."

"My God isn't there enough killing already?" she asked.

"Well, ...he didn't actually kill the brute, but he did take him down a notch."

Fr. Fagan came into the kitchen at this time and asked "What's all the fuss? Petr...me lad! What happened to your face?"

Petr took off his mittens and his hands were as bruised as the rest of him. He looked at the Priest sheepishly.

Maria caught herself as she reached for Petr. The skin on the hands was so swollen the flesh ballooned around the knuckles. She wanted desperately to offer some comfort, to ease his pain. She glanced at his face and saw him looking right at her. His eyes took on an azur hue she had never seen before. The ends of his swollen lips were lifting into a distorted smile. She sensed his pain took a hiatus.

Maria was turmoil personified. The raging storm outside was pale in comparison. Her feelings for Petr were swirling around unable to find a place to land. A mix of fear, pride, and God knows what tumbled like dice in a craps game. *What was this* she asked herself? She put her head down because she was afraid everyone was staring at her.

"Sir, maybe I should tell it," interjected the Corporal.

Fr. Fagan nodded his head in agreement.

"We have a guy at Camp they call The Ox. They should call him The Rock because he's as solid as one and about as bright. Has the brains God gave a doorknob. Anyway, he took a fancy to Petr's new mittens. Says he deserves a pair like that. Starts goading Petr, asks what he did to earn such a gift. Makes a few comments, I won't repeat, about Miss Maria's virtue. Calls Petr her little Polish stallion; maybe the Ox should visit her?"

Corporal Davis pantomimed two boxers. He bounced from one foot to the other, with his hands up.

"Petr reminds him an Ox doesn't have any balls and fists start flying. This lad here he's angry and fights like an animal. Strong as a bear and quick like a ferret. The Ox takes everything thrown at him. Petr even breaks a few of his ribs and it doesn't faze him. Both men go down a few times and each time it takes a little longer for Petr to get to his feet. He is getting weaker and Ox just smiles. Everyone's certain Petr is done for. Suddenly Petr shouts, something in Czech. He jumps in the air like one of those Chinese acrobats. Spins around and kicks the Ox right in the jaw. The man fell like a road apple. Knocked him flat on his arse, he did."

The Corporal paused to let that sink in. "As Petr's standing there looking at the bloke, one of the Ox's mates picks up a rock. I settled things with a warning shot from me revolver."

"Why didn't you stop the fight earlier?" asked Sister Veronique. "Did any of the other guards do anything?"

"Sure, they did."

"And what was that?"

"They took wagers, on the outcome. We have orders from the Commandant. We're not to intervene unless weapons are involved, or serious injury is apparent. Sorry ma'am, that's just the way things are. The Commandant knows there will be fighting. After all they are soldiers. He's fears if he clamps down too hard the fighting will happen where no one can render aid."

Maria looked toward Andrej. He was grinning and then said something in Czech. His speech was animated, and he kept pounding Petr on the back.

"This is my friend and I'm proud to know him," Maria interpreted.

Fr. Fagan looked at Petr and asked solemnly "So you like the mittens?"

In broken English Petr said "Yah… yes very much."

"What did you shout at the Boche?" the priest asked.

Petr shook his head like he couldn't say.

Andrej interjected, face beaming, "He say… He say…I'm not Polish you Kraut bastard."

The Priest turned back to the Corporal. "What happened to Ox, after the fisticuffs?"

"Infirmary... for a while they say. Jaw's broken; he be eating curds and whey, like Little Miss Muffet, for about a month."

Father Fagan nodded his head as if this is the way it should be. He then asked. "Sister Veronique, might we celebrate with some of that plum brandy you keep for medicinal purposes?"

Janos giggled from his bassinette, as if to second the suggestion. Everyone laughed. Petr's laugh was cut short with a grimace.

His stunted laughter reminded Maria that Petr had faced danger in part to defend her honor. Sure, he needed to fight for his possessions, but she sensed he did it as much for her as he did it for himself. Not only had he faced danger, but he triumphed. It could have been him now laid up in hospital with a broken jaw or worse. But he wasn't in hospital. He was here, and she liked that. Again, she asked herself *What is this I feel?*

She wasn't sure it was a good thing. Sure, she felt good right now, but what about later when he had to return to the Camp. And what would happen at the end of the War. She didn't even want to think about that. All hoped for the War to end soon. But what would that mean for her and Petr? Maria had her head down. Still convinced everyone was staring at her, anxiety forced her out of her chair.

"I'll get the scones," Maria blurted out nervously and stood up suddenly.

"Stay my child," Sister Veronique suggested strongly.

Maria caught sight of another nun, Sister X they called her, already at the oven. This nun moved with the sound of a shadow. Maria forced herself to remember the nun's name, Sister Xavier, from Brazil. She rarely spoke, as if a vow of silence had been taken. When she did it was in a language Maria couldn't understand. It sounded like Spanish but wasn't, Portuguese, that was it.

Maria forced herself to sit down and fought hard not to look in Petr's direction. With her head down slightly, she stared at Sister X as the plump scones were removed from the oven. The scent of fresh baked flour and shortening flooded the room. Prior to this the kitchen had begun to take on the smell of a damp blanket.

Maria's eyes locked onto the nun's every movements; like a collie on a sheep. She forced herself to focus all her senses on the nun's actions and surroundings. She did this to keep her mind on something other than a future with Petr. How could they have a future when their lives were at the whims of warring powers?

Sister X opened the fire box and poked at the peat log. Red, green and blue flames danced like angels in a bottle. The nun then closed the door and reached for a soup pot. The quiet woman filled the large pan with water from the pitcher pump. The first few pumps of the handle were not answered but faith prevailed; subsequent pumps forced fluid from the spout. The receptacle was about 18 inches deep and held over two gallons. Splash, blurp, splash, blurp; six or so ounces with each pump. The handle rose and fell 37 times and the pot was almost full. The pan had a blue-black sheen, with small white spots.

The older woman then added some herbs and placed the pot on the stove. Sixteen pounds of porcelain encased fluid. A sizzle escaped from under the pan as its wet surface hit the hot iron. Small bubbles lingered briefly at the bottom edge and then disappeared into nothingness.

Ten minutes later Maria was mentally drained as she had repeatedly attempted to count the small dots on the side of the pot. Try as she might she never made it past the halfway mark; she kept losing her place. Once she had counted as high as 212 but most times, she lost her way around 150 or so. She was rescued from this self-induced torture when Janos began to fuss. She stood abruptly and spun to the bassinette. It was only then that she realized someone had asked her a question and all were waiting for her response.

"What?" she asked hesitantly.

PARABELLUM: When you live in Peace, prepare for War
Jack Nanuq

"Would you help Sister Xavier tend to Petr's wounds?"

CHAPTER 11
December 4, 2000
Schenectady, NY

The clock in Carson bedroom read 2:14 and the green light for AM was lit. Liza Carbon was straddling his legs: again. And his body was responding; again. She truly was small, weighing no more than a snowflake. He was surprised he couldn't see the street lights shining through her ribs. He was again struck by her beauty, facial features so perfect they looked enhanced. But there was nothing artificial here except a little make-up; now smudged. Her hair just right, some of it matted with sweat and some of it flying off at strange angles, but all in a complimentary way.

She was running a manicured nail over his left thigh; tracing the many scars. Long lines, some straight and some serpentine, all intersected with hash marks showing where staples were used hold the skin together. The surface was dotted with dimples and divots where subcutaneous tissue was missing.

He was thinking back to five hours earlier. At 8:55 she had rung his bell; carrying a variety six-pack from a local brewery. He took her coat and found she was wearing a semi-translucent silk blouse and no bra. The look was perfect for her; not slutty at all.

She had jumped onto his kitchen counter and sat with her knees facing him. He took everything in. She had he body of a gymnast and the face of a siren.

She grabbed an India pale ale and announced "I've got to fly to Denver in the morning. I don't have time for you to go exploring like someone on a quest. We're gonna do what I like, and then, if we have time, we will do what you like."

She handed the ale to him. "I prefer dark beer," he told her.

"This isn't about you, it's about me. Then it's about you."

"Understood." *Understood? How lame is that*, he thought.

64

But that's all he had to work with. It was as if he went to the vocabulary cupboard and found it empty. Had she robbed him of everything but those three syllables: UN-DER-STOOD? For the next hour his only other tool was inflection. There was the barking UNDERSTOOD, like when he was at bootcamp and acknowledging a Drill Instructor's command. There was the meek UNDERSTOOD, like an admonished child. And then there was the excited UNDERSTOOD, like a scientist's eureka moment. About 10:30 they had drifted off to sleep.

When he woke a few minutes ago he found the vocabulary cupboard fully stocked.

"Don't you ever sleep?" he asked.

She seemed to be fascinated with the terrain of his leg. "It looks like a rail yard that's been carpet bombed."

"Really? I hardly noticed."

She then slid her hands up his chest, a wiggle or two and once again they were the beast with two backs.

Twenty minutes later she rolled off him. She reached for the bottle on the nightstand and took the last swig of pale ale. The fact that it was flat didn't seem to bother her. "I guess we never made it to the dark beer" she commented.

"No problem, but you owe me. Tell me something."

"What?"

"Anything, you know everything about me and I know nothing about you."

Over the next half hour, she gave him her life story. Divorced, with two grown boys. She had a master's degree in Mathematics and taught part time at her local community college. She had been Analyst with the Agency when she became a victim to cutbacks. The cutbacks, during the Clinton Administration, were known as Reduction in Force (RIF). "I got RIF'ed" . She now worked part-time, on-call actually, for USELESS. Yes, she used that term. She thrived on crosswords and brain teasers. And she liked him.

She then curled up in his arms and nodded off.

PARABELLUM: When you live in Peace, prepare for War
                                                    Jack Nanuq

     He kissed the top of her head and whispered, "I could
fall hard for you."
     In the soft voice of a dreaming child she mumbled
"Understood."

CHAPTER 12
December 21, 2000
Albany, NY

Carson crossed Manning Boulevard, to Nana's house. The Boulevard had two distinct personalities. This end was near Saint Peter's Hospital and the Albany Medical Center. The locals were mostly doctors, lawyers and other six figure incomes. The homes built in the early part of the 1900's and were modest and well-kept. This end of the block spoke of established money. The other end of Manning was occupied by people with few resources and the properties owned by absentee landlords. Nana had bought this place 50 years ago and he liked the neighborhood so much he bought the place directly across the street. Now the last of the Nowak line was walking from one house to the other.

His boots fell on pavement lightly dusted with snow. The air was a crisp and calm 28 degrees. The slight sharpness made him feel alive. He surveyed the yard and front of the house as he got closer. The previous week he and Newton had set out the obligatory plastic Santa and reindeer. Lighted icicles also hung from the eaves.

He then looked at the rusted Honda that sat in the driveway. The car had four mismatched all-season radials that should have been replaced months ago. One of them was bell-shaped and probably had a slow leak. *She's in for a surprise later*, he thought.

It also wore a bumper sticker that read I'D RATHER LOSE AT RUGBY, THAN WIN AT SOFTBALL. The hatchback belonged to Iris and she had told him the $600 car had come with the sticker. She didn't play rugby, but the decal described perfectly how she looked at life. She had come from adversity and challenge. That had shaped her into the woman she was. She was smart, driven and strong. She could take a punch and if need be, deliver one.

He continued around back and hoped to find Nana and Iris in the solarium. But that was not to be. He let himself onto the porch and the knocked gently on the back door. He had a key and could entered the house, but he respected Nana's space and didn't want to startle anyone. He knocked a second time and heard Iris say "Mr. Carson come in." She must have seen him walking down the driveway; she always called him Mr. Carson.

As he walked into the kitchen, he was surprised to find a bedsheet spread out on the table and a number of ancient journals scattered across the surface. Yellow sticky notes were also scattered about, some sticking from the books and others on index cards. Iris was using a handheld vacuum to suck up cobwebs, dust bunnies and other debris. As she moved across the books the sticky notes fluttered like Tibetan prayer flags.

"What's all this?" He asked.

"Recipes, madam, she translate recipes from the War." Iris waved a hand over everything.

"What?"

"Come, I show, you see. She say they are diaries from the War. See the boxes."

She used a finger to trace one of the hand-drawn squares on a random page. The box was filled with strange squiggles and numbers. It looked more like gang graffiti than actual words. The remainder of the page was filled with similar marks.

"She say it mini-hand, no I mean short hand. She say she keep records of her life."

"What?" Carson clearly bewildered asked "Where is she?"

"She sleep now, she had full morning and she very tired. She tell me many stories about her life. She tell me about her time in prison. She tell me about eating Seal meat with wild greens and living with nuns."

"Wait...that's not right, that can't be. Is she taking all her meds? She's not hallucinating? Prison? She was never in prison." Carson commented, clearly perplexed.

"*Oui, oui*, I'm sure she say prison."

He walked to the trunk, the one he had carried down a just a few weeks ago; the trunk that held the gun and the photo. To the best of his knowledge it had sat in this corner undisturbed since he carried it down.

The lid was open and about half its contents were on the table. He rummaged in the trunk and stacked the books on one side of the box to see if there were any more surprises. He jumped when he came across what he first thought was a dead rat. Its parchment-like hide was stiff leather. Upon closer examination he found it was an old leather mitten; its fur lining a shadow of its former self.

"What the hell?" he muttered. "Iris wait, I'm confused, tell me what happened this morning. Start from the beginning."

She aimed the Dustbuster at the trunk and waved it like a professor's pointer. "It started there. After breakfast the Madam she want to make pierogis. Did I say that right?"

"Close, *pierohi*, that's the Czech pronunciation. The word you used is Polish. She used to make them all the time, but now only at Christmas, go on."

"Okay. She get out flour, but then couldn't remember the recipe. She got into a frenzy, saying she's made them a thousand times but now she can't remember how. I scared for her, she very excited. I say it okay, I find recipe on the computer and she say no. I want my recipe. Then she started pulling the books out of the trunk. She page through one and lay it down, then she do the same with another, then another; she made a big mess and finally found what she was looking for."

Iris pointed to a journal with a green cloth cover. Sticky notes sprouted from its top like a misshapen daisy. A red star was drawn on one of the notes. She picked up the book and opened to that page.

"Madam, she tell me her recipe is on this page. But I say Madam I can't read this. She reads it to me in Czech and then in French. I write it down. Then I ask her what else it say on page? She tells me it say, 'TODAY IS CHRISTMAS 1916.' And then she tell me what happened on that day. She tell me she make pierogis for first time and she served them to some men from a camp. I think she say her sisters were there too."

"When I ask what else it say she waved me away. But then I think she feel bad for this because she started telling me about other recipes. She would turn to a page and read the recipe, she has all kinds of them. Seal meat with wild greens, blood sausage, roast goat, mint tea, even soap. As I write down the recipes, she tell me more stories about her life. The stories, they not all make sense and whenever I asked for more details, she say I tell you later, then she go on to another story, or recipe."

"Did you say she was in prison? I don't believe that."

"*Oui, oui*, yes, she say while on her honeymoon, in Egypt, the War break out. World War One she say and then she laugh 'the War that end all wars.' She and her husband were traveling on German passports and the British took them to jail. Thought they were spies. Imagine, madam a spy. They were shipped to an island somewhere and husband die."

"I tried to write it all down but she sometime talk too fast and other times too slow. She seemed to get lost in thought a lot."

"That's okay. Tell me more about how she acted. Did you believe her, did you believe the stories?"

"Of course, why she lie; she not confused. Just...how you say... nostalgia."

"No, no that's not what I meant. It's just that she doesn't talk about her life before coming to the States. I've never heard these stories. The only thing I've heard about was how a German banker foreclosed on her father's business. That's why she doesn't like debt, doesn't want to be beholden to someone else. Always says the borrower is slave to the lender. She came to this country as a war refugee in 1944. That's about all I know. Did you say she's sleeping now?"

"Oui, that right. She talked herself to exhaustion."

"Okay, let her rest. Let me help you clean this up, I want to talk to you about something anyway."

Iris looked up alarmed. "Did I do something wrong?"

His tone had been stern. *Damnit, I've got to work on that*, he thought. For some reason every time he needed to discuss business his voice deepened, his back straightened, and his tone told everyone he was the boss.

"No, no I'm sorry about that. You didn't do anything wrong, on the contrary. Let me ask you something. Do you like working for Nana?"

"*Oui*, yes, very much." Her tone was upbeat, but her face wore a look of concern.

"Are you sure, be honest?"

"Yes, yes, I like it here. Yes, she has her moments, but they are temporary, short lived."

"What does the nursing agency pay you?"

"Twelve dollars and hour. More if I stay late."

"Would you like to work her full time?"

"But I do. I'm here most days."

"But you work other places and other jobs to make ends meet, right?"

"Oui, I work other jobs so I can send money home to Haiti. Life is hard there and my family depend on me."

"I'd like it if you came to work for us full-time. I'll double your salary, with benefits and vacation. How's that sound? She likes you. Look at this." He waved a hand at the books. "You know more about her than I do, and I've known her my whole life."

"Oui, I would like that."

"Okay, it's settled. After the first of the year you will become an employee of Hawkeye Management. You'll be listed as the Company Nurse, but your only job will be to take care of Nana."

She looked at him, tears flowing from her eyes. "Is this real, you are not joking?"

"No, no joke" he said as he handed her a towel.

"Can I hug you?" As she held her arms up and moved to him.

He did the same and they embraced. They disengaged when they heard Nana stir in her room.

"You finish up here and I'll check on Nana" he said

Carson knocked on the bedroom door and asked, "You decent in there?"

"Yah, yah, come in."

"I had an interesting conversation with Iris. Can you tell me about the journals?"

"No!" she said forcefully. "Did you bring it?"

"Yes" and Carson handed her a legal-size envelope, then a pen.

She pulled out the document flipped it over and pointed to a set of digits on the back. "Is this correct?"

"Yes, Nana, I checked it yesterday."

The document was the Title to her 1990 Ford Explorer and although it was 10 years old it had less than 12, 000 miles on the odometer. She signed the back and announced, "Let's go, I make *pierohi.*"

"I think we need to clean the kitchen first."

"Okay, you clean, I watch. How was your day?"

"Good, but I want to know about your day."

"Iz nudding; lez go, I want to see the girl."

They walked into the kitchen and found Iris wiping tears from her face. Her eyes red and nose sniffling.

Nana looked at Carson with a sneer, "You make her cry! Wud you do? You bad boy!"

"No, no it's okay," said Iris "These are happy tears, he gave me best Christmas ever."

"Wud? You no give gift, I give gift."

Nana wrapped her arms around the younger woman and murmured, "Iz okay child, come with me, iz okay."

"You ladies go in the living room and I'll make coffee," Carson announced and waved them out of the room with an ancient aluminum percolator.

As Carson scooped roasted chicory into the pot's basket, he could hear the women speaking French. He couldn't understand a word and secretly admonished himself for not taking a language in high school. No matter, all was calm right now, as he stared at the little glass top hat on the percolator.

The water that bubbled against the glass was growing browner by the moment.

Another four minutes he thought as his pager buzzed. The digital readout announced **THE CUBE, TOMORROW 0800. FRED.**

No sooner had he absorbed this message than Iris screamed. He ran into the room and found her jumping around and waving the Title like a winning lottery ticket.

Nana watched Iris gyrate through her happy dance and thought about how much the young woman reminded of her in her youth. Far from home, in a foreign land learning, a new language, and yet not daunted by these obstacles. On the contrary, she embraced those challenges and responsibilities. And with all this the young woman had the capacity to care for others.

PARABELLUM: When you live in Peace, prepare for War

Jack Nanuq

CHAPTER 13
December 25, 1916
Isle of Man

Nana let her mind drift back to Christmas Day 1916...

Maria and a group of parishioners were milling about at the back of the Church. Everyone spoke of how beautiful sunrise service had been. Several of the women were also playing with Janos. They were commenting on how handsome he was in his little sailor suit; navy blue with white piping. He was fidgety under the constant attention and kept saying "Mama, mama...mama." The women thought this was cute and were pestering him to say something else. At 19 months of age his vocabulary was limited but this didn't keep the women from prodding him to say more than just this one word. One of the women; Maureen McAllister, was crouched on her heels and shaking a set of house keys in the little boy's face. She commented, "The lad should have a better command of his words; at that age me Colin could make complete sentences."

Janos did not like all the attention and repeatedly tugged Maria's dress.

"Mama, mama...mama."

Maria knew he was hungry. A creature of habit, he normally ate his breakfast right after morning Mass. Today's service had run longer than usual. To make matters worse she had forgotten to bring some biscuits, as was her custom. But she enjoyed the opportunity to catch up on the Island's happenings. She chatted with the adults and tried her best to carry her half of the conversation.

Janos scrunched up his face, as if to let out a scream. With the innocence of an uninhibited child announced, "Jesus done, let's go!"

The crowd burst out laughing. The spouse of the key jangler announced, "Aye, the Master has spoken, and truer words there never were."

"We must go… he hungry," Maria said in embarrassment. The adults nodded in acknowledgement and bid her a Manx Happy Christmas *"Nollick Ghennal."*

∞

An hour later the rectory kitchen was bustling with activity. Two nuns were stuffing a goose with sauerkraut and apples. Two others were washing dishes and another two were showing Maria how to make *pierohis*.

The only person not tasked with a chore was Janos who slept peacefully. Fed and wearing a clean diaper.

Sister Clarice spoke quietly to Maria. "The key to good dough is adding buttermilk to the flour and egg mixture. Then let the dough rest for at least 20 minutes. We'll make the filling while it rises."

While the fresh dough sat under a bowl the women moved to a small table near an open doorway. Although a light rain drifted outside, the door to the yard was open. With the cook stove going and the women working feverishly everyone was more than warm enough. Maria liked this spot, where the indoor and the outdoor air mixed; she got the best of both worlds. It also allowed her to glance down the path for the much-anticipated guests.

Sister Clarice mashed potatoes. Sister Xavier shredded cheddar cheese and Maria chopped onions. The dough would be wrapped around these Old-World staples. She paid close attention to all the details and wanted everything to be a success. She hoped to impress Petr with her cooking. He had shared with her that potato-stuffed *pierohis* were one of his most favorite foods. Aside from family, it was the thing he missed most from home.

During the previous year she had worked hard to develop and refine her kitchen skills. She learned to can vegetables, make jams, bake bread, and butcher livestock. The various nuns had lived and worked in over 20 countries. They were constantly sharing their worldly knowledge. They were all so helpful and she returned their generosity by taking it all in. By and large most of the culinary adventures were successful, except for the time she tried her hand at preparing eels. The slimy buggers were just too much for her. Sister Margaret had rescued her from that task, and the older woman joked "well, nobody's perfect."

In addition to helping with the meal, she'd also made Petr a new leather belt. She hoped he would not have to fight to keep this Christmas gift.

Maria jumped with a start and almost cut her finger when someone yelled a greeting. She turned to see the Corporal, Andrej and Petr walking her way. And Petr was pushing a bicycle, a canary yellow bicycle. The bike sported a large basket over the rear tire. She was confused by the sight.

Where did he get that from? Wasn't illegal for prisoners to have vehicles? Why was he pushing it and not riding it?

Maria wiped her hands on her apron and raced outdoors to meet the group. Petr held his treasure firmly. She could tell it was not new. The wheels were missing some spokes, and there were a few dents in the frame; but the paint was new. Petr then pushed the bike toward her. As he grew closer, she noticed the rear basket had holes cut in the bottom and held a small seat.

He stopped in front of her. "For you, Merry Christmas" he said.

"For me?" She responded with puzzlement.

"Yes, for you and Janos."

She then turned toward the kitchen door and sought Sister Veronique's permission. How could she accept such a valuable gift?

The Mother Superior nodded her head and added "Do you like it?"

"Yes, yes, very much. But how?"

"It's the season of miracles, let's leave it at that," the Mother Superior said.

Maria turned back to the bike and found Petr had secured the kickstand. Petr stepped away and it stood by itself. It was clear it had formally been a man's bike, but the top cross bar had been removed. She marveled at its transformation and her mind raced with all of its uses. She could now deliver her leather goods, for a fee of course. She could tour the countryside and bring home more items from the market. And with the modified basket, she could take Janos with her.

She admired the wonderful gift. She couldn't wait to try it out. But it had been years since she had ridden a bike. She wasn't sure if her first attempt might be a disaster and she did not want the group to witness such a debacle.

The rain increased and saved her from having to give a demonstration.

"Maybe we should all go inside and save us from a soaking" the Corporal suggested.

Before any of them could move she turned to Petr and wrapped her arms around him. "Thank you so much! Oh, so much! I don't know how you did it, but I love it."

He repeated his earlier greeting "Merry Christmas," and then in Czech "*Vesele Vanoce*!"

Maria would later learn the bicycle was rescued from a rubbish heap after it was struck by an Army lorry, but that did not matter to her. The fact that Petr spent weeks rebuilding it, was what mattered. She would ride the bike with pride and she would learn much during her trips around the Island. What she did not learn, until it was too late, was that Janos would develop such a passion for the wind in his face that it would have a profound influence on his life choices.

PARABELLUM: When you live in Peace, prepare for War

Jack Nanuq

CHAPTER 14
December 21, 2000
Schenectady, NY

At 7:55 AM Carson found the door to Fred's office open. The older man was typing on a computer. Carson knocked on the door frame and said, "You paged me?"

Without looking up Hutchinson said "Yeah, come in. Gimme a minute to shut this down." A few key strokes later and the screen went blank.

As Carson entered the office, he noticed it smelled of gun oil and cleaning solvents.

Hutchinson turned toward Carson and said "First, let me tell you your Security Clearance has been renewed. I thought it would take longer but that Carbon woman is on top of things."

You got that right Carson thought as he remembered the night they had spent together; *I'm such a whore.*

"The timing's perfect because we got an Op coming up and I want you on it. "

"Next, I want to talk to you about this." Fred pulled a red mechanics rag from a drawer. He unfolded the cloth and handed Carson the C96 Mauser pistol. The very weapon Carson had given to him just a few days earlier. The chamber was locked open and the weapon glistened with a fine sheen of oil.

"Hope you don't mind but I field stripped it. I went through it with a fine-tooth comb. It's seen some combat, but it's safe to fire. The ammo, that's a different story."

Carson remembered the tarnished and corroded cartridges and nodded his headed in agreement.

Fred pointed to a mark on the steel frame under the and edge of the wooden handgrip. The grip panel on the opposite side was hard rubber and appeared original. The wood appeared to be a battlefield substitute. "Looks like it got hit by a bullet or something, but it's only cosmetic."

Carson put the gun on his right hip, about where it would sit in a holster. The wooden grip was on the outside. He then moved the gun to the left hip, but with the grip forward. This simulated sitting in a cross-draw holster; again, the wooden grip was on the outside. "Hmm," he said as he pictured some poor soldier getting shot at. The gun probably saved him from a serious injury but not as one would imagine. The weapon had deflected a projectile, not fired one.

"That thing's got some history." Fred continued.

"It should, it's like a hundred years old."

"Not quite but close. Wanna know what I found out?"

"Sure," Carson said as he hefted the pistol. This distinctive handgun sported a box magazine in front of the trigger assembly. Star Wars fans would recognize a similarity to Han Solo's blaster.

"Yesterday I ran the serial number through the database; told me date of manufacture, 1919. That's it, nothing else. Not that odd for a war relic, no hits or wants, nothing. When I get back from lunch, I get a call from a contact at the BKA. That's the German equivalent of the FBI. The Germans keep records on everything. Your gun was originally purchased by the French Nationale Gendarme; in 1920. The Gendarme is their national police force. Who it got issued to is anyone's guess. No info until 1940. The French aren't so good at recordkeeping. In 1940 the Vichy government capitulates to the Nazis. All their weaponry, including this little beauty is seized by the Wehrmacht. This puppy's then issued to a motorcycle dispatch rider, named Janos Busch."

"Anything else?"

"Yeah a lot more. It was used to kill used to kill a Gestapo agent in Normandy; on June 5, 1944. That date mean anything to you?"

"D-day, no wait D-day, minus one."

"That's right. Now get this." Fred paused for effect. "Even with the invasion, the Gestapo investigated the death of their agent. When they went looking for witnesses, they discovered two people were missing. Corporal Janos Busch and a local girl named Maria Nowak. The Gestapo never located either person or the gun. The shooter was never positively identified."

"Jesus Christ!" marveled Carson. Suddenly seeing a completely different side to Nana.

"I'm not gonna ask where the gun came from, but you should know something."

"What's that?" Carson asked, clearly bewildered by this turn of events.

"My buddy at the BKA thought it was odd this file was still open. He's concerned; means someone has in interest in a 60-year old shooting. That can only mean Odessa, or one of their splinter groups. You know who I'm talking about, right? The gang of Nazi's that escaped to South America after the War. Got it? If that came from someone close to you, they could be in danger."

"Any chance I could talk to your contact at BKA?"

"No! And that means no, not no, with a wink and a nod! No! But here's the number for Archives at Langley. They might have something. Now let's go, we got a briefing downstairs."

The briefing involved Operation Peregrine and concerned two Bosnians (codename Kestrel 1 and Kestrel 2). This year the code computer was using bird names. The "birds" were going to be stashed at the cabin in Willsboro. Since Carson already knew the location of the safe house Fred wanted him to be part of the security detail.

Carson worked hard to maintain focus, but his mind kept spinning back to the gun and its relationship to Nana. As soon as they were dismissed from the meeting he raced to a phone.

"Archives," the woman with a southern drawl answered.

"Afternoon, I need bios on four names. Area of operation northern France. You may have to check the OSS files."

He then gave authorization codes for the request and his email address.

The first two names were the ones provided by the BKA agent. The third and fourth name were variations of the first two, Jon Nowak and Mary Novak.

"Suh, this may take a while. With the holidays, we're short staffed" said the woman on the phone.

"I'd be much obliged if I could have it in a week," Carson said with a manufactured soft southern twang.

"I'll see to it personally, suh."

"Thank you and Merry Christmas."

After that call he drove to the old woman's house.

∞

Carson rummaged through the freezer. There were three cartons of ice cream but nothing with chocolate. He closed the door and fished a $20 bill from his wallet.

"Iris, could you run to the store and get us some ice cream, maybe Rocky Road." He needed some alone time with Nana. When the younger woman was gone, he sat on the couch next to his great-grandmother.

"Can I talk to you?"

"Sure, sure, you okay? You no look so good."

"I'm fine, but I got to go out of town for a few days. I was wondering if you might like it if Newton stays here while I'm gone."

"Only if he wants too. I be fine either way. You take bag, you take two bags?"

"I'm taking two bags."

This was code. Somehow Nana had figured out he was doing clandestine work for the government. The multiple bag reference meant he was a taking a personal bag and a gear bag.

He thought back to when he was still in the Army. On one of the times he was home on leave he caught Nana rummaging through his personal bag. When caught she looked at him and said, "Where gun?"

"That's in another bag. When I deploy, I take two bags."

Now with her reference to two bags he had acknowledged he was putting himself in harm's way.

"Good boy, you make me proud." It was both a statement of affirmation, and a command.

He was humbled and simply said "Thank you; I will."

"You good boy."

"I need to ask you something?" He dreaded where this next part of the conversation would go. He wished he knew how she would react.

"Okay"

"Can you tell me about Grandpa Jon?" He had always thought Jon was short for Jonathon or Johan, but now he knew it was short for Janos.

"Vaat you vont to know and vie?"

"Was he in the Army, the German Army?"

"Yah, vie?"

"Was that his gun you gave me?"

"Yah; vie you vont to know these things?"

"Did he kill a Gestapo agent?"

"No! Not Janos, he good boy, he no shoot no one, he no kill Gestapo man...I did."

PARABELLUM: When you live in Peace, prepare for War
Jack Nanuq

Chapter 15
Derby, Vermont.
December 27, 2000

Operation Peregrine had begun more than 5 days ago, but Carson and his partner had only been actively involved in the op for about 48 hours. He parked the Dodge Durango at the only gas pump in the village of Derby Line, VT. He wasn't here to get gas, but something far more valuable. Even though the gas station was closed the area was bathed in light, for the 24-hour pump. Beyond the cone of light Carson couldn't see anything but silhouettes. He knew there were three other Durangoes hidden in the shadows.

He looked at his partner, Angie Rodriguez, and asked "You ready?"

"Born ready," she responded.

With that, they exited the SUV, placed their hands on holstered Glocks and stood ready to take possession of the package. They were 300 yards from the Canadian border and could hear the distant whine of snowmobiles. They could also hear a helicopter. The helicopter, on loan from Fort Drum and code-named Wasp 1, informed everyone the road was clear. Their headsets squawked and announced the package was about one minute away. Two snowmobiles broke through the trees, came down a snow-packed gravel road and pulled into the gas station lot. Each snowmobile had a passenger. The passengers dismounted and quickly walked to the Durango.

Angie said something, in Bosnian, to the two people and they climbed into the SUV without delay. They didn't even take off their helmets or jackets. With the mirrored face shields the passengers resembled space travelers.

Carson and Angie climbed back into the SUV and pulled out of the lot without any drama. The clock on the dashboard read 3:17 AM. They had another 4 hours of road in front of them. He wouldn't relax until he got them to the cabin, almost 200 miles away. Anything could happen between here and there.

A few minutes later he turned the SUV westward onto US 5. A set of headlights was about 100 yards behind him and a set of taillights about the same distance in front of them. The security convoy would spread out more as they got further from Derby. The Durangoes were identical in every detail, including the license plates. It was hoped, that if someone targeted a Durango, they would get the wrong one. Kestrel 1 and Kestrel 2 were very special and were to be protected at all costs.

Angie said something to Kestrel 2 and the woman in the backseat took off her helmet. She shook out a full mane of black hair. She was about 40 but looked older. Living in a war-torn country will do that.

She then turned to her companion and said something Carson could not understand but quickly deciphered. A teenage girl took off her helmet. Carson was surprised to see the girl was wearing a rainbow-colored Rastafarian knit cap. Aside from the gaudy headgear the girl was very plain looking, no make-up, no jewelry and no hair sticking out from the hat.

The older woman said something and reached for the cap. The girl pulled away and barked at her mother, not with hostility but firm, nonetheless.

Angie turned to Carson and relayed that the mom didn't like the cap and thought it looked ridiculous. The girl was exercising her sense of self by insisting it remain in place.

Kestrel 2 turned to Angie and added something new. Carson couldn't tell if her tone was sarcastic, mocking or just frustrated.

"Mom says the girl insists, as a Muslim, she should keep her hair covered and maintain a sense of modesty."

"I figured some of that. I guess mothers and daughters are the same everywhere," Carson said.

"I speak English," snapped the girl. "My mother doesn't but I do. You don't like my hat. Is everyone against me?"

"No wait," stammered Carson "I didn't say anything about your hat. I don't care what you wear."

"Good! I am Hana by the way, and my mother is Sultanija, but you can call her Sally. She wants an American name. Who are you?"

"I'm Robert Lake. Call me Robert" using his work name.

"Glad to meet you Robert, do we have far to travel?"

"About four hours; but we'll stop for breakfast in about two."

"Is it all like this?" pointing to the darkness outside.

"Yes, I'm afraid so."

Hana then turned to her mother and spoke something in their native tongue. The woman shook out a pill and then handed her a bottle of water.

Hana took the pill, chased it with some water and announced, "I take a nap now." She stripped her jacket off and turned it into a pillow. A short time later she was resting peacefully.

At 5:38 a.m. Carson, AKA: Robert Lake turned the Durango onto a bridge across a narrow neck of Lake Champlain. On the western shore a sign with the State logo read WELCOME TO NEW YORK. Angie Rodriguez pointed to the sign and provided a translation for Kestrel 2.

"Is anyone hungry?" asked Lake as he entered the Village of Rouses Point. The streets were quaintly decorated with Christmas lights. It looked like something from a Currier and Ives print.

Rodriguez repeated the question and the mother announced "Da."

Lake radioed ahead and informed the security detail of their plans to stop. He was sure the others would need to stop as well. A few minutes later they parked in the only municipal lot. The lead Durango was already stopped at a nearby gas station. Although Lake couldn't see the occupants, he knew they were scanning the area like a Secret Service detail. With dawn almost 90 minutes away the little village was like a ghost town. In the distance he could hear their air support. Carson could also hear a car driving on the slushy streets, he hoped it was the last Durango watching their tail.

Rodriguez walked to the back door and gently woke the sleeping girl. She whispered something to the teenager and the youngster's head bounced up and down. Angie then swapped the Rastafarian knit cap for a large checked bandana. A few bobby pins helped stray hairs stay hidden under the fabric.

Carson adjusted the ballistic vest that sat under his sweater. It was starting to chafe the lower part of his neck. The group then walked to a diner across the street.

As Carson, Angie and the Kestrels walked inside it was apparent they'd have the place almost to themselves. The only other occupants were two construction workers, wearing orange safety vests, and a single waitress. The men were starting their day with a plate of eggs and the waitress was wiping the counter near them.

"Morning, just sit anywhere."

Kestrel 2 whispered something, and Angie pointed to the ladies room.

"Can you find us a table in back?" she asked Carson and added "I'll stay with them." She then herded the women to the restroom.

Carson found a table as directed and noted the placemats cartoonish maps of the region. A ragged line of red maple leaves, near the top, showed the US-Canadian border. A single line ran down the middle showing Interstate 87. An X near the intersection of Route 11 and I-87 was marked YOU ARE HERE. The right edge of the map was blue and showed a caricature of a sea monster named CHAMP. The left edge showed the Adirondack Mountains and stickmen on skis.

When Hana returned, she was fascinated by the map. She whispered something to her mother and put her finger on their location. The mom said something that included the word skyscraper. Angie stifled a laugh.

"She wants to know where all the skyscrapers and people are," Rodriguez said out of the corner of her mouth.

"That's New York City. We're about 300 miles from there. This is Northern New York State. The best part of the State, as far as I'm concerned."

The mother asked something, and Angie responded "*Ne.*" Angie then put a finger near the lower right corner of the map and slowly said "Willsboro."

"I told her where we're headed to; how much further?" Angie said to Carson.

"About an hour," he responded.

The bell at the door tinkled and everyone at the table froze. Carson stuck his head up and he saw Fred Hutchinson walked to the counter. Neither made eye contact.

"Be with you in a minute" the waitress announced as she walked to Carson's table.

"Take your time" Hutchinson replied nonchalantly.

She couldn't have known it, but the waitress did exactly as they had hoped. It would provide Fred with the opportunity to loiter inside if any extra help was needed.

She handed out well-worn plastic menus and asked what they'd have to drink. Carson asked for an orange juice while the others ordered coffee.

Carson took an opportunity to carefully examine Kestrel 1 and compare her to the information in the case file. He scrutinized her with the intensity of a gangster casing a bank.

The girl, and that's what she was at 16 years of age, had cherubic cheeks. Her face was soft and pure, with no acne scars or any imperfections. Her complexion had a slight olive tint, testifying to distant Turkish blood. At one time her homeland had been part of the Ottoman Empire. She was wearing a heavy flannel shirt and the snowmobile bibs. If there were any pre-adult curves under there they were obscured by layers of fabric. Her hands were soft with short bitten fingernails. She was busily coloring the sea monster with a green pen. She beamed as if she didn't have a care in the world although she had seen and experienced unspeakable horrors.

Carson had trouble matching the angelic child in front of him with the purpose of this mission. This girl was on the verge of developing a revolutionary weapons defense system.

PARABELLUM: When you live in Peace, prepare for War

Jack Nanuq

CHAPTER 16
Albany, NY
December 27, 2000

"So, that was the day the fan hit the shit!" Newton told the laughing women.

Newton had just finished a story about the time, as a Navy Corpsman, he responded to a helicopter crash. The chopper was coming in for a landing when it suddenly lost power near a row of porta-potties and a honey wagon. The fuselage hit the holding tank and split it open "like an overripe melon" and the rotors shredded the fiberglass latrines.

By the time he was done describing the crash site as piles of "blue poop and soggy asswipe" Nana and Iris were in hysterics. Iris was cackling like a schoolgirl and Nana brayed like an asthmatic mule. Newton was actually concerned for Nana. Her face had flushed to the color of molten lava.

Suddenly Nana froze in place.

"Are you, all right?" Newton asked the old woman.

"Yah, yah."

"You look like you saw a ghost," Newton said with concern.

"Not a ghost, a devil." She ran a hand across her forehead. "Your story. It remind me of father-in-law. Can I tell?"

"Yes" Newton and Iris said in unison.

"We called him *Soudce,* which means judge. In our village he vaas judge, jury and executioner. He bad man, also banker and gangster. He rule our village like he mafia boss. Spring 1914, I vaas only 13 he came to our house for the first time. I sick in bed and hear the motorcar. I know it him, he only person in village with car. Papa vaas in cowshed milking. Dat was my job to do, but papa told me to rest. I sneak to window and hear them but not so good. Part I hear and part Papa tell me later. They talk about me marry Gregor, the son. Papa say '*nyet.*' *Soudce* say it would be good for my family but papa he say no. He say, I too young."

93

"Papa calm and repeat I too young. But *Soudce* insists and gets excited and yells. He startles cow and she shat; covers *Soudce* head-to-toe. Gregor's father mad now, very mad. He storm out of shed. He now look like giant *hovno,* a turd. He climb in car and drive away yelling. He be back."

"What happen next?" Iris asked

"Papa, he come in house and we all laugh. We laugh hard, so hard. We know it serious matter but it funny, so funny. That was the last time we laugh at *Soudce.* Someone come to our shed that night and slit cow's throat."

Both Newton and Iris sat there, stunned. "Is that why you married Gregor?" Newton asked, to ease the tension.

"Partly yes, partly no. I no want marry Gregor. But three weeks later some men, they beat papa and leave him in a ditch. Leave him for dead. I know then I must marry Gregor."

"The day they find my papa, *Soudce* come to house second time. He say he send for doctor if papa say yes to proposal. But papa not awake, Papa just lay there and moan. I say I marry Gregor if doctor come. *Soudce* say I smart girl. I marry Gregor one month later. My papa he never wake. He die, day before wedding. It good thing. After Papa die, my mother she sign over farm to *Soudce.* He say Papa owe him money. He promises to take care of her, but he lie."

"What was Gregor like?" asked Iris.

Nana paused and slowly shook her head in disappointment. "Gregor was bookish. He was a disappointment to *Soudce.* He lacked substance. *Soudce* want him to be lawyer. But Gregor he want to be arky... an arky..." She reached out with a trembling hand as if to pluck the elusive word from the air. "You know one of those digger men."

"An archeologist," interjected Newton.

"Yes, dat it. *Soudce* send us to the Levant, what is now called Middle East, after wedding. He think Gregor change his mind once he get taste of real work. *Soudce* right, Gregor he not like desert. All that dirt and stink and bugs. But we never make it home, we get arrested in Egypt."

"Arrested...you?" asked Newton.

"Yes, Egypt was British colony then. The fighting in Europe, they call The Great War. Had been going about five months. We were traveling under German papers and the government thought we be spies. We get arrested day after Christmas, 1914. They put Gregor in jail, but not know what to do with me. They send for Sister Veronique. She took me to convent. Months later we were sent to Isle of Man. Sister try to argue for my release but the Court say I have to accompany husband. Husband sent to Camp Knockaloe. She argue the prison was no place for young girl and Court agree. But say I need to be on same island as husband. She made arrangements for me to stay with a group of nuns near Camp. She come with us and like second mother to me."

"What happened to Gregor?" Iris asked.

"He die, but not before he give me a son."

"So, were you a spy?" asked Iris.

"No, no... not then, but later... later...yes."

CHAPTER 17
Isle of Man
July 28, 1917

"Faster Mama, faster. Yeeeeeeeeee" Janos screamed joyfully.

He was buckled into the basket on the back of Maria's yellow bike and waved his arms like a bird. "Faster Mama, faster."

Maria was taking a shortcut through a pasture and cascading down a steep path. The rutted trail was one mile long and she could cover the distance in less than two minutes, about 35 MPH, or 51.3 feet per second.

She wanted to get the news to the rectory. Mackerel were flooding the shoals. Fresh mackerel was Sister Veronique's favorite. As proof, her front basket was full of fish, caught by boys near the beaches. The fish were held in place by a by a makeshift cover fashioned from barbwire. Aside from fish, barbwire was the only thing in abundance on this island.

With her cargo secure she could concentrate on the trail. Maria fought the bike like a wild bull. It seemed to be drawn to every bump, hummock and pothole. Every moment threatening to pull loose of her grip and control. The hard rubber tires magnified the energy of every impact. The sensations were many; exhilarating, terrifying, muscle straining, and mentally taxing. But most of all freeing. Free to challenge the elements and laws of Nature. Gravity be damned.

Splashing mud plastered stray hairs to her face and eyes. She wanted desperately to wipe it away but didn't dare let go of the handlebars. The contraption more alive than any animal; fought to throw them free at the slightest bit of inattention.

Her eyes darted up and down the trail; mentally calculating the path of least resistance. Half a furlong in front a sheep crossed the path. No... wait... not cross the path but blocked it. A large boulder to the right and a large Hawthorne tree to the left; the beast right in the middle. The obstacles were about 100 yards in front; less than six seconds.

96

One second passed, 53 feet, before she fully processed the situation. She forced her eyes back to the path immediately in front. The bike bucked and swayed as it bounced from rock to rock. Her grip tightened against the handlebars. She pressed back on the pedals to engage the coaster brake. The chain protested this action by promptly snapping and flying free. The pedals spun wildly almost throwing Maria off balance. She fought to remain upright.

Again, she looked ahead, praying the creature had moved on; no luck. Apparently, tree buds were on today's lunch menu. It stood there munching on the greenery; oblivious to its impending doom.

Maria's head bobbled up and down to watch both the trail immediately in front and the stupid animal. She screamed curses at it. In her mind her speech was articulate but in the raging wind it sounded like, "aaaaaaaaaaahhhhhhhhhhhhhhhhh!"

Encouraged by the scream Janos added to the commotion by yelling "Faster mama, faster mama."

Two seconds to impact and Maria was certain it would be fatal, but for whom, the animal, Janos, or herself; maybe all three. What to do, her mind quickly processed her options, there were none. She was certain they would crash into the wall of mutton and it would be bad.

One second. The dim-witted animal looked up in bewilderment. A primitive survival instinct forced him to jump out of the way; so close that Maria could count the ribs on its newly shorn side. It dodged to the left and she to the right. Her right elbow smacked the boulder and the arm went numb. With no feeling in that arm, the other pulled to the left. The bike spun around the tree; right into a thick stand of saplings. Fingers of brush grabbed her with the strength of a cargo net and held her vertical. Not quite vertical but definitely not horizontal; and most importantly not corkscrewed into the ground.

Maria stood over the bike and tried to collect her thoughts; her breathing ragged and rapid. The adrenaline ebbed from her body and her leg muscle quivered uncontrollably. Her armed throbbed and blood dripped from the side of her head.

Janos giggled, "That was fun! Do it again! Do it again Mama!"

∞

An hour later the guinea hens in the churchyard announced Maria's arrival. The small spotted birds with their distinctive cackle were protesting Janos' arrival. The little bugger chased them every chance he could.

"Mama, I almost catched one."

"Yes, you did," Maria chuckled. If this was his version of "almost" the birds would live a long life. He never got any closer than ten feet.

Sister Clarice, working in the garden, looked up at the racket. "Oh, my child! What happened, are you alright?" she said as she ran toward the young mother.

"I'm fine," Maria mumbled but it was clear she wasn't. She was pushing the bike, her face was scratched, and her ripped blouse had spots of blood.

Janos, innocent of the averted tragedy, yelled "Momma made is go fast then she made us go stop!"

"Oh my" the nun said. "That sounds like an adventure". She added "Maria, are you alright? Did someone do this to you?"

"Dah. No…I'm mean no one did this to me. I fine. It my own fault. I was going too fast on the bike. I think I alright. My arm hurts and there is a thorn in my ear. But I think I all right."

"Let's get you inside and cleaned up" the nun said as she touched Maria's bloody ear.

"I need to see to Janos, he not have lunch yet."

"No, no don't worry about that, I'm sure Sister Veronique will see to his needs." "I'll get you cleaned up and you can tell me about your mishap."

Clarice looked into the front basket and saw the fresh fish. On top was the broken bike chain, coiled up like a treacherous snake.

PARABELLUM: When you live in Peace, prepare for War

Jack Nanuq

CHAPTER 18
Lake Placid, NY
March 22, 2001

This was Carson; AKA Robert Lake's, third trip up north in as many months. The Kestrels had settled into life at the cabin in Willsboro. The security team reported they were a joy to work with. Both Sally and Hana listened to all instructions and never asked for too much.

He'd also been told Hana's work was progressing well. The powers-that-be were ecstatic and wanted everything to continue. It was for this reason the Kestrels were permitted two days away from the cabin; a much deserved mini-vacation.

Carson had to admit the Kestrels had adapted well. Both had gained weight and were less haggard each time he saw them. Rumor had it that Hana had developed a liking for pancakes with real maple syrup.

Yesterday they spent eight hours on the slopes of Whiteface Mountain. Both Hana and her mother handled the moguls like champions. The security team was challenged to keep up with them. By the end of the day Carson's leg was screaming.

This morning they toured the US Olympic Committee Training Center in Lake Placid. A benign experience compared to the previous day's adventure.

Hana insisted they visit Lake Placid when she learned it had hosted both the 1932 and 1980 Winter Olympics. The city of her birth, Sarajevo, had hosted the Winter Olympics in 1984. That had been a year before she was born. Her country began to disintegrate a short time later.

Hana had a ball at the Center. She had an autograph book which at least 20 athletes had signed. She looked at them with the admiration most teenagers show rock stars. After visiting the Center, they spent the afternoon touring the Village of Lake Placid. Main St. was a collection of small shops and boutiques. Immediately behind the shops on the north side was a broad expanse. Under the snow and ice was Mirror Lake. Why it wasn't the Village namesake was a mystery.

Kestrel 2 whispered something to one of the women in the security detail. Angie Rodriguez turned to Carson.

"She wants to know if you need a break. Is your hip bothering you?"

"Is it that noticeable?"

"If you were a horse, we'd have shot you by now."

Carson looked at his watch. "I want to make one more stop before we go to dinner." At that he herded them into a shop belonging to Adirondack Chocolates. "You have to try the fudge covered pretzels."

The store was small, but cozy. The was air thick with the aroma of chocolate, mint, and spices. A counter top, with a dozen coffee carafes, ran along the front window expanse. A display case, that resembled a small greenhouse, ran down the middle of the store. It held dozens of treats, including the much-touted pretzels.

"I'm getting a cup of coffee while you girls' shop." Carson poured himself a cup and dropped a dollar bill into an honor box. A small note told patrons that all coffee proceeds went to local charities.

He then took a seat at the counter, with his right shoulder against the window. From this vantage point he could watch the interior of the store, as well as a portion of Main Street.

Angie took the seat opposite him.

"No chocolate for you?" he asked.

"Nah, I gave it up for Lent. Besides you need someone to watch your back."

"Well thank you, that's mighty nice of you," he joked. "Can I return the favor with a cup of coffee?" Carson breathed in the vapors drifting from his cup.

"That's ok. I'll get one later, for the road."

Carson's attention was drawn outside, to a man in a tattered camo jacket. His poor clothing stood out in the crowd of well-dressed tourists. The man was rummaging in a trashcan and collecting empty soda bottles. People avoided the scavenger as if he had the plague.

Hana plopped down in a chair just as the man walked in front of the store. "Is he a soldier?" She asked with concern, as she nodded her head in the man's direction. Her eyes were down and her body rigid.

"He might have been at one time, but not now," responded Carson. The jacket's raggedness indicated it had probably been picked up at a surplus store.

Hana relaxed. "I don't like soldiers."

"All soldiers, or just the ones from your country?" Angie asked.

"I guess just the ones from my country. They killed all the boys in my neighborhood." She said it so casually most would have thought she didn't understand what had just been said. But she did understand; she had lived through the ethnic cleansing of her country.

"Do you want to talk about it?" Carson asked, not sure if he wanted her to say yes or no.

Angie interrupted "Not here, let's talk about something else. Tell Mr. Lake about your moose."

Carson smirked at Angie's ability to divert the girl's attention; as easy as throwing a ball to a puppy.

Hana beamed and started the story about the moose. She had named the animal Moosey. What else do you call one of God's most ugly creatures. Hana was working to earn its trust. Last week they had seen it lounging near the cabin.

The story began about a month earlier. Hana, Sally and Angie were snowshoeing about a mile from the cabin. One sunny morning a cow moose blocked their path. Hana had been fascinated by the animal but had been talked into returning home. Angie explained moose could be unpredictable and dangerous, especially if they had a calf. The young girl left an apple as a treat. Since then Hana made it a point of leaving a different treat every day. And each day the treats were left closer and closer to the cabin. Hana was hoping that someday she'd be able to feed the animal from the back porch.

Suddenly Hana stopped her story and stared out the window. Her attention had been drawn back to the vagrant in front of the store. He had been pulling soda cans from the public trash can but was now holding a crumpled bag from McDonald's. He'd found a few fries in the bottom of the bag and gobbled them up quickly. Enlightenment dawned on Hana's face. She realized the man wasn't just collecting cans for extra money but for enough to buy a meal. She then turned to her mother.

"Momma, we should help him."

"Yes, we should" responded Sally as she fished a $20 bill from her purse. Sally's English skills had improved considerably since Carson had first met her.

Angie pulled a twenty from a pocket, quickly followed by Carson doing the same. Sixty dollars was nothing in the scheme of things; but would probably feed this man for a week.

"I'll take it out to him. Would you like to come with me?" Angie asked Hana.

"No!" interjected Sally.

"Ok, understood."

Carson watched the Kestrels as Angie walked outside and approached the man. Both were staring at the two people just a few feet away. The words were muffled but it was clear the man was grateful for the help. Carson amazed by how complex the younger woman was. She had the cherubic face of a child, despite being a refugee and a witness to genocide. Here she was helping a man she was frightened of only a moment ago. It was like staring at a rainbow, the beautiful product of a storm. A thing that was recognizable but hard to define.

The man turned toward the group, made eye contact with Hana and then made a heart with his hands. He held it over his chest, the universal sign for "I love you."

Hana blushed and turned away.

"That was very nice of you," Carson said to Hana. He was embarrassed that the youngest of their group was the first to recognize the man's need.

"Iz nudding," said Sally, blushing.

PARABELLUM: When you live in Peace, prepare for War
                                                    Jack Nanuq

    Carson laughed internally as that seemed to be Nana's favorite saying lately.

CHAPTER 19
Isle of Man
September 1, 1917

"Those bloody Yanks need to get off their arses. Don't they know our boys are dying in the trenches? What the hell are they waiting for? They declared war on the Boche five months ago and yet none have come to the fight!" The old man bellowed, not really expecting an answer. He crumpled his newspaper and threw it at the kindling bin.

"I'm sure they do, ya daft bugger. That... be why they are slow in committing," his wife responded. "Besides if their soldiers are as poor as their beer they might best stay home. Speaking of lazy arses, why don't you get off yours and pick up the bloody paper you just threw onto my clean floor. Was ya born in a barn?"

Maria felt like a hostage in the couple's home. She was fitting a new boot onto the woman's foot and couldn't even if she wanted to. The elderly couple was as coarse as marsh grass and it would never occur to them to temper their language around her. And yet as crude as their language was it was clear they cared very deeply for one another. The man had already been getting up when the wife fired her last shot. Maria liked the pair and they were always kind to her.

"Mrs. Kelly, how does that feel?" Maria said as she smoothed the leather over the woman's ample calf.

"It'd be feeling fine lass. But I be needing to put the other one on to give an honest opinion."

Maria grabbed for the other boot and hoped this pair would last longer than previous one. The last set had worn out prematurely, not because of Maria's workmanship but because this woman walked on the sides of her feet. A survivor of polio; her legs were bowed like barrel staves. As Maria slid the second boot on, she noticed the husband was by her side. He was there to help his wife out of the chair; all thirteen stone of her.

"Aye Maria, you've done well," the woman announced as she walked around the small cottage. "They be a little loose but that'll be good on the days I be holding me water. You've done fine work, girl."

She then barked at her husband. "Arthur, you be wantin to open your wallet now. She's done a good job and she deserves her reward, and don't be stingy about it."

"I hear ya woman. You need not be talking to me like that. Keep it up and I'll have the girl make a muzzle for ye."

The old man handed Maria the agreed upon price and an extra shilling. He then put a pot on the stove.

"You'll be staying for tea." It wasn't a question and yes, she would stay.

Tea really meant lunch and Maria could not refuse. Mrs. Kelly was the best cook on the island. The air was saturated with the rich aroma of rabbit and vegetable pie, cooking in the oven. Maria's mouth had been watering since she entered the home. "I be fool to say no. Dah, thank you" she said.

Maria marveled at the contrasts in this house. The occupants were as rough as the land, but successful. Mr. Kelly was one of the few beekeepers on the island and with the scarcity of sugar he had plenty of customers for his honey. They weren't wealthy but needed for nothing.

The cottage was a perfect example. The furniture was threadbare, but clean. Everything was spotless, not a thing out of place. And there were books, more books than Maria had ever seen in one place. Mrs. Kelly had told her once the books were her passport to adventure. With her handicap she couldn't see the world, so books brought the world to her. The walls were also lined with shelves; shelves that held mementos and photos. The photos showed the age progression of their four daughters, all grown now and working as nurses. There was much pride and love here.

The house was made of stone, stone floors and stone walls, and should have been cold; cold like a cave. But it wasn't, it was warm and not just because of the hearth. This wasn't just a house, it was a home.

An hour later the Mr. Kelly was helping Janos finish his meal. "Maria... have you given any thought to what you might do after the War? I don't imagine your people will welcome you home, especially with the wee one here."

"Jesus, you're a vulgar bugger!" interrupted the wife. "Please forgive me husband, sometimes he's got the manners of a goat." The wife then turned to back to the man. "You can't be talking to her like she's the village tart. The baby's not a bastard. The girl had a man, a legal man. They was married, with papers and everything. She's a widow for Christ sake, not a strumpet!"

"I said no such thing. It's just, there will be a fair number that will think she sat out the War in safety and comfort. There won't be many that will want her there. Not to mention that times will be hard, harder than they are now. The Crown will not be merciful to the Huns."

"Aye, I guess he's right" Mrs. Kelly agreed.

Maria sat there stunned. She had considered what her life might be like after the War, but how could she know for sure. It was like looking into fog. Who could know what lay ahead? It had never occurred to her, she would not be welcome home, not that she really wanted to go anyway. With her mother dead, there was nothing to return to. But was it true that her countrymen might hate her and Janos?

The three adults turned to Janos when he announced, "I'm not a basher, am I momma?"

"No sweetheart, you're not a basher."

CHAPTER 20
Albany, NY
March 31, 2001

Carson carried the ice cream cake into Nana's house. Tomorrow would be her 101st birthday. *How does someone live past the century mark*, he thought? As he kicked his boots off in the back porch he was greeted with the strong aroma of beer and broth. He recognized it as one of his favorite meals; the recipe called for a pint of Guinness and a meat few people ate anymore. He then heard the women working in the kitchen. When he stepped into the room the two looked up from what they were doing.

"Mister Carson, you're early," Iris said as she sliced a large green banana.

He walked to Nana, who was tearing apart a head of lettuce. Here was the answer to his question. *Eat greens every day and you'll live forever. Or die trying.*

He kissed her on the top of the head. "Smells delicious. Is that what I think it is?"

"Dah...iz hair spray," she gave him a look that read "gotcha".

Carson froze. At 100 Nana still had a quick wit. Remarkable, she could turn his words around and use them against him. She knew damn well what he was talking about. Now he had a second answer to his question. *She lived to aggravate him.*

Iris not sure what to make of this interaction answered "In the oven is Manx rabbit casserole, and I fixing *Lapen nan krèm*. My mama always made it for parties. It mean rabbit in cream but is really coconut milk."

As she said this a heavy cast iron pan sizzled and she ran to the stove to turn the pieces of brown meat. "Can you hand me that?" she asked, pointing to a plate of chopped vegetables.

He watched her slowly add peppers, onions, then others he didn't recognize. The hot oil popped in protest as it was cooled by the additions. Iris mixed everything, including the milk, and then added a heavy lid.

Carson pulled three beers from the fridge and took a seat across from Nana.

A journal, with sticky notes, lay between them. He quickly twisted the cap off two Genesee Cream Ales and pointed the third toward Iris. "Do you want one?"

"Oui"

He set one down in front of his seat, the second in front of Nana, and then walked the third to the stove. Iris moved the heavy pan to a back burner and turned the gas to simmer.

"Merci" she said as she took the beverage.

Carson took the seat directly across from Nana. She sipped her beer and stared at a new photo on the wall. Not exactly new, about 60 years old. The same one Carson had removed from the trunk, so many months ago. It was now encased in a cheap imitation brass frame, probably a thrift store find. He pointed his bottle toward the picture and toasted "To Grandpa Jon."

"To Grandpa Jon" Iris added, even though she wasn't family.

"To Janos" added Nana.

Carson sensed she wanted to say more, and he took advantage of this rare opportunity. "Tell us something about him?"

"Vaat you vant to know?"

"Anything. I only knew him as an old man, with a bad leg and a glass eye. When was he a soldier and why?"

"He no like being soldier, he conscripted." She paused and then continued. "But he love motorcycles, he love go fast! In the 30's he race many times. He win many races."

Carson didn't know how to take this information; it was news to him. His grandfather had been very quiet and never talked about his past. He knew the older man had served in the War; everyone of that age did. But Carson never knew it was in the German army. Carson kept up the momentum. "So he was good, I mean with the racing?"

"Dah," she said proudly. She then said something to Iris, in French, and the younger woman left the room.

A few moments later Iris returned with a small package wrapped in brown corduroy. It was tubular, maybe the leg from an old pair of pants.

Nana's hands were animated as they unwrapped the package. The liver spotted fingers seemed to dance, with a life of their own. She took out a small notebook, similar to a pocket-sized bible. Flipping through the book she found an old newspaper clipping. Yellow and brittle cellophane tape held it in place. "Here," she said. The article was in French.

"What does it say?" Carson asked as he handed it to Iris.

She took a moment to read the article. "It says a man named Jacques Lapin won 20 francs in a local motocross race."

"Who is Jacques Lapin?" Carson asked.

"It was Janos" interrupted Nana "he not want me to worry so he used a *faux nom*, a fake name. And it was secret. Petr knew but I not know for years. This is Petr's book. They were very close; more like brothers than father and son."

Jacques Lapin, in English that would be Jack Rabbit Carson thought.

Iris continued "it says the crowd roared as he crossed the finish line a full minute ahead of the closest rival. The race lasted 97 minutes, with average speed of 73 kilometers per hour."

"When, and where?" Carson was intrigued

Iris pointed to a number and hand-written note, next to the article "1-7-31 Le Figaro"

"We live near Calais, in France, at da time. It was July 1st, 1931 and the newspaper was the Le Figaro," Nana explained. "Janos worked as a mechanic then. But on Saturdays, he and Petr would go off to races. They kept it a secret for long time."

"How you find out madam?" Iris asked.

"Two years later," she tapped a finger on another article, "he crash and break leg. Petr had to tell me then. I was

110

so angry, but I was proud, but I was angry. So many emotions." She was misty-eyed and the fingers that only moments ago were twirling like circus acrobats were now locked upon themselves. Her eyes stared into a distant past. The face was that of stone and the body rigid.

Carson looked to her chest to see if she was still breathing: she was. He wanted so much to see what she saw. He was the last of the Nowak clan and knew so little about his family's past and accomplishments. Growing up, he would ask questions about the family and was always heard "Someday I tell you." Now the somedays were running out. His grandparents were gone, his parents were gone and now this remaining archive was on borrowed time.

He reached for the small book. The handwriting was cursive and meticulous; not Nana's. At least it did not match the scratching in her journals. This writing had distinct characters with marks over some of the letters. Could it be that Petr, whoever that was, had written it in plain script? "Can I borrow this?" He asked as he palmed the book.

Nana responded with a slight head nod; her mind still lost in the past.

A plan began to unfold in his mind, but he would need the help of Iris, and maybe one other.

PARABELLUM: When you live in Peace, prepare for War

Jack Nanuq

CHAPTER 21
Ilion, NY
April 7, 2001

The clock on the dashboard read 6:44 and Carson could see the sky in his rearview mirror starting to lighten. He again found himself driving one of the Durangoes. This time they were last in line and about a mile behind the other two.

"Should we be this far from the team?" Angie Rodriguez asked him.

"I'll close the gap, a little but I don't want any cops noticing three identical SUV's"

"So where are we right now?"

They had left Albany almost ninety minutes earlier and were traveling westbound on the New York State Thruway. Mimicking a cheesy tour guide Carson responded with "off to our left are the lights of Ilion, home of Remington Arms. The oldest gun maker in America."

In a gear bag on the back seat was a Remington model 870 pump shotgun, similar to the ones millions of sportsmen carried around the world. Although Carson's gun wasn't high tech like a as a sub-machine gun or an assault rifle it was no less lethal. How ironic was it that they were on a trip to test a weapon system that would transform modern warfare?

Carson's headset buzzed, and he turned to Angie "I got to take this." He then tapped a button and answered his phone. "Go for Lake" he said.

"It's Liza. You got a minute?"

"Always got time for you"

"I had some guys look at the notebook you sent me. We've only had about a dozen pages translated but I thought I'd let you know what we found."

"Great, let's hear it."

"It's written in Czech. There's a number of slang words and abbreviations we can't figure out. But it speaks about a woman named Maria and a boy named Janos; seems they all lived in France. Petr worked in a rail yard and Maria ran a bistro."

"Anything else?"

"Yeah…, it's not a diary, at least not in the traditional sense. It seems the author only made an entry every few weeks or so. The book covers about a 15-year span, basically the years between the Wars. We've got a lot more work to do but should be done in about a month. I'll send a transcript of what we've got so far."

"Great. What do I owe you?"

"Nothing right now but I'll think of something. I hear they're bringing a PF Chang's to Albany."

Just then Carson hit a large pot hole and the headset bounced free.

Angie grabbed for the gadget and missed. It bounced around like it had a mind of its own. As it hit the floorboard Carson shouted, "I'll call you back."

∞

Two hours later the caravan pulled up to the North gate of Fort Drum. A blue and white sign read HOME OF THE 10TH MOUNTAIN DIVISION. A large contingent of MPs was waiting for the group, which was escorted to an out of the way bunker.

When they arrived at the bunker, they found four ominous looking black Chevrolet Suburbans already on the scene. The tint on the windows was almost darker than the paint on the fenders. The glossy glass resembled the eyes of a giant beetle. As the Durangoes rolled to a stop, ten men stepped from the Suburbans. All were wearing dark trench coats and aviator sunglasses. They couldn't have looked more like G-men than if central casting had been involved.

The concrete structure was dome shaped. At about 50 feet wide and about 12 feet tall, it resembled a giant igloo.

The entire group descended a set of stairs and were greeted by an unpleasant aroma as they emerged below ground. Both Kestrels crinkled their noses. It was an imbedded mix of cigarette smoke, sweat, adrenaline and anxiety, with a hint of Pine-Sol. It reminded Carson of a sleazy night club.

Opposite the entrance was a bank of video screens, a computer work station, and a lectern. Thirty or so folding chairs were in the middle of the room. Two of the MPs were organizing food and drink on a shelf to the right of the entrance.

"I'd like to welcome you all to Fort Drum," said a captain standing by the table. "If you could all step over here, I have some paperwork for you to sign." The captain wore no name tag, but Carson knew him as Mark McAlister.

The trench coat mafia pushed their way to the front of the line. Each grabbed a clipboard scanned the document and scribbled a signature. Carson knew the document was a confidentiality agreement. It was full of legal verbiage that promised a million years of incarceration should today's events be disclosed to unauthorized parties.

The men in trench coats were an unsettling group and made more so as they kept their sunglasses on. They made no attempt to introduce themselves or socialize. They moved en masse toward the coffee bar, without saying a word. Carson wondered if they communicated telepathically.

After signing the document, Carson escorted the Kestrels to the snack tray where he found the coffee carafes empty. He sent a vile glance toward the thieves, sipping on their caffeinated nectar. Not only had the trench coats taken all the coffee, they now dominated the front row of chairs. The Kestrels grabbed two bottles of water and Carson picked up a large navel orange.

Video screens blinked to life and drew everyone's attention in that direction.

The captain spoke up again. "Everyone take their seats, we'll get started now."

One of the screens read PROJECT PARABELLUM, and in smaller script it read "When you live in peace, prepare for war."

Carson and the Kestrels took seats in the second row. Hana was beaming with pride. She held her mother's hand, not in fear but in triumph. She had worked for months to help bring this project to the testing stage. Sally was stuck behind one of the men-in-black. His wet wool coat smelled like a damp dog.

The video screen now showed an outdoor panorama. Snow blanketed the ground and dry weeds danced in the wind. A set of railroad tracks ran horizontally and a large concrete cube about 5 feet wide sat near the middle of the vista. A tripod with a flat panel, stood on the block.

"Folks, if I can get you to look at the tracks outside, we'll get started with the testing."

Hana should be in the front row; this is her baby, Carson thought. *But no… we gotta stare at the backs of these yahoos.* Carson leaned forward with his fruit and sunk a thumbnail into the thick rind. Citrus mist sprayed the back of a yahoo. The victim was oblivious to the assault.

Sally stifled a laugh and as the air took on the scent of an orange grove she whispered, "Thank you." Carson simply shrugged like he didn't know what she was talking about.

McAlister raised a remote control and another screen flashed to life. A small railcar slowly moved into view. It appeared to be traveling about five miles an hour. The image zoomed in and showed a close-up. On the car was glass jar holding what looked like a jelly bean. "On the concrete block we have a RF transmitter. It's similar to the anti-theft devices found in a department store. The kind that makes an alarm go off if someone leaves the store without deactivating. In the jar we have the Parabellum. It is a passive receiver and micro switch. Let's see what happens."

The railcar picked up speed and when it got about fifty feet from the block the jar exploded. It was an impressive display, but Carson wondered what all the fuss was about. The railcar continued off screen and thirty seconds later it returned from the opposite direction. This time a 60mm mortar round was on the car. When it was about ten feet from the tripod it too exploded.

"What exactly are we looking at?" said one of the men-in-black.

116

"As I said earlier the Parabellum is a micro receiver, but what I didn't tell you is it is mated with a small explosive charge. When placed inside a larger weapon said weapon will FUBAR if it gets too close to the transmitter. Our long-range goal is to shrink the Parabellum to the size of a grain of rice" McAlister explained.

"How is this supposed to be a good thing? Wont our troops blow themselves up?"

"It's not for our troops. Maybe I should have the brains behind the project explain the concept?" At which time he pointed to Hana. "Miss, would you like to come up here."

Hana stood nervously and side-stepped to the end of the row. She then took a position next to the lectern.

Sally leaned toward Carson and whispered, "What a FUBAR?"

"Fucked up beyond all recognition."

"I like it," she said.

Without preamble Hana said "As the captain said our goal is to shrink the Parabellum. I think we can get it even smaller than a grain of sand. Then it can be introduced into the manufacturing process. Now picture this. The government makes a bunch of TNT, RDX or Semtex, seeded with parabellums. Then it gets sold to the Chinese, the Iranians, and other bad guys. The bad guys use the tainted explosives in their weapons, artillery shells, RPGs, etc. They test a few of the weapons and everything works fine. They even fire them at their enemies and they work fine. But! They fire them at our troops and poof; they self-destruct. That will really mess with their minds. They will think the US has some type of Star Wars force-field."

The group mumbled with pessimism. Hana got their attention when she said, "They'll be stuck there with their dick in their hands."

"Where does she learn such language?" murmured Sally, to Carson.

"Our troops or theirs," said someone in the front row. The group broke out in the laughter.

117

"Will this really work?" asked someone else.

"Yes and no," said Hana. She paused until everyone became silent. "As you saw, it will work in its current configuration and in a controlled environment. But there are a lot of variables that we need to account for. Especially, when we start shrinking the device. The problem isn't with the micro receiver it's the explosive coating. Military explosives are stable; must be to survive in combat. Because of this stability they need a strong primer. My hope is that if there are enough of the parabellums inside a charge it will set off a chain reaction. Plus, we need to account for the thickness of the casing over the charge and the speed of its travel."

"So, this is a defensive weapon?" asked one of the men-in-black.

"Defensive and offensive. If we surround a military installation with the transmitters, it's defensive. Maybe truck bombs will become a thing of the past. If we put the transmitter on aircraft, it can be offensive. Get the transmitter close to a weapons stockpile and it's gonna suck to be a bad guy."

"Where does she learn these things?" Sally asked no one in particular.

PARABELLUM: When you live in Peace, prepare for War

Jack Nanuq

CHAPTER 22
Isle of Man
November 10, 1918

"All Bunny?" Maria asked tentatively.

"Close enough" said the American who was helping her harvest potatoes. Fr. Yates had told her he was from the capital of New York State, Albany.

Maria liked conversing with this American; it distracted her from the lousy working conditions. She could not remember being more miserable. Wet, cold and sore from head to toe. Her clothes, gloves and boots were soaked from a steady drizzle not much above freezing.

The harvest was very late this year, as laborers were scarce. Every able body had been called to the fields to dig the crop before it rotted in place. Nature and monotony conspired against the harvesters.

The process went like this. Step down on the fork, pry the potatoes from the ground, stoop to pick up said potatoes, slip into sack, drag the sack a few feet and repeat as necessary. Step, pry, stoop, drag... step, pry, stoop, drag... step, pry, stoop, drag. Tears flowed from her eyes, but no one noticed. The pitchfork was more rust than steel and she wished it would break. Then at least she would have an excuse to stop.

"Christ!" Maria screamed as she got her wish, but not in the way she hoped. The pitchfork broke in the heavy clay soil. As she stepped on the shoulder of the fork, for the 200th time, or was it the 2,000[th] time, it disintegrated. The tine snapped off and the top of the tine pierced her instep. The pain was indescribable. She leaned against the tool so as not to fall in the mud.

"What happened?" asked Yates.

"I'm hurt" she grimaced and looked to her foot. It was speared in place like a fish on a gaff.

"Don't move," he told her as he looked around for some help. The ragtag harvest crew consisted of mostly young children and a few adults not accustomed to manual labor.

Everyone seemed to have their head down, protecting their face from the cold stinging rain.

She could not afford an injury and yet here she was crippled like a lame mule.

"How bad is it, can you move your foot at all?" asked the priest.

"Iz bad, iz stuck" The pain blocked her proper use of English.

He grabbed her by the shoulders, so she could take some weight off the foot. He yelled at two young workers about three rows away. "Boys, you over there, boys come here, come here now!"

The youngsters jumped as if struck with a whip and ran to them.

"She's hurt, help hold her up." When he was sure they had her he got down on his knees and using only his fingers he dug the tine from the cold ground. He then braced her foot against his knee.

The image of a crippled mule returned to Maria's mind as she remembered a farrier cradling a horse's leg in a similar manner.

With both of his hands grasping her ankle he lifted the foot and tine clear of the ground. Drops of blood leaked from the sole of her boot. "Hold her boys, don't let her fall."

"Aye Father, we've got her," said one.

"Maria... listen to me carefully, we've got two choices. First, I can try to pull that tine free right here and we can see if you can walk to the cook tent."

"I no like this plan," Maria grimaced.

"Or I can carry you to the tent and we will remove the shoe and tine there."

"Dah dis much better plan," she said.

"Okay, here we go." He crouched and put her over a shoulder, like a sack of grain. He stood, lifting her clear of the ground. "Boys run to the tent and tell Mrs. Kelly we're coming. Tell her to boil some water."

"Aye father." Both took off for warm sanctuary.

Twenty minutes later Father Yates reached the tent. Maria was now in agony. Not only was her foot throbbing but her ribs were bruised, and she was having trouble breathing. Her chest banged against the priest's shoulder. She wasn't sure how much more she could withstand.

By then some men had come from the village but Fr. Yates would not share his load. He was exhausted but would not let her down until he was assured there was a clean and comfortable place for her to sit.

"She'll not be sitting anywhere," screamed Mrs. Kelly, "set her on the table."

"Please don't cut my boot," Maria whispered. The tine stuck out from the bottom like a pirate's peg leg.

"We'll do what we can," Mrs. Kelly whispered back. "Now lay back and relax. Let me take a look at this mischief. I should throttle that Thomas Cregeen." Mrs. Kelly was referring to the lease holder. "He had no business planting taddies in this heavy ground. That land is holding onto them tighter than a Scotchman with a five-pound note. The sod must have thought he could get cheap help, from the Camp, to dig the ground. The greedy bastard." With concern in her voice she added "When we get you cleaned up, we'll get you home."

∞

Maria woke with a start and pulled her head up from the desk. She was shivering and disoriented. The candle she lit over an hour ago had burned down to a nub. The small flame threw little more light than a glowing match. She leaned forward and as she put weight on her feet, they felt odd. She looked down and found them soaking in a bath of Epsom salts. She now remembered she was back in her room. After her wound was cleaned, she was fed a large bowl of stew and helped back to her quarters. She'd been told to soak her feet.

There was a time the water had been so hot it had been difficult to lower them into the saline bath but now it was causing hypothermia. She jerked her legs from the bath water and found they resembled a beached sea creature; wrinkled sponges, lacking any color. As her feet touched the stone floor,

122

she couldn't feel the surface. Stomping them had little effect. Even the wound it barely registered.

She opened a small tin box and pulled a new candle from the container. She grasped the wax stick like a club because her fingers wouldn't work individually. With palsy-like finesse she attempted to light the new candle off the old one. As the first candle sputtered the new wick flared to life but was threatened with extinction by the shaking hand.

Maria held the candle on its side and worked to get dripping wax to form into a small puddle. Wax sprayed over a wide swath but slowly coalesced into a small ball as she lowered the flame toward the wood surface. She cupped her free hand around the flame and felt life altering warmth. As the sensation built, she was able to use this hand to steady the other and the secure the base of the candle to the desk. Cupping the flame with both hands sensation and dexterity returned to her digits.

A knock on the door pulled her eyes away from the flame. "Maria, Maria are you awake?" called Sister Xavier.

"Dah" she mumbled.

"Can I come in?"

"Yah, please...I need help."

When the nun entered the room, it was clear she had been crying. This woman who rarely showed any emotion, had clearly suffered a loss. Before Maria could say anything, the nun spoke swiftly. "Our Lord has taken Sister Clarice. It's the flu, she went fast." She said this quickly as if to drag it out would be unbearable.

"What...what?" Maria questioned.

"Sister Clarice has passed on."

"How can that be? I spoke with her this morning. I know she was sick but she ... she..." Maria couldn't find the words to finish her thought. A kaleidoscope of the nun's kind deeds flashed through Maria's brain. The sadness and loss she felt was hard and sharp and heavy, like a blanket of barbwire.

"I know... He works in his own way."

"Momma, I cold!" At this point the women were reminded they weren't alone. The small boy stood next to them. He had made no sound as he walked from his cot.

"Janos, you should be in bed," Maria admonished.

"But I cold, I can't sleep."

"Why... why is it so cold in here?" the nun asked.

"The fire must have gone out."

The older woman turned to the child. "Janos do you want to help me make a fire?"

"Can I? Momma says it's dangerous."

"It is dangerous, but we will be careful. Do you think you can do that?"

"I think so... Can I Momma?" he asked, as he ran toward the coal stove.

The nun then put a hand on Maria's shoulders. "You stay put. Once we get this room warm, we'll look at after those feet of yours."

"Thank you." Maria

Ten minutes later a tea pot was whistling, and the room was more hospitable. Maria had wrapped her feet with the only clean garments handy and was embarrassed when Sister X stared.

"Maria, why are there knickers on your feet? Are you starting a new fashion trend?"

The humor broke the tension that had come to the room.

"Here, let me have a look."

Maria was happy to see the color and shape had returned to her calves and feet. She was reluctant to look at the soles.

"Momma, can I have some tea?"

"No, you need to get too bed, it is after 10. We've got a big day tomorrow."

"But I hungry, I worked hard today."

"You can have a biscuit... then... then you go to bed."

"Can I have two?"

"Yah but be sure to offer one to Sister Xavier."

"Sister, do you want one?" He asked as he pulled the biscuit tin from a cupboard.

"Give mine to your mother. She needs it more than me. She worked hard today, as well."

"Here Momma."

"Thank you," she said as she took the sugary wafer. "Now go to bed."

Janos did as he was told.

"Now child," the nun said to Maria, "let me look at your feet."

Maria cringed as she lifted her wounded foot off the floor and placed it over the opposite knee. The circulation had returned, and the pain was incredible.

Sister Xavier gently pulled the undergarment from the foot and gasped. The sole was a flayed mess. Numerous blisters had formed and then been shredded by the work, wetness and friction. Fortunately, no serious damage had been done below the surface. The tine had only penetrated about an inch.

"I was afraid of this... I think your boots are not built for digging potatoes. Do you know a good shoemaker?" she joked.

"It might be I, that is not built for digging potatoes" Maria responded.

"Nonsense, no one should be working in these conditions. That field has more clay than dirt. Add to that it hasn't stopped raining for a week. It's a wonder more aren't crippled. No work for you tomorrow, maybe the whole week."

"But sister, I must..."

"Nonsense; you are to remain in bed. It will be only God's grace you don't end up walking like Mrs. Kelley. You've done enough."

By the time Sister Xavier had left Maria was comforted to know tomorrow would be a day of rest. The room was pleasantly warm as the nun had filled the coal stove. Maria now had her second wind. She pulled out her journal

Today I met my first American, Fr. Yates. He is a distant relation to Sister Veronique. Things in America must be good. He

carried an extra stone of weight and wore new clothes. I cannot remember the last time I saw new clothes.

He is an interesting bloke. We dug potatoes, all day, and he worked as hard as anyone. The harvest is late this year because half the Island is sick with the flu. There is no help from the Camp as it is on quarantine.

It has been a very hard month but there may be hope for an end to the war before the New Year. There are rumors the German navy has mutinied and the Kaiser has abdicated the throne. I can only hope that is true.

But I must ask myself what next? Last week we lost Andrej to the flu. Today we lost Sister Clarice and now I hear Petr is sick. Oh please Lord, don't let him die; if not for me then for Janos.

Please let us all get through this, so that we may be a family, if that is your wish.

With that she closed her journal.

PARABELLUM: When you live in Peace, prepare for War
Jack Nanuq

CHAPTER 23
Albany, NY
May 13, 2001

Carson watched Nana navigate the golf cart through the crowd, Iris seated next to her. He and Newton walked a few steps behind. The Albany Tulip Festival was in full bloom. Washington Park was alive with the scent of the flowers and the hum of happy people. For more than 50 years Nana had been spending Mother's Day at the Festival. She was the unofficial Grand Dame. Over the years she had donated thousands of dollars and just as many bulbs.

The festival had started as a celebration of Albany's roots and its Dutch founders. In recent years it had morphed into more of a carnival; food booths interspersed with games of chance, interspersed with art vendors.

The crowd today was moderate, and Carson was thankful for this. It slowed Nana to a reasonable pace. Given the chance Nana had a heavy foot and would drive the cart like it was NASCAR.

As Nana approached the booth for the Young Republicans a man, about 19, stepped in front of the cart.

"Ma'am would you like a BUSH-CHENEY bumper sticker for your ride?" The poor man had no idea who he was talking too or her deep-seated dislike of the resent occupant of the White House.

"No, I not. Vie you ask such thing?"

"He's our President. I thought you might like to show your support."

Her face flushed with anger and she shouted. "He steal election, he thief and cheat. You not know this? You not know how dangerous he iz?" She emphasized this with rude noise that sounded like a cow fart.

"But the Supreme Court ruled he won the election fair and square," the young man responded. The Supreme Court's decision in BUSH v. GORE was about six months old and it still irritated Nana.

"The Court iz dumb as you. You watch Bush. He bad for Country. He will cause much problem and much misery. He war mungler."

"You mean war monger."

"You see, you agree."

The young man stammered. "But his father was good for the country."

"He not his father. A copy iz never sharp as original. I done with you. Keep your sticker."

Carson placed a hand on her shoulder. He half anticipated Nana was about to tell the young man where to put his sticker.

The man wasn't done. He must have felt the need to best the old woman even though he had no chance. He took a cheap shot. "What do you know? That accent tells me you're not even from here."

Carson pulled his hand away. The kid should have let it go. He now deserved anything he got now.

"No, I not from this country. I here because of Busch family. All of them bad, back to Old Country, all bad. They all thieves and cheats, and cause much hurt, for many people. They no care for people, only themselves." She continued, "I not from this country but I do much for this country. You stupid boy, for support Bush. You think you do good for this country, with you stickers and signs? You not know real world."

A moment ago, Carson was ready to restrain Nana but was now glad he hadn't. He was enjoying the show. It was nice to see Nana tear into someone other than him.

The kid was turning red and his body language spoke volumes. It was clear he didn't take kindly to having an old woman insult him. And he didn't want her to have the last word. "You're nuts lady!" he yelled at her.

She stopped suddenly, and the boy smiled. She took three carefully measured breaths and when she was sure she had his attention, announced. "You should sell brain. Could sell as new, as it never used. We go now." She stomped on the accelerator.

He jumped out of the way, lest she roll over his toes.

Carson stifled a laugh, but Iris couldn't help herself. Her laughter added salt to a raw wound. Carson turned around and saw the young guy slink back to his booth. *That poor son of a bitch never had a chance*, Carson thought as his cell phone rang.

He was pleased to see the number belonged to Liza. With a flip of the wrist the phone opened. "Hold on" and covered the mouthpiece with his hand. "Nana let's get some lunch. I'll meet you at the Explorer in ten minutes." She nodded acknowledgement and sped away as he returned to the phone.

"I'm back."

"You busy?" Liza asked.

"Not really," he snickered.

"Am I missing something, wanna let me in on the joke?"

"It just that Nana just tore into some schmuck about our illustrious leader. I wish I understood why she hates the President so much."

"Seriously…you've no idea?"

"I've got no clue, I guess it's just part of her personality."

"Seriously, no clue whatsoever?" she asked again.

"No, not a clue …wait… You know something, don't you?"

"I do but I can't believe you don't. Her first husband was Gregor Busch. It's spelled differently but I guess a Bush is a Bush."

"How do you know that?"

"The notebooks you gave me, we're still working on them, but I know that much. I'm surprised you don't."

"No, the only husband I know of was named Nowak, Petr Nowak."

"That brings me to why I called. Next weekend I need to be in Boston, I was figuring I'd drive into Albany a few days early. You gonna be around?"

"Yeah, I'd like that. I owe you a dinner."

"You do, but all kidding aside I want to talk to you about something our big-eared friends heard recently." The folks with the "big ears" referred to the National Security Agency (NSA).

"Anything I should know about?"

"Yeah," she answered. "But I don't want to discuss it over the phone. I'll be in town on Wednesday. We'll talk more then."

"Any clues?" he asked.

"It may not be anything but just stay close to Nana for the next few days; and keep your Glock handy."

Perfect, just perfect.

Twenty minutes later Carson and the group walked into a Vietnamese noodle house. The restaurant smelled of beef broth and fresh vegetables. Soft tinny music played from a back room. The proprietor of <u>20-Pho-7</u> greeted his favorite customer.

"Mrs. Nowak, you gone long time, we miss you much." His words were launched as if on a tightly wound spring.

He turned to Carson. "Why you no bring her more, you no like our food? She number one cussamah!"

The proprietor; Nguyen Quang Dong was dressed in his standard uniform of polished oxfords, pressed gray slacks, a short–sleeved white dress shirt and a thin black tie. This uniform only varied on cooler days, with the addition of a long-sleeved shirt. He walked with a slight limp, half of one foot was left in a rice paddy, near a Viet Cong booby trap.

The interior of the small restaurant was festooned with both American and Vietnamese memorabilia. Photos and knickknacks were arranged in a chronology that told the story of the Nguyen family.

He and his wife were born in rural villages. Later, he served in the Army of the Republic Viet Nam (ARVN). A photo showed him standing with a group of Green Berets; his dress uniform festooned with medals. Next were photos of a wedding. Then photos of US Navy warships crammed with refugees. The Nguyen family and countless others were briefly known as Boat

People. Thousands were forced to flee, when it was clear Communists would take their control of the country.

One photo seemed out of place but wasn't. The photo showed Nana and the owner cutting a large ribbon across the front door of this same restaurant. Since 1975 Nana had done much to help the Nguyen family. She rented them an inexpensive apartment; she provided financing for this restaurant and also helped Quang Dong with other business ventures.

The small, plain-looking man that greeted them was actually a multi-millionaire He owned two other restaurants, car washes and apartment buildings. Of all his holdings he liked this restaurant, his first, the best. He did all his business from a backroom.

Mr. Nguyen yelled something in his native tongue and a teenager brought a plate of shrimp spring rolls to the table.

He then turned back to Nana. "Madame, you look well. Would you like the usual?" He now spoke French, to her. Much of Southeast Asia was a French colony for over 100 years.

Nana responded in the same language "Oui".

And with the manners of a true gentleman he then turned to Iris. "And you m'am'selle?"

Iris knew the menu by heart and asked for tripe pho, with extra bean sprouts.

He then turned to Carson, but in English asked, "What I get you?"

"Just coffee."

Mr. Nguyen would never take any money for their meals and Carson was never comfortable asking for anything other than coffee.

"And you monsieur?" he said to Newton.

"Coffee's fine with me also."

"Okay," he said and looked to the server. The boy nodded acknowledgement and scurried for the kitchen.

"Anything else, maybe whiskey?"

"No, we're good, thank you," said Carson.

"Okay, I leave now, but you call if need anything."

"We're good," Carson repeated. But Carson wasn't good, he was jumpy and nervous. Liza's last words kept replaying in his mind and each time these words passed through his mind they were followed by questions. *Why is Nana in danger? It had to be the gun? What had he done? How could I have known running its serial number would set off this chain of events? How much danger is she in? Maybe it's nothing? What should I do next? Should I stay, even though unarmed? Should I leave and get some firepower? Should I call for reinforcements?*

He latched onto an idea. "Ladies excuse me, I need to go to the men's room," he said as he stood.

He walked past the bathroom and knocked gently on Mr. Nguyen office door. A video camera was mounted above the door. A buzzer, like a bumble bee on steroids, sounded and the electric lock clicked open.

Carson stepped inside quickly and pulled the door behind him. Mr. Nguyen sat at this desk. "I need to borrow a gun" he said softly.

Mr. Nguyen responded with "You need borrow, or you need keep?"

"Just borrow, I'll have it back to you tomorrow."

"You need big gun or you need small gun?"

"A handgun, maybe a nine-millimeter?"

"Come."

They walked to a wall safe, the size of a refrigerator. A few twists and turns of the dial and the door opened with a pop. Inside was a small arsenal; dozens of handguns were stacked on shelves.

A Beretta model 92, in a pancake holster, grabbed Carson's attention. The holster had a clip on the right side and was designed to be worn inside the pants. He took off his windbreaker and picked up the hardware. He checked to see the automatic was loaded and then slid it back into the holster. He then loosened his belt and slid it between the belt and pants. He didn't want anything digging into his skin. He adjusted it over the right hip and covered everything with his windbreaker.

"Thank you" he said as he was buzzed out of the office.

"Madam, in danger? She good people, that one. You call if help need," Mr. Nguyen directed, as the door closed.

CHAPTER 24
Willsboro, NY
May 12, 2001

Hanna sat on the porch of the cabin. She had panoramic view of Lake Champlain and was working on a watercolor. A light breeze stirred whitecaps and she was trying desperately to catch the motion. Her mother sat nearby, pulling yarn from a skein and winding it into a ball for her current project. Although they were approaching summer Sally was already knitting a winter sweater.

One of the women on the security detail was cutting the front lawn with a battery powered mower. The machine made no more noise that an electric razor. It reminded Hanna of the buzz a dragon fly makes.

"I like that smell much," Sally said to her daughter. She worked on her English, every day. Sally rarely used it in public but practiced around the cabin.

"Do you mean the fresh cut grass?" Hanna asked.

"The grass, the water, the flowers, everything. To me it smells of freedom."

"It is momma... we are free."

"Are we ... really? I know ... but sometimes it doesn't feel that way. We are surrounded by armed guards, we live like hermits and you have no friends. You should be able to enjoy your youth, it will be gone soon. And ... and you no forget about your project; your secret project. A girl should not make bombs."

Hanna responded, "The Americans say, freedom is not free." Hana hesitated and continued "I guess this is our price of admission. It is not so steep a price. Look at where we were last year. Would you rather be in that refugee camp living on donated peanut butter?"

"No, but ... that smell, that smell reminds me of all we have lost... Your grandfather used to have a dacha like this.

When I was young, we would go there and eat fresh caught fish, and watermelon, and sip dandelion wine."

"Your papa was not a good Muslim. Alcohol is not permitted."

"There is more to life than religion. Life is about living, about experiences, about choices and memories. My papa was a good man. Maybe not a good Muslim, as you see it, but a good man. It is good that he died before the troubles. It would have ruined him to see what happened to the family; and to his country."

"Enough talk of old times" Sally continued. "Are you ever going to name that thing?" She then pointed to a kitten that had jumped into the yarn basket.

The kitten, a calico, had shown up a week ago. At that time it was no bigger than a coffee cup, malnourished and soaked from a rain storm. No one knew where it had come from. Had it not been rescued by Hanna it surely would have perished. In the last seven days it had doubled in size and had boundless energy.

The kitten hooked a claw into Sally's skein and pulled not so gently.

"Should I name it Mystery?"

The woman and the animal were engaged in a tug-a-war for the yarn. "You should name it Trouble."

"How about Mischief, or maybe Miss Chif?"

"How do you know it girl cat?"

"The color, all calicos are females."

"Okay Miss Chif it is. Now get her out of my basket... before it frays something." Sally jerked a long section free of the animal and then quickly wound it onto the ball she had in her hands.

"Momma! That's it" Hanna yelled as she jumped up from her painting. "You just solved my puzzle."

"The what?"

"The puzzle, the Parabellum puzzle, you just solved the problem with my bomb. I now know how to shrink the trigger."

"I did? How did I do that? What I do?"

"The ball of yarn! Look at it! If I stretch the nano-receiver into a thin strand it can then be coated with the primer. Then I wrap it into a tight ball like your yarn. If I'm right, we can shrink the trigger to the size of a grain of sand."

Hanna grabbed a nearby sketch pad and began scribbling notes and diagrams. The kitten thought it was a game and jumped on the pencil. The key drawing to Hanna's new design would be forever marked with a jagged lightning bolt line where the cat had done her mischief.

"Glad I could be some help," Sally said to herself, as she returned to her knitting.

PARABELLUM: When you live in Peace, prepare for War

Jack Nanuq

CHAPTER 25
Albany, NY
May 16, 2001

At 5:45 AM Carson sat in his living room and paged through a file. The room was cool as he had the windows open. A light rain fell as the day dawned, the outside air temps in the fifties. As he read, he also listened intently to the heartbeat of his neighborhood, as it woke. Occasionally cars traveled the wet street and it was easy to follow their progress. There was a rhythm to things and he was alert to any changes. Had a car slowed anywhere near Nana's house he'd be up like a shot. Heaven help anyone that showed interest in Nana. This time his Glock was handy.

A pager buzzed in the bedroom, but it didn't belong to him. A moment later he heard Liza talking on her cell phone. He carried the file into the kitchen and turned on the coffee maker.

He set the file down on the table and pulled a bottle from the fridge. Unscrewing the cap, he poured a glass of his favorite breakfast beverage.

"Do you have enough to share?" Liza asked. She was wearing one of his shirts but hadn't bothered to button it. Though it hung like a tent, on her small frame, it was sexy with a capital S.

"Sure...you drink this stuff?" he asked as he pointed to the dark brown liquid.

"Yeah, I love Dr. Pepper. Never had it for breakfast though."

"I took you for a coffee drinker."

"Oh, I drink coffee, especially on campus, but I love Dr. Pepper," she stretched out the word love.

"I started drinking it in Kuwait," Carson added.

"Sounds like there's a story there," she countered.

"Everything has a story. During Desert Storm we sort of liberated truck load of it."

"Go on," she said.

"Well, some Iraqis were trying to sneak back home in a delivery truck. Those guys used everything to get out of the country. After it was clear the Coalition was in control. My unit caught them on an open stretch of road and they ran the truck into a ditch. They scurried out yelling 'George Bush number one... Bush number one... USA number one, USA number one'. It was hysterical. That was all the English they knew. When we looked the truck over, we found it was crammed to the gills with cases of Dr Pepper. We debriefed the Iraqis and they thought the cases were medical supplies. Seems one of the soldiers recognized the letters DR and knew that stood for doctor".

"What did you do with them?" she asked.

"Oh, we let them go. They were conscripts and were just trying to get home. They never wanted to fight. Their guns didn't even have bullets. They had to walk though, the truck axle was broke. We pointed them toward Baghdad and sent them on their way, each with a case of Dr. Pepper. We drank the rest."

Liza drained her glass. She then picked up the file and asked, "What do we have here?"

"It's Nana's recruitment file".

"Her what?" she asked.

"Her recruitment file... she was codenamed Shakespeare. Take a look".

The manila envelope held Xeroxed pages of microfiche documents.

"That top page is the most interesting," Carson went on. "I'm headed for the living room," he said as he carried his drink out of the kitchen.

OFFICE OF STRATEGIC SERVICES

INTER OFFICE MEMO

TO: Mr. Charles Cheston

DATE: December 3, 1942
FROM: Capt. Charles Pouliot
SUBJECT: Agent recruitment in the Normandy area

SECRET

SHAKESPEARE – the asset hereto referred to as SHAKESPEARE, is a 41-year old woman, of Czech descent, currently operating a café near Calais, France. She is fluent in Czech, German and French (but with a heavy accent). She has limited English skills.

Although considered a foreigner by the local populace, she appears to be well liked and has numerous ties to the community.
She has limited schooling but a well-developed intellect and what one would call street smarts. She is a devout Catholic and attends Mass on a regular basis.

The café is popular with the local residents and it is reported the food is very good. Due to this, it is also popular with German soldiers assigned to the area.

She has a deep-seated hatred of the Boche. It is rumored she was orphaned in 1914 and was forced to marry a German National. Her father-in law then acquired her family assets. Her parents are deceased, and she has no known siblings.

From 1914 to 1919 she was interred on the Isle of Man. As the island did not have internment facilities for females she resided with a Catholic Order. At age 19 she and a second husband (hereto referred to as CORDUROUY) moved to Calais.

It is suggested efforts be made to recruit SHAKESPEARE. Her position as a café owner, her ties to the community, her dislike of the Axis and her language skills enable her the ability to provide us with information on coastal defenses, troop deployments, and other intelligence.

CORDUROUY – the asset hereto referred to as CORDUROUY is a 43-year old Czech national and married to SHAKESPEARE. Although a Czech National he has resided in the area since 1920. He speaks Czech, French and German.

At age 15 CORDUROUY was conscripted into the German Army. He was taken a prisoner shortly after being deployed to a frontline unit. From 1915 to 1919 he was interred at Camp Knockaloe, on the Isle of Man. Records indicate he was a model prisoner.

He is currently employed as a mechanic in a local rail yard. His skills are such that the Nazis have left him in place. It is suggested efforts be made to recruit CORDUROUY. His position as a train mechanic, and his language skills give him with the ability to provide us with information on troop movements, armor and equipment deployments and other intelligence.

INDIAN - the asset hereto referred to as INDIAN is a 25-year old son of SHAKESPEARE. He has both German and British citizenship. He is currently serving in the Wehrmacht as a motorcycle dispatch rider. His duty station is unknown at this time, but it is believed he is currently on the Eastern Front. His loyalties are unknown at this time and no effort should be made to contact him until further information can be obtained.

SECRET

When Liza was done reading the documents she walked into the room and said, "So the whole family was spies?"

"Seems that way," Carson said. "This is getting weirder by the day."

"How do you think they came by their codenames?"

"Oh, I don't know, maybe she got the name because her English sucks. Maybe Petr liked corduroy pants, I don't know.

142

It's probably no more complicated than that". Carson stopped mid-breath and his eyes locked onto a man walking down the street.

PARABELLUM: When you live in Peace, prepare for War
Jack Nanuq

Chapter 26
Albany, NY
May 16, 2001

Nana tossed fitfully in that ether world of dream and memory. Images raced through her mind like a poorly put together picture show. Frames were missing or juxtaposed on another or out of time or out of order.

She saw Janos ride up on his motorcycle. But it wasn't her son, but it was. He was much older than when she had last seen him. And the eye patch. What was that about? And the soldiers; why was he in a motorized column of German soldiers? She tried to call out to him, but no sound escaped. She prayed for him to see her, but she was on his blind side.

Then she was inside her café. The noise was hideous. Who told the Germans they could sing? They couldn't. What were they celebrating? And why were there so many? She then remembered they were supposed to be there. But couldn't remember why.

And the smell! She was cooking something. No, wait...they were...they were boiling their laundry. Damp clothes hung everywhere. But now these were different soldiers, Brits. And then there were French soldiers with their big rifles and funny helmets. The French weren't made for fighting. They were made for eating croissants and drinking wine.

And horses, the horses were everywhere, all sizes and colors. She didn't know there were that many in all of France.

Then came the bombs. The bombs came from the sky, like what? What was term they now used...acid rain. Yes, the bombs fell like a toxic rain. And she was in a hole or was it a cave... no, it was her root cellar. She was afraid and hiding underground like a mole. But Petr was with her and he held her. Her beloved Petr was there. He held and told her it would be alright. But it wasn't alright. There were more bombs, and the screaming. Men screamed for their mothers. And the horses screamed, and others screamed. She recognized one of the voices; it was hers.

Then someone grabbed her, and she screamed louder. Fear like never before. The hand on her shoulder grabbed with more intensity and terror raced through her body. She screamed again and the hand relaxed. Then there was the voice, but who's voice?

"Madam…madam…madam, please wake up."

Now the hand was back, but it was gently touching her face and wiping away her tears. It was Petr. She was safe.

"Madam…madam… please wake up, please wake up".

No it wasn't Petr… it was Iris. She opened her eyes, and it was Iris! She was home; she was safe.

"Madam, you have nightmare. You screaming, you scare me. You want I Carson?"

"No, not now, I need shower, I afraid I pee myself."

Both women froze as they heard two men talking in the front yard.

∞

Carson approached the man as he stepped onto Nana's front lawn. The man was forty-five but looked sixty. He reeked of incense and was dressed like a beach bum. Definitely an oddity in this neighborhood of manicured lawns, and designer fashions.

"Smokey… how you doin this morning?" Carson said to the man he'd known for years.

"I'm cool dude. How's the C-man?" At this he set a newspaper on Nana's porch.

"I need a favor," Carson said.

"Anything man, just name it."

"I need you to keep an eye on the neighborhood, especially Nana's place. Let me know if you see any strange cars or people lurking around."

"Sure, can I ask why or is it on the down low?"

"Oh, everything's cool. It's just that I went out with this chick a couple of times and discovered she's psycho. I broke up with her and now she's pissed. Said she's gonna send her brothers after me. She thinks I live with Nana."

"No problem man…bitches be crazy!"

Carson handed him a business card and a twenty-dollar bill. "Call me if you see anything strange."

"You got it, man." Smokey sauntered away, carrying his bundle of newspapers to the next house.

Carson scanned the neighborhood; all clear. He then took a glance at the lawn. The grass was ankle high. He'd send a grounds crew over later in the day, regardless of the weather. He'd see to it there would be plenty of eyes on Nana for the next few weeks, at least.

He then crossed the street to his house. He'd check on Nana in an hour. First, he had to take care of a few things.

"Who was that?" Liza asked. She was still wearing his shirt but now it was buttoned up.

"That's Smokey, our paperboy" Carson replied.

"A boy? He looks a hundred years old. Why do you call him Smokey?"

"He's a pothead, he likes his ganga. I asked him to keep an eye on Nana."

"You put a doper in charge of Nana's security? Are you nuts?"

"He's not in charge as you say it. I told him to keep an eye out for any strangers. No one's more paranoid than a pothead. He'll call me if he sees someone that doesn't fit in the neighborhood."

"And what about when he's done with his paper route, what then Einstein?"

"Oh, he won't be far. He lives down the block, with his mom. And he does odd jobs around the area. He's always out and about. Enough about Smokey. What do you want for breakfast?"

She walked to him, hooked a finger in his waistband and said, "I think you've got too many clothes on."

Thirty minutes later, Carson took a seat in Nana's kitchen as Iris put a plate of poached eggs in front of him. He sprinkled his breakfast with Tabasco sauce. The pungent aroma woke up his senses. He could hear the shower running.

"Shouldn't you be with her, Iris." It was more of a comment than a question or criticism.

"No, she insist she take shower by herself. She has chair in there and she likes to be alone. She will call me if she needs me. She so independent, I not argue with her. Besides she very upset today. She not sleep well, she have ... how you say, night horses?"

"Nightmares, you mean," he corrected.

"*Oui*, nightmares. She have wartime memories. She say she want talk with you. I not know what about."

"Is she alright? I mean her heart and everything?"

"*Oui,* she fine. Her pulse a little racey this morning and blood pressure a little high but not danger level. The shower helps. She sits in the chair and lets the water run over her. It seem to wash away fear." As if on cue, they heard the water shut off. "I go help her now."

Carson sat at the table in consternation. He wondered what had Nana so upset. He would hear what she needed to tell him and then he would decide. Decide whether or not to tell her about the stalker.

A few minutes later Nana shuffled into the room. Carson got up, gave her a hug and kissed her forehead. She smelled of sandalwood and baby powder. He helped her to a chair.

"Iris tells me you've been having bad dream..." He let the sentence drag out, afraid of providing an option that might shut things down.

"Yah, lately I dream a lot about Petr and Janos and France. I think I have much to tell you. Maybe I should tell these stories long ago? Maybe now I have PST"

"You mean PTSD".

"Yah, but why? I old woman, I not fear anything anymore."

Carson searched her face, for clues to her nightmares. "We all have fears. Maybe you're afraid you'll take the stories to the grave?"

148

"Could be...maybe you right? Yes, you right...you smart boy, you know that."

"I had a good teacher." They were straying into uncharted waters and he felt nervous energy building. It forced him out of the chair and he poured her a cup of chicory coffee.

"Thank you. You know why I drink this... this ersatz coffee?"

"No why?" He thought he knew but wanted her to start with a safe subject.

"In First War we not have coffee, only tea and not much of that. So we make ersatz coffee. Lots of different recipes, some use acorns, some grain, some dandelion root and some chicory root. At first, I no like any of them, but I learn to like chicory, with milk". Her trembling hand was reaching for the creamer.

Carson interjected "I'll get that".

"By time war over I like chicory coffee. I have real coffee first time in 1920 and no like, it give me headache." She gripped the cup with both hands and lifted it to her lips. She sipped it mindfully.

Carson wasn't sure if she was testing the temperature or just taking a break from the story; maybe both.

∞

An hour later and Carson was still at the table. He couldn't believe what he was hearing. Nana; a refugee, a spy, an assassin? Well not exactly an assassin, but definitely a killer. War was a dirty business. The dogs of war were more like the hounds from Hell. It unleashed the animal in us all. Sure there were acts of bravery, gallantry and maybe even justice. But those were rare events. War was dirty, and violent and evil. The actions of Cain and Abel magnified by the generations that have passed since Genesis. "Ours is not to reason Why, ours is just to do and die..." so much truth in that quote, Carson mused.

Carson turned from the old woman in front of him and tried to picture her as a vibrant young mother. He had to turn away, not because he was embarrassed or ashamed but because the image in front of him did not jibe with tale he just heard. Most of his life Nana and the rest of the family's saga were unknown to him. She had just unburdened her soul. Almost like a war chief's death song. A chronology of her accomplishments and deeds, for all the world to know before their death. Well maybe not the whole world, at least not yet. Right now the three people in the room were the only guardians of this truth.

Soon it would be his turn to share and he did not relish that endeavor. He needed to tell her that death, but not natural death may be lurking just around the corner. Wait was there such a thing as natural death? What an odd way to put it.

∞

Carson laid out what he knew. It wasn't much but he shared everything Liza had given him. Radio transcripts from South America had told of a plot to kill an "Old woman", in Albany. None of the transmission mentioned Nana by name but one gave her address. The address had been given in two parts and the analyst almost missed it. No specific time frame was provided. But the tone of the messages indicated an urgency.

Nana sat for a full minute before speaking. It was a painful silence, at least for Carson. He wondered if she understood the danger. His lips quivered as if to say more. He froze when she held up her hand for more time.

"This news does not scare me, should it?" She said slowly. "But you must promise me something," she added as her gray eyes bored into Carson.

"What is it?"

"You must protect this one," she said as she pointed to Iris. "No harm must come to her. I no fear for me, but she is just girl."

"I don't want any harm to come to either of you," Carson said.

"You no understand. I now ready to die. What more do I have lived for? But she... she has her whole life. If someone is hunting me that is one thing. But no one, no one will hurt the girl. If someone want to kill me, that fine. That between him and his God; I ready. You do what you must. What you do? You protect her. You hear this?"

"I don't know what to say," Carson stammered.

"You say you promise. You promise to keep her safe, she precious."

"I'm not worried," Iris said, reminding them of her presence. "You no remember I from Haiti. We have bad guys in my country. I can protect myself. If Madame is not afraid, I not afraid. Let them come!"

"Jesus, you guys are too much. Maybe I should move you somewhere?"

"No," both women said in unison.

Nana added "This my home, I not run."

"Ok, can I get someone to stay with you?"

"Who you suggest?"

"Maybe Newton?"

"OK, if he want, that iz fine".

"You got to promise not to eat the dog," Carson added to lighten the mood.

"OK, I like this plan. But he must want to come, you no force him." Nana then turned to Iris and added "You like this plan?"

"Oui"

"Agreed. I'll call him in a minute. You, " he said directly to Nana, "You can listen in and know I'm not twisting his arm."

"Iz good, I trust you. You go now, don't keep your lady friend waiting," she said as she pointed a finger toward his house.

"How'd you know I have a woman waiting for me?"

"You forget, I was spy, I know these things. You go. You treat her good."

PARABELLUM: When you live in Peace, prepare for War

Jack Nanuq

CHAPTER 27
Willsboro, NY
May 16, 2001

Angie, Hana and Sally were bushwhacking their way along a path that wasn't much more than a game trail. The route was choked with deadfalls and thick vegetation. Angie led the way with a compass and topographic map. They were headed to a group of remote ponds on the back side of a private forest reserve. The land, some five thousand acres, was owned by a paper company. The company no longer harvested the trees. It was now cheaper to get pulp from other sources.

The property was located along the eastern edge of the Adirondack Park, but the vegetation was so thick it felt as if they were in the heart of an Amazonian jungle. The group had set out that morning because Sally said she had a craving for fresh trout. Angie suggested they try this spot. She had warned them it would be rough going. Since then she'd repeatedly apologized for suggesting this route.

"Son of a bitch!" screamed Hana. She stumbled backwards into Sally as a cedar bough slapped her in the face. Sally caught her daughter and kept her from hitting the ground.

"I got you. You okay?"

"Yeah," at which point Hana turned toward her mother. Sally gasped as blood poured from the side of Hana's face.

"Angie! Angie help! She hurt."

"I'm fine Momma."

"No, no… you bleeding, sit down." She said this as she guided Hana to a log.

"What happened?" Angie asked.

"Tree branch… hit her face... she hurt."

"I'm fine Momma, don't worry, I'm fine."

"Let me look at you, tip your head back," Angie said.

Hana did as she was told, and blood dripped from her hair.

"This is gonna hurt" Angie said as she ran her fingers along the girl's scalp. Hana grimaced as Angie probed the wound. Angie's finger brushed against a small twig that was imbedded in the skin and Hana pulled away from her. "Easy now, you're gonna be fine."

"I know I will! You don't need to talk to me like a child," snapped Hana.

"How bad is it?" Sally asked.

"Not bad. Head wounds always bleed a lot, but I've got to get that sliver out of her scalp." Angie said this as she rummaged in her daypack, for the first aid kit.

A few minutes later the three of them were resting on the log. "You sure you don't want this as a souvenir?" Angie asked. She pointed the twig, about the size of a match stick, toward the grimacing teen. It was held firmly in place in a pair of tweezers.

"No, I said I'm fine" Hana snapped.

"Okay then. Let's get you cleaned up."

"I'll do that" Sally said as she reached for a canteen.

"I'm fine, Momma."

"No you are not, and I not mean the tree branch thing. You have been walking like you were in a fog, what's wrong with you today? Is it... how you say... a lady day? You will tell me and then we will go, but we not go anywhere until you tell me."

"No it's not a 'Lady Day' as you call it. It's my project, it's not working. It should work, but it won't, and I can't figure out how to make it work."

"How you know it not work? I thought you sent plans to The Rock?" Sally was referring to the Red Rock Arsenal.

"I did, and they sent me an email that it's not working. I feel like a failure and I'm scared."

"Why are you scared?" asked Angie.

"I'm afraid if I can't get it too work, they will send us back...back to Bosnia."

"Could this happen?" Sally asked with terror in her eyes.

"No, it won't. The government is going to give you both citizenship. You will not be sent back. The powers-that-be recognize Hana has a brilliant mind. They want you both here and safe. Now walk me through your project. Maybe we can figure this out together. Pretend like I don't know anything about it." This wasn't far from the truth.

"Okay, my parabellum is like the primer in your pistol cartridge. The cartridge will not detonate until the primer is struck and begins a change reaction."

"Go on."

"Okay, as you know military explosives, RDX, TNT, that kind of thing, are very stable. They have to be to survive in combat. Think of them like sawdust, I mean stable like that, like sawdust."

"Go on."

"Okay... I guess I'm saying okay a lot, but I'm nervous, okay?"

"You're doing fine. I'm with you so far."

"Okay... um... okay now picture my parabellum as a kernel of popcorn, hidden inside sawdust."

"Go on."

"I can send a sound wave, like in a microwave oven to get the kernel to pop. But not with enough energy to light the sawdust, or in my case to get the explosive to detonate."

"How big is the parabellum?"

"About the size of a grain of sand."

"Can you make it bigger?"

"Yes, and it will work then, but it needs to be small. The parabellum needs to be tiny. So that it can't be seen, or at least not with naked eye. But when we shrink it there's not enough...enough mass, for reaction."

"I follow you. Don't worry about getting sent back, you're safe here."

"Are you sure?" both Kestrels said simultaneously.

"Absolutely. If it's only a size thing, somebody will figure it out. Just look at computers, they used to be the size of a house. Now they fit in your phone, which fits in your pocket."

155

"But what if someone else figures it out?" asked Sally.

"Don't worry about it, the government believes in Hana. They know she's smart. They would rather Hana work for us instead of them."

"Who are them?"

"Them that's not us."

"Okay" said Sally.

"How's your head?" Angie asked as she turned back to Hana. "Should we go back?"

"It hurts but I'm fine. Let's keep going."

"Okay, ...okay, now look you got me saying it...Damn" snickered Angie.

∞

Two hours later all three women had at least one fish and Sally had limited out at five. Fresh trout would be tonight's dinner entree. Sally walked over to Hana and noticed only one fish in her creel.

"You need relax. Iz not difficult. Cast out farther...reel in slower. Let the fish find the lure. Not get run over by it. Relax...now cast. Further next time. Now reel in slow...slower. That it, now do it again, cast further and reel slower. Let the fish come to you. You can do it...easy...easy. This nice, you and I. Mother and daughter bonding."

The pond they found was about 20 acres in size and they had the entire place to themselves, save for the loon on the opposite side. The water was clear as the proverbial mountain lake and the fish were hungry.

"Ladies come here!" yelled Angie. She was holding a pair of binoculars to the face.

"Are we in danger?" asked Sally.

"No, but there's something strange in the woods." Angie had the binoculars pointed at the base of a cliff. The granite face towered about 100 feet.

"What is it?" asked Hana as she approached Angie's side.

"I think it's some kind of box. Here you take a look. Do you see the black square at the bottom of the rock face?"

156

Hana placed the binos to her face and pointed them in the general direction. "I don't see anything."

"I know it's hard, the bushes keep moving in this wind. Do you see that large tree that's tipped over, resting against the hillside?"

"Okay, I see it...but I don't see a box."

"Look between the base of the tree and the hillside, look for a black square. Look carefully, whatever it is, it isn't natural. It's only about a foot or so in size."

"I see it, no wait...damn brush keeps moving."

"Watch your language," spouted Sally, who was now at Hana's side.

"Here momma, you take a look. Just like Angie said. It's near the base of that tree."

"Okay, I look. But why is box so interesting?"

She took a moment to examine the hillside. "Yeah, I see it, no wait...yeah I see it. Wait...it window...yeah it a window. I don't see house, but I see window."

"What?" Hana asked.

"You look, look close, it window. It four pane window and one iz mizzing. It look like window into side of mountain. I no see house or cabin, but it definitely window."

"Can we go see, can we?" Hana asked.

"You ask Angie. I don't know, maybe we shouldn't."

"Let me look again," Angie said as she slid her hand over her Glock.

A few minutes later Angie rendered the final verdict. "Yeah, it looks like a window, but I don't see anyone around. I think we can check it out."

∞

They stopped just outside of the well-hidden cabin. The exterior was sided with wood slabs. Installed in a vertical manner, some of the bark still in place. The siding was perfect camouflage, as from any distance the structure looked like a stand of trees. Adding to the effect was a thick layer of moss that covered the roof. The large uprooted tree Angie used as a landmark had fallen against the hillside about 15 feet above the cabin and provided additional protection from the elements.

The group slowly walked around the outside of it. It was three sided. With the rock face acting as the back wall. The only window was the one that faced the lake. It looked like something out of a fairytale.

The door, opposite the window, had fallen into the structure. The leather strap hinges were dry rotted and frayed.

"Hello… anyone home…" Angie asked tentatively. The question was clearly unnecessary, but she felt a need to ask it.

"Stay here," Angie told the two women as she reached for her Glock.

Sally put a hand on her. "I don't think that needed."

"You're right but stay here anyway."

"Okay," Sally said as she gave her daughter a commanding look.

Angie stepped gingerly on the door, as it lay flat on the floor. The wood creaked, and an alarm chatter sounded. The sound, like a playing card in a bike spoke, rattled everyone's nerves.

"It's okay, it's just a red squirrel" Angie said, to calm everyone. "Let me move this" as she picked up the door, "and you guys can come inside, be careful though."

The interior of the cabin was in shambles. At first glance it might be called a hovel but upon closer inspection it was clear the structure had been well built. The interior framing was post and beam construction. The walls looked straight and true. An assortment of leaves, pine needles and other forest debris littered every flat surface. Cobwebs filled the corners and eaves. Woodland creatures had made this place home for years. The dirt floor was bone dry and dusty, except for near the woodstove. It was clear the roof leaked near the stovepipe, but the rest of the structure was solid.

"What's that smell?" Hana asked, from the doorway.

"Possum poop, or coon poop, or squirrel poop. You get the point" said Angie.

The three women took in their surroundings. An old crosscut saw, other tools and some wire snares hung on one wall. A table, two chairs and a bed rested against another wall.

"Is this a trapper's cabin?" asked Sally.

"I think so," responded Angie.

"What's that?" Hana asked as she pointed to another door, a door that appeared to lead into the mountainside.

"I don't know, maybe a root cellar" Angie replied. "Let's leave it alone" anticipating the girl's next question.

"I agree" added Sally.

Hana walked toward a calendar hanging above the bed. Some type of creature had shredded much of it, but an image remained, of an old John Deere tractor. She brushed away some dust. "January 1935. This is cool! It's like a time capsule."

"I don't know, maybe we should not be here? What you think Angie?" Sally asked with trepidation.

"I don't see the harm."

"Momma its fine, no one lives here, look around."

"I know... but it not feel right... it feel...how you say...creepy."

"It does feel a bit creepy. I can't believe no one has been here in 65 years. But I think it's okay," Angie added.

"I think we should open that door. What can it hurt?" Hana announced.

"No" the other two women said in unison.

"I think we go now," added Sally. She pointed out the doorway "It getting dark, we go, we go now."

"What do you mean it's getting dark? It's only 2 o'clock" Angie said.

The three women looked outside as it began to rain lightly. Then the sky opened up and it came down in buckets. The temperature dropped significantly and there were no breaks in the clouds.

"Crap, I guess we're here for a while. We go out in that and we'll be soaked in a minute. Let's see about getting a fire in the stove," Angie directed.

Thirty minutes later the cabin was toasty. Angie had wedged the door into its frame helping to cut down on drafts. The fuel for the fire was a mix of pine cones, leaves and sticks collected from inside the cabin. Collecting this debris had the added effect of cleaning the interior. The structure was now more livable.

"Sally let's let the fire burn down to coals. Then we can cook the trout. I'm hungry" said Angie.

"Good idea. Hana clean table please. Then get mess kits from Angie's pack."

"Okay. Will we stay the night?"

"I hope not but the rain hasn't let up." Angie dug out a satellite phone from her pack "I need to make a call. Let them know where we are. In case we have to spend the night. If we do, it won't be comfortable, but it beats being outside in that mess."

∞

The next morning all three women were stirring at the first hint of daylight. The rain had stopped a few hours earlier, but dampness hung in the air. It had been an uncomfortable night. They had spent it wrapped in foil space blankets.

"I feel like I slept in a potato chip bag." Angie commented. From the looks of the other two it was a shared sentiment. "I'll be right back" she added.

"I got to go too," said Sally.

"Me too," chimed Hana.

All three women walked into some weeds and answered the call of nature.

"Now what?" asked Sally.

"I'll make a call. Then make some coffee and then we'll get the hell out of here."

"I want to look behind that door. It bugged me all night not knowing what's behind there," Hana said.

"We know," both of the other women said.

"You must have said hundred times. I admit...I now curious. We will look, before we go," added Sally.

160

The coffee was black and hot, as Sally insisted the stream water be boiled for more than ten minutes.

So, you were Girl Scout, is that good thing?" Sally asked of Angie.

Yeah. It taught me to always be prepared. That's why I keep this," she patted her daypack, stocked with emergency supplies. Like the space blankets, the first aid kit and this coffee."

"Iz good plan, we should do same. When we get home. First, we see what behind that small door. Maybe Hobbit?"

All three women stared at door as they sipped their brew.

Angie squeezed the empty Nescafe packets, like a worry ball.

"I think it's a tunnel. Maybe it goes way under the mountain," speculated Hana, stretching out the words "way under".

PARABELLUM: When you live in Peace, prepare for War
Jack Nanuq

CHAPTER 28
Isle of Man
February 1, 1919

Maria watched the priest take another draw on his pipe. The air was rich with the sweet aroma of imported tobacco. Maria followed Fr. Fagan's gaze as he looked out over the distant hills. They were a mottled greenish brown. Frost-killed grasses lay like frayed hemp over green bases ready to spring to life with the first hint of warmer weather. That was still two months away, but the dormant tufts reminded everyone that richer days were ahead.

A change was in the air and even the animals sensed it. The yard rooster crowed to his flock, some of which had become broody on small clutches. A fat calico cat, her belly swollen with soon to be delivered kittens, worked its way through a nearby hedgerow. Songbirds flitted from branch to branch in the search for a mate.

"Petr, do you know the term orphan?" Father Fagan asked.

"Da, I mean, aye sir, I do," Petr said as he worked on Maria's bicycle. Since the Armistice had been signed Petr could move about the island without an escort.

The four of them; Petr, Maria, Sister Veronique and Father Fagan were seated around a table in the yard. It was a bit cool, but at least it was not raining. Petr had arrived about an hour earlier to help Maria with her chores, but Father Fagan insisted that could wait. He announced today was for leisure and contemplation.

The priest exhaled through his nose. Maria thought he resembled a kindly dragon. Tendrils of smoke drifted from his nostrils.

"If Maria was a child, we would call her an orphan. But then again she's not a child." The priest said to no one in particular, but certain everyone heard him.

Sister Veronique chimed in with "You are right she is not a child. She is a woman, and a fine one at that. And she is the mother of a fine boy. I couldn't be more proud of them both if they were my own."

Fagan spoke again and added "Petr; you too are an orphan, am I correct?"

"Yes sir, my family, they are all gone. Some in the war and some to the flu, but all are gone. I have no one."

"Oh my son. But you do have someone, you do indeed. She is seated at this table. It is not a secret, you are fond of Maria," the priest continued. "What are your plans? When the Crown sends you home."

"I have none, I wish I did but I know not what I will find when I return."

"A man should have a plan" the priest continued. "You are handy with machines, are you not? With skills like that you could go anywhere. The world needs tinkers."

"Aye, true. And as you say...I have feelings for her." He glanced slyly at Maria. "But I have nothing to offer and have no... how you say? Way to provide for her... and Janos. It is wrong that I care for Maria, she needs man that has future. I should not have these feelings, it is wrong."

Fr. Fagan took a long pull on his pipe and contemplated what had just been said. Petr and Maria looked at each other, knowing there was some truth in his statement.

Sister Veronique spoke up. "I'll be leaving for France soon."

"What?" stammered Maria, with alarm.

"My sister...she lives near Calais. I am old and that is where I want to live my last days." The nun exchanged a glance with Fr. Fagan and he picked up the conversation.

"This war has caused much heartache and suffering. It is my guess there will be more struggles to come but I think you two should be wed." He said it with certainty. It wasn't an order or mandate but a certainty.

The four sat in silence. Maria looked at the two adults and knew they had discussed this earlier.

Fr. Fagan continued "As Sister Veronique has said she will be moving to France soon. We will miss her very much. But she has made her decision and I wish her well. She would like you two to join her."

"What?" Petr and Maria asked in unison.

"My sister, she has a café, but has no children. She is old like I and needs help. I have told her you can cook and she is willing to give you a job. The café is near a rail yard. There will be work for Petr. There will be challenges, many of them but I think you both can handle them. The French are slow to welcome foreigners, but they will come around."

"This is a lot to think about," stuttered Maria.

"Petr, I suspect you feel the same way," said the priest. "Sister, I think we should go inside and let these young people talk." With this he knocked the ash from his pipe and stood up.

Sister Veronique also stood and walked toward the rectory. Nothing more was said until the two of them were inside.

Maria would remember the following conversation for the rest of her life. It was the first time she had spoken in Czech in over four years. It was the only way they could communicate clearly.

"Petr" she said with trepidation "this is a lot to think about."

"It is… and it isn't …I love you. Yes, I do. I know I do." He let the statement hang there. "I think I knew it the first day we met…but you need a man that can provide for you…I have nothing… even the clothes on my back are not my own. They were given to me by the Camp. And Janos…what do I know of being a father?"

"But Petr…" Maria could not say anything more. Emotions would not let her mind make words. But the words were, or at least the feelings behind the words were there. She had thought about this moment…for how long…for months, no it had to have been years. She discovered the feelings for him were like windblown snow. Each thought and emotion like single snowflake; individually they had been insubstantial but over time they had coalesced into a barrier or was it a weight? Now that weight had piled up against the doors of her mind.

Sensing Maria's distress Petr continued "I am like...
like that cloud" pointing to a white mass in the middle of a blue
sky. "I am like that. Present, and maybe even pleasant to look
at" trying to lighten the mood with humor. "And someday that
cloud may form into something of substance. But now it is
nothing but...nothing but a downy image."

Maria was stunned, this man who she now knew she
loved with her entire being was telling her he didn't want to be
with her. No wait, that wasn't what he was saying. He was
saying he couldn't be with her. No, that wasn't right either...*Oh
Jesus please help me*, she prayed.

He took her hands in his and the feelings almost
overwhelmed them both. With tears in his eyes he said "I love
you, with all my heart, but..."

Maria interrupted, in her mind she could see herself
shouldering past the barricade of chaos.

"No... don't say any more...it is my time." She
hesitated "It is my time to speak, I love you too and there is no
but. We will do this, we will. The priest and the nun have said it
should happen and I believe them. We will make this work, all
of us. You, me and Janos, we will make this work."

They looked at each other and an electrical circuit was
now complete. Energy flowed from one being to the other and
then back again. They were now One, a heavenly creation, a
work of mystery and all that is Holy. They knew in their hearts
they would make this work, they didn't know how but they both
knew they would make it work.

Petr pulled Maria closer, and then closer and then...

The mood was broken when the rooster jumped on the
picnic table and startled them both.

Without a moment's hesitation Petr asked, "Can we
take the bird with us?"

They both burst out laughing; the dam of emotion had
been broken. The laugh they shared was far more intimate than
any kiss.

PARABELLUM: When you live in Peace, prepare for War
Jack Nanuq

CHAPTER 29
Albany, NY
May 17, 2001

The truck beeped irritatingly as it backed Newton's trailer down Nana's driveway. Newton stood next to Carson as he used hand signals to guide the driver alongside the house. Demon barked incessantly from inside the trailer.

Newton tapped Carson on the shoulder and muttered. "You got company," pointing to a car as it pulled to the curb.

It was a blue Ford Crown Victoria, a model marketed to law enforcement agencies all over the country. Although it had no markings, it screamed cop car. Carson made eye contact with the driver. He then turned back to the truck and trailer. As the truck came to a stop and the back-up alarm ceased Carson heard the car doors open.

"Can you see to the rest of this?" he said to Newton, as he pointed to the RV. "And keep Demon in the trailer until I figure out what these guys want," Carson added.

"Got it."

"Mr. Nowak, Carson Nowak?" one of the men asked. The accent was classic downstate; maybe New York City or Long Island. The first syllable was drawn out and emphasis on the last. It sounded like "Caaah-Sun Nooo-WHACK!"

He turned around and saw both men wearing dark suits. They had pulled aside their jackets to expose the eight-sided badge of the New York State Police, on their belts.

"Yes... what can I do for you?" Carson replied.

"Investigator Ron Matthews, we'd like to talk to you about a threat against your grandmother," said the taller of the two. He carried a briefcase.

"You mean my great-grandmother," Carson corrected.

"Mary Nowak...she's your great-grandmother, wow," said the other.

"Yeah...Mary Nowak. Everyone, everyone except you two that is, calls her Nana. What can I do for you?"

"Your grandmother, I mean your great-grandmother, may be in danger. Can we talk inside?" continued Matthews.

"Let's go across the street to my place. I'd rather talk in private, and then we'll talk to her."

"Okay… I guess we thought you lived here."

"Yeah, it's a common mistake. She signed the house over to me a few years ago."

"We'll be back later," Carson yelled to Newton.

∞

As Carson opened the front door to his home, he looked across the street and saw Demon running around the unmarked cruiser. The dog lifted his leg near the front driver's tire and marked its territory. If the other two men saw this, they didn't say a thing.

"Coffee?" Carson asked.

"Only if it's already made," Matthews, clearly the senior man, said.

"No, but I'll make a pot anyway. I have a feeling we'll be here awhile. Not to mention… you won't like Nana's coffee."

"I got to say, you're pretty calm about a threat against your grandmother" said the other.

Carson wasn't going to let on he knew she was in danger or how he might have known. "Well, she's made some enemies. Not many that is, but a few, over the years. You know…disgruntled tenants, unhappy contractors, business rivals, it happens."

Matthews continued "I'm afraid this is a little more serious than a disgruntled tenant. We have reason to believe she may be the target of a death threat."

"Go on, I'm listening" Carson said as he poured water into the coffeemaker. "Maybe you should start at the beginning."

Matthews laid his briefcase on the kitchen table. "I'd like you to take a look at some photos. Do you know this guy?" The shot was clearly pulled from a surveillance camera. It showed a tall, blond- haired man, wearing a Yankees cap. The blurry image only showed a portion of the man's face.

169

"No, but that could be anyone."

"Yeah, I know. How about this guy?" This image was much clearer and showed another white male, also with blond hair. This one was lying on a stainless-steel table.

"Dead?" Carson asked rhetorically.

"Very," said the shorter investigator.

"I didn't get your name," Carson said.

"Sorry…Petersen … Art Petersen" he said, as he slid a business card across the table. Matthews did the same.

Carson looked at the cards. "Bureau of Criminal Investigation – Special Investigation Unit… You guys are a long way from home. It says your office is in Manhattan."

"Yeah, we drove up this morning" Matthews said. As he said this, he slid some more photos across the table. These men were also lying on stainless steel tables. All were Black, with multiple tattoos.

"Ever seen these guys?" Matthews added.

"No."

"I didn't think so, but thought I'd ask. We don't think the last three guys are involved, but you never know."

"Involved in what?" asked Carson.

"We think Blondie number one and Blondie number two are assassins from South America. The others are local gangbangers. The Black guys picked a fight with the first two. It took place at Penn Station. The guy in the first photo escaped, but not without some injuries. The second also tried to make a run for it but died at the scene. Lead poisoning, if you know what I mean."

"And the others?" asked Carson.

"They were poisoned," responded Matthews.

"What?"

"Yeah poisoned. Blondie number two, name unknown, because he had multiple passports. This guy had a knife dipped in snake venom, a venom cocktail, actually. We think his partner had a similar setup. The gangbangers never had a chance, once the knife broke the skin. The Medical Examiner found four different types... of venom that is. Two attack the nervous system and the other two close off your windpipe."

"What happened?" asked Carson.

"Witnesses and video say the gangbangers tried to rob the two South Americans. They must have looked like easy pickings... boy were they wrong. The gangbangers circled the blonde guys. Two of the gangsters pulled back their jackets to show guns and suddenly both blondies pull out these little knives and start stabbing away. One of the gangsters..." Matthews looked at a notepad to confirm the name. "Orlando Jackson... yeah Orlando Jackson... AKA Puppet, got off a couple of shots. But he was dead and just didn't know it yet. He drops about 50 feet from the scene. When paramedics got there, he and the other two were squirming like worms on a hook. All three were dead within an hour."

Matthews continued "When NYPD and the Transit Authority cops look over the blonde guy, they find he had a homemade knife and sheath. The knife, not much bigger than a paring knife, was razor sharp on one edge and had a serrated edge on the other. The sheath held the toxin."

"So, what does that have to do with Nana?" Carson asked. He was pretty sure he knew but if he didn't ask the question it would be suspicious.

"The Transit Authority searched a nearby backpack and found a computer printout and directions to your grandmother's, I mean great-grandmother's house. And there were some notes, written in Spanish, which makes sense since they flew in from Argentina. The notes said to kill the woman, in the house." Matthews held up air quotes when he said the word woman. "The cops run the address through the computer and come up with Mary Nowak. Seems she's a bigwig here in Albany so they call us. Plus, it's outside of their jurisdiction."

"So why does someone want to kill Nana?" Carson asked.

"That's my question. His fingerprints got sent to Argentina and Interpol. Who knows if we'll get a response?

What can you tell us? No offense but she doesn't seem to warrant this kind of attention."

"Not a clue." To tell them anything would have opened a can of worms and Carson didn't want to go there. "No offense taken. Maybe they got the wrong address?"

"Maybe...but not likely. You sure you got nothing? Don't forget, there's another one running around. Here...look at this." Matthews said, as he slid more photos of Blondie number two. The photos were of the man's torso. The chest and shoulders clearly defined by hours of gym time. The muscles looked like woven ropes, no body fat visible. Another photo was a close-up of a tattoo on the inside of the right bicep. The tattoo was a line drawing of a running dog, superimposed over a swastika.

"This," Matthews continued, as he tapped a finger on the dog . "This mark here. That's stands for Galco. It's a bastardization for the Spanish word for greyhound, Galegos. But it means more than that. It's an offshoot of Odessa. You know...the Nazis that escaped from Germany? These are dangerous people. That mark means they will run their enemies to the ground. They fly under the radar, most times that is. They are professionals, with a capital P. If it weren't for this little mishap, we might never know they were in the country." Matthews took a breath. "Are you sure you got nothing to tell us?"

"Nah...I got nuthin. What now?"

"Not sure," continued Matthews "seems pretty strange a pair of professional killers fly five thousand miles and have the wrong address."

"Yeah, seems strange to me too," interjected Petersen. "I say we talk to your grandmother."

"Great-grandmother," the other two men said in unison.

Carson's cell phone rang, and he looked at the display. "I gotta take this. Finish your coffee and we'll go talk to Nana."

He stepped into the living room and mumbled "What's up Fred?"

"Can you talk?" Fred Hutchinson whispered in response to Carson hushed tone.

"Kinda, what's up?"

"I just wanted to remind you about the upcoming trip to Utica. Both the Kestrels want to visit the SUNY campus." SUNY stood for State University of New York. SUNY-Utica was an up and coming technology school.

"When are we going?"

"In a few days. At first we thought tomorrow, but the girls are exploring some garnet mine."

"What?"

"Apparently Angie took them fishing and they found a cabin in the middle of nowhere. Inside the cabin was a door to a garnet mine. Angie says it's pretty wild. Like something out of a fantasy novel. I told her to be careful."

"And?"

"And... she has orders to check in no later the 2100 hours."

"You're worried, aren't you?"

"Is it obvious, what gave me away?"

"You used military time, normally you would have said 9 p.m. But you use military jargon when you get nervous."

"Truth be told, I'd rather they weren't playing around under some mountain. I'm in real shit if they get lost or hurt. Angie said that won't happen, but these things do happen!" Hutchinson's voice had risen in volume.

"Easy Fred, you'll give yourself a heart attack. How about we let this run its course? I'm sure they'll be fine. You call me five minutes after you hear from Angie. Okay?"

"Yeah... you're right. Take care of whatever you got going and we'll talk later. Over."

Carson snapped the phone closed and returned to the kitchen. "Gentleman, let's go see Nana."

∞

"A galco... a galco you say... Is that not the lizard that you see on TV? That sells insurance?" Nana asked.

Carson snickered at this. He could tell she was having fun with the investigators. They were now in her kitchen and she was in her comfort zone. He glanced at Newton and Iris and could tell they were also enjoying the show.

"No ma'am...that's a gecko," said Petersen impatiently. He added "This is important. You have no idea why someone wants to kill you?"

"I do not. I am old woman. What do you do you think I should do with this information?" She paused and then in a poor imitation of Arnold Schwarzenegger she said "You vaant I should hurt someone?"

"No ma'am, we just thought you might have some information. We don't know what we should do next."

"You don't know...you don't know... I know what you should do. But should I tell you? I not sure. Why should I?"

Matthews interjected "Mrs. Nowak, if I may be blunt?"

"Go on... you be blunt." Nana was clearly enjoying herself.

"I had my office do some research on you. And..."

"And vaat?"

"And I know you were a war refugee..."

"And vaat, you think I got Nazi treasure hidden in my basement? Maybe I give birth to Hitler's baby...or maybe...maybe ...I know not what? I not see vaat World War Two have to do with this. Dat was more than fifty years ago. I now tell you vaat you should do. You should, you should..." She paused and when she was sure she had both men's full attention she said "You should investigate! You should go out and get information, not bother me. You know where bad man was yesterday, and you know where he is going. Or should I say where is coming? You go find bad man, that your job... But I old woman. Maybe I not worth such things? You go, I done now!"

As if to echo this command Demon growled menacingly. The dog was curled in a corner and vigilant. The growl could have curdled milk. His ears stood upright and the lips were pulled back. Petersen slid his hand to his gun.

"Demon down!" ordered Newton. The dog relaxed his lips and laid his chin on his paws, but his eyes remained locked on Petersen.

Matthews broke the tension. "You're right. We should look into this further. And that's what we're going to do. I was going to suggest we post a car in front of your house, but I doubt anyone's getting near you as long as the dogs by your side."

No sooner had the men left, and Carson closed the front door, did Newton and Iris break into laughter. The sound was so loud that Carson was sure their guffaws could be heard by the men as they climbed into their car.

∞

"You should be ashamed of yourself" Carson said to Nana, who was wearing a grin like the Cheshire cat. "Those men have a job to do."

"Then they should do it, not bother me. Let them go find bad guy, the gecko."

"That's Galco, not gecko. Jesus you're infuriating. I wanted to hear your story. Why didn't you tell them?" Carson worked to keep the frustration out of his voice, but it was impossible.

"Because it my story, not theirs, they not need hear story. They need do their job; find bad guy. They spoke to you first, vie you not tell them story?"

"Because…as you say, it is your story. I have no idea why someone is hunting for you and whether or not it has anything to do with the War."

"You vaant I should tell you then?"

"Yes I vaant you should tell me," Carson mimicked her ancient voice.

175

PARABELLUM: When you live in Peace, prepare for War

Jack Nanuq

CHAPTER 30
Pas de Calais
April 1, 1920

Petr rolled over in bed and whispered "Happy Birthday. How does it feel to be 20?"

The words were spoken in Czech. When they were home and sure not be overheard, they spoke in their native tongue. Maria loved the sound of his voice but still found it strange to share her bed with this man. Even after a year of wedded bliss she found the shared space to be a strange land. The first man to share her bed was a brute. He had been bookish in public, but a brute in bed. In the back of her mind she wondered if Petr may someday change into that kind of person. She doubted it and knew that it was no more likely that the oak tree in her yard would someday change into a pine tree.

"Good morning, Happy Birthday" Petr said again.

"Good morning, to you too" she responded in the same language.

"I have a surprise for you."

"What? I said no gifts, we cannot afford it."

"Nonsense, it is a little thing."

She snuggled up to him and replied, "I do not think it is that little."

"Oh... no, not that, but it makes me happy to hear you say that. I have something different for you."

"What is it?"

"It's a surprise, you will see later."

"But later you will be at work; tell me now."

"That is part of the surprise, I traded shifts. I have today off, no work today.

"You won't get in trouble, will you, please tell me you won't get in trouble."

"No, the bosses at the rail yard like my work. Tomorrow I will work double shift. Today we have to ourselves."

"And you are sure? Just the other day you said they don't like foreigners. This is not some way to trap you?"

He pulled her closer. "No, you should not worry. It is true the French, do not like foreigners, but they are romantics. When the superintendent asked why I wanted the day off he was thrilled to hear about your birthday. I do not think it is a trap as you say. He seemed quite pleased. He said he was young once, although that is hard to believe. He remembered being in love with his wife. He no longer loves her, but they are together, nonetheless. He said he hopes we don't have the same fate."

Maria playfully pushed him away. "But you forget I have the café, I have to work."

"No, you don't, I have spoken with Bridgette. She will cover your shift today. The day is ours, to do as we see fit."

"And Janos...what about school, did you get someone to copy his lessons for him?"

"Sadly no, I spoke to the Headmaster. He tells me Janos must go to school today. He say Janos can spend Sunday with us but during the week he must go to school like all the others. He said, 'Where would the world be if all the children skipped school for birthdays?' He seemed to think it would lead to chaos. I think not but who's to say in these matters."

"So it's just us for the day? What shall we do?" she said as she moved back into his arms.

"That must wait until later," Petr said as he pushed her away playfully. "Janos will be awake soon."

As if on cue they heard Janos walking down the hall to the water closet. The old floor boards squeaked in protest even though his footsteps were light. A short time later they heard him pull the chain and the toilet flushed. The floor sounded again as he padded back to his room.

Maria turned toward Petr. "Can you get some nails from the landlord and tack those boards in place?"

"I'll see what I can do. We better get up now."

∞

Bacon sizzled in a pan as Janos walked into the kitchen "Happy Birthday Mamma, I made you something."

"Thank you" she said and took the large piece of brown butcher paper. On it Janos had drawn three stick people, each with a large red heart. "It's beautiful."

"That's you and me and Papa."

"Look Petr, it's wonderful." She was making a fuss over the picture. This simple gift touched her heart.

"You are very talented, maybe we should send this to the Louvre?" Petr commented.

"The loo?" Janos looked confused.

"No, no," Maria laughed. "Not the water closet...the Louvre." She then spelled the word. "It is a famous art museum, in Paris."

"This French, sometimes I don't like it. It is much harder than English. Like this word Louvre, it sounds like where you crap."

"Young man, watch yourself," Petr snickered. "Yes, it is sometimes difficult. But don't let a Frenchman hear you think it is harder than English. They think French is the only language that should be spoken. To do otherwise is barbaric. Someday you will realize it is good that you speak more than one language. You may want to travel when you are older. Your English is good, and you will have French. Your momma teaches you German, and we speak Czech at home."

"Maybe...maybe I can borrow momma's bike and ride to a Czechoslovakia? And I can ask directions in those languages and not get lost."

"You're right, you could. That is, if mama lets you use her bicycle."

"Momma, can I, can I?" Janos asked excitedly. His faced beamed with adventure.

"I think so, but that's a long way off, maybe you will have your own bike by then."

"Oh really, ..., you are getting me a bike, oh yeah!"

"Slow down Janos. Today is your mother's birthday. She's the only one getting a gift right now."

179

"Okay," a slight frown of disappointment crossed his face. "Did you get momma something?" The face brightened again.

"I did, but that's later. It's a surprise," Petr said as Maria slid a slice of bacon onto their plates. A croissant with some jam completed the meal.

Maria said "We are going to walk you to school today. Hopefully by the time you get home Papa will have seen fit to give me this great surprise. He's a man of mystery."

The walk to the school was pleasant. It seemed like all of nature had conspired to celebrate Maria's birthday. A warm breeze came from the south and the path was dry for the first time in a week. The sun was a distinct orange ball and radiated warmth and life. Songbirds, recently arrived from Africa, sang their melodies in celebration of the new day.

∞

The motorcycle ride was unlike anything she had ever experienced. It reminded her of the time she was speeding through the sheep pasture, on her bicycle. Only this time things were under control. Or at least she hoped Petr had things under control. He seemed to be in control. The bike motor made a hit and miss sound under her legs and she could feel some of its heat. Her arms were wrapped around Petr and wished she had gloves as the breeze caused by their travel was stripping the heat from her fingertips. She slid her hands under Petr's jacket and leaned her head over his shoulder. She looked and saw the speedometer. The gauge read a little over 30 KPH. Not fast but faster than most people could run for any distance.

"Where are we going?" she yelled.

"You'll see. It's a surprise."

"No more surprises." She didn't really mean it. She wanted more surprises, lots more. Not just today but all the days to come; pleasant surprises that is. She couldn't help but wonder where they were going. It must be far, or they would not have needed a motorcycle.

And the motorcycle; what a surprise that was. When they came out of morning Mass the machine was waiting by the back door. Maria still went to Mass daily and whenever possible Petr could he went with her.

Petr told her he had rented it for the day. She suspected there was more to that story but figured he didn't want her worrying about the cost. She couldn't help herself. Frugality had been hammered into her by the past few years. This past year had been especially tough. They always had enough to eat, thanks to her job at the café. But everything else cost money. She had thought she could make extra money by making shoes but the one thing in abundance in the area was shoemakers. The locals would never go to a foreigner for such a luxury.

She did not blame the locals; things were hard for them also. The land had taken a beating. Shattered tree trunks stood in stark testimony to the destruction and suffering experienced during the war years. To add emphasis to this thought she saw a one-legged farmer yelling at a sheep dog.

The bike continued down a rutted road as they neared the coastline. On either side of them were fruit trees; apples and pear and peaches and who knew what. Some of the trees were in bloom, some past that stage and some just starting to bud out. The salt air blocked any fragrance, but Maria reveled in the sight, nonetheless. Here was a sign things would get better. As the trees bloomed the people would prosper.

∞

On the ride back home, Maria was both excited and concerned. She was now wearing a haversack that had been fashioned out of a feed bag. The backpack held small wooden box, with a rare and precious cargo. The pack vibrated. Maria was sure of this. But was it vibrating from the rutted road or the cargo? Never in her wildest dreams would she have seen herself on a motorcycle in the French countryside, carrying a box of bees. Honey bees and a queen bee. Given to her, by a distant relative of Mrs. Kelly.

Good old Mrs. Kelly. *That sneaky old woman, I love her*, Maria thought. The woman had reached across the Channel and called in a family favor. Maria was now the benefactor of that favor. Maria would do everything in her power to do right by the old woman. She would read every book she could get her hands on and make a prosperous hive. She could almost taste the sweet honey as she thought about this.

She wondered how quickly she could make one hive into two and then two into four. Honey and beeswax meant cash money. She did not know of any other beekeepers in her area. She would have a commodity the locals would buy from her. She warmed to the thought of having a little extra coin to put away. She warmed to the thought of having Petr as her husband. A man who took a day off so that they could embark on a new adventure together.

PARABELLUM: When you live in Peace, prepare for War
Jack Nanuq

CHAPTER 31
Albany, NY
May 19, 2001

Carson was finishing his morning run as he passed a bank's digital reader board. It read 5:19 a.m. 53 degrees F. He turned south onto Manning Boulevard, slowed to walk and took in the sights around him. The morning was beautiful. A brief shower had stopped about an hour before he left the house, and everything wore a glimmering coat of water. The sounds of waking songbirds seemed to come from everywhere.

He briefly debated walking down Nana's side of the street but stayed on his side. She was safe and he could view the neighborhood from this side as well as from the other side. He scanned each parked car as he approached them. Except for breaks at the ends of driveways the cars seemed to be parked bumper to bumper. Parking was at a premium. This neighborhood had been developed long before families had three and four cars. Each car glistened with watery marbles from the earlier storm.

Then he saw it. About a hundred yards from his home, and Nana's, was beige Nissan Sentra. Its skin and windshield devoid of water. To the untrained eye it fit right in the neighborhood, but Carson knew it had to have been parked within the past hour. He approached it cautiously. There were no occupants. He noted a small green sticker in the corner of the windshield. It was the letter "e" and stood for Enterprise Rental Cars. There were all sorts of innocent reasons a rental car had been recently parked in the neighborhood, but Carson's nerves were on edge. Without missing a stride, he glanced into the car, as he passed it. The rear seat was packed with boxes.

When he was sure no one was hiding inside he looked toward Nana's house. No one was in view but that didn't mean anything to Carson. About two doors from his home he stopped and was about to cross the street when he saw the stranger. But the stranger wasn't at Nana's home they were at his. And the stranger was leaning against his car as if they belonged there.

184

In the half-light of early morning he couldn't see the person's face. The fact they were wearing a hooded sweatshirt didn't help either. But something about this person seemed familiar.

It was the size, yes it was the size. The person looked like a child. No, not a child, maybe a teenager? The person then turned toward him and pulled back the hood. *Son-of-a-bitch, it's Liza.*

As he approached, she twisted the top off a Dr. Pepper and handed it to him. "I thought you might like this."

"I'd like this better," and took her in his arms. He kissed her passionately and ran his hands down her back. When Carson got to her belt he stopped and pulled away.

"Aren't you full of surprises? First, you show up here unannounced and now I find you wearing a gun. What's up?"

Liza looked him in the eye. "I heard about what happened at Penn Station and want to help. I didn't call because I wasn't going to take no for an answer."

"Fair enough, but I'm not a Neanderthal. I wouldn't have said no. Nana's safety is paramount to me. What do you have in mind? Hide in a closet and jump out when the boogeyman shows up."

"Don't be a smart ass... that's your job. Seriously though, I brought some electronic gear."

"That your car... that Nissan?"

"Yeah. I hope you don't mind but I brought some motion detectors, infrared cameras and alarms."

"No landmines or rocket launchers?"

"Jesus, you're an ass. Here drink this, before it goes flat" she said as she tapped on the plastic soda bottle.

"Thanks. Sorry...I make jokes when I'm nervous. I appreciate your concern for Nana. Let's go inside, she's safe for now. She's not even home."

∞

When Carson got out of the shower, he found Liza in his living room, cleaning her gun. The aroma of solvent was potent but not unpleasant.

"So you like the Walther," he asked?

"Yup, the iconic Walther PPK. If it's good enough for James Bond, its good enough for me."

"Nice choice."

"With my tiny hands I don't have many options. It fits me perfectly." She said this as she reassembled the weapon.

"I'm going to make a call. How many people will we need to install your equipment?"

"Three or four should do it. With that many we should have everything up and running by lunch time. Where'd you stash Nana?"

"I didn't stash her anywhere. She decided to take a trip to Cooperstown. She has a place on Otsego Lake. She loves it down there and she took her two nurses. She'll be busy playing tour guide. They've got an opera company, the Farmers Museum, the Fennimore Art Museum and don't forget the Baseball Hall of Fame. And the barbecue chicken at Brooks'. She's a woman of eclectic tastes."

"I'm surprised you got her to leave town."

"She wasn't going to go until she learned about the Galcoes. She told me 'I not run away, iz just that…best way to survive punch iz not be there when it arrive.' She was more worried for the safety of her nurses. They will take good care of her and she'll take good care of them. It wasn't really that hard to get her to go."

"I've got to meet her sometime."

Carson chuckled. "Be careful what you wish for."

∞

Liza was wrong. The installation work wasn't completed until late afternoon. One of the crew members was vacuuming odd bits of plasters and dirt when Carson announced, "Dinner's on me."

An hour later the crew, all of them smokers, were eating their *banh mi* sandwiches in the yard. Inside, Carson and Liza were having spring rolls and soup at Nana's kitchen table.

Liza picked up the bag from 20-Pho-7 and said "This name cracks me up. I love the play on words. I'm guessing it's open round the clock."

186

"Yup," Carson mumbled as he fought to speak and not spit out food.

"Sorry, my bad, I should have waited for you to finish."

"It's okay. You're right its open 24 hours, every day of the week. Mr. Nguyen is a big fan of idioms. It's kind of his way of showing off his command of the language. Which is really funny because his English sucks. Nana says his French is perfect, and I can only guess his Vietnamese is also. But he learned English working with American GIs; need I say more?"

Changing the subject, Liza asked "How long is Nana going to be out of town?"

"About two weeks. Which is a good thing since I have to be on escort duty for the next couple of days. Maybe while I'm gone someone will catch the bastard." Carson's voice roughened. "It won't be good if I get my hands on him. I don't want to talk about that. How's Nana's journal project coming along?"

Liza finished off a spring roll before answering. "Great, I'm having a lot of fun with it. No wait that's not exactly true, sometimes it's a royal bitch."

"Welcome to my world."

Liza waved her hand dismissively. "Seriously though, the challenge is just what the doctor ordered. I was getting into a rut with my job. This little project has been interesting. It gets the juices flowing. I've got some new material in my car. I'll go get it."

Carson sipped an iced tea as he paged through the new material. There were still some gaps in transcripts, but he was astounded by all the information that was on these pages. "This is amazing, I can't believe what's here. How did you decipher it? Nana's writing looked like Sanskrit or something."

Liza looked pleased at the compliment. "It's been a bitch, but in a good way. The recipes are the key. We are using them like the Rosetta Stone. First, we compare the translated recipes to the ones in the journals. Then we know what some of the squiggles and symbols mean. Then we scan the journals and insert the words we know. That's the easy part, next comes the fun part because we only have about 10 percent of the information. If we're lucky we might get three or four words close together and we might be able to figure out a sentence from that. Sometimes that helps us translate other symbols. For instance, one of the recipes uses horse meat so we knew the symbol for horse. Then we were able to figure out the symbol for saddle and leather."

Liza clearly relished talking about this. "And don't forget about Petr's journal. That helped a great deal. His was easy to translate and his story is fascinating. When he was 14, he was leading a pig to the market. He and the pig were arrested by the local militia." She used her fingers to make air quotes around the word arrested.

"They accused Petr of stealing the pig. The next day a magistrate found him guilty and sent him to the Army. To fight for the Kaiser. He was on the front less than a month, before he was taken prisoner. A mortar shell knocked him unconscious. He got shipped off to a POW camp. Camp Knockaloe, on the Isle of Man. His journals were written in a very basic manner, almost like a child might write. It was puzzling until I came across an entry that told how he couldn't read or write until he got to the Camp. At the camp he got some basic schooling. His friend Andrej taught him to read and write. His notes are in that green folder."

Liza turned so she was sitting lengthwise on the couch, with her feet tucked under Carson's left thigh. "Do you mind if we don't fool around tonight? I'm beat," she said.

"No problem. Do you want a blanket?"

"No, I'm good."

∞

Carson slept fitfully that night and it had nothing to do with the fact he was on Nana's other couch. He had spent many nights here. He and the couch were old friends. Yet he tossed and turned repeatedly. Each time he woke he looked across the room to Liza. She slept soundly, wrapped in a quilt, with a fluffy pillow under her head.

She had drifted off shortly after she said, "I'm good." He stayed next to her until almost 9:30, by then his bladder was ready to burst. He hadn't dare to move any distance, for fear he'd disturb her. Each time he reached for a new folder he thought she might wake. She was so beautiful sleeping there. She had a cute little snore, like a kitten's purr. He wondered if she knew she snored.

He was falling for this woman. No wait that wasn't right. The fall had already occurred. When he wasn't looking someone had stuffed his heart and soul into a barrel and launched it over Niagara. Now everything was swirling around in a whirlpool at the base of the Falls. In those dangerous and fickle currents. That place where he could easily get slammed against a rock and drown or be trapped and run out of air. If the Fates were kind, they might pluck him from this turbulence and let him drift to calm waters.

He had to wonder if it was fair to get involved when he had to deal with this Galco issue, not to mention his responsibility for the Kestrels, and his responsibilities at Hawkeye. And she lived in Baltimore, would a long-distance relationship work?

At 3:55 a.m. he had enough of this convoluted thinking. He went into the kitchen and did some stretching exercises. He then left her a note.

Liza;   *20-May-01*

Duty calls and I must be out of town for at least a day, maybe two. Please help yourself to anything in the house, Nana won't mind.

We never got around to discussing your plans. I am leaving you my spare house key. If you are going to be in town for a while please stay at my house. I'll worry less if you are across the street. Please excuse the mess.

Call me when you get up.

Yours;

Carson

PS: There is a new toothbrush in the top drawer of the vanity in the bathroom.

With that mission completed he laid his key on the note. It wasn't a spare key, it was off his own ring, but he had a spare in his yard. Had he looked he's probably found a spare in one of Nana's kitchen drawers. He wondered momentarily if there was some significance to him lending out his original. No, he wasn't lending it. He knew she could have it forever.

With that he jogged across the street for a shower and change of clothes. Fred would pick him up in less than an hour.

PARABELLUM: When you live in Peace, prepare for War
Jack Nanuq

CHAPTER 32
Otsego Lake, NY
May 20, 2001

They couldn't have asked for a better day. The sun was directly overhead, and white puffy clouds littered the sky. The air was a calm 65 degrees and although a slight fishy odor drifted toward them it wasn't unpleasant.

Nana and Iris sat on the deck of Nana's vacation home. They had a view of Otsego Lake. Both women were watching Newton and Demon play on the beach. Time after time Newton threw a piece of driftwood into the water and the dog would retrieve it. His retrieval style was all his own. He would swim after it, bite down firmly and bring it back to the beach. About ten feet from Newton he'd stop. He'd chew on the stick until he was sure it was subdued. Then he would prance the remaining distance to the man and drop it at his feet.

"That's hysterical," said Iris as she snickered at the dog's antics. "It's beautiful out here."

"You like?" Nana asked.

"I do. It's so peaceful and relaxing. I can see why you bought this place."

"You like?" Nana repeated.

"I do," answered Iris, wondering if Nana had not heard her.

The conversation was interrupted as the dog bounded up the stairs to the deck, with Newton close behind. Demon jumped onto the cushion next to Nana.

"Demon! Get down," yelled Newton.

"No iz good, he good dog, he fine," responded Nana. "You ugly dog, but I like you," she said as she patted Demon on the head. She gave the dog a fig newton from a nearby plate.

Newton took a seat next to Iris and picked up a fig newton for himself. Before biting into it he offered it to Iris.

Nana repeated her earlier question. "You like lake house?"

"I do," Iris responded tentatively. She then turned to Newton "No thank you".

"I give you," Nana continued.

"What, no I can't ...I can't."

"Vie... vie not, you say you like... I give you."

"But, but...I don't think..."

"Vaat... you afraid ... maybe people think you take advantage of old woman...they not know me. I not feeble minded, they feeble minded if they think that way. "

"It's just that you have already given so much, first the job, then the truck, and now..."

Nana then turned to Newton "You like lake house?"

"Yeah, but I couldn't... Carson should get this."

"No, no Carson have his own place up in Adirondack. He no need this place. He like mountains better than lake."

"But..., but..." Newton stammered.

"I give you and I give to her," pointing at Iris "call it early wedding gift."

"What?" Iris exclaimed. Newton sat there dumbfounded.

Nana turned to Iris. "I see how he look at you, and how you look at him. He look at you, like my Petr look at me. You foolish girl, you no accept gift, you think about it. And you too" she said pointing a gnarled finger at Newton. "Lez get lunch" Nana said to signal the conversation was over.

∞

An hour later they were waiting at Brooks' House of Barbecue, in Oneonta. The air was rich with the smell of charcoal smoke, vinegar sauce and grilled meats. The waiting area was packed with people. Apparently, others thought this was the perfect place to spend a Sunday afternoon. Iris held their place in line while Nana took a seat on a wooden bench.

Newton sat next to her. "You need to take your meds" and handed her a rainbow assortment of pills.

"Damn pills. If I take those I vont have room for chicken."

"I know, but the doctors say you need your meds. Now take your pills or we're not taking the house," he said winked at Nana.

"Okay I do this for you and you do this for me."

"Deal. Now take your pills, Old Lady. Why does everything need to be a struggle with you?" he said jokingly.

A waitress came forward and announced their table was ready. Newton and Iris helped Nana to her feet.

During the meal Newton said, "We need to talk about the elephant in the room. Or should I say the Galco?"

Nana dipped a piece of chicken into some sauce and shook her head.

"Seriously, we need to talk about this."

"You vant I say I scared...okay, I scared. I talk tough in front of Carson but yes...I scared. I not afraid of death. But I afraid I meet God and not know what to say. I live good life but yes, I kill a man. I do so to protect Janos, but I not sure if God agree. What then?"

"That's not what I meant. I meant how long do we stay here and what do we do when we go home? As for the other thing this might not be the best place to talk." He scanned the nearby tables to see if anyone was listening to their conversation.

"You in hurry get back home? You say you like lake house."

"We do," interjected Iris, "but I think ...I think we are wondering ...what happens if they don't catch the Galcoes?" "That, I not worry about. I was hard on State Police boys but they good at their job. And Carson is there, and Carson has friends. They catch bad guy or bad guys. Maybe two, maybe three weeks but I sure they catch them soon. Until then we have fun. Tomorrow we go to Fenimore Art Museum. Do you know museum?"

Newton spoke first "Let's see ... that's where James Fenimore Cooper was born, right? He wrote The Last of the Mohicans."

"Gold star for you...yes. Last of Mohicans is my most favorite book. That why I name company Hawkeye." Nana turned to Iris and continued "Why you not call your sister? Next weekend is holiday weekend; Memorial Day. Have her bring kids to house... we maybe rent boat, go fish, have big picnic, and good time. This is vacation."

Newton's phone rang and they all stopped.

He looked at the display. "Speak of the devil" he muttered as he flipped open the phone. "Carson, we were just talking about you... speak up...I can't hear you, speak up.... no wait." Newton turned to the women. "I need to take this outside."

In the parking lot, the phone conversation continued. "Is she driving you crazy yet?" Carson asked.

"Kinda," Newton responded and listened to the echoe-y sound of a car on a highway.

"What'd she do now?"

"She wants to give us the house." There was a pause on the line. The highway noise continued. It was clear Carson was in some type of vehicle.

"Which house? The one in Albany?"

"No, the lake house. She said we should get married."

"What'd you say?"

"I said no to the house thing but didn't know what to say about the second thing."

"You're gonna have to say yes to both things," Carson laughed. "You may have to... just to shut her up. Unless you want to hear about the pretty babies you and Iris will make."

"Jesus, I didn't think of that. This thing just keeps getting worse."

"Ah come on now. It's not that bad, it's not like you'd make ugly babies."

"You're not helping" Newton said exasperated. "Did you call for a reason? Or did you just sense my discomfort."

"Yeah, I wanted to tell you I'll be out of town for one or two days. I'm checking to make sure Nana doesn't want to come back already."

"Naw… you might not see her all summer the way things are going. She's having a blast. She's a little concerned about the Geckos, as she likes to call them. But she figures between you and the cops someone will find them. How are you doing, any sign of them?"

"No... but I've got the house wired and they are in for a surprise when they do show up. If Nana changes her mind and wants to come home early make sure you call first. You can reach me on my cell phone." There was a pause. "I got another call, I got to go now."

"Okay, take care," said Newton.

Carson looked at his phone and didn't recognize the number. But since it was his personal phone he answered, "Go for Carson."

"Dude," said a strange voice. "Dude, I saw that psycho bitch" continued the voice.

Carson recognized the voice. "Smokey, Smokey slow down…What are you talking about?"

"I saw that psycho you asked me to watch out for. She just left Nana's house. She got in a Nissan and left. She was alone though, no guys with her. You want me to check on Nana?"

Carson knew what happened but wanted a clearer picture. If for no other reason than to tell Liza how on top of things Smokey was. "Describe her for me."

"Short, and cute but tiny. I kinda thought it was a girl scout until she drove away. You want I should check on Nana?"

"Nah, don't worry about it. I know that chick and it's not the same girl. But thanks for the call. I'll settle up with you next time I see you."

"It's cool, just thought you'd like to know."

"Thanks, gotta go." Carson burst into laughter as he hung up the phone.

PARABELLUM: When you live in Peace, prepare for War
Jack Nanuq

CHAPTER 33
Utica, NY
May 20, 2001

"What the hell was that all about?" asked Fred as he took the exit for Utica.

"This day just keeps getting better and better."

As the Durango turned onto Genesee Street Carson asked, "So, what's on today's agenda?" He looked in the side mirror and confirmed the other two Durangoes were behind them.

"First, we're going to pay a visit to some professor at the college. He's some type of metallurgist" Fred responded.

"Something to do with the Parabellum, or shouldn't I ask?"

"I'm not exactly sure, whether you should ask or not, but I don't see the harm. You've been with this since the beginning. I told you about the garnet mine the girls found; right?"

"Yeah, go on."

"It seems Hana brought back a bunch of garnet ore, and the ore contains a rare earth element ...or something like that."

"Do you mean rare earth metals?" Carson corrected.

"Oh, looks who's been watching the Science Channel, or did they mention it on Sesame Street? Do you want to hear what we're doing or not?"

"Go on."

"Anyway, this guy's supposed to be some type of expert in the field. I guess they use the rare earth metals in cell phones and that kind of technology. Hana seems to think it might help the conductivity of the trigger mechanism."

The conversation was interrupted by a beep of a horn. Carson checked his mirror and saw the Durango behind them flash its headlights. The right turn signal showed the SUV was going to pull into a FASTRAC gas station.

"Looks like someone needs a potty break," Carson joked.

"Good... they read my mind; too much coffee this morning" Fred said matter-of-factly.

Twenty minutes later they were back on the road. Carson was now driving the SUV with the Kestrels in it. Angie Rodriguez was in Fred's car and taking a much-needed break, after driving almost 5 hours.

Carson checked the rearview mirror and saw Hana working on a sketch pad. She sported a set of earbuds and seemed oblivious to the adults surrounding her. He cleared his throat and said, "I heard you guys found some cool rocks".

"Dah" Sally said. "We went how you say... spellbunking?"

"Spelunking," Carson corrected. "Tell me about it," he continued.

"We find cave in woods, no...it was mine, garnet mine. You know little red gems? Most rocks..." she continued "Or maybe you say stones? They are small, but some are bigger. Some have black mine-rails. No... no, I mean minerals. Around them and they look like donuts. Hana says she wants to refine mineral, use for her bomb. We see scientist today. See if it possible."

"What was the mine like?" asked Carson.

"I'm glad we return from there...it scary place. Bats, spiders, other bugs. I no like that, and dirt, and muck... not good." Sally continued "But this trip not just work. After we meet professor, we have fun. I want to see zoo. It been long time since I see exotic animals. I want Hana see animals. She love pandas."

"Do they have pandas?" Hana asked, her attention now on the conversation.

"Kinda," Carson responded "Not the black and white ones. But they have red ones, called Fire Pandas. No wait, that's not right, it's called a Lesser Panda. They kind of looks like a raccoon."

"You've been there?" Hana asked.

"Yeah, a few times, it's a pretty cool place. We don't have a zoo in Albany. Whenever I get over here, I stop in. It's a nice place to unwind."

"Unwind... unwind what are you unwinding?" asked Sally.

"Sorry...it's a saying. It means to relax."

"Okay, I like this saying. I need to unwind after trip inside mountain."

∞

The group entered the waiting area of Professor Maarsten's office. The walls were festooned with photos of mountain bikers. There were photos of desert landscapes, jungle trails and even a group of cyclists cascading down a snow-covered hillside. Interspersed with the photos were awards and certificates recognizing various achievements; crossing the Continental Divide, biking the length of the Appalachian Trail, and the completion of various endurance runs. Stacks of cycling magazines filled the corners of the room. It was clear this man had a passion.

The receptionist, a red-haired coed said "He's expecting you, but he's running a little behind. He'll be out in a minute. Please have a seat."

The couch wouldn't hold all of them so Fred said, "I'll wait in the hall."

A mere minute later, the door to the professor's office opened and the man himself walked out. He was clearly an athlete. Well defined thigh muscles stretched the seams of his charcoal gray Dockers. A muscular chest filled a blue polo shirt. He had shoulder length hair, was worn in a ponytail. His tanned skin had that elastic quality that made judging his age a near impossibility. He was somewhere between his late 20s and his early 40s.

"Paul Maarsten," he announced and reached out with his right arm. "Sorry. I can't shake hands." The hand, wrist and most of the arm was covered in a lime green cast. The fabric was decorated with graffiti, flamboyant signatures, wishes for a speedy recovery, hearts and smiley faces. It resembled a truck that had been left in the wrong section of town.

He waved the appendage and joked "You know what they say. It's all fun and games, until someone gets hurt. Then its fuh..." he paused as he looked at Hana. "It's, frickin hilarious."

His voice had a slight accent. *German* Carson thought. "Follow me, my lab's this way." Without waiting for a response, he stepped into the hall and crashed into Fred. "You with them?" the professor asked rhetorically as he bounded away.

Maarsten held his ID badge next to a card reader and entered a code. He made another rhetorical statement. "I take it you're all cleared for this?"

The door slid open and Carson was surprised by the interior. He had expected it to resemble a high school lab with Bunsen burners, beakers, test tubes and other paraphernalia. But this was state-of-the-art electronic habitat, nothing old-school, about this work area. Computers, keyboards, and digital screen surrounded them.

"Professor, before we get started," Angie broke the silence. "Are we alone? I need you to sign some paperwork."

"Yeah...yeah we're alone."

Angie handed him the security disclosure agreement. The professor mumbled some of the words "under penalty of..." as he scribbled his signature. "You know, I think I've signed about a hundred of these" he said to no one in particular.

He turned to Hana and said "I've been read in on some of this. But I want to hear what you have to say about your project. And what did you bring me?"

Hana explained her idea. How the Parabellum is supposed to start a chain reaction when it receives a RF signal. "Think of the filament in a lightbulb," she said as she pulled the garnet and rare earth rocks from her day pack. "Thomas Edison had to find just the right element, tungsten. Before he could get his light bulb to work. The tungsten excites the gas and gives off light. My parabellum needs to charge the element

PARABELLUM: When you live in Peace, prepare for War

and make the explosives go boom. I hope these minerals will do it. Or at least help do it."

The professor hefted one of the rocks. It was about the size of a baseball and weighed nearly five pounds.

"Do you have a name for this yet?" he asked Hana.

"What do you mean...it's a rock?"

"No, no, let's give it a codename."

"Well, no...I guess... it looks like a muffin but...but I like biscuit better. Can we call it a biscuit?"

"We can call it anything you like...a biscuit it is. We'll call the raw material a biscuit. As we refine it, we'll come up with other names."

Hana beamed. This was the first time an adult had let her put her very own stamp on something. Prior to this moment, the adults around her recognized her talent but no one had given her any ownership. They made decisions around her and the project but had simply given her lip service when asking for an opinion.

Up until now all her input had simply been insights and hard work. This was the first time an adult, other than her mother, had treated her like an equal. Coming up with the codename BISCUIT may not be a big deal to others but it was a very big deal to Hana.

The professor picked up the smallest of the rocks, this one about a pound and said, "Let's see what in this". He carried the biscuit to a machine that looked like a coffee grinder on steroids. A minute later the raw material was reduced to the consistency of powdered sugar.

"If I understand correctly, this will be the catalyst for the Parabellum. Am I correct?"

"Yes" Hana said, still euphoric over the earlier triumph.

"Well, it needs a name. What should we call it?" the professor asked.

"If it's a catalyst, how about yeast?"

"I like it, yeast it is. So from now on the raw material is biscuit and the ground material is yeast; agreed?"

"Agreed," said Hana.

PARABELLUM: When you live in Peace, prepare for War
Jack Nanuq

CHAPTER 34
Albany, NY
May 22, 2001

The motion sensor woke Carson at 2:47 AM. He scanned the computer monitor and saw the bad guy hiding behind Nana's garage. The monitor screen showed the infrared image of the Galco. That was 33 minutes ago and the man hadn't moved. The bad guy was definitely a professional; patient and cautious. Carson was certain the Galco would not make his move until he was sure no threat existed. Little did he know Carson was a professional also and the bad guy was in serious danger. Carson had the home field advantage and held all the cards.

The Galco had begun his move toward the house. The man took slow and measured steps. He moved along the back fence and kept to the shadows. The Galco moved slowly, painfully slow. As he approached Nana's bee hives, he crouched so that his body was no taller than the boxes. His head swiveled from side to side; like a heron searching for prey. It took almost 10 minutes for him to cover the 100 feet from the back of the garage to the back of the house.

As the Galco approached the back-door Carson took a position, on the carpet. He stretched out flat and set up a sniper's nest on the floor. He then reached over and pulled the laptop next to him. He swept his eyes from the back door to the laptop.

He then tapped a button on his laptop. The image from the camera covering the back door went from infrared to daylight. He did this to get an idea what the neighbors might see without the aid of electronics. The man was nearly invisible; dressed in dark street clothes. A fleece jacket that was probably Navy blue, a hooded sweatshirt under that and newer jeans that covered his lower half. Clothes that would allow him to melt into the night, but not draw attention if he was seen.

Two minutes after testing the doorknob the Galco picked the lock and stepped into the solarium off the kitchen. Carson shut the laptop and focused his attention down the length of the house. He lay motionless on the living room floor. With a clear view of the kitchen door and what lay beyond. The upper half of the kitchen door was plexiglass and provided Carson with an unobstructed view of the intruder.

The Galco opened this door and stepped into what cops call the fatal funnel. The wedge between the doorjamb and the doorknob. A half second later a shotgun exploded like a grenade.

Carson pulled the hood from the man's head and stared at the wriggling form. The Galco struggled for breath; as if trying to inhale and exhale at the same time. The blue polyethylene tarp, under the prisoner, crinkled irritatingly with each movement. The sound resembled that of someone walking on potato chips.

Carson pressed the muzzle of his shotgun against the man's sternum. A painful grunt was uttered, and the trespasser curled into a ball. "Let me tell you what just happened" he whispered. He then pressed the gun against a bleeding ear. "I shot you... but you've probably figured that out by now. But I shot you with a rubber bullet...right in the chest...right in the sternum to be exact. That's why you're having trouble breathing. The impact overwhelmed the nerve bundle that controls your diaphragm." Carson then jammed the barrel into the ear and the man let out another grunt.

"When you fell, I dropped a hood over your head and bound your wrists. Then I grabbed you by the ankles and dragged you down the stairs. After all that bouncing you probably feel like someone threw you into a cement mixer. You can't see it, but your face looks like shit. And I bet you have a bunch of bruises under that jacket of yours." To confirm his suspicion, he ran the barrel of the gun over the Galco's back. The man squirmed every time the metal touched a sore spot.

"Now we find ourselves in what I'll call the blue room. Look around, construction tarps on the walls, ceiling and floor. It's amazing what criminalists can do with DNA evidence. I can't chance you leaving any in Nana's house." Carson said all this with a menace Anthony Hopkins used in the movie "Silence of the Lambs".

The man groaned. "f….f… f…uk you" came a strangled response.

"Good boy," Carson said "That shows you're getting your breath back…good, very good. Means you're not going to die, at least not now…We can't have that."

He cringed when he thought about what would happen over the next few hours. He was a soldier at heart, not a cretin from the Fingernail Factory. He didn't relish the task at hand. But would do what was necessary to protect Nana and Iris, and anyone else.

Carson watched the Galco's chest. The man's breathing had evened out. Now it was time for the duct tape and before he could change his mind, he muzzled the man. He put the man's hood back on. The technical term for this stage of the interrogation as Sensory Deprivation. Carson preferred to think of it as a Mind Fuck. Once deprived of visual stimulation the brain would provide its own stimulus. It would conjure up its own images; all of which would be disturbing. The man's fears would rise to the surface.

Carson thought back to his time in college. A professor explained the psyche was often times its own worst enemy. Although it could put someone in their "happy place" more times than not it would create its own hell. Phobias and fears would chew on the body like a self-devouring cannibal. Psychosis and terror would be this man's roommates for the duration. With the right kind of encouragement, the man would do or say anything to free himself of the demons.

Carson then ran a chain from the man's wrists to his ankles and suddenly the Galco was trussed like a steer at a rodeo. Carson again looked at the man's chest. The breaths were rapid but steady. Carson would not ask any questions until he felt the time was right. "I'll be back," he said as he left the room.

Forty-seven minutes later Carson carried a metal chair into the blue room. Then came a metal table, then came a power saw. Carson let the saw drop onto the table with a crash; a crash that sounded like a Buick hitting an oak tree. Then came a heavy tool box; another crash as it was tossed onto the table. A pipe wrench, a hammer, a tank of compressed gas, more crashes. The Galco cringed with each collision.

Carson undid the chain and removed the hood. "Get in the chair" he said in a flat voice. This was the first of many tests. It was important for the Galco to get in the chair voluntarily. A mind game that would demonstrate how compliant the man would be.

The Galco didn't move so Carson walked back to the table and picked up the saw. "Not sure if you can see this from down there but it's a circular saw. I picked it up at Sears about a year ago, paid 40 bucks for it. It works great, at least on lumber, plywood, and that kind of shit. I'm not sure how it works on muscle and bone though." At that he let the saw fall to the table. "I'll make you a deal. You get in the chair and I'll never pick it up again."

The Galco rolled onto his knees and then stood up. Carson watched as the man walked tentatively to the chair. The Galco glowered at the chair with unadulterated hatred. As if the chair was responsible for this development. Within 30 seconds the man found himself bound into the chair and facing the table. The Galco could now see everything on the table. Carson walked around the table slowly and ran his hands over each item. Some of the items he would caress like that were rare treasures and others he would push away like they were trash. But each time he touched an item he would look at the Galco and read his face. The Galco tried to make his face blank but there were small tells, even with the duct tape. This was another mind game and both men knew it.

The Galco let a smile show across his eyes, when Carson picked up the man's knife. "Nah, that's too good, too fast for you. Or maybe you think I might cut myself? I know what's on the blade."

Then Carson picked up the jar on the front edge of the table. This was an item that clearly disturbed the Galco. Carson

207

gave the jar a shake and the swarm of bees tried to attack Carson's hand.

"Good thing those little stingers aren't diamond tipped," Carson said as he set the jar down.

He then put the hood back on the Galco. "I'll be back," Carson said a second time and left the man to stew in his own private hell.

Three hours later Carson got the Galco's attention when he yanked the hood away. The man was twitching and squirming by then but Carson doubted he was ready to talk. Carson took out his phone, dialed a number, and hit the speaker button. As the phone rang Carson yanked the duct tape from the man's mouth.

On the third ring the Galco heard "You speak English?" in a heavily accented voice. "You speak English?" said the voice a second time.

"Answer her damnit, answer her," Carson said as he slapped the man.

"Puta!" the Galco yelled in Spanish.

"Ah, he speaks. That sounds like...like... how you say...false bravado. But I think not....I think you very brave man.... you must be very brave. You leave your home and you travel thousands of miles... to...to hunt old woman. Yes I think you very brave." There was a pause. "No comment...that okay, you no need to talk. I talk now. You will need much bravery... much, much bravery. I the one you hunt for... but I not there... but you know that. That no good for you."

She paused a second time. "I talk to Carson now...Carson turn off speaker."

"Yes ma'am," he said with deference. This was no time to be joking with her.

"You no kill bad guy. You hear me?"

"What?" he said with astonishment.

"No... you no kill bad guy. I did that once... years ago and it not good. I no have you carry that burden for me. You do what you need to... to get information...to protect Iris and Newton, but you no kill him. You good boy. I know you good boy and you stay good boy. This will be difficult but…but…but manageable…if you no take his life. You take his toes if necessary, but not his life."

"Yes ma'am," he said as he clicked off the phone.

Carson was perplexed. For him it would be easier to kill the man than torture him. He'd never tortured anyone before and he wasn't looking forward to it now. But he would do what Nana wanted. Besides simply killing the man wouldn't remove the threat. His bosses would just send another hit man. Carson needed information. He needed information to short-circuit that contingency.

Now what do I do with this asshole, he thought?

∞

The next evening Carson took special interest in a news story about an unidentified man found wandering in Washington Park. The commentator told how "When found by police the man was blind due to multiple bee stings, nearly naked and ranting "no mas, no mas."

This man may be unknown to the general public but Carson knew everything about him; well almost everything. The man tried to lie but Carson was sure he had everything; name, aliases, birth place, drop boxes and the chain of command. The only thing Carson wasn't sure of was the name of the head man. The Don, so to speak. By the time Carson got the Galco to give up this name the poor man was spent, and so was Carson. Carson took as many notes as he could but the Galco was babbling in Spanish. Since he didn't speak Spanish, he spelled things as best as he could.

Carson had a name; Dolph Bauer. Or was it Rolf? And he thought Bauer meant farmer in German. So maybe it was a nickname, Rolph the Farmer. When he went back to his notes, he found a mess. Sometime after the interrogation he had put a sweaty palm on that page. The salt water combined with the weight of the hand turned the page into a Salvador Dali print. He could no longer make heads or tails of what had ben put down on paper. *Damnit.*

PARABELLUM: When you live in Peace, prepare for War
                                          Jack Nanuq

CHAPTER 35
Lake Otsego, NY
May 23, 2001

Nana watched as a life flashed before her eyes. But it wasn't just one life it was two. First it was Janos as an infant, then as a toddler, then it was Janos with Petr. Then Petr teaching Janos to ride a bike, then the both of them working on a motorcycle. Then both of them collecting honey. Then there was Janos trying to teach Petr to play the guitar; not a successful endeavor.

Now there was an image of Janos in the Wehrmacht uniform, but no Petr. Thank God for that. But that uniform and more importantly the sidecar motorcycle helped both Janos and Maria escape from Nazi held France. That rainy night as they sped across the countryside with the Mauser in her lap. The gun seemed to hold the heat of its sin for the entire trip.

Next, Nan saw Janos, many years later, at his job at General Electric, in Schenectady. He made parts for jet aircraft. He'd been proud to help keep the world safe. Or at least that's what he told everyone.

Finally, she saw Janos as an old man, in the hospital after his last heart attack. She remembered him in that frail state. "I go see Papa now." The cardiac monitor beeped in alarm as the life force dissipated. She reached out and took his still warm hand and the only sound was the chirp of the alarm. And then Petr was there. Not the real Petr, but the ghost Petr. Dressed in his Church clothes and that stupid beret. He always wore the beret and said it made him look "more French". Ghost Petr placed his hand on hers and nothing was said but much was communicated. How long did they stay like that? Was it a minute, an hour or a lifetime?

The chirp continued. "Madame, your tea is ready. Madame are you awake? Do you want your tea?" said Iris.

Nana was pulled back to consciousness. She was in her recliner at the lake house. She must have fallen asleep. How long had she been out; was it a minute, or an hour or a lifetime?

"Yes, yes, I have tea now," she responded. "Thank you".

Just then Newton and Demon came into the house. Both were soaked from the rain. Newton immediately wrapped the dog, with an old towel, before he could shake. He rubbed the dog vigorously as the animal tried to squirm free. It was the end of May, with summer was just around the corner, but today was damp and cold. Just like that night of the escape.

Nana turned to the side table and reached toward the plate of Fig Newtons, but there weren't any. Someone had swapped them for dog biscuits. How long had she been asleep?

Iris came into the room as Nana was reaching for the biscuits. "Newton say no more cookies for dog. They give him gas. Here your tea... careful it hot." Nana then realized the alarm she heard in her dream was the timer on her microwave.

"Did you get some rest?" Newton asked her as the damp dog made a beeline for the side table. Demon sat as soon as he reached the old woman's feet.

"You good boy," Nana said and handed it dry biscuit. Demon gave her a look like "What the hell is this?" But took the treat anyway. "Sorry, boss's orders," she added and pointed a finger at Newton.

"I sorry" she said, and turned to Newton, "What you say?"

"I asked if you got a nap," as he unrolled a blood pressure cuff. "You look winded to me. Are you feeling okay?"

"I old, I always look winded...I fine."

"Nonsense," he said as he placed two fingers on the inside of her wrist. "Tell me the truth. But first be quiet so I can take your pulse."

Thirty seconds later he said, "Alright spill it, how are you feeling?"

"I fine... really...I just have dream again...I think I see Petr and Janos soon."

"You mean in your dream?"

"No, no, I think soon I go be with them...for good. You no worry about me." She pointed to a chair and told Iris "You sit, I need tell you both something."

"135 over 92" Newton said as he took off the blood pressure cuff and made a note in a book. "Make it short. I want you to get some more rest."

"No, this will be long story." She said as she took a sip of tea. Fortunately, the beverage was in a travel mug or the shaking hands would have spilled it everywhere.

"You know word Parabellum?" She first looked at Iris and then at Newton. Iris shook her head no but Newton nodded.

"What you know?" the old woman asked.

"It's a pistol cartridge. The Germans put it on their 9-millimeter cartridge," Newton said.

"Yes and no...it Latin word...it mean...When you live in Peace, prepare for War."

She took another sip of tea. "Much of my life was peace, but some of my life was war. During first world war I live on prison island, but life not bad. I have Janos and I meet Petr. Then I live in France, with Petr and Janos, and life good...very good. Then second war come and I lose Janos, then I lose Petr, then I get Janos back, but not Petr. Then we come to America and life good. I build business, Janos have family. I soon have grandson, and then great grandson. Not big family but good people and we help others. But now I old...and tired...and can no help others..."

The long pause was interrupted by a dog fart. It was so loud it startled Demon and he jumped up. Under other circumstances all three people would have burst out laughing but no one made a sound.

Nana continued. "I old now, and I not say this for pity. I say it because it true. I go see my Petr and Janos soon. But I tell you this...you now live in peace, but I think war come soon...I know not when but it come. It might be big war, or it might be small war."

"What?" Iris asked.

"It might be small war. Carson...he take care of Galco, or at least one Galco. Maybe more come for me, or for you? I no think I be here when or if they come... But you here and

Newton here and Carson here. They will want to harm you, kill you."

"But I think a bigger war coming. In America we live good life. Not all...but most. There are those that hate us for that. Imagine hate someone because he have good life. It no make sense but it real. Just like that rain outside, it real. They want to take it from us. Not to help themselves but so to hurt us. It no make sense, but it Parabellum. When you live in Peace prepare for War. So I want you be ready."

"What should we do?" Iris asked.

"You be ...what is word? Vigilant, yes, vigilant. You be alert, but also prepared. No take fight to others but if fight come to you...you be ready. You have weapon, and food and ...and skills. And you be ready to help others, others that need help. You do this for me...Please."

"We will...Now you get some rest." said Newton, with concern in his eyes.

∞

Carson was in his office at Hawkeye Management when the intercom squawked. "Boss, there's a trooper, actually an investigator, from the State Police to see you. Says he talked you about a week ago. Name's Matthews, Ron Matthews."

Carson had expected this but was wondering why only one of the investigators was here. He remembered Matthews as the taller of the two men and the more mature. Maybe worldly was a better word. "Thanks Stephanie. Send him in."

"Gotcha boss."

About 30 seconds later Stephanie escorted the investigator into the office. Carson stood and was reminded that he was correct. This was the taller of the two lawmen. What Carson had forgotten or maybe hadn't noticed during their first meeting was the way this man carried himself. Professional, with a capital P. A charcoal gray suit, a white shirt and a blue power tie. People rarely dressed this way, outside a corporate boardroom.

And the man had bearing; a presence. *How did I miss that?* Carson thought.

Matthews reached out and said, "Thanks for meeting me." The words were said with a calmness that softened the man's edges.

Ah, that's how I missed it. He can turn it on and off. Be careful, be very careful, Carson reminded himself.

"Pleasure." Not really meaning it. "Did you find something?" Carson asked with his best poker face.

"Yes, we did, but I'd prefer to discuss this in private." Matthews said, looking toward Stephanie.

"I'll be out of your hair in a minute," she said, as she opened a cabinet. Carson watched as she tore open a vacuum pack of Folgers. She poured the grounds into a state-of the-art coffeemaker. The office was immediately filled with the rich aroma of malty caramel. He loved that smell. *If only coffee tasted like it smelled I might drink more of it. Careful Carson...stay focused...stay focused,* he reminded himself.

"There you go, gentlemen. It'll be ready in about three minutes. Can I get anything else?"

Carson paused, waiting to see if Matthews would try to exercise some power here. But the other man remained silent. Carson sensed the other man purposely chose not to speak, so as not to assert any authority. Not because he couldn't but because he knew this was not the time to.

"We're good..., thanks Stephanie," Carson said

As the door closed Carson walked to the chairs at the opposite side of the office. He wanted to have their conversation on neutral ground. He wasn't going to hide behind his desk. He wanted to convey the message he had nothing to hide; even though he had lots to hide. *Be careful, be very careful,* he reminded himself again.

"Now, where we?" Carson asked as he took a seat.

"We think we found your Galco."

"What do you mean? My Galco!" Carson asked struggling to hide all tells.

"I guess he's not your Galco. I'm sorry...I phrased that wrong."

Carson was certain Matthews had phrased it exactly the way he meant it to be. He was also certain Matthews wasn't sorry about it.

"I just came from the Psych Ward at Ellis Hospital. The Albany cops picked up a John Doe with a greyhound tattoo. Just like the dead guy at Penn Station. Remember the line drawing of the dog, with the swastika in it?"

"Yeah, I remember. Kinda hard to forget."

"Anyway…he was a basket case when the cops found him. He's sobbing and not making much sense. It didn't help that he was only speaking Spanish. At first, the cops think he's having a bad trip on LSD, a really bad trip. The EMT's get the guy sedated and things go a little smoother, not great but a little better. They get him admitted and do an ID check. The guy had no identification. Fingerprints come back NO RECORD FOUND. My office gets a call when they enter the tattoo. So here I am."

"And…?" Carson asked tentatively.

"And, and it's pretty strange. My partner, who speaks Spanish, spent the morning with the guy. The Galco's story is pretty weird. We're not sure how much is fact and how much is fiction." Matthews paused as the coffee maker hissed to signal the brew was ready.

Carson got up but Matthews said, "I'm good." He sat back down.

"Go on."

"Okay, the guy's story is pretty weird. One of those tinfoil hat type stories. He says he was tortured by a giant bumblebee in a blue room."

"It does sound like a bad acid trip," Carson agreed.

"Yeah, sounds that way. Funny thing is he was covered with bee stings, but they weren't random."

"What do you mean?" Carson asked.

"They were places they shouldn't have been if he had simply stumbled into a hive. For instance, in between his toes, in his armpits, and in the center of his eyeballs, dead center. Maybe someone did work him over?"

216

"And?" Carson asked again.

"And...and technically there's a crime here, multiple crimes actually. But..." He let that word hang in the air.

Carson took this moment to get a cup of coffee. With his back to the investigator Carson asked "But?"

"But, there's no victim here. At least not one that could ever testify. He's messed up. That boys gonna need therapy; years of it."

"And you're here...why?" Carson asked, now facing the investigator.

Matthews let out a sigh. "Before I answer that, let me tell you about what we do at SIU, the Special Investigations Unit. Our mission is to investigate matters that are close to prominent citizens. Your nana is a prominent citizen. We're schooled in the political ramifications of our actions. That's not to say we are told to look the other way. It's just that...sometimes matters pertaining to prominent people can cause chain reactions and have unintended consequences. We have wide discretion when investigating these things. My thought is that there's no reason to poke a stick at something, that doesn't endanger the fabric of society..." He again let his statement hang. "I'm here because...I want to make sure there are no more bumble bee incidents."

"It's my experience bees are pretty docile, unless agitated. They only attack when they're in danger. They're not predatory. They don't go looking for trouble," Carson responded with slight irritation.

"Yeah, that's my impression. Most times they serve the collective and just want to be left alone." Matthews interjected, and then added. "I did some checking. You and your grandmother excuse me your great-grandmother keep honey bees. Mater-of-fact, you are the only two people licensed to keep bees in the City Limits." He pulled a small envelope from an inside pocket. "You can keep those, I've got more."

"What's that?" Carson asked.

"Stingers, bee stingers. The doc saved some of the ones he pulled from the Galco. There's probably enough genetic material to match to your hives...But..."

"But!" Carson responded sharply.

"But I don't see any point in that. I just wanted you to know...to know...that I know. I don't see any point in putting any more effort into this thing. The way I see it, the Galco is no longer a threat to anyone. As for the giant bumblebee. We'll just call it an unexplained phenomenon, like the Bermuda Triangle."

Carson saw no point in arguing with the man and simply said "Understood."

With that, Matthews stood "I'll see myself out."

As Matthews left Carson's alpha-pager buzzed and read "Cheeseburgers at four o'clock".

"*Shit*" Carson thought.

PARABELLUM: When you live in Peace, prepare for War
Jack Nanuq

CHAPTER 36
Schenectady, NY
May 23, 2001

Carson parked his Subaru in the lot of the Schenectady Central Library. "Cheeseburger" was the codename for this meeting spot. In many ways it was a perfect meeting spot. People came and went without notice. If they met inside, they could and should talk in a whisper. A nearby police precinct kept unwanted persons at bay, another advantage. The only disadvantage was the video cameras covering the lot. But nowadays it was nearly impossible to find a spot not covered by cameras. At least these didn't go into a central feed, the recordings were kept in-house.

Today the weather was miserable. But Carson knew his meeting with Fred would take place in the lot. He no sooner had this thought when Fred's mini-van pulled into the spot next to his.

The passenger window rolled down and Maggie Post barked "Get in the back!" It was an order. An order given with the authority of a mafia don. Carson did as he was told. In the few seconds it took him to get in the van he was soaked. Partly from the rain but mostly from the anxious sweat that shot from his pores.

"You got something to tell me soldier?" The look on the woman's face was a mix of anger and disappointment.

"Ma'am?" Carson said tentatively.

"What the fuck's a Galco? Didn't your momma never to teach not to piss in the kitchen? Jesus, I can almost see Ellis Hospital from here. Now speak!"

"Ma'am, the Galco doesn't concern the Agency... it's a personal matter."

"Bullshit! If it concern's you it concern's the Agency! We're in the middle of an op. Do you need me to take you off that op, so you can take care of a... personal matter? Don't answer that! I can't take you off the op, nor do I want to," she softened slightly. "Jesus Carson, you should have come to me.

You shouldn't be doing that kind of thing," waving her hand in the general direction of the hospital. "We have people for that."

"But it's not Agency business."

"Think again! There are only about a dozen people that know where the Kestrels are and what they are working on. And you're one of them. Something happens to you and that puts us in a bind. You end up dead and we don't know if you're compromised. You end up missing and we don't know if you're compromised. You end up with your brains scrambled and we don't know. We're the C-fucking I-A, and we don't like not knowing. And... on a personal note... I'd feel bad if something happened to you. So, spill it! Tell me why some South American lizard is hunting for your nana?"

"It's a long story, goes back to before D-day," Carson responded tentatively.

"No, no, the Reader's Digest version and how it affects us today?"

"Okay, back in the War, Nana killed a Gestapo agent and some distant relative is trying to avenge his death. Something about family honor."

"Why now? That was like 55 years ago. Why the hell now?" Maggie asked.

"That's my fault. I found the gun she used and ran it through the system." There was no need to mention Fred's part in this matter.

"Maggie, that's only partly true," Fred interjected. "I ran the check and knew there was a problem with it by the end of that day. I should have come to you but didn't see how it meant anything to the current op. I guess I didn't see the full picture. It won't happen again."

"Damn right," she said and then continued. "Here's what's we're going to do. You got a go-bag in your car?" pointing a finger at Carson.

"Yes ma'am."

"You got anyone to feed your cat?"

"I don't have a cat."

"Okay. You're going to Willsboro for a while, a week at least. Angie Rodriguez needs some R & R anyway. You can run your office remotely, right." It was a rhetorical question. She then picked up her phone. After two rings she said, "Bring me a Durango."

Carson clearly heard the man on the other end say, "Yes ma'am."

When she hung up the phone she continued. "When the Durango gets here you are taking it north and it's not to come south until I say so. Fred will leave your car at your home. You need anything...meds, clothes, anything?"

"I'll manage," Carson said.

"Good, I'll do damage control here. Something tells me the lizard's getting a free trip to Buenos Aires. His people will get the message."

"Ma'am I should probably tell you he's a Galco, not a gecko."

"Okay, I'll bite. What's a Galco?"

"It's Spanish for greyhound."

"Hmm, never cared for that breed, always favored Rottweiler's. There's a dog that's bred for work, for doing a real job, not chasing bunny rabbits, or old ladies."

"Never mind," Carson mumbled.

PARABELLUM: When you live in Peace, prepare for War
Jack Nanuq

CHAPTER 37
Willsboro, NY
May 23, 2001

Four hours later Carson backed the Durango into the driveway of the cabin. Angie Rodriguez was standing in the front yard when he arrived.

"Hey. This looks nice," Carson said as he jerked a thumb at the new garage. The building was a huge for a garage, more like a small barn. With its mansard roof that's exactly what it looked like.

"Glad you like it, after all you paid for it. You, as a tax payer that is."

Of course, Carson knew of the construction. Since Hawkeye Management was listed as the owner, his company paid all the bills. The Agency had asked for an outbuilding to hide the cars and also provide r more housing accommodations. Hawkeye was reimbursed for these expenses with "Consulting Fees".

Carson reached into the backseat of the Durango and pulled out his rucksack and a smaller plastic bag. "Here I brought you some groceries."

"Oh, I love you, I've been jonesing for one of these lately" said Angie as she fished out a Slim Jim jerky stick. "The little one's been on a Halal kick. The only meat she wants in the house is fish; which isn't exactly meat anyway."

"What's Halal?" Carson asked.

"It's kind of like the Muslim equivalent to Kosher. Unless meat is butchered a certain way, it's considered Haram; forbidden. She'd rather it not be in the house."

"Has she been a problem?"

"No, not really, and I'm not gonna stand in the way of her beliefs. She…or I should say both of them, lost everything when they escaped from Bosnia. I'll not infringe or impinge on her keep her religion. She's not fanatical about it. But a few of her beliefs she holds onto pretty strongly. Sally thinks it's a phase she's going through, but we'll see."

224

"Teenagers," Carson added.

"Yeah, it could be that simple," Angie said, as she gnawed on a jerky stick.

"So, anything else new?" Carson inquired.

"Yeah…I think Sally's got a boyfriend."

"What?" Carson asked, surprised.

"It's Dr. Maarsten. They've been trading emails back and forth ever since we got back from Utica. I think it helps that they are both refugees. He came here as a teenager, when his parents left East Germany."

"How do you know that?"

"I read their emails."

"Ok. That makes sense," Carson added as they walked into the back door of the new garage.

They stepped into a heated work-out room. The room smelled of fresh paint. Everything, but the weight bench, was state-of the art. They had a Stairmaster, a Treadclimber and a stationary bike. Carson walked over to the weight bench. The bar had two 50 lb. plates on each side. He did some quick math. With the weight of the bar he came up with 245 lbs.

"Yours? I'm impressed," he said.

"Yeah. It was the first thing I had moved in here. I really missed working out. There's nothing like pumping iron to make you feel alive."

"May I?" Carson asked, as he laid on the weight bench.

"Sure be my guest. But be careful I don't have the locking pins set." This allowed the lifter to tip the bar to the side and spill the plates off if there was a problem.

"Gotcha," he said as he dropped his rucksack.

On Carson's fifth lift Sally came into the gym. "Angie, there's a problem with the computer again. Oh, hello Mr. Lake."

"Please call me Robert. We've been through that," Carson corrected Sally. He set the bar on its hooks and took three breaths before sitting up.

As Angie left the room she said, "I'll be right back."

Sally looked at his rucksack and asked, "You be with us, for a while?"

"Yeah. Angie has to go home for a few days. I'll be staying in the apartment upstairs. I hope you don't mind?"

"No, iz no problem, Hana likes you. She needs male, how you say; role model. I afraid she think most men are bad. Since we have to leave home. "

"I understand, I hope I can live up to her expectations."

"You will. She have low expectation. No wait…that not sound right. What I mean is she likes you. She not trust most men. I try tell her all men are not bad. Her father was good man. She knows this but our experience… it make it… confused."

"I think I know what you mean. I got to take this upstairs," pointing to his rucksack.

"Now I think I make you uncomfortable, I sorry."

Carson realized his mistake immediately. He sensed sensing she wanted to talk. He sat back on the bench. "I'm sorry. That was rude. I don't need to go right away."

Sally paused "You sure, you no have to go?"

"No, no I'm good. I should have asked how you are doing. How are you doing? This has all been a big change for you. Do you miss home?"

"A little bit, but mostly no. It was hard when we were I refugee camp. But…but we were there more than five years. I get over it. Besides homeland not what it used to be. I no want to go back now. It would be nice if I could go back to what it used to be. Does that, sense I make? Maybe my words not good?"

"I understand… Here you sit. Where are my manners?" He emphasized his point by standing.

"No, no iz okay. I sit most of day, I need to stand. I know you have hip problem, you sit."

"I'll sit, if you sit."

"Okay, but you no romance me, okay?"

"No, I will not romance you. I have a girl back home."

"Iz good you have wife."

"No, no, not wife, just a girlfriend."

226

"Iz serious? This girl."

"I think so."

"Why you not know? I sorry, that iz rude. I should not ask this question. Iz not my place."

"No, you can ask. Let me see...Why don't I know if it's serious? I think it's serious because I never felt this way before. But I don't know how she feels. It's new for both of us. I think."

Sally nodded her head.

Carson continued "You can always ask me anything. If I can't give you the answer, I'll be up front with you. That means be honest with you. It must be tough living in this security bubble, where everything is hush-hush. So I'll always share whatever I can with you."

Sally said "I like we talking like this, iz good we talk. You may ask same question of me."

"Later," Carson responded, "First tell me how you are doing, up here in the wilderness?"

"Life here sometime hard. We live like cloistered nuns. But we are safe. So that is good. And it is only temporary. We just learn Hana go to college next year and we will be in city."

"That sounds great, what college?"

"Utica, SUNY. She go college in fall. We move to Utica. After last visit we talk long time and make decision. I tell her it important she be around people her own age. Maybe then she learn to...to unwind. Did I say that right?"

"Yes, you did. Your English is getting good. You've been practicing?"

"Yes, I practice. I watch talk shows and it helps. Angie and I then talk about show. I also like JUDGE JUDY, that not talk show but I learn lots about Americans. I also learn slang words, but I no use slang. I not know the right time to use these words yet."

"I'm impressed. You've come a long way."

"Thank you...I should go now. You look tired."

"Kinda. If you don't mind, I'm going to head upstairs and get settled in. I'll be over to the cabin in about thirty minutes."

"I no mind. Thank you for being…up front. Did I say that right?"

"Perfect. I'll see you in a half hour."

PARABELLUM: When you live in Peace, prepare for War
Jack Nanuq

CHAPTER 38
Otsego, NY
May 24, 2001

Nana woke to find her sheets soaked. At first, she feared she had an accident but then realized her nightgown, especially around her shoulders was wet. She was covered in sweat. Muted light from a not yet completed sunrise streamed into the bedroom.

"Iris, Iris, I need help," she cried feebly.

She heard Iris stir in the next room, but it was Newton that came to her rescue.

"What's wrong?" he asked.

"I cold, I wet, I need help get from bed," she said, with fear clearly evident in her voice.

"Okay, I got you, I got you," he said as he reached under her shoulders. "Slow down, I got you. Let's just get you sitting upright, okay?"

"Yes, yes, I need sit, get from wet blankets. I have bad dream," remembering what woke her.

"Another one? Maybe I should call Father Mike?" he said as he reached for her wheelchair.

"No, you not call him. I not need Confession, just need dry clothes."

"They say Confession's good for the soul," said Newton, only half in jest. "I'm worried. You've had dreams every night this week. You can't go on like this."

"What's wrong?" Iris asked as she entered the room.

"Iz nudding, just bad dream."

"Another one?" Iris said.

"That's what I said" Newton interjected, concern etched on his face.

"I be fine, just need clean clothes, I fine."

"*Rete*" Iris said in Haitian-Creole. "Stop!" she added for clarification. She then unleashed on the old woman in her native tongue. The tirade went on for over a minute. When she was done, she was out of breath.

The Creole, a French derivative, provided Nana with enough vocabulary that she understood what Iris was saying.

Newton stood there stunned. He had never seen Iris so much as raise her voice; let alone tear into the old woman with such ferocity.

"I don't speak French, but I think I got the gist of that," Newton said.

"I not child, you no need to speak like that," Nana said with false indignation.

"No, you're not a child, you are a stubborn old woman. You drive us crazy. You might be done with this world, but it not done with you and we not done with you!" Iris shouted, tears running down her face.

Newton pushed the chair up against the bed but didn't say anything. He was going to take his lead from Iris.

"You right. I sorry, I stubborn, and…and foolish. I should not give you trouble." Nana said as she reached up to brush the tears from Iris' face. "I sorry, I no mean to make you angry."

"I'm sorry too, I love you, but you drive me crazy. We need to find a way to get rid of these dreams. They cause you pain and worry…they cause us pain and worry."

"Okay. Help me to shower. When I get dressed, we will talk about dreams. Maybe I make tape for Carson? Tell him life story. I never tell him much when he growing up. He should know story. You should know story too. I feel better now."

"Oh, great…she feels better now," Newton mumbled sarcastically.

"I hear that," Nana said, "but you right."

Thirty minutes later Iris wheeled Nana into the kitchen. Nana had showered and changed into clean clothes. Newton had a cup of tea, a small bowl of oatmeal and the morning dose of meds waiting for the older woman.

As Nana ate her breakfast, Iris and Newton had a cup of coffee; real coffee. The tension at the table was still present and no one said a word.

Nana broke the silence by suddenly yelling "Boo!"

"Jesus Christ!" shouted Newton, grabbing his chest "You about gave me a heart attack."

As he said this Iris was pinwheeling her arms trying to stay in her chair. The effort was futile and gravity took over. The chair tipped to one side and crashed to the floor; taking Iris with it. As she hit the linoleum, she grunted a curse in her native tongue.

"You okay?" Newton asked as he scrambled to her side.

"Yeah, I okay. Can we kill her now?"

"No...no...not until we get the lake house," he said jokingly. He turned to Nana "What the hell was that for?"

"You should see your face. You want to yell, but you want to laugh, and you want to yell. That why I did it. You should see your face. That why I did it."

"I want a raise," he said. He righted Iris chair and helped her from the floor. As he stood, he noticed spilled coffee covered the table top and was threatening to leak over the edge.

"I should make you clean this up," he said as he grabbed a dishrag. He shook it at her "Never a dull moment."

"Okay, I clean, you give me rag."

"No, no, you've caused enough chaos for one day. Iris, why don't you take Madame into the parlor," Newton said, mimicking a British servant.

"Okay, I take her. I hope you done with breakfast," Iris said to Nana.

The rubber wheels made an eerie squeak as they left the room.

Iris parked Nana near a window that faced the lake.

Nana pointed a finger at a large hutch and said, "I think tape recorder in bottom drawer. It might need batteries."

Iris asked, "You still want to do a tape? I not think it good idea?"

As Iris reached the hutch Newton walked into the room and crouched next to her.

"I got it," Iris said as she pulled a faded and cracked cardboard box from the drawer.

"This thing's ancient. Any chance you've got something newer?" Newton asked.

"No, no, that fine, that work. At least I think it work."

"You better hope so or I'm calling Father Mike."

Iris tipped open the box and four Duracell batteries spilled out, then came an older style cassette recorder. Then came a paper bag of tapes.

"Are these blank?" Iris asked, holding up the tapes.

PARABELLUM: When you live in Peace, prepare for War

Jack Nanuq

CHAPTER 39
South Burlington, VT
May 24, 2001

The scene in the departure lounge of the Burlington airport was akin to a family sending a cherished member to war.

"I promise, I promise I'll be back next week, the following week at the latest." said Angie Rodriguez to the two other women.

The Kestrels were crying and hugging and crying. Angie was crying and hugging and crying. She had been with the other two almost night and day for the past six months. The bond that had developed was as fixed as concrete.

"You promise, you promise?" pleaded Hana.

"Yes, I promise, even if I have to walk. I promise."

A loudspeaker announced the boarding of "flight 2165, to O'Hare". "That's me. I got to go." She then turned to Carson. "You take care of them. You hear me, Mr. Lake."

"Roger that," he said using military jargon to hide his emotions. He was on the verge of tears also, but only because everyone else was sobbing.

Get a grip, he reminded himself, *it's not like yawning, you don't have to cry just because everyone else is.* "Have a safe trip, we'll be here when you return," he forced himself to say, matter-of-factly.

"Now seating rows 15 through 35" the loudspeaker announced.

"I gotta go," Angie said as she gave the Kestrels one last hug. "Keep up the good work," she said to Hana.

As they cleared the airport parking lot Carson, AKA Robert Lake asked, "how about we do something fun?"

"Like what?" Hana responded

"How about we go off-roading?"

"What be off-roading?" asked Sally.

"There's a Land Rover driving school a couple hours south of here. How about I sign you guys up for a lesson?"

"I can't drive," Hana said with disappointment.

"We don't say can't. You can't drive now. But I bet be the end of the day you'll be having the time of your life. What do you say mom?" he asked as he turned toward Sally.

"I say we go… Step on it," she said jokingly.

Carson made it to the Equinox Resort in two hours and 20 minutes. It only took about 15 minutes to fill out the paperwork. Sally had to sign a separate release for Hana as she did not have a driver's license. Just a technicality for the insurance company. Not a problem for the school, or the State of Vermont, as she would not be on any public roads.

Within a half hour of arrival, they, along with the instructor, were seated in an almost brand-new Range Rover. Hana was beaming as she adjusted the steering wheel and mirrors to fit her.

"Okay now. Look at your left mirror. Tell me what you see," the instructor, said in a thick British accent. He was recent import from London.

"I see trees." Hana responded.

"Okay. I guess that's right. We are parked in a wood," he said cheekily. "Look at the right edge and tell me if you can see your rear bumper."

"I can. Yes, I can."

"Okay then, now look at the mirror on my side and tell me if you can see the bumper," he went on.

"Yes, I got it."

"Okay, here we go. Put your left foot on the pedal in the middle. That's the brake and turn the key."

The sport utility vehicle barely made a sound as the engine idled.

"Now careful. Keep your foot off the brake, shift the lever here into Drive.

Whe she did this the SUV made a small roll forward. "Now lift your foot off the brake and lightly touch your right foot to the pedal on the right. Lightly."

The engine raced and the car jumped forward.

"Easy! I said, easy! Foot off the gas. Left foot now, brake, brake." He said calmly, but forcefully, as the SUV stopped just short of a large oak.

Over the next hour the two Kestrels learned to navigate steep terrain, avoid trail obstacles and negotiate wallows. By the time they were done mud and debris covered the Rover and some had even seeped inside.

This little adventure was just what the doctor ordered. Both of the Kestrels' moods had changed radically, and for the better. Hana was so happy when the lesson was over, she volunteered to clean the Rover.

"Aye, that be mighty nice of yee, but I'll manage," the instructor said.

On the return trip home Sally asked Carson "Robert, do you think you could give me some driving lessons? On real roads, that is?"

"Sure."

"And me too?" Hana asked.

"Oh boy. What have I started?" Carson chuckled.

Sally continued "Yes. She should learn also. I used to drive but it was almost six years ago. I be tarnished. Iz this right word?"

"You mean rusty." Carson corrected.

"Yes, yes rusty. And Hana, she is 16. Every teenager should be knowing to drive."

"Yeah, I'll teach you guys to drive. It will be my pleasure. I think we'll start in some parking lots if you don't mind. You young lady," turning to Hana "had me pretty nervous a couple of times."

"I'm sorry."

"No problem, I've seen worse" thinking back to the time his helicopter crashed.

"Then we'll go on real roads," Carson continued.

"Thank you, Mr. Lake," Hana said as they turned into the driveway of the cabin.

PARABELLUM: When you live in Peace, prepare for War

Jack Nanuq

CHAPTER 40
Lake Oswego, NY
May 24, 2001

"His name was Gustav Busch." Nana started the story. "He was evil man. Most people they have both light and dark side but he only have dark side. Black heart, black eyes, mean, he be Gestapo." Nana started to shake as she recalled the man and his leather trench coat. "He send my Petr to Peenemunde. You know this place? This place where Nazis build rockets. After Petr sent away, he tell me he some type of cousin to my first husband. He say he not responsible for Petr going away. He lie. He then say it not good for me to married to Petr. I was widow and should stay widow. Then he tell me maybe I be widow again. He was devil I tell you. He get much pleasure from others suffering."

Newton seeing her in increasing distress asked. "Maybe we shouldn't do this?"

She waved a hand. "No, no, I be fine. I know he dead, he can't hurt anyone any more. He only live in my mind. I know he not hurt me. But memories, they are not nice. I say I do this and I will do."

Iris interjected "Yes, they are only memories. They can't hurt you, especially if you share then. Get them out in the open."

"Okay, you right. I tell you Petr sent to Peenemunde. They first say he and other workers needed for secret project. They say they need skill laborer and pay well. But that lies. They need slaves, slaves with skills. And Busch he let me know he choose Petr personally."

"He send my husband to his death so I no longer have husband. But then fate return Janos to me. That happy day for me. I was hanging laundry and I remember it like yesterday. I was behind café and he sneak up behind me. He grab me and put a hand to my mouth. I scared at first, I think I being attacked. He was wearing German uniform and have eye patch. I not recognize him. But then he speak; he tell me not to scream.

He tell me he can't stay long but he wanted I know him safe. I hug him and I cry and he hold me. He was gone five years and I not hear from him all during that time. I thought he dead too."

Where was he, I mean before this?" Newton asked.

"That long story too. In 1938 he go on motorcycle tour to Czechoslovakia. He arrested when there. But I not know this. He missing more than five years and I think him dead. Like my Petr, he made to go in army. I tell that story later."

"He tell me he now in army but doesn't want to be. He first serve in Poland. A general learn he know motorcycles. So Janos made dispatch rider. He do good job, not fight or shoot, just deliver messages. Then he hit with bomb. Mortar, I think he say. He injured and go hospital. After…they send him to France, to heal. He now only have one eye and his leg not work right so they keep him on motorcycle. He still dispatch rider. We only spend 15 minute together that day but I very happy. Very happy, I know my Janos is alive. I not care about injury, just that he alive."

Nana was smiling broadly as she recounted the story. The joy she felt almost 60 years prior had returned and filled her entirely. Iris pulled her chair closer and took Nana's hand in hers.

"Keep going, tell us more," Iris said.

"We hugged and hugged, hiding behind hanging bed sheets. He tell me 'Momma I miss you very much. I sorry I gone so long, but I here now.' He tell me when he visiting relatives in Sudentland…That in Czech Republic now. He tell me he get arrested, in 1938. Later he part of group that invade Poland, but he not fight. A General learn he know motorcycles. The General make him dispatch rider. He try many time to get word to me that he alive. But he could not."

After he get to France, he work for transfer to Calais area. Then he come find me. That was 1943. That day he could only spend short time with me but over the next year he visit often. Sometime he visit café with other soldiers and we not able to talk. But at least I know he safe. I slip him extra food when I can."

"I can't imagine having to be there but not talk to him" interjected Iris.

"You do what you have to," the older woman said. "Someday you have children and you understand…you do what you have to." She paused and took a deep breath. "I just so happy he now back in my life. Yes, I miss him much when he gone but when he there I…I…I can't find the words, it…it just good."

"I understand," said Iris.

"So for a year we like that. He come for talks sometimes and for meals other times. He very sad much of time. He no like be in army. He like his soldier friends but he good boy. He no like the death, the destruction. He especially not like Hitler and Nazis. Many soldiers feel same way. I hear them talk in café. They not know I speak German and they have loose tongues. It then that I realize all Germans not bad people. The government; it be bad. The army it do bad things but most soldier not want to be there. They miss home and family and maybe girlfriend. They no like war like, like… I no like war."

"Do you need to take a break?" asked Newton.

Nana ignored hm and continued. "No, no I feel good. I should have told these stories long ago. I feel lighter now. I keep going."

"Okay," Newton acknowledged "but if you need a break…"

"About one month after Janos find me, he get soldier friends to share their sugar ration with me. I combine sugar with my honey and I start making treats for soldiers. Then I get more and more soldiers come to café. And more sugar. Sugar very rare, during war. I make more treats and more soldiers come. And I learn much about army stuff, troops, guns, tanks, divisions, and defenses. I learn much, but I not know what to do with information until St. Bernard come."

"You got a dog?" Newton asked, clearly perplexed.

"No, no, not dog, a priest. His name Father Claudio but I call him St. Bernard and he call me Shakespeare. He priest but he also work for Allies, like spy. He pass along information."

"Weren't you afraid?" Iris asked.

"Yes, yes I was. Especially when Gestapo come to café. First time they come I almost have heart stop. But they only there for food. I serve them but I no like them, they all bad. I serve them many times over year. They always ask for treats and never pay. One day I get idea to put sugar in their gas tank. I not do it, but thought of doing it make me happy."

"Be a waste of sugar but might be worth it," Newton mused to no one in particular.

"So, one day I tell this to St. Bernhard. It was really a suggestion more than plan. How you say, thinking out loud? He tell me it very bad idea. Yes, it would be good that Gestapo car break down somewhere but it nothing more than inconvenience. And someone would be made to pay. They shoot people, he reminded me. I know this, and I tell him I not serious."

"Go on," Iris said from the edge of her chair.

"I go back to Janos. He come to café as often as he can. If no one in café we talk about trying to leave. But I cannot leave. I have no travel papers. Plus, there was much army traffic during winter of 43-44. Spring of 1944 especially bad, much traffic. And much bad weather, much rain and much cold. We have lots of soldiers in café then. Much talk of Channel invasion. Much, much talk, most rumors. The soldiers they gossip more than school girls. No one really know anything. But all are sure Allies will come soon. They not know when or where but know it soon. They talk much about this and they complain it always cold, and always raining." Nana pulled her arms around herself. It was clear she was feeling a chill.

"Can I get you a sweater?" Iris asked.

As she said this Demon came into the living room, dragging a bedspread. "Demon, bad dog!" shouted Newton.

"Don't be mad at dog," admonished Nana. "He know I cold and he bring me blanket. I take blanket, I no need sweater."

"How about some tea?" Iris asked.

"Okay... I take more tea."

242

PARABELLUM: When you live in Peace, prepare for War
Jack Nanuq

CHAPTER 41
Willsboro, NY
May 24, 2001

The digital display of Carson's clock read 4:02 a.m. as he replayed the previous day's events. The trip to the driving school was a real hit and it helped both girls develop some skills. Sally knew how to drive but her skills had atrophied. The trip had helped her renew them.

As for Hana, it was as if Carson had let her fly a jet. She had never before driven anything, not even a go-cart. She beamed the entire way home and couldn't stop talking about it. She must have thanked him a hundred times for the experience. To Carson it was both flattering and uncomfortable. He was flattered that he had been able to provide her with so much enjoyment. It also made him wonder what he would have to do to maintain his hero status. More driving lessons would definitely need to be in the near future. But they couldn't keep making trips to Manchester.

He thought back to when his parents first let him drive. Every night for a full month either his mother or his father drove him to a cemetery. There he would climb behind the wheel and practice accelerating, braking, negotiating turns and even parking. Forty days later he got his learner's permit and his father let him drive on public streets. He would follow the same routine with Hana. During that time he would also talk to Maggie Post about getting both women driver's license.

At 4:07 a.m. Carson was done contemplating his responsibilities and told himself to get up. There was a brand-new gym downstairs, just aching to be used. He slipped on some sweats and running shoes.

At 5:47 a.m. Sally walked into the gym. She was wearing a sweat suit emblazoned with a US Olympic logo.

"Where'd you get that? The suit I mean." Carson asked her as he paused on the treadmill.

"The internet, I order it after we get back from Lake Placid. It help me remember trip. Do you remember trip? Do you remember chocolate pretzels?"

"Yeah, I do, and I remember how Hana treated that soldier guy. She's a remarkable young lady. You have a lot to be proud of."

"Thank you. Yes, I be very proud of her. She is everything to me. I happy she turned out good. She could be not good and has every reason to be that way but she good girl. We here now and things will work out. She get her life back on track and maybe someday she do other good things in life."

"Can I ask you ask you something? How did you get here? I mean get the governments attention and get the kind of sponsorship you did?"

"Yes, yes, you can ask. I not exactly sure how we got here. I tell you what I know. It started in refugee camp. I used to be an acupuncturist. One of my patients was an Army nurse, male nurse. He had bad back and I help him with pain. He become regular patient. One day he talk to Hana. On another day they have secret conversation. I not like this at first and I have long talk with her about being with men. She tell me 'it not like that Momma, I tell him about my idea for bomb.' He come back for more treatments and they talk more also. Then he bring other soldier men. I learn later they engineers, and they talk to Hana for long time."

"So they asked you to come to the U.S.?" Carson asked.

"No. Not at first. At first, they just have long conversations with Hana. When they come, they bring us food, tea and gifts. I think at first maybe them just being friendly and give us gifts for our time and Hana's information. At that time I not know much about Hana's idea. I not pay attention. I think it like science fiction. I not think it real. I happy for extra food and treats, but I never think we get more."

"So what happened?" Carson asked with genuine interest.

"One day a Colonel come, I not know he Colonel at the time. He had regular clothes, street clothes on. He talk long time to Hana. He, and translator talk long time to me. He tell me Hana have bright future. Maybe we think about come to U.S. He tell me Hana idea workable, but not safe to work on project in Camp. Maybe we think about come to U.S. I tell him we have no money to come to U.S. He say this not problem. Government, US government, will sponsor both of us. I say I must think about this, I must sleep on it. He say he understand but he warn me not talk about this to anyone else."

"So you decided to come?" Carson asked.

"Yes, but I have dream first. I have dream about mountain with presidents' face on it. You know this mountain?"

"Do you mean Mt Rushmore?"

"Yes, yes that one. It funny dream. I see presidents talking to Hana. When I wake up, I know we must go to U.S. The next day I get word to the colonel and tell him we come."

"You're pretty brave."

"Not really, I really have no choice. We could not live in Camp forever. I could not expect this thing to happen to us. But from first day in Camp I know we must eventually try to get out. To make real life for ourselves. This thing that happened is like winning lottery. We get free trip to U.S. We get free housing, and now Hana get free college. Once Hana get on with life then I also get on with life. Maybe go back to school and become nurse."

"Do you think you will make Utica your home?" Carson asked.

"I not know that yet, but I like what I know. It nice city and have other Bosniaks there. Hana could even go to mosques. She like her religion. Maybe she even meet boy or boys?"

"That's pretty open-minded of you," Carson said.

"No, no, I think it good thing she meet boys her own age. She smart girl. I no think she do shameful things, but she must learn about boys. I hope she meet good boy, and eventually good man. She be woman soon, she will need to think about future, and future husband."

"You talk about Hana's religion but you're a Muslim also. Aren't you? Yes, but it not so important to me. I mean, pray five times a day, fasting, and so many holy days. I believe in Allah. But...but I not so sure about all Mohammed have to say. There are things about Islam I like and there are things I no like. I believe we should believe in a creator, help others, and live a good life. The rest is just...is just stuff. I no think Allah have exact formula to get eternal blessing. Maybe that not make sense to you?"

"Makes perfect sense to me." Carson agreed.

PARABELLUM: When you live in Peace, prepare for War

Jack Nanuq

CHAPTER 42
Lake Otsego, NY
May 24, 2001

Nana finished her tea and continued. "It was June 3rd, 1944, Saint Bernhard he bring me travel papers. They say I cook for Rommel and must travel for party for Rommel's wife. The papers say I must travel with military escort, Korporal Janos Busch" Nana started. "Saint Bernhard tell me Allies come soon. He not know when but know it soon. When he leave, he say he must find Janos."

"How did he get you those documents?" Iris asked

"I not know how, except I know it gift from God. I remember it very cold that day, very wet, rainy, but I no care. I feel so much warmth. I can escape with my Janos. I so happy."

"What happened?" Newton asked

"All day I wait to hear from Janos, but he no come nor send word. And I not see Saint Bernhard after this. I very worried, but I excited at same time. I know it will work out but not know how or when. I just believe it." Nana paused. "You know what I remember most from that day?"

"What?" asked Iris and Newton, in unison.

"Trucks...; trucks and rain. There was much truck traffic that day and it cold with much rain. Many soldiers stop at cafe that day. I serve much Hunter Stew that day. I have reputation for good stew." Nana turned toward Demon and gave him another treat.

"It was cold day and soldier very hungry for warm meal. You know what I put in Hunter Stew?"

"No," Iris said tentatively. She wore a look of confusion.

Nana handed another treat to Demon. "Dog meat, yes dog meat. I tell soldiers it rabbit or squirrel but it dog. I feel bad about that, but it war time. I had to make do. That why I spoil this one," Nana said as she scratched Demon's forehead. "Many people eat dog and some cat during war, it very tough time."

Nana paused, lost in thought. She was coaxed back to the present when Newton asked, "tell us about the travel documents."

"Not much to tell, they forgeries. Dat much I sure of. But all they say is I must travel with Janos, for party. But Janos, he no show that day. I very worried for him. I think maybe he get arrested. But I also busy feeding soldiers stew and treats."

"When did Janos arrive?" asked Iris.

"Next day, he show up first thing the next day, the 4th. He say he cannot stay but would come back after dark; we go then. He say he must return to his unit but would be back at end of day. I beg him not to go but he say he must. He say all will be well at end of day. He then ride off into rain. He leave but trucks keep coming. They stop at café, all day."

"I remember soldiers all wear heavy great coats, heavy wet wool. The café it smell like sheep barn. It was June but feel like winter. The rain it make everything so cold." Nana shivered as if she was there.

"Are you sure I can't get you a sweater?" Iris asked.

"No, no, I fine. I drink my tea and I be fine." Nana paused again, the only sound was that of the rollers in the cassette recorder.

"Do you remember how many soldiers you served that day?" Newton asked to get the conversation started again.

"Maybe a hundred, maybe two hundred. I not know, some parts of that day are blur. What I remember clearly is when Janos show up, second time. It almost 9 o'clock, and I was almost out of my mind. The café was empty then and we almost ready to leave when another truck pull up."

"I bet you were exhausted," Iris said.

"Dah, but I excited and anxious also. But when that truck pull up, I was almost at breaking point. Janos helped me though. Not help as in fix meal but he talked to soldiers as I fixed food. His presence was reassuring."

"How long did those soldiers stay?" asked Newton.

"They not leave, they stay forever."

250

"What?" Newton and Iris asked in unison. Both wore a suspicious look.

"No, no, not what you think. You think maybe I poisoned them?"

"Never crossed my mind" said Newton with a mischievous sneer.

"I fix them big meal." She swung her arms out to the side. "I make big fire in stove. It was very warm in café. So warm they all fall asleep. I think this good. Now we can make escape."

"Janos and I go outside and he say he want to look in truck for supplies we might need. He look in back of truck, He see barrels of petrol, gasoline. He open one barrel. I think maybe he steal extra fuel for our journey," Nana paused. "We should have left then. But no, he say we need to sabotage fuel. He say it help war effort. He tell me get sugar from kitchen. I try to tell him no. He not listen to me. I his mother but he not listen to me. He tell me if I no get sugar he would go. I tell him I go. I afraid he make too much noise climbing in and out of truck. I go back inside café and check on soldiers. They all sleeping hard. Most just put their heads on the table and snoring. The café very warm, the fire in grate burning very hot still. I very scared but they sleep like babies. I get sugar and get back to truck."

"It raining hard at this time. I can't see Janos inside of truck. I call to him and not see him until he stick hand out of canvas. I give him bags and then I hear him crawling over drums. At first, I think he make too much noise. I beg him to be quiet. Rain pick up, it fall harder. The wind and rain drown out the noise. He make much noise and he tell me he stuck."

"I think we get caught. Maybe soldiers wake and come to noise. He say he okay. Just stuck between barrels. Then I hear him say he free, as he crawl toward me. I think we go now. His arm come out of truck but not him. There something in his hand. I beg him to keep coming and he say no, 'take this'. He give me holster and gun.

"Imagine…Me with gun. Later he tell me he needed to take off holster to get unstuck, but he not tell me that then. I very scared. I beg him to go and we leave. He say he not done yet. I say we go now and he say, 'just one more minute."

Nana paused again. With shaky hands she sipped her tea from a covered mug. "Then I see headlights come up road. I not hear car because of storm. So car is suddenly there. I duck around truck just as car stop near café. I tell Janos to be quiet and I not sure if he hear me."

Nana took another sip and continued. "I hear car door open and then boots on the wet ground. I hear squish, squish, and then man shout. He upset truck is unguarded and he yelling. Then I see torch and he walking toward back of truck."

"A torch?" Iris asked. Newton quickly interjected "A flashlight." Iris nodded her head with understanding.

Nana continued "I run into brush on other side of the road just as man come to back of truck." Nana's breathing was ragged and sounded like a leaky bellows. She paused and held her tea to her lips.

"Janos loved that Indian" Nana continued.

Iris and Newton turned toward each other with a look of bewilderment.

Even Demon looked perplexed, but that might have been due to his recent admonishment for stealing a cookie.

"What Indian?" Newton asked.

"His motorcycle," Nana responded. "In 1932 we had a group of Americans come to the café. They had spent weeks touring the area on motorcycles. On weekends Janos helped them keep the bikes, as they called them, running. When they left one of men gave Janos his Indian motorcycle. The man told him he didn't want to pay to ship it home. If he sold it, he'd have to pay taxes, which he didn't think the French government deserved. Janos loved that machine, more than a man could love a woman."

The phone rang and ended the conversation.

"I got it," Newton said as he stood.

252

"Morning" Newton answered the phone. "We're doing good....Yeah she's right here. We're just here shooting the breeze."

Newton handed the phone to Nana, "It's for you."

"Carson" Newton mouthed to Iris.

"Dah, I fine. We telling old stories. No, that not right. I tell old stories, they listen. They listen good, even dog listen. We make recording for you. Will we see you soon...No? Okay, you be safe. You good boy, I love you."

PARABELLUM: When you live in Peace, prepare for War

Jack Nanuq

CHAPTER 43
Willsboro, NY
May 24, 2001

"What?" Carson asked with astonishment. For years "You good boy" was code for "I love you". Carson could not recall the last time she used those three words, I love you.

"I say you good boy," Nana repeated.

"Yeah, that's what I thought you said," responded Carson.

"He want talk to you," she said and handed the phone back to Newton.

"Yeah she's a real chatter box today." Newton responded to Carson's question.

"Do we have a number we can reach you at?" Newton continued. "Okay, you said a couple of weeks…Maybe? Okay, take care."

∞

No sooner had Carson ended the call than his phone rang. Thinking Newton had called him back about something he answered without looking at the caller ID. "Forget something," he said nonchalantly.

"And good morning to you too," said the woman on the other end of the line.

A startled Carson looked at his phone, LIZA. He gave himself a mental head slap and said, "I'm sorry… thought you were someone else."

"One of your other girlfriends?" she said jokingly.

"Please don't bust my balls," he said with exasperation.

"Rough day, or rough week?" concern evident in her voice

"Rough week. I kind of got myself in a jackpot but can't talk about it. Not over an open line."

"You want me to come up there?"

"No, well that's not true, I'd love to see you. But I can't have you come up here. I kind of got deployed. Can't talk about it and have probably said too much already. It's good to hear your voice." He paused and then continued with "Are you calling for business or pleasure?"

"Kind of both. I called to tell you I found something interesting about your grandfather."

"Grandpa John, what is it?"

"I'm holding a copy of an Arrest Warrant; for one Janos Augustus Busch."

"What?" Carson asked, clearly perplexed.

"The warrant's not valid anymore as it was issued by the Nazis, in 1944. It says he is wanted for the murder of a Gestapo agent."

"Can you tell me more?"

"Yeah, I can tell you lots more. I've got the whole file."

"A whole file. What the hell?"

"Yeah, I hope you don't mind but I've been like dog with a bone on this. I found a small museum; dedicated to the French Resistance that has all kinds of Gestapo files. The custodian found a file that mentions both Nana and Janos."

"Jesus," Carson said with astonishment.

∞

A light mist began to fall as Carson walked into the cabin. Upon entering the kitchen, he was warmed by the sight of Hana cooking pancakes. The kitchen smelled of bubbling batter, fresh coffee and maple syrup. The aroma of home and normalcy, not a secret bomb factory. Well, it wasn't exactly a bomb factory, maybe he should call it an anti-bomb factory.

"How you take coffee?" Sally asked.

Carson cringed and paused before answering. It was only natural she assumed he was a coffee drinker. He was craving a Dr. Pepper but instead said "Light and sweet. If you don't mind, I'll do it. A little cream and a little sugar."

"Sure, how you say, no problem?" responded Sally. Hana interjected "How many pancakes, Mr. Lake?"

At this Carson smiled. Being in the Adirondacks stimulated his appetite and he could never get enough of Hana's pancakes.

"Three please. I want more but have to watch my figure." He said jokingly. The remark wasn't that far from the truth. He could feel his belt stretch from the big meals he had eaten since coming to the cabin. Plus he wanted to take Hana for a driving lesson and didn't want to be falling asleep behind the wheel. He lifted the cup to his mouth.

Sally sat at the table and patted the seat next to her. "You sit, we talk about what we do today?"

"What do you have in mind?" Carson asked as he blew on the hot liquid.

"First, we take walk in woods. Maybe we find Moosey, last time we saw her she looked like she have baby soon."

"That would be a sight."

"Yes, but I okay if she have calf on her own, she no need our help. I like walk in woods anyway. If we walk to beaver pond, we maybe see loons. They are nesting and laying eggs now. They my favorite birds."

"They're one of my favorites also. The black bodies, with the white polka dots are so cool. But their calls are so eerie."

"What is this word, you use? 'Airy'?" Hana asked.

"No, eerie, E-E-R-I-E. It means spooky, almost ghostly."

"You are right," Sally said. "The first time I heard it, I thought it was woman crying, or maybe a baby. It sent chills through me." She paused. "Is chills the right word?"

"Yes, I understand" Carson confirmed. "Your English is getting very good."

"Thank you, I practice every day."

"She does" Hana said as she put a plate of pancakes and eggs in front of Carson. "I'm very proud of her."

Carson paused. It was so odd to hear a child speak proudly of their parent. Normally the roles are reversed.

"And I proud of her" Sally said as she pointed a finger at Hana.

After breakfast the three of them shrugged into their rain gear. The earlier mist had changed into a steady drizzle.

Carson felt the familiar throb in his hip but pushed it away. *If the girls can be out in this so can I,* he thought.

"Here, put in pocket" Sally said as she shook a handwarmer packet. "It for hip, you no want it cold."

"Thank you, I should have thought of that."

"You male, you, not smart. I mean, I mean…you no think that way. You man, you think you tough. I mean, I mean…"

"That's okay" he said to ease her consternation. "I know what you mean, and you're right."

"You need woman in your life," said Sally.

"But not my mother," Hanna interjected good naturedly.

"You're right, I need a woman in my life. Any suggestions on where I might find one up here," he said as he gestured toward the wooded mountains.

"Sorry, it's the wilderness. If you don't bring it with you, you won't find it here" Hana teased him.

"Okay, Miss Smartypants, let's go find your Moosey." Carson marched across the yard and slid his holster backward so that he could get the warmer pack into his pocket.

"You know," Sally said, "there were times in the camp we would have to wait in food lines in weather like this. We had no choice if we were to eat. I did not like being cold and wet like that. But now I don't mind. Now I am free. I am free to go out in rain, if I choose." She turned to Carson and asked, "Is that odd?"

"No, I understand" he replied and then thought *If they can do this, I can do it.* At that the pain in his hip disappeared.

PARABELLUM: When you live in Peace, prepare for War
Jack Nanuq

CHAPTER 44
Willsboro, NY
June 1, 2001

The phone woke Carson at 2:07 a.m. The caller ID read NEWTON. "Yeah," Carson said groggily.

"She's gone, she's with Petr and Janos."

Carson could hear someone crying in the background.

"She passed in her sleep, she went peacefully," Newton continued "Are you there?"

"Yeah, I'm here," he said, as he sat up and rubbed his eyes. "Just trying to process it. I knew it would happen someday, but now it's here. You said she went in her sleep?"

"Yes, peacefully. It was time. She left you something."

"What…, what did she leave me?"

"Tapes, cassette tapes, lots of them. She told us stories all week long. I never heard her talk so much. I think we have more than a hundred hours of tapes. She made it clear she wants you to have them; very clear."

"Okay, have you called the police yet? Or the undertaker, I'm not sure who to call in a case like this." Carson wasn't yet fully awake and was trying desperately to pull all the pieces together.

"No, I called you first. I'll call the Sheriff's Office in a few minutes, but I thought you should know first."

"Thanks. Okay, call them. I'm going to get a shower and I'll call back in an hour. Then we'll talk about what to do next. How are you doing?"

"I'm okay sir. But Iris, she's a mess. She's the one that found Nana. She got up to check on her, said she knew something was wrong. Guess she was right."

"Newton."

"Yes sir."

"Thank you, thank you for everything. I'll call in an hour."

"You're welcome sir."

It was clear to Carson that the stress of the situation had forced Newton to revert his military training. Hence the "Yes sirs". Carson rubbed his temples as he digested everything. He knew this day would come. But that was like knowing that someday the sun would burn out. It just didn't seem real, but it was real. She was gone. He felt tears roll down his cheek.

Carson's phone rang again at 2:17 a.m. *What the hell?* he thought.

He looked at the caller ID and said "Yeah Fred...you heard. You monitoring my phone?" There was a sharpness in Carson's voice. He didn't want to talk right now and was taking it out on Fred.

"I'm sorry buddy, I really am. I know she was special to you. I'm coming up there."

"You didn't answer me?" He couldn't help himself. He was in pain right now and wanted to share it; regardless of Fred's motives.

"Yeah, we are, you know that, or should. Think about it." Fred responded. "Did you hear me when I said I'm coming up there?"

"Yeah, I heard you, but I got it under control. You don't have to come up here." There was a hitch in his voice as he said the last word. *Keep it together*, he thought.

"Carson, listen to yourself. You don't have it under control; nor should you. She was pretty special and she's the only family you've got."

Tears were flowing freely now, and Carson was glad his friend couldn't see him. He wasn't sure if he could do much more to keep things in check. He was vacillating between the first two stages of grief; denial and anger.

Fred continued "Carson, I'm calling as both your friend and boss. I'm coming up there. You need to get home and take care of the arrangements. I'll take your place and see to the Kestrels' safety. You're gonna have a lot on your mind. I can't have you distracted. Come home, do what needs to be done, and we'll talk about what should happen next."

PARABELLUM: When you live in Peace, prepare for War

Jack Nanuq

As Carson listened to this, he felt like his emotions had been kidnapped. They were stuffed in sack and thrown into the trunk of a car. He was being driven down a washboard road. His psyche and soul were being tortured as the fictitious vehicle bucked along. He gave Fred a noncommittal grunt, as he didn't trust his voice. Now to make matters worse someone in the kidnapper's car had turned on Don McLean's "American Pie".

In the ear closest to the phone he heard Fred speaking but in the other ear he heard or more correctly felt the lyrics of this haunting song.

A long, long time ago...
something touched me deep inside...
The day the music died.

"I'll be there about 0700 hours; we'll talk then," Fred informed him. "Now, and this is an order. You need to let it go. You need to grieve, and you need to let it all out. It sucks she's gone and it's gonna suck some more before you get through it. Now, hang up the phone, have a good cry, and I'll see you in a few hours. Copy that?"

I can't remember if I cried....
The day the music died.

There was no response.

"Soldier, do you copy that?" barked Fred.

"Yes sir," Carson said meekly.

As he hung up the phone it was as though the kidnapper's car came to screeching halt. His very being was ejected from the trunk. He crashed, and everything broke loose. He cried, he screamed, he howled, and he sobbed. His body shook violently as the pain poured forth. Twenty minutes later he found himself curled on the bed in a fetal position. He couldn't recall doing this. His T-shirt and the bedspread were soaked with sweat and tears.

He remembered Fred's last words. He stumbled toward the bathroom. He needed to get a shower, call Newton and then get other things in the works.

He was thankful his room was above the garage and away from the cabin. He was glad he hadn't woken the Kestrels.

Before he could leave his room, the phone rang again. *What the hell?* he thought as he looked at the caller ID. LIZA.

"You heard," he said with a raspy voice.

"Yeah," she said with concern. "Fred called me. I'm sorry. I want to come up there. Is that okay?"

"Of course, why wouldn't it be?"

"I guess, I guess...I just thought I'd ask before I made the trip."

"Yes, please come. I want you here. Wait, that came out wrong. I mean, I mean...oh shit, I don't know what I mean."

"It's okay, I understand. Should I fly into Albany, or maybe somewhere else?"

"Albany. I'm not there now but will be tomorrow. Wait, I mean later today; it's already tomorrow."

The phone clicked, and he looked at it. INCOMING CALL read the display. "I've got another call coming in. See you later," he continued.

"Okay, let me call the airlines. I'm sure I can get a flight in sometime today. I'll call when I hit the ground." She paused, and an unsettled silence lingered on the line.

The phone clicked a second time and Carson said "I got to go. I don't recognize the number, I should take the call."

"Love you," Liza said quickly.

The phone line clicked again, and he pressed answer. As he did this he whispered, "I love you too."

"What?" said the other voice.

"I'm sorry." Recognizing the voice, Carson continued with embarrassment "Angie, ignore that."

"Okay. Normally I have to get a guy drunk before he tells me he loves me," she said jokingly. "I'm sorry, maybe that was insensitive. I'm calling to say I'm on my way. I should be there sometime in the afternoon. How are the Kestrels by the way?"

"They miss you. We've had a good week, but I get the feeling they prefer your company. Probably a girl thing, no offense."

"None taken. You okay? All Fred would tell me was you had a family emergency."

"Yeah, something like that. I'm fine."

"No you're not. I can hear it in your voice. Must be a guy thing, no offense."

"None taken," he replied. "Have a safe trip. I've got a few things to take care of."

"Okay…If you need anything."

"Yeah, thanks," he said as the phone line went dead.

∞

At 6:01 a.m. he called his assistant; Stephanie. She picked up the phone on the third ring.

"Boss, you okay? Something wrong? You never call this early."

"Yeah…I'm afraid so. I wish I had other words, but Nana passed away." He paused and let that sink in.

"What?" she squeaked.

Carson suspected this wasn't a question that needed an answer. It was her way of venting. Releasing the pressure of an incomprehensible event. He gave her some time to process things.

"Steph, Steph, you there?"

"Yeah boss. Yeah, I'm here." Her voice quavered.

Carson thought, *there she is; my dependable Stephanie. Good girl.*

"I need you to take care of a few things. I'll be back today, but probably not before noon. First, I want you to send an email, to all employees. Tell them the news and give them the day off. Unless something is an emergency no one has to report to work. If something needs immediate attention, I'll pay double time. Got that?"

"Yeah"

264

"Next, I need you to start on a press release. Don't send it out before I can look it over, but I need it done by the time I get back."

"Do we know when the service will be?" she asked.

"I'm thinking next Friday, the eight, or maybe Saturday. That will give people plenty of time to travel. She knew people everywhere. I won't be sure until I speak with the funeral director."

"Boss, I got another question. You doing okay?"

"To be honest...No, but I'll get there. How about you?"

"I'll get there too. I got to go, got things to do. I'll be near my phone if you need anything else."

"Thanks Steph, I'll be back this afternoon."

PARABELLUM: When you live in Peace, prepare for War
                                        Jack Nanuq

CHAPTER 45
Albany, NY
June 7, 2001

For Carson the week, went by in a blur. Monday was spent with the funeral director, Tuesday he met with attorneys. And there was three days of viewing. In those days he shook so many hands he now had a blister.

Today was a bitch. The funeral, then the luncheon and then was the informal reception put together by the Mayor's office. This last event was excruciating. It was now 8:09 PM, Friday the 8th and he was home, with Liza. As he slipped off his dress pants, he heard himself say "I never want to do that again."

Liza grabbed the pants and checked the pockets before she put them on a hanger.

He continued "The politicians, the contractors, the blood suckers and the ass-kissers. I can't believe we got them all in one room. I don't care if I never talk to another person the rest of my life."

"What's this?" Liza asked.

"What's what?" Carson replied as he turned to her.

She was holding a business card. "It says INTERPOL."

"What?"

"The card, it says INTERPOL; Jan Krueger. What does he want?"

"I don't know, what does he want?" Carson asked; clearly perplexed.

"That's what I'm asking you. What does he want? There's a note on the back" She said with exasperation.

"What's it say? I don't know him. Where did you find that?"

"In your pants dumbass. In your front right pocket," Liza announced. "You don't remember taking it from him?"

"Let me see that." He turned the card over and in neat handwritten script were the words PLEASE CALL. The phone number written below showed a local Area Code.

Carson was both perplexed and aggravated and said "Let's see what this is about," as he dialed the number.

The phone was answered on the first ring. "Hello," said the voice on the other end.

"Is this Mr. Krueger?"

"Yes, Mr. Nowak, it is. I see you got my note. I'd like to meet with you." The voice had a slight German accent, but words were crisp and perfect, similar to a BBC newscaster.

"What about? I don't know you. What this is about?"

"I'm staying at the Marriott on Wolf Road, they have a nice lounge. I really think we should meet."

"Didn't you hear me? What's this about?" Carson asked angrily.

"I'd rather not say over the phone. I can tell you...I am named for your grandfather."

"I'll..." Carson tried to consider all the angles. "I'll be there in an hour," Carson replied.

At 9:04 p.m. Carson waited in the parking lot of the Marriott. He scrutinized the main entrance of the hotel. Ever alert and vigilant, he wondered. *What is this meeting about? Is it some ploy for the Galcoes to lure him into a trap?* He had done as much research as he could, on Inspector Krueger, in the limited amount of time he had. The man appeared to be legitimate. Maybe he was on their payroll? Carson had taken some precautions for his safety, but the risks were still there.

Frank Christian, an employee from The Cube, exited the hotel. A newspaper in his right hand. This was the ALL CLEAR signal. Had the paper been in the left hand the meeting would be aborted. Christian continued to his car without looking at Carson.

Carson walked into the lounge a few minutes later. He scanned the interior and let his eyes adjust to the lowlight conditions. As he did this, a man in a blue sport coat stood and walked in his direction. He immediately recognized the man from the wake and funeral. This person had attended all three days of viewing; and Carson had noticed him. Early 50s, about 6 foot 2 inches, with a muscular build. His dark hair was

268

peppered with gray; giving it the appearance of weathered asphalt.

"Thank you for coming," the stranger said as he reached out to shake Carson's hand. The other hand held a well-used leather briefcase. "I have something for you."

"Maybe we should get out of the doorway," Carson said as he scanned the small crowd. About a dozen patrons were scattered around and none were overtly suspicious. Not at this time at least. Soft jazz music streamed out from hidden speakers.

"Yes. I have a table over here." The man had a confident and comfortable manner.

As they sat a waitress appeared immediately. "Two Dr. Peppers," Krueger said to the young woman.

"Impressive. You've done your homework," Carson said, with suspicion.

"I have, I'm sorry we have not met before now. I feel like I know your family. I heard stories about them most of my life." Krueger said as he laid the briefcase on the table.

"Then you have me at a disadvantage. Is the card you gave me genuine?" Carson continued.

"You know it is. I'm sure you Googled me. I would have…had you approached me."

"Good guess. I checked a few other sources also. Former Lt Colonel with the German Polizei; Hamburg specifically. Now attached to Interpol, and stationed in Lyon, France. Age 52, divorced, four adult children, favorite hobbies skiing and scuba diving. Shall I go on?" Carson asked rhetorically.

"And…I remember you from the wake. Who goes to a wake, all three days? Who does that? Who spends three days mourning an old lady? An old lady you probably never met. Forgive me, it's been a long week," Carson added, with sarcasm. "You said you have something for me. And you said you were named for my grandfather." Carson's tone was menacing.

"I apologize. First, let me give you this," he said as he handed a photo album across the table. "A gift from my father to your family."

"What is it?" Carson asked with a genuine interest.

"Let me start at the beginning. Your grandfather saved my father's life; multiple times actually. They served together in the War."

"Go on," Carson said, tentatively.

Krueger fiddled with the latch of the briefcase. "My father was an odd person. Nowadays we might say he had Asperger's Syndrome, albeit a mild form of it. But people weren't as enlightened back then. My father had trouble making friends. Plus, father was the youngest in his platoon. He joined the army at 16. He was attached to a panzer unit in Normandy. That's where they met. At the time your grandfather was about 10 years older. I believe your grandfather was a dispatch rider at the time. They sent him to France after he was wounded in Poland. Janos took father under his wing because my father was an outcast. Plus, they shared a love for engines, machines and other gadgets. They spent a lot of time working on Janos' motorcycle. Developed quite a friendship, they did."

"That's the backstory, as they say. On the night before D-day my father's platoon drove a truck to a café, near Pas de Calais. Years later he learned the café belonged to Janos' mother, your nana. No one knew that then. My father's unit had spent the day transporting equipment and fuel. By the end of the day they were exhausted, cold and wet. Their sergeant let them stop and get a hot meal. They found Janos there. No one thought it odd as he spent a lot of time there. Everyone liked him. He was always going out of his way to help them and others. That night he volunteered to guard their truck as they ate. After finishing their meal all fell asleep. The warm café, the heavy meal, it was all too much to resist. As you Americans say, they crashed."

PARABELLUM: When you live in Peace, prepare for War

Jack Nanuq

Carson watched the story teller with intensity. His mind was spinning as he was trying to fit this puzzle piece into his family's collage. "Go on."

"On the night in question my father was asleep about an hour when he woke to gunshots. Even though they were in a combat zone and were familiar with taking fire, these shots were different. He yelled at everyone and told them what he heard. They ran out to the truck, thinking partisans had shot Janos. They found a Gestapo agent dead, but no Janos. They had no idea what happened but knew they could not be found anywhere near a dead agent. They left immediately and took an oath of silence. They came up with a story they never made it to the café because the truck broke down. They all stuck to their story, and no one was ever the wiser."

"It was my father's belief Janos had shot the agent to protect the group. Had they been found sleeping then bad things would have happened; firing squad or shipped to the eastern front. My father felt your grandfather saved their lives. Later he learned Janos had spiked the fuel barrels in their truck. Maybe protecting himself but that didn't matter to father. The events of that night set in motion other events that helped my father get through the war unscathed. Even though he ended up as a POW."

"Tell me more. Nana was a POW, of sorts," Carson said.

"It's strange really. Kind of a twist of fate. The fuel Janos spiked got into a bunch of lories. Trucks, as you Americans say. My father was in one of those trucks. It quit running, on the way to the invasion beaches. His group was taken prisoner, by the British, as they were working on the truck. They were so engrossed in getting it working they never heard the paratroopers, until it was too late. They spent the rest of the war locked up, but safe. Something like a dozen other trucks broke down on the way to the beaches. I, as well as father, always wondered how many lives were saved because those trucks broke down. Later, when my father thought about this quirk of fate, he thanked Janos. Maybe he should have thanked the gods of war. But…but he knew Janos had saved his life; again."

"Can I look at this?" Carson asked pointing to the album.

"Yes, it's yours. There are photos of father and Janos. I think you will find the first page the most interesting."

"What's on the first page?" Carson asked.

"That is a letter Janos sent to father in 1946. This was the third, maybe fourth time your grandfather saved his life."

Carson looked at the letter, it was written in German, of course it was written in German. Carson didn't speak, let alone read German. Carson rudely said "I'm afraid I can't read this…in the low light and all. I'll look at it at home." He was self-conscious about his limited language skills.

"Shall I tell you what it says?" His beaming face showed a keen desire to share.

"Sure," Carson said.

"The note itself is short and simply asks about his health and well-being. A query basically, asking if my father made it home from the war. It was sent to my grandmother's home, in Hamburg. But it came from the United States. The letter was brief, but the envelope contained a few other things. First, was a sheet of airmail stationary, with a stamp and most importantly five US dollar bills. It doesn't seem like much today, but it was like winning the lottery. Back then US currency was like gold. That and British pounds were the only thing accepted on the Black Market. Goods were very scarce in Germany at the time. At the time the letter arrived Father and his family shared one blanket. They had no coal for the house. And had to scavenge food, wherever they could find it. Things were very hard."

"I can imagine," said Carson with sincerity.

"I'm glad you can. I can't… and I grew up there. Things were so scarce my father had to go to the neighbors to borrow a pencil to write the reply." Krueger took a sip of his drink.

Carson had been so engrossed in the story he never saw the waitress bring their order.

Krueger straightened up and looked Carson in the eye. "My family owes your family a great debt. Once my father responded and Janos knew he was alive care packages came on a regular basis. Everything...from aspirin, to vegetable seeds, to clothes. Your Nana even sent hand-stitched leather gloves and mittens every Christmas. I wish I had come sooner. I would have liked to have met your nana and grandfather. But life gets in the way and things happen."

Carson felt a pang of sadness, at the reminder Nana was gone. "That would have been nice, but she would have told you not to feel indebted to her. She would have asked you to pay it forward, help others. That's the type of person she was. You know my grandfather passed away more a decade ago. You do know that?"

"Yes, she told us in a letter. My father was so heartbroken his health began to fail. He was diagnosed with cancer shortly after that. It was a long battle and he wanted to come here but was never well enough to travel. He made me promise I would come someday. In hindsight I should have done it the day after his funeral. But...as I said...life gets in the way."

Carson paged through the album. "I don't know what to say. I want to say don't worry about it, but it clearly bothers you. If it's any consolation I understand completely." Pointing to the album Carson added "This is incredible. Did your father save every letter?"

"Yes, every one, and they are all there. Now onto another topic," Krueger said, clearly switching gears. "As you said, I never met your nana. Yet...I was at the wake all three days. I was there to pay my respects, but I was also there to help ensure your safety."

Carson perked up. "I'm all ears."

"My office, at Interpol is responsible for tracking Neo-Nazi groups. Most are simply annoying and troublesome. We refer to them as mushrooms. They pop up somewhere, feed off the decay in their neighborhood or region and then disappear. But there are others that pose a real danger. One of these groups is known as the Galcoes. I think you are familiar with them; are you not?"

"Go on," Carson said cautiously.

"They are assassins of the highest order and they never forget an attack on one of their own. The group was founded by Julio Busch. He's half Argentinian and half German. And he is the grandnephew of Augustus Busch; the murdered Gestapo agent. You have recently been put on their radar, so to speak. They want revenge. We've learned they paid your nana a visit, but she wasn't home. We're not sure what happened, but their guy then shows up in Buenos Aires mumbling about a blue bumble bee. A short time later the local cops found him in a vacant lot; dogs were feeding on him."

Carson struggled to keep his face impassive. "And what does this mean for me?"

"I'm surprised you have to ask, but okay. Since they can't get their pound of flesh from Janos, and they can't get it from your nana" He let this hang in the air. "And the rest of your family has passed away…You're the last of the Novak clan."

"Not much of a clan is it," Carson stated rhetorically. "And it's pronounced Nowak."

"Not originally. In much of Europe the W is pronounced as a V, but I digress. My office knows you are in danger, a lot of it. I feel a need to help protect you."

"That's not necessary."

"Maybe not. I know you have resources available to you. But as I said my office is tasked with investigating and disrupting Neo-Nazi groups. The Galcoes are a Neo-Nazi group hence they fall within my purview. If my staff can help dismantle their organization by removing a few members from the planet then so be it. If that helps protect you, then all the better."

"So, you assassinate the assassins, is that correct?" Carson asked.

"I can neither confirm nor deny that rumor," Krueger said, with a twinkle in his eye. "I'll let you in on a secret though.

You see those two people sitting behind me? The ones with the martinis."

"You mean the ones that have spent the night playing with the olives, moving the glasses around and even bringing the glasses to their lips, but not drinking. Are those the ones?"

Krueger chuckled. "Exactly... they are with me. When you leave, they are going to follow you to your car. Don't be alarmed. After you pull away, they will blend into the night."

"They're not gonna follow me home?" Carson asked sarcastically.

"No, I have other people for that."

"That's not necessary, so no. I understand about all this," lifting the album off the table "But no, that's not necessary. I can take care of myself."

"You'll never see them."

"I saw those two," pointing to the ones behind Krueger.

"I'll let you in on another secret. You were meant to see them." Krueger said smiling.

"I'll let you in a secret," Carson whispered, as he stood. "It wasn't Janos that shot that agent, it was Nana." With that he looked at the two, behind the martinis, like they were errant children, and barked "Come on we're going now!" And marched to his car.

PARABELLUM: When you live in Peace, prepare for War

Jack Nanuq

CHAPTER 46
Albany, NY
June 7, 2001

Liza was sitting in the dark, her pistol nearby, when Carson returned home. She was dressed in Hello Kitty pajamas. "How'd it go?" she asked.

"Weird, really weird. Why couldn't I have been born into a normal family? You know... one that was peppered with alcoholic rednecks. Not these secretive spy types. Seems Nana and Grandpa Jon helped support some family in Germany, after the war." He emphasized this by dropping the album on a coffee table.

"I take it you had no idea?"

"Not a clue. Not really surprising when you think about it but I always thought Nana hated the Germans. Now I find out Grandpa Jon had a little buddy over there. And that little buddy is Herr Krueger's father! And now Herr Krueger has some of his office mates looking out for my well-being. At least that's what he says."

"You don't believe him?"

"Hell...I don't know. All these layers of secrets are driving me crazy. It's not like I never spent time with my family, or Nana. We talked about everything, politics, work, school, even girls. But did anyone mention we had some kind of foster family in Germany? A family that feels as though they have a blood debt, to our family. No, no they didn't! You can't make this shit up."

"Wait...start from the beginning. I'm confused" Liza said.

"You're confused? I'm confused. I don't even know where the beginning is. Krueger told me his father thought Grandpa Jon shot a Gestapo agent to protect his army unit. He feels as though Grandpa Jon saved his life. Said Grandpa Jon saved his life, multiple times."

"But Jon didn't shoot the agent, Nana did. Or did she?" mused Liza.

"Good question, who the hell knows? I don't know what to believe anymore."

"Do you want a beer, or maybe a scotch?" Liza asked trying to change the subject or at least calm Carson.

"Yeah, that sounds good."

"Which do you want?"

"Both," he said as he walked to the front window. There was no one on the quiet street.

"Okay, one Boiler Maker on the way."

"I'm sorry I'm so grouchy. Now I'm acting like Nana" Carson said with embarrassment.

"Then stop it. You are your own man. Act like it." She said jokingly.

"How did I get so lucky?" he said turning to her.

"Not sure," she said she slid her Walther into her purse. "Have a seat on the couch. I'll bring the drinks in a minute. You're wound up like a long-tailed cat in a room full of rocking chairs."

"Southern witticism, I love it," he said as he took a seat closest to the window. He listened for any passing cars.

She took the seat next to him, and said "Relax, put your feet up. Now let's look at this book. What's in here?"

"Pictures and letters."

"Naked pictures?" she asked jokingly. Trying to lighten the mood and calm him.

"Don't know, haven't looked." His mood improving by the minute.

∞

"So, you speak German! Of course, you speak German. Am I the only one that can't speak a second language?" Carson asked. They had just spent more than an hour going through the album.

Liza stifled a yawn. "There's a joke that goes something like. What do you call someone who only speaks one language? …An American."

Carson finished his beer. He leaned forward, putting his elbows on the coffee table and his head in his hands. This was a lot to take in. He pushed the day's events to a dark corner of his brain. He focused on his breathing, and his body. He was aware of the alcoholic tingle in his lips and tongue. He then focused on how the booze had softened the sharp edges of his nerves. He stayed like this for a minute; or was it an hour, or a lifetime.

He was brought back to the here and now when Liza ran her hand up his back and through his hair.

"Can I offer a pleasant distraction?" she asked.

"Mmmmm, I'd like that."

∞

Carson woke at 4 am as usual but felt less than rested. The few hours of sleep he did get were troubled. Now that he was awake the tension resurfaced. He looked at Liza. Asleep and at peace; angelic. This helped ease his anxiety.

Nana what have you gotten me into? And Grandpa Jon you're not blameless in this either. And then he thought about his parents, both killed in a car accident on the night of his high school graduation. *Did you guys know about any of this? I guess it doesn't matter, does it?*

He climbed out of bed and walked over to his computer. Opening his email, he saw a note from Krueger was at the top of the list.

> *Mr. Nowak;*
> *I must apologize for the way this evening's meeting ended. My people are experts in their field. They will not interfere with your daily activities, in any way. I would like to ask that they be allowed to do their job, for at least a few days. As I mentioned the Galcoes are tenacious. It may be years before they try to even the score, but I think not. When, not if, they return to the area it will be soon. If we can agree to work together then maybe, we can put a dent in their organization. A win-win, as you Americans like to say.*
> *Sincerely;*
> *Jan C Krueger*

279

Carson thought long and hard about how he should reply. He was still confused and angry, maybe he should wait. *Yup, that's what I'll do, wait. I'm going back to bed.* He forwarded the email to Fred, before returning to bed.

∞

"Morning sleepy head" Liza chirped as Carson opened his eyes. She was dressed, and it was clear she had been up for a while. Sunlight streamed in the bedroom window.

"What time is it?"

"10:19...in the morning. Saturday morning, the 9th; to answer your next question."

"Wow, I haven't slept in this late since I had the flu, last year."

"You've had a long week, you need your rest. They say Rest is Best."

"Who are you; Dr. Quinn, Medicine Woman?"

"More like Nurse Ratched" she responded. "You better be nice to me, or I'll take your temperature and it won't be in a good way."

"Does everything have to be a joke with you?" He said sharper than intended.

"No, it doesn't," she responded in the same tone. "But it helps release stress and right now you are under a ton of it."

"How about you?" he said in a more conciliatory tone.

"How about me... what?" she responded, still on edge.

"This can't be easy for you. You drop what you are doing to be here. As long as you're here, you're in danger. Plus, I can't be that fun to be around. Aren't you anxious?"

"Yes, yes, yes and yes, but I can handle it. I'm here because I want to be. If you haven't noticed I've got feelings for you. As for the danger I can deal with that. It's the fact that you are in danger that's driving me nuts. As for being fun, we'll get there. I repeat, I'm here because I want to be."

"I'm sorry, I'm a shithead sometimes. For what it's worth I have feelings for you too. I love you...there I said it. I love you! But I don't know what that means for us. You live in

280

Baltimore and I live here. I worry you'll get hurt if you stay. But...but I don't want you to leave. And now I've got Krueger's goons lurking in the shadows. Plus I don't know what this means for my status with the Agency. There are two others I need to think about, but I can't tell you about that. I want to...but I can't. You haven't been read into that. Can this get any more bizarre or complicated?"

Carson's anxiety saturated the room.

"Slow down big guy, slow down. We'll get through this, all of it. First, we'll figure out how to deal with the Galcoes. Then we'll figure out how deal with us. We'll figure it all out, all of it, I promise. Now... do you want some breakfast, or are you going for a run?"

"I'm gonna skip the run and get a shower first. I need to call Fred. We'll go out to eat. How's Huevos Rancheros sound? I know a great Mexican place. My treat."

"Great...Sure...Can I use your computer while you're in the shower?"

"Have at it," he said as he walked into the bedroom.

Twenty minutes later he returned to the living room, running a comb through his still wet hair, wearing jeans, a polo shirt and a zippered sweatshirt.

Liza pointed to his feet and said, "Wrong shoes, put some hiking boots on. We're gonna spend some time in nature, after we eat."

"What have you got in mind?"

"You've got three choices. Thatcher State Park, The Christman Sanctuary or Vrooman's Nose."

"You made that last one up...admit it."

"I did not; it's about an hour southwest of here."

"Oh yeah, I remember now, it's right near booger nugget mine."

"Do you have to make a joke of everything?" she barked.

"I'm sorry," and reached out to hug her.

She pushed him away and shouted "I just want to go someplace where we can get some fresh air and exercise. And not think about the Galcoes!" As she said this, she removed the Walther from her purse and slid it into the holster at the small of her back.

"I'm sorry; Vrooman's Nose it is." He held up his arms a second time. This time she surrendered to his advance. They hugged each other tightly.

CHAPTER 47
Willsboro, NY
June 8, 2001

The cabin smelled of baking bread and toasted caraway seeds, as Sally kneaded a lump of rye dough into another loaf. Three hours had passed since this project began and six finished loaves sat on the counter cooling. Three more were in the oven. She was in a rhythm and enjoying the fruits of her labor. Hana was at the kitchen table and light jazz music came from the laptop the girl was working on. She looked out the back window and watched chickadees and juncos search for tidbits in the yard. For the first time in a very long while she felt at peace. All seemed to be right with the world and this little sanctuary felt like home. She knew this feeling wouldn't last but she was determined to enjoy it for as long as possible.

"Look at this momma!" yelled Hana as she pointed to the computer screen.

"Another stupid cat video?" Sally asked with exasperation. "I busy, you no see that."

"I see, but I think you need to look at this. It …it's Mr. Lake, only it's not. He has another name."

"What you mean?" she asked as she grabbed a towel.

"I'm reading the news, from Albany. There's a picture of Mr. Lake, he's at a funeral. It says he's the grandson of a real estate mogul. She died at the age of 101 and the funeral was a really big deal. Hundreds of people attended."

"Can I see that? Sally asked.

"Should I call Angie? She's lifting weights, in the garage."

"No, no, I first read article."

"There's a bunch of articles. She owned a company called Hawkeye Management, and lots of properties. And supported charities, and, and well you read… you see."

"I'm coming, I'm coming" putting the towel down, Sally felt herself getting anxious.

Ten minutes later Sally had read the articles and looked at all the photos. Mr. Robert Lake AKA: Carson Nowak was wearing a suit in every one of them, but it was him. It was amazing how much a formal suit changed a person's appearance, but she was certain it was him.

"Why did he lie about his name?" Hana asked her mother.

"For safety reasons, Angie's probably fake name too, don't be mad. Give me some time, I read articles again. Then I figure out what to say to Angie. I will have questions for her. I need know if it will affect our status."

"What? Why would it? Affect our status. Did we do something, something wrong, I mean? You're scaring me."

"Calm down. Maybe not status but maybe if we to stay here, or not. Let me think," Sally said as she absorbed the information on the computer screen. "We talk with Angie, maybe even Angie boss." The buzzer on the oven announced the latest loaves were done.

"Get that." Sally said, pointing to the oven "Please."

As the oven door opened so did the rear kitchen door. Angie walked into the cabin. "That smells great." She said, loudly smacking her lips. "May I?" she asked as she pulled a bread knife from a wooden block.

"Yes, yes, but save some crust for the birds," Sally said. "I have butter in the fridge, you want?"

"No, no, when it's fresh like this it's perfect. Warm, moist, and delicious. Gotta hand it to you, you've got a knack for breadmaking. It's a shame Hana's a secret agent, or you could open a bakery," she said jokingly.

"Yeah, she secret agent lady. What every mother dreams of."

The phone rang and startled the three women. Angie looked at the display and recognized the number. "I gotta take this." She picked up the handset and walked into the living room.

The other two listened with interest to one side of a muted conversation. Only a few words made it through the wall

284

but both Hana and Sally understood Angie was speaking with Dr. Maarsten.

A few minutes later Angie returned to the kitchen and announced "Ladies, I've got good news. We're going on a road trip".

"Where to?" Sally asked suspiciously.

"Utica, that was Paul Maarsten. You remember him, don't you?" Angie asked rhetorically, as she looked at Sally.

Sally's cheeks took on a rose tint at the mention of the man's name. She knew Angie was playing with her, so didn't respond.

Angie continued. "He says he has made a breakthrough with the Parabellum. He tried to explain it to me but then said he'd rather show you." She pointed at Hana at this last comment.

Hana, with mischief in her eyes, asked "Will Mr. Lake be coming with us?"

"No, no I'm afraid not… something's uh…well…well… he won't be coming along. But we'll have plenty of protection. I'll make a call. We'll hit the road in about an one hour or two. And we'll spend the night in Utica, if no one minds."

Sally cleared the computer screen. "Sounds great" she said. And added "Hana go pack some things. And clean the cat box. We don't know how long we'll be gone. I'll fill the food bowl."

"I need to take shower but need to finish this first" she said as she pointed to the lump of dough, she had been working on only a few minutes ago.

"Take your time. I need to call the guys and get everything worked out" she said as she carried a slice of fresh bread to the yard.

Sally rebooted the computer and checked the weather in Utica. If conditions are right maybe she and Paul could make time for each other, even if it was just for a bike ride.

∞

Five hours later the group was arrayed in Maarsten's lab. Angie was with the girls, but the rest of the security detail remained in the hall. The doctor used a Power Point presentation to demonstrate how the addition of a key element, in a certain configuration would enhance the Parabellum's performance.

The screen on the wall showed amplified images of the prototype design. The first few showed how the raw elements were teased into strands and then woven into Hana's original design. The small bundles resembled a skein of yarn. Subsequent images showed Maarsten's contribution. Images showed him working in a clean room, wearing a Tyvek suit.

"So if we encapsulate the individual strands with magnesium, we will create an object similar to the lightbulb. Kind of like the Edison design Hana spoke of. More accurately though, this will be more like a flashbulb. At this time making these little buggers will be extremely tedious. As we start building them though I'm sure we will find short cuts." He looked at Hana and asked, "Do you think you are up to this?"

"Yes," she said, nodding with excitement. She had the energy of a puppy with a new toy. Her project was coming to fruition.

"First things first. We will need more Biscuits". He was referencing the code name for the raw ore they brought back from the garnet mine.

"How much?" Sally asked.

"Tough to say exactly. I think we will need at least fifty kilograms. Is that possible?"

Sally turned to Angie and without saying word, used her face to ask the same question.

Angie hesitated for a moment before saying "I think we can do that. We can bring it out in forty-pound packs...but we may have difficulty getting more...with our present system."

The women were quiet as they contemplated carrying heavily laden backpacks over the foot trail, and through the ever-present black flies.

"We'll cross that bridge when we get there." Angie continued.

"Bridge, what bridge, I no remembering bridge?" said Sally.

"Mama, it's a figure of speech," Hana whispered.

"Okay, okay I understanding now. But why she not say it clearer...without picture words?"

More serious now Angie asked "Doctor, how much ore do you think we will need to make this project feasible, not just experimental?"

"I'm not sure right now. I think we'll need about one ounce of ore for every pound of explosive that you want to taint. I'll take a wild-ass guess and say five to ten tons, maybe more."

"Tons?" Sally asked. The enormity of the project sinking in. She then turned to Hana and gave a "what did you get us into" look.

"That's assuming there is that much ore in that mine," Maarsten added.

CHAPTER 48
Albany, NY
June 10, 2001

The 70-pound heavy bag danced violently and erratically, like a piñata with a seizure disorder. It was under assault. Each strike sounded like a handball hitting wet concrete. Every impact punctuated with a splat. It was the blood. The bag was covered in Carson's blood. It dripped from the surface and poured from his body. He charged and punched and screamed and dodged and struck and screamed. It wasn't just punching it was the encyclopedia of close quarters combat; knee strikes, head smashes, sidekicks, haymakers, you name it. He was favoring his injured leg, but it didn't slow him down. Strike, scream, kick, punch, scream, dodge. "God damnit, why...why...why'd you have to leave?" Kick, scream, dodge, strike, scream, dodge, head smash. The bag swung from the ceiling of the makeshift workout area behind Hawkeye Management. Blood was everywhere, on the floor, on the bag, soaking Carson's clothes. The bag was ready to give out and one of the support straps had broken.

The three spectators stood in silence. Iris and Stephanie were bewildered but Newton understood Carson's actions. This is how he was grieving Nana's death. For a moment Newton was back in Beirut. It was a month after they pulled him from the rubble of the Marine barracks. One minute he was talking to a chaplain about returning to the States and the next minute he is attacking the office. He punched sheetrock, threw a desk, broke windows, smashed phones. He hurt, and he wanted the world to know his pain. He was the living, breathing definition of berserk. It took four MPs to restrain him. And here he was watching Carson do the same thing. But Newton didn't have any MPs. He would have to try a different tactic.

"How long's he been like this?" Newton asked Stephanie.

"About an hour, that's why I called you guys. I was at my desk and heard him scream. I came running and found him like this. I thought he'd tire himself out, but here we are."

"You did the right thing," Newton lamented.

"I know I sound calm, Stephanie said, said with concern, "but I'm freaking out inside. He's not gonna have a heart attack or something. Is he?"

"He be fine. I give mouth-to-mouth, if he collapse" Iris said jokingly. No one laughed.

"That won't happen," Newton assured her "I'll put a stop to this. Steph can you find a bucket and some ice?"

"Yeah, anything else?"

"Yeah, some Dr. Pepper." Newton said as he stepped toward the swinging bag. As he closed the distance blood splattered onto his shirt. "Carson, Carson buddy, come on now."

Punch, scream, dodge, kick, yell, strike. Carson was in a fugue state.

In a voice that would make a drill instructor cringe Newton boomed "Sergeant Nowak, stand down! Stand down soldier!"

No response.

"Soldier, soldier, I said unfuck yourself, and do it now!" Newton boomed again.

Carson stopped and slowly turned his head toward Newton. He moved like an automaton. Something out of a Terminator movie. His face was a mess. Tears, blood and spit dripped from his chin and jawline. He dropped his arms to his side; in surrender.

Newton stepped to him and gripped him in a bear hug. "It's okay, we got you, it's okay, you're safe." Newton was echoing the words of that chaplain so many years ago. And he meant it. He had Carson and he would see that everything was okay.

Newton looked over his shoulder and to Iris he said, "find a chair."

Iris unfolded an old lawn chair and slid it behind Carson. Newton lowered his friend into it. It took all of Newton's strength as Carson had lost his ability to focus. His 200 plus pounds had turned to dead weight. Iris understood immediately and helped hold Carson in the chair.

"I couldn't find a bucket, will this work?" Stephanie asked as she returned with an Igloo cooler, ice rattling in the bottom.

"Yeah, perfect. Thanks," He turned to Carson and said, "I need to look at your hands, you hear me?"

Stephanie gently placed the cooler on the ground and gripped Carson's right arm. She made eye contact with Iris and then added "We got ya boss. Newton needs to look at your hands. Can you do that?"

Carson slowly nodded his head in recognition. "What's wrong with me?"

"Nothing," Stephanie whispered, "you're just hurting. She was special to us all, but to you most of all. Now let Newton look at your hands. Can you move your fingers?" She glanced at Newton "Okay to say that?"

"Yeah, you're doing great. Carson, listen to Steph. You're safe, we got you. Open your hands move your fingers."

"It hurts," Carson mumbled, as he uncurled his fingers.

"Where? Your hands or inside? I think you broke some fingers. We'll try something different." Newton said as he opened the ice chest.

He pulled out the sodas and carefully placed the cooler in Carson's lap. "I want you to put your hands in the ice. It'll stop the bleeding and help with the swelling. I got you buddy, it's okay, it's okay." He said as he gripped Carson's shoulders.

∞

The next morning Carson's phone rang promptly at 6:00 a.m. After the fifth ring Carson picked up the receiver and groggily said "alloooo?" It had been a year since he slept past 4 a.m., but in the past week he'd done it twice. "Allooo," he repeated. He cradled the phone loosely in his swollen bandaged hand.

"Mornin sunshine, you up for some company," chirped Fred.

"Um, what, what, who is this? Oh Christ never mind, what do you want, Fred?"

"I heard you got a little banged up yesterday. You okay with me stopping by?"

"Yeah, Yeah, I guess. Can you give me 20 minutes?"

"Sure, can I bring anything, coffee maybe?"

Carson ran his tongue around his dry mouth and under his swollen lips. "Yeah but make it iced coffee."

"Deal; see you in twenty."

At 6:19 Carson, in his boxer shorts and a t-shirt, opened the door to his friend "You're early."

Fred took in the racoon eyes, the broken nose and the bandages. "Jesus, what's the other guy look like?"

"Not sure, don't remember much. But they tell me I did this too myself, with the help of a heavy bag."

"Ya wanna talk about it?" Fred asked as he moved toward the kitchen.

"Not sure what to say. Not really sure what happened. One minute I'm walking to the yard behind Hawkeye and the next I'm sitting with Newton bleeding on everything." Carson paused as he steadied himself at the edge of the table. "I remember throwing a few punches at the bag, but I hadn't gone there to work out or anything. I was still in my street clothes. I threw a few jabs, and a couple of roundhouses. I think they were roundhouses. I felt a little sting in my hands and that felt good and it fed on itself. A wave of pain washed through me, then another. The pain felt good. I can't explain it, but it felt good. And the better it felt, the harder I hit the bag, and the harder I hit the bag the better it felt. And so on, and so on."

"So how do you feel now?" Fred said as he pulled out two kitchen chairs.

"Not sure …to be honest. It's bizarre. I'm having trouble wrapping my head around her not being here anymore. I didn't even feel this way when my folks were killed. She was just there, or I should say here, for so long. She was an anomaly

291

my entire life and I was just getting to know her. Now she's gone. After all these years I was finally learning about her history. It's surreal." Carson grimaced, as he lowered himself into the wooden chair.

"How are things at Hawkeye?'

"Pretty good. I've got great people all across the board. It runs like a well-oiled machine. There's days I feel like I'm in the way."

"You up for a little project, maybe something to get your mind focused?"

Carson held up his bandaged hands and said, "You're shitting me, right?"

"Nah, it's simple assignment. I'll drive."

"What do you have in mind? Carson asked.

"A little house hunting. We need to find a new place for the Kestrels, in Utica. Some place nice, but not over the top. The little one is gonna start college in the fall and Momma Bird is getting pretty tight with Dr. Maarsten. She might even go back to school, maybe nursing. I was thinking if you wanted to take a trip you might be able to find the perfect place. If you're not up to it, I can have the people in Housekeeping find a place."

"You know they'll screw it up," Carson said with little emotion. He was referring to the folks in Housekeeping.

Fred grinned. "Exactly why I called. You've spent time with the Kestrels and have the best idea of what would suit them and still be safe. What do you think?"

"Yeah. I'm game."

"Great, let's go."

"Now?"

"Yeah now! Unless it's gonna conflict with your needlework class?"

"Jesus, you're a piece of work. No compassion, none." Carson said sarcastically.

"Yeah, they call me Heartless Fred."

"Can I at least get dressed?"

"Throw some sweats on, you got 10 minutes. We're burning daylight."

Carson looked out the window and saw the sun had crested the neighboring houses. Fred was right. "Okay" he said as he walked toward the bedroom. "And don't drink my coffee."

PARABELLUM: When you live in Peace, prepare for War

Jack Nanuq

CHAPTER 49
Herkimer, NY
June 9, 2001

The Durango made a pleasant sound as it hummed westward on the NY State Thruway. They were about an hour into their trip when they passed Canajoharie, the giant sign for Beechnut Foods, looming in the mist. Fred turned on the windshield wipers as the rain started. "I think we picked up some company" he mentioned nonchalantly.

"Yeah, I see them. A dark motorcycle and a blue Jeep Wrangler, soft-top I think" Carson responded. "How do you want to play it?" he continued.

"Let me ponder this a bit," Fred mimicked an old western movie star.

"Okay, while your feeble brain works on this quandary, I'm gonna make a call." Carson then pulled his phone from its holster. He scrolled through the directory and found Jan Krueger's number. His swollen index finger poked at the highlighted box.

"Hello," a cautious voice answered on the second ring.

"Good morning sir. Do you know who this is?"

"Yah, how can I help you?"

"I have a question, maybe a few questions"

"Go ahead," Krueger said in a business-like tone.

"Any chance you've got a couple of people following me?"

Krueger sighed. "No, my people are in your neighborhood. I told you we would not interfere. Are you in danger? Should I send someone to you?" Krueger asked in concern.

"No, I've got it under control."

"Are you certain, I can send help. Just tell me where you are?" The concern evident in his voice.

"No, I'm good and have adequate help. Thanks for your time. Wait...one more question. Have your people seen any suspicious vehicles, near my house?"

"Are you sure you don't need help?"

"No, please... just answer the question."

"As a matter of fact, there was a motorcycle; a black Kawasaki. It cruised through the neighborhood a few times this morning. The number plate was covered by a backpack. I've encouraged my people to make contact if he returns. But we haven't seen him in over an hour."

"Any chance they saw a blue Jeep?"

"No, no Jeeps. Are you sure you don't need help?"

"No, we're good, thank you." Carson folded his phone closed and turned to Fred. "Those aren't friendlies behind us."

"I gathered that. Fred responded. "I've got plan. I'm gonna get off at Herkimer."

"And?" Carson asked.

"How do you feel about being bait?"

∞

Forty minutes later they pulled into the parking lot of the Herkimer Wal-Mart. The rain was steady and most of the cars were parked near the store. No one loitered in the area. The few customers in the lot were moving about with their heads down. Fred stopped in a spot toward the far end of the lot. He parked in such a way that he occupied four spaces. There were at least 10 spaces between the Durango and the closest car.

Fred watched as the Jeep stopped about four rows behind them. The motorcycle parked in a shopping cart corral. The corral had a small roof and offered some protection from the elements. Fred then turned to Carson. "Are you armed?"

For the second time in a day Carson held up his bandaged hands. "You're shitting me, right? You kind of rushed me...and besides". He wiggled his stiff fingers.

Fred reached under the seat and pulled out a weapon. "Here take this."

"Oooh, I like it," Carson said as he caressed his newest possession.

"Yeah, thought you would. The Galcoes like to work up close and personal. This is perfect for that."

"Got that right."

296

"Now climb in the back seat and stay put."

"What?"

"Climb in back, the tinted windows will hide you. Play possum and that might draw them in. I'm gonna walk toward the store and then circle around behind them. I'm not sure how this will play out so stay on your toes."

Carson moaned and whined as he squeezed between the bucket seats. "I'm getting too old for this shit."

"Aren't we all. Now get comfy and stay put. I'll adjust the mirrors, so you can watch your six, let me know when I get them right," Fred said as he reached for the button on the driver's door. "I think I can get the Jeep in the mirrors but not sure about the bike."

For the next few seconds the only sound was the whir of the small motors and the rain hitting the roof. "How's that?" Fred asked, as he craned his neck toward Carson.

"The passenger side needs to move more to the right... perfect." Carson said as he situated the weapon in his lap.

"Okay, now sit tight, play dead and maybe you won't end up that way." Fred chuckled.

"Very reassuring, thanks," Carson said sarcastically.

Fred turned his head and said "Wait...the guy on the bike is moving toward the Jeep."

Carson moved slightly and said "Yeah, I see him. It's a bit fuzzy with the water on the mirrors, but I see him."

"Okay, we'll stay with the same plan and see what happens. Sit tight, and I'll circle around. Don't worry, I got your back." At this Fred reached behind the driver's seat, collected his Carhartt jacket and exited the SUV. He threw the coat over his head not so much to protect himself from the elements but to hide his face from the parking lot cameras.

Carson tracked Fred as he walked toward the store but his main focus was on the mirrors and the Galcoes. As Fred closed in on the store, he stepped behind a transit bus that stopped in the fire lane. Carson then saw the man with the motorcycle helmet start walking toward the Durango. The driver of the Jeep stayed inside.

PARABELLUM: When you live in Peace, prepare for War
Jack Nanuq

 Mr. Helmet walked nonchalantly toward the Durango. To do so otherwise would have brought attention to himself. In this weather he couldn't linger anywhere, and he couldn't run toward the SUV. Carson pressed his back into the seat and made sure his upper body lined up with the headrest. He was pretty sure the Galco couldn't see him. The heavy tint on the windows was commonly referred to as limo tint. In spite of this Carson wasn't going to silhouette himself.

 The black helmet moved toward the Durango, about 50 feet and closing. The Galco had slowed slightly; not readily apparent to the average person but clear to Carson.

 Forty feet, then 35, then 30, then 20, then he was within a car length. His pace even slower now. His steps purposeful and cautious. Carson saw the man home in on the passenger side mirror. Even with the rain drops on the window and mirror Carson could clearly see the Galco. By his expression Carson could tell the bad guy was handicapped, by the tinted window. *What a great advantage. I can see him but he can't see me.*

 The Galco moved up the rear of the SUV. He stopped and tested the back hatch, just like a police officer would. The vehicle was locked and the door held firm. The Galco turned his head side to side. Carson glanced into the driver's mirror as the Galco was now blocking the other. Fred was moving on the Jeep in a manner similar to the way this Galco had moved on Carson.

 This might just work. Carson thought. He again caressed the weapon in his lap. "Closer, closer, closer" he whispered as the Galco took a half step, then another, then he cupped his hands around his face and lowered his head to the rear passenger window.

 As the Galco pressed his hands to the window three things happened simultaneously. First, the glass exploded outwardly like Mount Saint Helens on Mother's Day 1980. Next the tip of the Galco's right pinky finger popped like an overripe pimple. Third, and most importantly the Galco's right eye socket shattered in a starburst pattern. The 24-ounce framing hammer, Carson had been holding, connected with over a ton of force. The impact overwhelmed the neuro pathways and the body fell backwards.

As he burst from the backseat, he heard a small pop in the distance. The door barely cleared the body. Carson needed to make sure the assailant was down for the count. He drove his size 11 Nike into the opponent's crotch. No response, not even a groan. With the man down, he loosened his grip on the hammer.

He looked around. If confronted by anyone he was ready to say the Galco had tried to break into his car, but no one was around, and no one took notice. He glanced toward the Jeep and saw Fred moving his way, in a hurry, with the Carhartt jacket held at his waist. Fred closed the distance in no time and said, "Let's go." Carson didn't need to be told a second time and climbed into the front passenger seat as Fred clicked the key fob.

Fred pulled away slowly, so as not to draw attention. Carson scanned the lot and saw the Jeep move forward in a lurch. A passerby might think the driver was drunk. As they left the lot Carson saw it stop near the fallen Galco. He lost sight of the vehicle as Fred turned onto Route 5.

"Where are we going?" Carson asked as he threw the hammer to his feet.

"Back home, I want to get this," Fred pointed at the dashboard, "indoors and out of view as soon as possible. Looks like we'll have to get to Utica another day. Keep an out for the cops and get Maggie on the phone."

The SUV continued eastbound and Carson added "the Thruway's the other direction."

"Yeah, I know but I want to stay on the backroads. I don't want to get trapped on the interstate if the cops are looking for us."

"Got it, ...I should have thought of that." Carson said, as he hit the button for Maggie.

As the phone rang Carson handed it to Fred.

Carson heard Maggie's muted voice say "Hello".

"We've had a code 13, with two down in Herkimer" Fred said curtly.

"Are you injured?" Carson heard.

"You hurt?" Fred asked, as he turned to Carson.

"No."

"That's a negative." Fred squeezed the phone between his ear and shoulder. Carson could no longer hear Maggie.

"They were Galcoes, both are down. One with a bullet in the hand and the other...well...well the other's down also."

Carson envisioned the now hectic activity in the Cube. Maggie would be snapping her fingers and pantomiming her desires. The commo people would be tuning into the radio frequencies of the Herkimer Police department, Sheriff's department and even the State Troopers. When the staff and Maggie got a clearer picture of what happened someone would call the PD and pretend to be a reporter. The Cube could never have enough information.

"We're are headed back to Albany. We're on Route 5, eastbound, about 15 miles, maybe less from St Johnsville. That noise? That's an open or should I say missing window. No... I repeat we're not hurt." Fred then turned his head slightly to Carson and said, "She wants to talk to you."

"Ma'am?" Carson said cautiously.

"You okay?" she asked.

"Yeah, same with Fred."

"Can you tell me what happened in 10 seconds or less?"

"Yeah, two bad guys followed us to Herkimer. We then suckered them into an ambush. I left one in a parking lot and the other is wounded in a blue Jeep. I'm not sure if we should pass that info to the locals. That's your call."

"What's your ETA?"

"About 90 minutes, maybe less."

"Can you drive? Is anyone following you?"

"No...I don't know where the Jeep is but it's definitely not behind us. And no one else is either."

"Was that no, you can't drive?"

"No ma'am, I mean yes ma'am. I can drive."

"Good, tell Fred I want you to stop somewhere and switch. And take his gun. You're both on an adrenaline high.

You maybe less than Fred. If he shot someone, I don't think he should drive. He'll understand."

Fred must have heard this as he nodded his head in acknowledgement.

"And don't stop anywhere else unless you need gas. Get back as soon as you can, without drawing any more attention to yourself. I gotta call Angie and tell her to ditch her Durango. I don't want her caught unawares. Call me if you get into any trouble. If I don't hear from you, I'll assume you're on the way."

"Copy that," Carson said and then pointed to an upcoming gas station.

Fred nodded his headed and signaled to turn into the lot.

"One last thing, ...be careful."

"Yes ma'am, over"

"Over, out."

Fred pulled up to the pumps. "I'll go inside and pay, you fill it up. Stay close to the car and keep your head down... I don't want anyone to see your swollen face or bandages."

"Got it." Carson replied.

With Carson now behind the wheel Fred was able to examine his jacket. "Son of a bitch, I liked this coat!" He said as he poked a finger through a bullet hole in the sleeve. The edges of the hole were frayed and cottony like an overripe cattail seed pod.

"I don't think you can flash that thing at me." Carson said jokingly, as he turned to Fred.

"You wish...your just jealous. Wish yours was this big." Fred said as he pulled the index finger from the hole. It was quickly replaced by his middle finger.

"So what happened to the jacket and what happened at the Jeep?"

"I had to use the sleeve as a poor man's silencer. I moved up on the passenger side of the Jeep. The Galco was staring at your position. His situational awareness sucked. When your window blew out, I told him to freeze. I had my Glock in the sleeve and he must have thought it was an empty threat. He made a move and I shot him in the hand. That changed his priorities right quick. What do the cops call it? 'Pain compliance'? When I was sure he wasn't a threat I hot-footed it to the Durango. How about your guy; did you kill him?"

"Not sure and don't care."

Fred slid his pistol from its holster, ejected the magazine and put both in the glove compartment. He then rolled his jacket into a pillow, and as he did this a spent casing rolled to the floor. "Sorry buddy, but the adrenaline's all gone. I feel like I've run a marathon. Can you wake me when we get near the Cube?"

"Copy that."

Carson's eyes flicked from one mirror to the other, to the other but he was now more relaxed. The rain had stopped, and the sun was now blazing. Steam rose from the pavement. Carson glanced at the thermometer on the dashboard; 79. Although his nose was swollen was able to take in a lung full of air. The air had that summer washed clean smell. To Carson it smelled of victory.

PARABELLUM: When you live in Peace, prepare for War
Jack Nanuq

CHAPTER 50
The Cube
Schenectady, NY
June 9, 2001

Maggie Post started "First things first." She turned to a grandmotherly type seated about halfway down the conference table. "Katy, we need to get all the Durangoes off the road. Call Fleet Services and trade them for something newer. Any color but white, maybe gray."

"Got it ma'am."

Maggie then turned to Fred, "You said you left yours in a storage shed near Erie Boulevard, get her the address."

"Right here," he said as he slid a yellow sticky note toward Katy.

"Is there anything in it I need to know about?" the woman asked.

"Not sure, you might want to spray some luminol in it. We collected the floor mats. They had some blood on them. We didn't see any spots anywhere else, but you might want to double check."

"Thanks," she said in a business-like tone. "If there's nothing else ma'am; I'll get on this right away." she said as she gathered up her notes.

"That's all for now. This is a real cluster. I want these guys gone," Maggie continued.

Both Carson and Fred misconstrued this and stood.

"Not you guys, I mean the Galcoes. Sit down!" she barked. "Bobby, what do we know from Herkimer?"

The man she turned to was a tall African American who wore Buddy Holly glasses. Bobby was their electronics and communications expert. He was also their resident marathoner; Boston, NYC, etc. He joked he was good at running because his ancestors had to be quicker than lions.

"Well...we know more than the cops. They're still scratching their heads. The call first came in as a hit-and-run.

A witness said a blue Jeep hit the man in the parking lot. Seems they saw the Jeep near the man down and put two and two together and got five. The driver of the Jeep left the scene, without ever getting out."

"Go on."

"The man in the parking lot was transported to St Luke's Hospital in Utica; something about a head wound."

"What about Fred and Mr. Lake here?" She used Carson's work name.

"That's where it gets good, but weird. Seems the cops then took a look at the video of the parking lot." He turned to Fred and Carson "You guys dodged a bullet there. The cops saw the Galco move on the Durango and you" he pointed at Carson "kick him". But the video is fuzzy due to the rain. All they know is they are looking for two white guys, in a white Durango."

"No plate info?" Fred asked.

"No, the cameras couldn't see much and no one on the ground saw anything. I called personally; said I was from the Mountain Gazette. The desk officer was a real chatterbox. Said they didn't know anything about the white Durango until they looked at the video. They're not sure what happened but kind of think it was maybe a drug deal gone wrong."

"What about the guy on the ground?" Carson asked.

"They've got him id'd as an Aaron Sanchez, with a Missouri driver's license, but it's fake. So, they're not sure of his name. Last I knew he was in surgery. No clue on the other guy; he never got out of the Jeep. They think the license plate is from Pennsylvania, but they're not even sure of that. They're basing that on the color of the plate but it's just a guess, on their part."

"Anything else?" Maggie asked.

"Not at this time ma'am."

"Okay, call them again in about four hours and see if there's more."

"Copy that, ma'am. Permission to leave?"

"Yeah, thanks, and…good work."

Aside from Carson and Fred there were now four other people in the room. One of which was their in-house counsel.

Turning to this man Maggie asked "Mark, where do we stand on this?"

Mark ran a hand through his wild gray hair. Hair that gave him an Einstein look.

"Unfortunately, we're in a gray area. Based upon the totality of the circumstances Mr. Lake can argue self-defense. But...but I don't think we want to sell that argument to the local District Attorney. We'd have to give out too much info, to get them to buy in. If push comes to shove then we'll take that route, but I think we should let things play out. If the locals think it was a drug deal, they may not push too hard."

"And if they do push too hard. Wait...don't answer that. I'm just thinking out loud," Maggie said.

"If we're just thinking out loud...then we could always have Bobby put a worm in their computer and erase the files. Just a thought."

"Let's not go there...at least not now."

"Understood," the lawyer said.

Maggie turned to Carson. "Now...let's start at the beginning. I want to know everything. About these Galcoes and how they came to fuck up my op. And I don't just mean today. I want to know everything you know. Everything mister!"

Carson spent the next 20 minutes telling everything. From Nana's gun, to what he knew about the death of a Gestapo agent, to the Trooper visit, to the Galco visit, to Nana's death. "And then I got a visit from Interpol."

"Interpol. Jesus, why is Interpol involved? No wait, not why, but how?"

Then he spent another thirty minutes telling the story of his grandfather, the War, and how Jan Krueger came to be named after Janos "and as a hobby his group hunts Galcoes."

"Do they know you work for this office?"

Sheepishly Carson answered "Not sure. He made a reference to me 'having resources' but that could just mean employees at Hawkeye."

"This day just keeps getting better and better. I take it you have a way to contact him."

"Yes ma'am. Would you like a meeting?"

"A meeting, a meeting, do you mean he's still here?"

"I think so, he has people parked near my house."

With exasperation Maggie said "Okay, see if he'll meet with us. If you can make it happen, we'll go as a group, and until then you are to stay here at the Cube. Do I make myself clear?"

"Yes ma'am."

"Okay then... I got to call Langley. And Mr. Lake...one last thing..."

"Ma'am?"

"Thanks for not getting killed. We'd really miss you around here."

"Thank you, ma'am."

"You guys..." Maggie turned to the last three men. They could all be mistaken for prize fighters. "You stay on him. He's to stay indoors until our meeting and then you will be on him like stink on shit. Understood?"

"Understood" they said in unison.

"What did I say? she added.

"Like stink on shit?" they again said simultaneously.

∞

At one p.m. Carson found himself seated at a table in the banquet room of <u>20-Pho-7.</u> Now Herr Krueger was giving Maggie a crash course on the Galco Organization.

"Around 1955 was the first time anyone heard the term Galco. It's believed to be a group of former SS troopers and officers. Some still had a blood lust and needed a way to make a living. So they became hired guns. High dollar hired guns. Most of the original members are long dead and what we have now is their offspring and grandchildren. For about 20 years no one could confirm their existence. They were good, think of them as Nazi Ninjas. Their preferred weapon is a poison tainted knife. Sometimes they would leave the knife at the scene, and if they did that was the only evidence. In 1974, we got a break."

"What kind of break?" Maggie asked.

"However, in 1974 a rabbi was killed in his apartment. Not too far from here...in New Paltz."

"Does the rabbi have a name?"

"I'll get it later, but it doesn't matter to this story. As the assassin is leaving the building he trips on a cat. Falls down the stairs, breaks his neck and dies. When they examine the body, they find a knife and the greyhound tattoo."

"A cat, really, a cat?" Maggie commented.

"Yes, it happens to the best of us."

"What?" one of the body guards said.

"Sometimes, life just gets in the way." Krueger continued. "My first wife used to say, 'God does not like ugly'. I think that applies here. From the body, the knife and some documents they tracked him backward to Buenos Aires. The killer owned a travel agency there."

"What else do you know?" Maggie asked.

"Mostly that they are tenacious and patient. In the case I described, that killer took a flight from Buenos Aires, to Mexico City, to Los Angeles to Buffalo. Then he took a bus to New Paltz, then stole a car and drove to the victim's neighborhood. This seems to be their...how do you Americans say it? Their MO, they operate the same way in Europe."

"And they always use a knife?" Fred asked.

"Almost always. A poisoned tip knife is preferred, followed by just poison. Some victims have been shot, but that is rare. They like to keep a low profile. That's why they travel by bus. No one pays any attention...to someone on a bus. To stay under the radar, so to speak. But..."

"But what?" Maggie asked

"Based on what you told me, I think they will come gunning next time. Today was the second attempt, there will be a third."

"Great. You got any good news?" she asked rhetorically.

"It will be up close and personal."

"What?" Carson asked

"To our knowledge they have never used a sniper. They know that, unlike the movies, too many things can go wrong. And they don't use bombs. That draws too much attention, there is too much evidence." Krueger sipped a spoonful of broth.

"How is this good news?" asked one of Carson's bodyguards.

No one answered him, and they let him think about it.

In about 10 seconds he said, "Forget I asked that...I see. Up close and personal." He slapped his forehead, like a V-8 commercial. "They have to get through us," he pointed at the security team.

Krueger cleared his throat. "Madam, I would like to ask a favor." Krueger said and then continued "I have a sketch artist that would like to sit down with this man here," he pointed to Fred. "We would like some information concerning the one that got away."

PARABELLUM: When you live in Peace, prepare for War

Jack Nanuq

CHAPTER 51
Fort Drum
Watertown, NY
June 13, 2001

Carson woke to the sound of a muffled radio transmission. For a moment he couldn't place his surroundings. There was a digital clock on the opposite side of the room, not next to the bed like at his home. The time was 4:02; of course, it was. He tried to stretch out but there was a lump in the bed. Liza, it was Liza; of course, it was. He remembered he was at Polaris. Maggie Post's codename for Fort Drum. To ensure mission integrity he and the Kestrels had been moved to Polaris. He was now bunking in guest quarters on the base. A lot had happened in the days since he had been exiled to this location.

First, had been the long trip here. Fred drove him north to Lake Placid, then Malone, then west along the Saint Lawrence River. Using the backroads, it had taken more than eight hours to get here. Carson joked that Daniel Boone could have crossed the State faster.

Then Liza surprised him with a visit. Liza explained Maggie had reached out to her and suggested the visit. This was for Carson's mental health, after all he'd been through. Maggie explained this was conditional to not discussing why Carson was at Polaris. Any discussion of sensitive material would have serious consequences. Liza, the former CIA analyst, understood the need for compartmentalization and agreed willingly.

As he lay in bed his attention was divided between Liza's breathing and the radio transmission that woke him. He was sure it was his security detail but the events of the past few days had him rattled. He ran a still bruised finger down Liza's back and was rewarded with a kitteny "mmmmmmmmmmmm." He wished he was running his finger along her bare skin instead of the cotton t-shirt. But he had a rule. After sex they got dressed. Not completely dressed but t-shirt and shorts at least; a safety precaution. He explained that in the event they had to bug-out or god forbid get in a firefight you didn't want to do it buck naked.

He took a few more breaths and contemplated his situation. They were now staying in the safest place, this side of the White House. Matter-of-fact they were probably safer; as the White House staff always had to worry about getting stabbed in the back. The bungalow they were in sat on a cul-de-sac. Across the street was an identical structure that housed Hana, her mom, and Angie. The remaining houses were all vacant at this time. A chain-link fence and numerous sensors surrounded the neighborhood, while at the opposite end of the street was a guard post, manned 24-7. Two military police officers were also stationed in the front yard.

Carson leaned over and kissed the top of Liza's head as he slid from the bed. As his feet touched the floor he was startled by a burble, bubbling sound. After his heartrate returned to normal, he realized it was just the coffeemaker. Liza must have set it. After his shower he would take some coffee out to the security detail.

"Good morning Mr. Lake," snapped one of the MPs, as Carson stepped out the front door. He had flashed the porch light twice to give them a heads up. "Good morning…," Carson took a moment to read the name on his uniform. The man stood just at the edge of the cone thrown by the porch light.

"Mornin…Frazier is it?"

"Correct sir."

Carson took in the other MP. She was standing about 12 feet to the left and in the shadows. He couldn't read her name tag or see many of her features, in the low light conditions. *She's good* he thought, *using the dark to her advantage.* He immediately flashed back to the moment he was hiding in the back of the Durango.

"What?" he said, bringing himself back to the here and now.

"I said…do you have authorization to wear that?"

He padded the zippered sweatshirt that read ARMY. "This, yeah, I do."

"Not that... that!" With her left hand she pointed to the bulge above his right hip. Her right hand was wrapped around the pistol grip of an M-16. The barrel was down but she was ready for action.

Without thinking Carson slid his hand toward his Glock.

"Don't!" she barked.

"Easy Martinez...he's cool," said Frazier.

"Says you, how do I know that? All I know is we're here to guard them. Why do we have to...if he's packing? They don't tell us shit, it's all need-to-know crap. I'm tired of it. Last month it was the ragheads and before that the fat Russian bastard."

"It's cool, I'm telling you it's cool. He's one of us or used to be at least."

"It's alright...she's just doing her job. Makes me feel a lot better, actually. Can I make a peace offering?" Carson said as he held out a thermos and bag of Styrofoam cups.

"Are we good?" Frazier said to Martinez.

"We're good...thank you sir. Sorry about that."

"We're good," Carson said, as Frazier took the peace offering. "I heard some radio chatter earlier."

"Did it wake you?" Martinez asked with alarm.

"No, I'm up at four, every morning. Was just wondering if there's anything I need to know?"

Before anyone could respond they, all heard a Chevy Suburban moving down the street.

"Speak of the devil...here comes the boss," said Frazier.

The man that stepped from the SUV was squared away. He had spit and polish on his spit and polish. He wore the chevron of a First Sergeant and both MPs stood at attention. Even Carson stood erect with his hands at his sides. Old habits never die.

"As you were!" he commanded.

All three relaxed.

"Mr. Lake, I didn't expect to find you up so early."

"I was just telling them...I'm up at four every day. Rain or shine, summer or winter."

"Good to know, since you're up, can we talk in private?"

"I... I have a guest... First Sergeant." Carson said, like a college kid that had just been caught with a girl in his dorm room.

"Yes, I know. Liza Carbon...maybe we can talk in my vehicle?"

"Yes, First Sergeant."

The man turned to his MPs. "Anything to report?"

"No First Sergeant!" they said in unison.

He then looked at Martinez. "Anything to report?"

She glanced at the bulge on Carson's hip.

"No First Sergeant."

"Very well, carry on. Mr. Lake, this way."

∞

At 7:55 a.m. Carson knocked gently on the front door of the bungalow directly across the street from his. He could hear the women moving around inside. Angie Rodriguez shouted "Coming".

"No hurry, it's just me." Carson said to the closed door. He listened as two deadbolts and a crash bar were moved out of place.

As Angie opened the door Carson said "Transport to the test range will be here in an hour. Will everyone be ready?" He then looked down as the cat brushed against his leg. "Jesus, what are you feeding her? Moose meat? She's gotten fat since I last saw her."

"Come in and don't let her out. One of the MPs is allergic." Angie continued.

Carson used a foot to corral the animal and shut the door behind him.

"Sally's in the shower but the little one has been up since six. Like a kid on Christmas morning. I really hope this goes well."

"Good morning Mr. Lake," Hana shouted from the kitchen. "You want breakfast, we've got pancakes?"

The small house had that malty smell of batter frying in butter. He could almost picture the little bubbles rising to the top.

"Nah, I got to get back across the street," he turned to Angie "I Just wanted to make sure everyone will be ready. The MPs run a tight ship."

As he exited, he saw a pewter-gray Durango, headed in his direction. *It has to be Fred,* he thought.

The SUV circled the cul-de-sac and he saw Maggie's profile in the passenger seat. . The Durango parked in front of his bungalow, facing the exit.

∞

The conversation took place in the street at the grille of the Durango. "Sounds like you want me to build a coffin," Carson said to Fred.

"Not exactly, or should I say not in the traditional sense." Maggie explained, "Since you're gonna be on base for an indeterminate length of time, I thought we'd put you to work."

"An indeterminate time frame! I got a business to run." Carson said, testily.

"Easy boy, what she means is we need you here for a while, maybe a week, maybe more. You can do that. Right?" Fred said.

"I'll be honest with you," Maggie continued. "We are working on getting to the source of the Galcoes. Herr Krueger has been invaluable; his office has tons of info. Plus your notes from your time in the blue room." She held made air quotes as she said blue room. We are going to find the head of the group and tell them you are off-limits, then we will nuke their HQ. I have the full blessing of Langley. No one will lose sleep over their departure. But until then I need you here. I know you can run your business from here. But we also have a project for you."

"What'd you have in mind?" he said, resigned to his fate.

Fred explained "The Parabellum project is moving right along, better than expected. The guys from Rock Island just delivered some prototypes. Today we're doing speed tests. Hana will get to see this thing in action. The completed package even has its own codename; Marlin."

"Like the fish or the person?" Carson asked.

"The fish" interjected Maggie "This year the computer is using fish species for codenames. Last year it was birds, and this year it's fish. It wasn't the first choice; the first codename was tuna. But I wasn't gonna be known as the Tuna Lady if this thing goes south."

"I like Marlin, and I see your point," Carson concurred.

"Anyway," Fred continued "they have a group of carpenters and engineers on base that build things. Things we can't buy on the open market. With the project moving along at breakneck speed we are gonna need some ammo crates."

"And you want me to supervise them?" Carson asked.

"Not exactly, seems most of them are working off-base on some other project. All hush-hush and above my pay grade. No idea when they will be back. So, we need you to build the crates."

"Can you manage?" Maggie asked while glancing at his wrapped hands.

"Yeah, I guess so. The bandages are more for show, just to hold the salve and ointment in place. The hands are still a little stiff, but some work will help limber them up. I'm game."

"Great, now go tell Liza you'll be back at five. Then I'll introduce you to Clyde," said Fred.

∞

Carson was dropped off in front of the bungalow at 5:03 PM. Liza sitting on the front porch. The MPs on the lawn moved across the street to give them some privacy. "What are you doing?" he asked.

"I'm smoking a pipe. What's it look like?"

"You don't smoke?"

"I thought you said I was smokin hot?"

"There's that, but I mean a pipe...a pipe?"

316

"I came out this morning and found Martinez smoking and it reminded me of my dad. He used to smoke. And...and he used to let me share his pipe. So yes, I do smoke...its rare, but yes."

"Martinez? ...Martinez the lady cop? She smokes a pipe? Wow!"

"Be careful what you say about my new friend. She and I are thick as thieves now. She even invited me out to a ladies night tomorrow. I hear... she almost shot you this morning." Chuckled Liza.

"It was nothing." He almost wanted to mimic Nana "Iz nudding," but didn't. "She's just, she's just ... a little ..."

"Control freak."

"Your words, not mine. The First Sergeant gave me a little background on her. Seems she served a tour in Kosovo and was a K-9 handler there. About a week before she was to come home the dog died. And she's still grieving."

"Died? How? Was there an investigation?"

"Of course, there was an investigation, this is the Army. Seems the dog's heart just quit one night. Anyway, she blames herself, even though it wasn't anyone's fault. Just one of those things. He said she's wrapped a little tight and sometimes over reacts. He kinda said to just be careful around her."

"Good to know," Liza said. "Enough about her tell me about your day. You know you're covered in sawdust, right?"

Carson brushed at his clothes, self-consciously. "Yeah, my day was weird, but in a good way. First, I got to tell you about the guy that runs the workshop; Clyde. He's an odd duck. Long arms, short legs, barrel chest and stringy red hair."

"Sounds like an orangutan, not a duck."

"My thoughts exactly. All day long I kept thinking about that old Clint Eastwood movie, <u>Every Which Way but Loose</u>."

"The one where he has an orangutan as a sidekick. Clyde...Right?"

"Bingo."

"So is it his given name or a nickname?" she asked.

317

"I couldn't bring myself to ask. He's another control freak; very exacting. He's got me building some ammo crates, this is kinda hush hush."

"Mum's the word," she said as she made a locking motion over her lips.

"So I'd spent thirty or so minutes building each crate to exact dimensions. Everything had to be perfect, even how the stencils were applied. Then I'd hand it over to him and he'd beat the crap out it with a chain and sprinkle it with coal dust and used motor oil. Was like some deranged priest doing a blessing."

"He was aging it? Wasn't he?"

Carson ran his fingers through his hair. Sawdust fell like snow. "Gold star for you. It took me awhile to figure it out. I was really confused when he dressed some of the boxes with kimchi. Said he wanted to give it an authentic aroma."

"Did it have a North, or a South flavor?"

Carson cupped his hand around his mouth and mumbled "North, but don't tell anyone."

She repeated the earlier gesture of buttoning her lip. "Come inside, I have a surprise for you." She stood and tapped the pipe on the porch rail.

Carson watched the tobacco ash fall into a flower bed.

"Another surprise, now what?" he said as he followed her into the house.

"I've been cooking."

"You don't cook, wait…what's gotten into you lady? Who are you and what have you done with my Liza?"

"Well, I was kinda feeling nostalgic. No, that's not right, I was kinda bored. Not exactly bored either. I've been going through Nana's notes. "Seems her first meal with Petr was seal meat and greens."

"We're having seal?"

"No, the PX was fresh out so I had to settle for a roast. But I did make a wild green salad, it has dandelions in it. And I tried my hand at pierogis."

They walked into the kitchen and Carson immediately noticed it looked like a bomb had gone off. Mixing bowls were piled in the sink, spoons and measuring cups lay strewn along the counter top and everything seemed to be dusted with flour and greenery.

Carson was almost speechless. "I...I...I've never had dandelions," was all he could say.

CHAPTER 52
Fort Drum
Watertown, NY
June 20, 2001

Liza and Carson were sharing a shower when she grabbed him by the middle and said, "I found a love handle, where did that come from?"

"It's all the pierogis you've been feeding me."

"Not the cheesecakes?"

"Well, yeah...those too. How'd you know cheesecake was my favorite vegetable. You've become quite the Julia Childs, in a week."

"Silly rabbit. Cheesecake is everyone's favorite vegetable. Enjoy it while it lasts. I've got to get back home, in a few days."

"What...What's up, anything I should know about?"

"Ya mean like my other boyfriend? No, ...but I am scheduled to teach a summer school class after the Fourth. I need a few days to prepare."

"Do you have another boyfriend?" Carson asked; emphasis on the word have. He hoped for a no.

"Don't be silly, unless you count my sons. They're gonna forget what their mother looks like."

A knock on the front door interrupted their conversation.

"Damnit," they said in unison.

"Will they go away, if we ignore them?" Liza asked.

"No, just the opposite. They'll probably kick the door in."

"Then you better answer it. Promise me, you'll put some clothes on first," Liza said with a twinkle in her eye.

"Do I gotta?" Carson whined theatrically.

"Yes, you gotta," drawing out the word gotta. She gave a him a look like she was admonishing a child. And then added, "I'll start breakfast."

MP Martinez was at the door when Carson opened it. "Sir, I need you to accompany me to the guard shack. You have a phone call. ASAP sir."

Carson instinctively patted his pockets for his cell phone. He was still getting used to the fact that no electronic devices could pass the check point. "Thank you, Martinez."

"This way sir," as she pointed to the Humvee parked in front of the house.

Thirty seconds later he was escorted into the guard shack. A female MP he had never seen before, handed him a sealed envelope. "The number's in that. Sir, please use the secure phone." She pointed him to a glass booth at the far end of the shack.

As he stepped into the booth, he tore open the envelope and recognized Fred's number. The booth had a musty smell and a few dust bunnies were hiding in the corners.

"Mornin sunshine," Fred said, as he answered the phone.

"This had better be good." Carson hit back.

"It is. You sitting down." Fred asked excitedly.

As if it was an order Carson took a seat in a standard issue gray steel and vinyl office chair. "I am now, what do you got?"

"It's what we've got. We've got the Jeep. The Galco Jeep."

"Really, where? Was the Galco in it?"

"Nope, no Galco, just the Jeep, but we do have part of his trail."

"Start from the beginning," Carson said.

"Okay, the Jeep was found at the bingo hall on the Akwesasne Reservation," Fred continued.

"The Akwa who?" Carson asked.

"The Akwesasne Mohawk reservation, you might know it as St Regis. It sits on the St Lawrence River. We drove through it on our way to Watertown. The Jeep was found abandoned at the bingo hall. No sign of the Galco, but we've people up there checking on things."

"Why do you think he left it there?" Carson asked. The bewilderment clear in his voice.

"There's a possibility he crossed into Canada."

"What, how?"

Fred continued "The reservation sits on both sides of the river. Half in the US and half in Canada. There's an old treaty that lets the Mohawks cross from one side to another, without going through Customs. That and some Sovereign Nation bullshit I don't understand means it's a smugglers paradise. You name it. Cigarettes, booze, drugs, guns and people move freely across the border. A few years back some Pakistanis drowned while coming south to the US but most people don't know about that. Most of the human traffickers move people North to South but with the right connections someone could easily do the reverse. That's what we think happened here. But as I said we're checking on it."

"I had no idea. You don't think about smuggling on the Canadian border. The Mexican border yes. I see that but Canada? I guess that makes sense." Carson said.

"Are you still sitting down?" Fred asked.

"Yeah, why?"

"We found a medical bracelet in the Jeep. He cleaned the Jeep pretty good, but this was stuck under the seat and he missed it. Our boy was hospitalized for a few days after the attack. Seems he got to a medical clinic in Syracuse. He told the Emergency Room staff a forklift crushed his hand. They should have known it was gunshot and reported it but the clinic is run by a group of anti-violence crusaders. They rarely call the police. Think they are doing the community a service by not involving the authorities. Anyway, our guy gets there and gets some help. They get him stabilized and drive him a few miles to St. Joseph's Hospital. By then all evidence of a gunshot is gone. Couple of days later he sneaks out of St. Joes. And a couple of days later they find the Jeep at St. Regis."

"Are we sure it's his Jeep?" Carson asked.

"We are now. Our guy on the ground, up there, sent me some photos. There's damage to the steering wheel about where

I shot him. It has Pennsylvania plates and a parking decal I remember."

"How'd they know it was the Jeep, no one had a plate number?"

"As much as I wish we could take credit for it I have to give it to a Tribal cop. He's a real straight shooter and top-notch investigator. He saw the Jeep had a busted side window and checked on it further. He matched it to the BOLO the Herkimer cops put out. He called them, and we knew about it right away. Our people got there before their people, but we kept a low profile."

"Where does this leave us?" Carson asked with the enthusiasm of a bird dog on a hunt.

"Easy boy. It leaves you right where you are. At least until we figure out whether or not the Galco went to Canada. We're working on it, I promise. By the way, the other Galco…"

"Yeah…" Carson replied.

"He's brain dead. Never regained consciousness. They're gonna pull him from life support. You okay with that?"

Why wouldn't I be?"

"Just checking…"

"I got a favor to ask." Carson hesitated for a second. His personal life and work life were getting too comingled.

"Shoot, name it, and I'll see if we can accommodate."

"Liza just told me she has to get back home in a few days. Any chance we could give her some protection? Maybe put someone in her math class?"

"Do you think it's necessary?" Fred asked.

"No, well I'm not sure. I might just be a Nervous Nelly. And I'm not sure if she be okay with an escort. Maybe just put someone close. I'll talk to her later."

"She lives in Baltimore, right? I might have just the guy. He's kind of cooling his heels at Annapolis. I'll see what I can do. Anything else?" Fred asked.

"No, that's more than enough. Keep me informed?" Carson said.

323

"We're cool, I got your back. How are the Kestrels?"

"Their doing good. I think Hana is having so much fun with the testing she's oblivious to everything else that's going on. Momma on the other hand is getting a little stir crazy, but she's used to be detained. She's got tricks to help maintain her sanity. She's been teaching Liza to cook and they use me as their Guinea pig."

"Oh, you poor boy, my heart bleeds for you," Fred teased "and how are things at the shop?"

"How much time do you have?" Carson chuckled. "Where did you find that nutcase Clyde? Yesterday he had me shredding potato chip bags, at least I think they were chip bags. Every time I asked why he said, 'Just do, no ask'. I felt like what's-his-name in that Karate Kid movie. Wax on, wax off, just do."

"Yeah, his communication skills are lacking but he knows what he's doing. He had you making pocket litter. Stuff they put in the shipping containers to give it a taste of authenticity. Just hang in there, big guy. It's for the greater good."

"You sure?" Carson sounded doubtful.

"No, but what choice do you have? I'll tell you what. I'll speak to Maggie about a day pass. Maybe you can take Liza out for a nice dinner, before she has to get home. How's that sound?"

"Sounds fair. What choice do I have?" Carson said with resignation.

"One last question before I go. Is that Mauser still in your desk, at the Cube?"

"Yeah, why?"

"I found some ammo for it. How about I bring it with me the next time I'm out there? We'll go to the pistol range."

"Sounds great, looking forward to it."

"Alright, I'll call you when I'm on my way or if I have some news. Take care."

"Take care," Carson replied.

∞

As Carson walked back to the bungalow he took in his surroundings. There were worse places to be sequestered. If you could look past the chain link fence the surroundings were idyllic. They were far enough away from everything that even the everyday noises of the base were muted. The yards were well maintained. Deer and turkey were often roamed in the area.

He looked at his watch; 6:15. About two hours before his ride to the shop. The morning sun was b ruining off the light ground fog. He couldn't remember if today was the first day of summer. Was that tomorrow? Either way the day was shaping up to be a beautiful one.

He'd have to let Liza know what was going on. But he wasn't sure how she would react to having a bodyguard. Well not exactly a bodyguard, maybe he could call it a shadow. Carson was pretty sure she would be safe at home. How could the Galcoes know about her? Better safe than sorry.

They still had a couple of days together and he vowed to make the most of them.

PARABELLUM: When you live in Peace, prepare for War

Jack Nanuq

CHAPTER 53
Fort Drum
Watertown, NY
July 4, 2001

Carson watched as the sky as it exploded with fireworks. If anyone knew how to celebrate Independence Day it was the military. There was no better place in the world to watch the display than on an Army base. And the crowd agreed, all 3,000 of them. He'd just read a news article where President Bush labeled the 10th Mountain Division was "Unfit for deployment". What did he know? They would deploy anywhere at any time and had done so for the past twenty years.

With each burst of color or bang the crowd oohed and aaaaahed. He, the Kestrels and their security escorts were seated in an open-air grandstand watching the festivities. The night was perfect, about 65 degrees, clear and dry. For a moment Carson forgot this was his third week of exile. The only way the night could have been any better if he could have spent it with Liza.

The day had been perfect also. He and Fred had spent the morning at the range, with Nana's pistol. That old Mauser shot well. Holding the broom handle grip properly took some getting used to, but he got the hang of it. of it. Each time he loaded a fresh clip of ten rounds he wished the gun could speak to him. He wished it could tell him what really happened on the night before D-day, or about its travels with Grandpa Jon, then known as Janos. Had it been with him in Poland, when a mortar shell blew Janos off his bike? Maybe it had been wounded when Janos was wounded.

In the afternoon he and Fred shared some beers as they listened to Nana's recordings. The stories were fascinating. Petr an Janos collecting honey, from the beehives in Calais. Janos with his first motorcycle, the Indian. Or cooking Hunter Stew, and it's primary ingredient. Boil twice and then deep fry.

The stories were fascinating, as well as frustrating. She would start one story and then veer into another, then another.

Then back to an earlier one. Even jotting notes and timelines on a legal pad was little help. Although she was gone the sound of her voice helped soothe some of his grief. He wished she had lived longer or started telling the stories at a younger age. There was so much more to know, and he had so many questions. He couldn't wait to share the stories with Liza. He smiled as he realized so many of the good things in his life now revolved around her.

His mind switched gears and he now thought about Hawkeye. He spoke to Stephanie every day and was glad to hear things were running smoothly. This was good as he never wanted to be indispensable. He wished he could take the credit, and some might rightly be deserved. But much of it was Nana's. She had a knack for putting the right person in the right job. Since Hawkeye didn't need his constant attention, he would think about moving to Baltimore, be closer to Liza. He could run the business remotely. The thought of this buoyed his spirits even higher. Yes, he would talk to her about this. Thinking of her reminded him he hadn't heard from her since noon. The last he knew she and some friends were driving to DC for the festivities. He reached for his phone; which he had access to now they were outside of the secure neighborhood. During the afternoon he had left her a couple of voicemails, but she had yet to return the calls. This wasn't like her but maybe she was caught up in all the fun.

At precisely that moment the phone buzzed. Before flipping it open, he looked at the display: LIZA.

"I was just thinking about you," the excitement clear in his voice.

"I doubt that," said a strange male voice. The voice had a Spanish accent and an evil tone.

"Who is this, where's Liza?" concerned and confusion now replaced the excitement.

"You know who this is. And…she is right here."

"If you've hurt her…" he couldn't finish the sentence.

"Of course, I hurt her. This is not some Disney movie. After I collected her, I needed some, how should I say...recreation. Yes, recreation, I like that word." Menace oozed from the phone.

"Put her on, god damnit, put her on the god damn phone!" Carson struggled to maintain his composure.

"Do I hear panic in your voice? Or maybe anger, or confusion?" the voice asked in a mocking tone. "If you are worried, that is good, that means I have your attention. I think I put her on the phone now."

Carth...,th...th...zun, Carthzun, hepp...happ me."

Carson's blood pressure hit a dangerous level. "Liza, Liza, babe, babe..." and he struggled to sound calm. He was failing miserably.

"Carthzun, hepp...happ me."

"I will babe, I will, I promise." He had no idea if he could live up to this promise. "I want to talk to the man; can he hear me?"

She made a grunt that he couldn't understand.

The man with the Spanish accent came back on the line. "I have your attention now, I think."

"You do but I don't think it's her" he lied. "I want proof. That could be anyone."

"Proof, you are stupid, of course it's her?"

"No, I want proof, how do I know that's her...that could be anyone?"

"Proof, maybe I should send her head to you? Maybe?"

Carson's brain screamed *"No!"* He paused and with a very deliberate tone said, "Ask her a question."

"Or what, will you hang up? I dare you. You Americans are so stupid. Maybe you play too much poker, this is no game. Why gamble with her?"

"Ask her a question. Ask her a question, so I know, I know without a doubt."

"I know you know but okay we play your game. What is your question?"

∞

As Carson closed the phone he felt like an ant. A small, useless, inconsequential ant. How could he hope to save Liza?

329

The Galco held all the cards. He even told him so. The Galco had taunted Carson by saying it didn't matter if he got Fred or other Agency people to help. The Galco would decide when and where they would meet. "I will come to you." the man said. Carson was sure those words would haunt him for the rest of his life.

Roman candles and mortars exploded above the grandstand, but they no held no appeal for him. He looked around and saw people staring at him; except Fred. Fred was on his phone. How could Fred be oblivious to his pain? His best friend in the world wasn't even looking at him.

Fred turned to him and Carson saw his face was ashen. As ashen as Carson felt. Something was wrong, and it wasn't just Liza.

"They've got her," said Fred somberly. "They killed my friend and took Liza. That was Maggie on the phone."

"I know, I know" Carson said as the full weight of it hit him.

"How, how do you know?" Fred asked, clearly concerned.

"I just got off the phone. He's got her, he's got her." Carson was starting to boil now. "He's got her god damnit, the bastard's got her. I need a car, I need a car." Carson stood so fast his head began to swim.

Fred grabbed Carson. "Slow down, slow down...I got you."

"The Galco's got her, I need a car, I need to get to her. Get me a car or for Christ sake's I'll steal one."

"Slow down, I said slow down and I mean it. The cops are on it. He killed my friend and left him in a parking lot. The cops are on it."

"The cops, the cops!" Carson said derisively. "These guys have been running around the world, killing people, for more half a century and never been caught. What do you think the locals can do? What the fuck can they do?"

"Hey, watch your mouth," shouted a woman from the crowd. The crowd around them was mostly comprised of women and children. The mothers pushed the children away as the men's voices rose.

Fred turned to the woman, "Sorry about that. We've got a situation."

"Okay, listen to me," Fred said, turning back to Carson. "We've got to get the girls to the bungalow, and then you can go." As Fred laid out a game plan he had to stop. The fireworks had reached the finale. The thunder, bangs and cheers from the crowd drowned out his voice.

The moment the fireworks stopped Fred took control of the situation. "Hana, Sally, Angie, let's go, let's go, we gotta move! Carson follow me!" There was no need to say this twice.

Ten minutes later Martinez was clearing a path through the traffic with her lights and siren. Another ten minutes and they were at the guard shack. Everyone, in the car, had put their phones into a plastic bag by the time they reached this spot. The bag was practically thrown at the MP on station.

Enroute to the bungalow Carson had tried to explain he couldn't afford this delay. Fred countered that Maggie insisted they get the Kestrels "Locked down and safe" before Carson could leave. Carson was out of his mind by the time they got to the cottage. "I've got to get home, I've got to get home. He only gave me four hours. I only have four hours!"

CHAPTER 54
Albany, NY
July 4, 2001

The drive home was excruciating. The night was full black, with not a star in the sky. What a change in just two hours. When he got past Syracuse, he turned eastbound on the Thruway and ran straight into heavy thunderstorms. The rain cascaded from the heavens in biblical proportions. A liquid blanket formed an opaque curtain on his windshield. The wipers flew left, right, left, right, left. Carson could only glimpse the roadway for about a second.

Water glazed the pavement and the truck was threatening to hydroplane. And he wasn't alone. Traffic around him was moving in erratic patterns with different drivers moving at different speeds. He skated from one lane to another like a downhill slalom racer. The rear of the truck slid from side to side. Any minute now Carson could find himself in a ditch or rollover. He forced himself to slow down. The speedometer read 79 MPH which incensed Carson as it felt like the truck was crawling. He kept looking at the clock on the dash. "Get your eyes back on the road," he screamed at himself. He looked up to see a kaleidoscope of red tail lights. He needed to slow down. "Slow the fuck down!" he screamed inside the cab. He grabbed the right leg of his jeans and pulled his foot off the gas pedal.

He looked at the clock and did the math. He had two hours and five minutes to cover more than 100 miles. He could do this, he had to do it. Fifty miles an hour and he would make it. Failure was not an option.

To help distract himself from the time constraint he thought about the question he had asked the Galco. He would never again eat cheesecake, ever. That was the question. What was his favorite vegetable? He sort of heard Liza's response but what he clearly heard was the Galco's anger. The man hadn't understood her answer and yelled for her to repeat it. He struck her, the sound of the slap coming clearly through the phone. "Are you playing with me?" he screamed.

Carson thought he was being cunning when he asked the question, but it backfired. Liza paid the price. He heard her cry out, "Thease, theease don't hit me anymo, anymo...theeease!" How could Carson have been so stupid? What had he been thinking? What the fuck had he been thinking?

The brake lights immediately in front of him flashed and he was forced to hit his own brakes. He stomped on them so hard he felt the anti-lock system chatter and the pedal stuttered under his foot. From the corner of his eye he saw his gear bag and shotgun slide off the seat and hit the floor. His right arm shot out and grabbed the cigar box, that held Nana's pistol. The truck came to a complete stop about a foot from the car in front. At least it looked like a foot through the curtain of water. He was trapped. A flat-bed semi was parked to his right and a tour bus parked to this left. Everyone was at a standstill.

Carson screamed again and then realized the screaming wasn't helping. While holding the cigar box to his chest he felt, not heard, but felt Nana say "Iz nudding." It hit him like Newton's command, so many weeks earlier, "Unfuck yourself!" A calm determination washed over him.

Now in a different frame of mind he thought about what he knew. Fred, enroute to the bungalow, laid out what he knew via Maggie Post.

Around 2:30 PM a woman called the local cops after she saw a stabbing and kidnapping. An unidentified White male, the cops described as the assailant, but Maggie knew was a Galco, jogged up behind Fred's friend. With Baltimore's proximity to the seat of power and so many military installations, joggers were as common as leaves on the trees. The friend, named George Sycamore, was talking to Liza and seemed oblivious to the jogger. They were on her college campus and standing between Liza's car and a Mercedes SUV. The boxy kind, that looked like a military jeep. The assailant side stepped behind George and stabbed him in the base of the skull. Liza was then hit and thrown into the Mercedes. Some grainy video backed up the reporting party's statements.

333

Maggie added that the assailant had hit Sycamore with so much force the knife was lodged in a vertebra. He had to leave it at the scene. "I bet it's covered in that tarry poison crap" she added.

The BOLO described the SUV as gray, or light blue, with Maryland plates, beginning with the letter G or possibly the number 6. The assailant was described as a White male, mid-thirties, with short, collar length, brown hair. Medium build and wearing a dark green, maybe black, track suit.

After leaving Fort Drum, Carson called Maggie directly. She told him she had people working on it. She promised to give him all the technical support she could but was sorry to say she could not provide him any personnel or equipment. There were legal constraints she couldn't bypass. She repeated she would do everything she could do, inside the law. She had people pinging Liza's phone. The call had been placed from a rural road near Lancaster, PA, moving in a northerly direction. She had passed this info to the FBI; kidnapping cases were their jurisdiction. Right now they couldn't locate the phone. Either the Galco had destroyed it or put it in a Faraday bag. She promised to call as soon as she heard anything.

After hanging up the phone he contemplated calling Investigator Matthews, with the State Police. No, not yet he decided, maybe later. But he did place a call to Herr Krueger.

"I am aware of your situation. Ms. Post has been in touch. We are working on it." Krueger told him. Krueger then told him all of his people had left the Albany area shortly after Carson had gone to Ft Drum. "I'm sending a couple people your way. But they are hours from Albany. Arrival time around 5 AM."

"Thank you," Carson said, not sure how much help they'd be.

Traffic began to creep forward; 13 MPH, 19 MPH, 27 MPH. "Come on, come on, give me 50," Carson begged. Within a mile he got his wish and then some. Not much but some. He paced the car in front of him and his speed fluctuated between

52 and 54 MPH. The rain showed no sign of lessening, but now the speedometer blinked 57, 56, 57, 58, 57, 58.

Drivers were getting their sea legs. Traffic moved a little more smoothly. The traffic to his left, the passing lane moving slower than the right lane. The right lane appeared to be mostly semi-trucks and trailers. Clearly these drivers were used to driving in the rain. Carson stayed in the middle lane, the speedometer now reading 59. He could live with this.

∞

Carson reached his neighborhood with 13 minutes to spare. Just enough time to circle the block and check things out. Not thoroughly, but since he had some time, he'd take advantage of it. He wasn't sure what he might find. Would the Galco be there? Not physically possible.

Would he have a friend waiting? Would there be a note on his door, or maybe a body? Carson pulled to the curb in front of the house and ran to his front door. He found nothing. He raced inside and did a cursory search of the interior. Again nothing. Nothing out of order, except the dishes he'd left in the sink.

When his brain registered that he was alone, his body reminded him of an urgent need. He jogged to the bathroom and peed for almost two minutes. As he listened to the water splash against water, he had a random thought. *How do fighter pilots hold it that long?*

As he pulled up his zipper his home phone rang. He knew who it was but couldn't help looking at the display as he grabbed for it; LIZA.

"You are home, no?" the male voice asked. Before he could respond the connection was lost. *God damnit*, Carson thought. For an excruciating 45 seconds nothing happened and then the phone rang again. Carson answered on the first ring. "I'm here" he shouted.

"That is good," the other man said. The Galco continued. "Do you know Middleburgh?"

"I've heard of it." It was an hour south, not far from Vrooman's Nose.

335

"Good, that is good. About five miles south, on Highway 30, there is a futbol field. Drive past the concession stand and to the creek. I will be there. You are to come alone. I will be watching. If you don't come alone, I kill your lady. Do you doubt me?"

"No." Carson the supplicant said. "Wait...Highway 30, south of Middleburgh." Carson was trying to buy some time. "Is she alright?" Carson couldn't bring himself to say Liza's name. Part of him feared she was dead already.

"That is relative, but she is still breathing. You will see her soon, if you follow my instructions. Be there by 3 o'clock."

"Let me talk to her."

"You are wasting time, 3 o'clock remember no later. But I let you talk to her."

Carson could hear her trying to talk. "Cartthun...Cah, Cahthun."

"It's okay babe, don't. You don't need to say anything. I'm coming for you, I love you. It'll be okay, I promise." Again, he wasn't sure if he could fulfill that promise. But...if he could delude himself then maybe she could do the same?

"3 o'clock, do not be late." The Galco said. The phone went dead again. Did he hang up or did they lose the connection?

Carson's waited, one minute...two minute...three minute... As Carson wondered for the hundredth time if he should get moving the phone rang again. "I'm here." Carson barked after the first ring.

"It's me," said Maggie Post. "We know he called you. What did he say?"

"First, tell me where he is!" Carson said.

"He was in a hamlet called Grand Gorge. It's in the middle of nowhere, in the Catskills." She was referring to the mountain range south of Albany. "I'm surprised he reached you. There's not much cell coverage down there. What did he say?"

"He wants to meet in Middleburgh, at a soccer field, on Highway 30, but I think he meant Route 30. I know I've heard of it but can't place the town." When he stopped talking, he could hear someone typing in the background.

"Hold on, we're checking on that."

Carson then heard Maggie snap her fingers. He was listening so intently it sounded like a pistol shot. She was motivating whoever was in the office at this late hour.

"Here it is. Got a pen and paper?"

"No, wait!" Carson screamed in frustration.

"Calm down, I'm not going anywhere. Take it easy, we'll do this together."

Carson grabbed a piece of junk mail and pulled a pen from his shirt pocket. "Okay, I got it, go"

She read off some coordinates. "You can't miss it. At the only traffic light in town, you'll make a jog to the right and follow the Route 30 south, to the field. It's just over a bridge, and it will be on your left. It's closer to seven miles than five."

"Got it, traffic light, then seven miles south. Thanks."

"You got Fred's truck, right?"

"Yeah, but I was gonna use my car."

"Screw the car, take the truck. It's got one of those newfangled GPS systems. It'll save you from having to look at a map. You've got enough to do. I'm assuming he said to come alone. Can I do anything else?"

"Can't think of anything right now." Carson's mind raced. "Wait…call Investigator Matthews, Ron Matthews, with the Troopers. He's in their Manhattan office. Let him know what's going on, but not where I'm going."

"Okay, I'll find him. Let me know if you think of anything else."

"Call Krueger. Let him know where I'm going. I'll be in Middleburgh long before they can get there. I'm not worried about them getting in the way."

"Then why send them?" Maggie asked.

"Maybe they can fix things, if it goes bad."

"Copy that." Maggie said and hung up the phone.

CHAPTER 55
Middleburgh, NY
July 5, 2001

The clock on the dashboard read 2:49 when Carson saw a light pole, by a concession stand, in an almost empty field. He turned onto a narrow gravel drive that wasn't much more than a goat path. Actually, two goat trails, with a strip of grass and weeds in the middle. It had stopped raining, but the evidence of the storm was everywhere. His headlights reflected off puddles and mud splashed up from depressions.

Carson took inventory of his equipment. His Glock sat in a holster on his right hip, the shotgun was within reach and the cigar box rested against his right thigh.

About 300 yards in front of him a set of headlights flashed on. He couldn't miss them as they were the new High Intensity Discharge lights and threw a blue beam. He accelerated in that direction. The truck began to slide from side to side, in the wet grass. Green confetti flew past his periphery. He hoped he wasn't on the soccer field but didn't care.

About a hundred feet from a barely visible tree line the headlights blinked again and then stayed on. Carson stopped about fifty feet from the boxy SUV. He put the truck in Park and turned off the engine. He left the lights on. Carson held his hand in front of his face to guard against the bright light, of the other vehicle. *It's a Mercedes alright; G class*, he thought. Price tag around $100,000. *This thing's got all the bells and whistles*, Carson couldn't help but think. He climbed from the truck in a slow and measured manner. Hands in front of him. He didn't want to startle the Galco.

"Led me see you gun." The Galco's accent was stronger now. *Is that a sign of fatigue?* Carson wondered.

"What?" Carson asked, stalling for time.

"I say step in front of truck. Led me see you gun. I know you have one. Maybe you have more than one?"

338

Carson did as he was told. Stepping in front of his own headlights he lifted the hem of his jacket. He turned his right side toward the Galco. *Is this how it ends?* Carson asked himself.

"Trow it away, trow the pistol in the weeds. Now!"

"I want to see her, this is just between us. Let her go."

"She here, she go nowhere." At this the Galco cut his head lights. With the driver's door open the dome light was on. Carson could see into the SUV. Liza was in the front passenger seat. He was shocked by what he saw. Her face was a bloody mess. Her lower lip was torn from its mooring and hung like a piece of flank steak.

"Liza, Liza, Babe, I'm here, you'll be okay. Babe look at me, please look at me."

Her head moved, and her chin rose. Carson could now see she was missing some front teeth. She then lifted her duct taped hands and gave him a thumbs up sign. Carson breathed a sigh of relief, *at least she's alive.* The Galco held a large black revolver against her head. The driver's door was open, and he was half in and half out of the SUV.

The blue lights flashed back on and the man barked "Okay, now the gun, trow it to your right. Easy, or she die. If you do as I say she live. I want that. I want to see her watch you die. Beside, maybe if I kill her now you run away and hide. Maybe you coward if she dead?"

What could Carson do? He had to comply. He had to buy more time. With the blue lights on he could no longer see either Liza or the Galco. The bright light formed a solid wall, as opaque as concrete. He had no chance of making a snap shot and hitting the Galco. He was still stalling when his brain screamed *No! Let's get this done, let's get this done.* For almost six hours this bastard had been torturing him. *Let's get this over with*, even if it meant his death. Let's get this done! Carson moved his hand to the gun at his hip. He drew it from the holster and flipped it to his right. He tried to watch where it landed but once it passed out of the cone of light it was lost to him forever.

"Lift your jacket. Led me see your belt. Turn around, all the way, 360. Okay, now you lift pant leg. No ankle holster, I surprised. You Americans seem to like those."

The blue lights were shut off again. The interior dome light showed the Galco was still in the same position, half in and half out. *Damn it*, Carson thought. The Galco stepped from the SUV but remained close enough that the dome light cast a glow on him. With great theatre he made a show of emptying the cartridges from his revolver. The bullets went into a pants pocket and the gun was thrown in the back seat. The Galco then threw a blue Wal-Mart bag at Carson. "Pick it up! We settle this like men!"

Carson opened the bag and found a brand new Rapala filet knife, and sheath. He grabbed the wooden handle and slid it from the sheath. The blade was about eight inches long, about as thin as a razor and just as sharp. Not ideal for a knife fight but dangerous just as well. A weapon with more heft and substance was preferred. Carson felt a knot in his gut. He hadn't done any knife training since bootcamp. Although he carried one for years, he had always used it as a tool; opening boxes, cutting string, etc. Never as a weapon. He tried to recall the lessons given 20 years earlier. All he could remember was hold he knife low, in front and with the sharp edge upward. He knew there was more, but the lessons and memories had been tossed into a dusty corner of his brain, like a neglected yearbook.

"You look confused." The man shouted. "You no like knife. It all store have in stock. I have to leave my favorite knife in you friend."

The Galco left the headlights off and stepped away from the SUV. The lights from Fred's truck provided enough illumination.

"What's your name? It's only right. I should know our name." Carson shouted.

"Me name... me name is Max Weber."

"You're shitting me, right? Doesn't sound very Spanish to me."

"No, I agree. It do not and it was not meant to. I am Argentinian by birth but German by blood. I am proud German and proud Aryan. But I no expect you to understand."

"Yeah, doesn't look that way. All I see is someone that kidnaps little ladies. I bet your momma's proud. You're just an asshole to me, a thuggish asshole." Carson couldn't help himself.

"You forget about her bodyguard. She was not alone when I take her."

"So okay, you're good at sneaking up behind someone. Just a chicken shit, couldn't even look him in the face. Proud Aryan my ass." Carson was trying desperately to get under this guy's skin but couldn't tell if it was working.

Weber stepped in front of the SUV and Carson looked him up and down. The man was about 5 foot 8, with ropey muscles, maybe 180 lbs. He was wearing a skin-tight white T-shirt and a cast on his left hand. A souvenir from Fred's handywork. Carson also noticed the muscles on the left side of the body were slightly more defined. *This guy's left handed. Can I use that to my advantage?*

"Let us do this, enough talk. You want, take your jacket off?" Weber held a twin to Carson's knife, in his right hand. About belt level, with the blade upward.

"No, I'll keep it on." Carson was wearing his ARMY jacket and a sweatshirt under it. He kept these layers on because he hoped it would hide the contours of his ballistic vest. He needed every advantage. Carson had barely finished his sentence when the Galco dodged to Carson's left and parried. He didn't connect, and Carson knew he'd done this as a test. Had the Galco known this was his weak side, and the side of his bad hip? Before the thought fully registered Weber did it again. This time, he moved all the way around him and smashed the cast into Carson's left ear. Stars exploded inside his head. Carson barely acknowledged a pinprick on his right side.

Weber was now in front of Carson. "Diss is no fun. I expect you be better. You move like old lady."

Carson was nervous, and Weber was right. He had barely moved in the time it took the Galco to circumnavigate his body. Carson lunged forward but it was like stabbing at a shadow. One minute Weber was there and then he wasn't. This time he moved to Carson's right. Weber bounced on the balls of his feet and shook his arms out to the side. He showed no signs of concern. He looked more like he was warming up for a volleyball match, not a life and death contest. Carson tried to mimic the same actions and then dodged to the left. His right hand shot out again and again he hit nothing but air. Weber moved again, and Carson slashed at him. Weber again used his cast as a club and smashed it into Carson's right hand. Carson was able to maintain his grip on the knife, but just barely. The pain was intense. Then there was a stinging pain in his left thigh. *Shit!* Then a stinging pain in his right hand. *Fuck!* Blood sprayed from his hand, but the pain was minimal. The blade was scalpel sharp.

Weber hopped backward and let Carson assess his wounds. Before he could stop himself, it occurred to Carson this is exactly what the Galco wanted. Carson saw blood had saturated his pant leg. Weber jogged in place, just out of reach. *This bastard's good, and smart. He's using psychological warfare on me. He wants me to know I'm wounded. And wants me to panic. Get your head in the game. God damnit, for Liza's sake, if not your own. Focus, focus damn it!*

Weber dodged to the right, then the left, then the right, then the right again, and right again. This forced Carson to pivot on his bad hip and wounded leg. His right foot slipped on some wet grass, but he caught himself. It wouldn't do to end up on the ground. When he came to a stop, he felt the bite of the blade in his right thigh. *Shit!* Weber was playing with him and this was confirmed by the man himself.

"I wrong, this is fun. Not a challenge but fun. You die soon Yanqui. I think it will take longer for your woman to die."

Carson tried to respond but couldn't find enough air to power the words. *What the hell?* His right side suddenly hurt more than it had earlier. Try as he might he couldn't get more than half a breath.

"Sucking chest wound," the Galco explained. "You think I no see you wear bulletproof vest under clothes. But vest have no side panels. Iz you too cheap to pay for side panel? You stupid man. No you…you retard. You die soon. Maybe I just stand here and watch. Just like your woman, she watch you die."

At that moment Carson's body felt like it weighed a ton and his legs buckled. His knees bent, and he used his left hand to steady himself and keep his ass off the ground. He was now in a crouch and resembled a three-legged stool; his body leaning to the left. *Get it together, man up, soldier on. For Liza. For Liza!* A story from Nana's recordings flashed into his mind. The story of when Petr jumped up and kicked the bully in the face. Carson tensed his leg muscles and prepared to jump, jump like he was dunking a basketball. *Ready, Ready, Go!*

If this was a Hollywood action movie Carson would have been propelled off the ground with super human strength. The film would immediately switch to slow motion. The audience would then see Carson execute a perfect crescent kick, where the instep of his right foot would connect with the bad guys face and knock him unconscious or kill him. Either way the fight would be over. This is exactly what Carson had pictured in his mind when his feet left the ground. But this was not to be. The oxygen starved muscles and the muddled brain cells couldn't pull it off. His feet made it about knee high before the Galco swept them up and over. Carson lost his balance and fell flat on his back. The vest cushioned his fall but he felt blood squirt from his side.

Weber couldn't contain himself and burst out laughing. The laughing must have deprived his muscles of oxygen as well as he had to lean against a tree. "You are a retard. What the hell was that?"

Carson heard Weber taunt him but Carson's ear, close to the ground, heard another sound. A sound he couldn't quite place. A sound like a fan, and then a sound like a fan on steroids.

343

The Mercedes shot past him. It struck the tree Weber was leaning on. A brief scream was mixed with shattering glass and tearing metal. Then the whoosh of the airbags.

PARABELLUM: When you live in Peace, prepare for War
Jack Nanuq

CHAPTER 56
Middleburgh, NY
July 5, 2001

The driver's door of the Mercedes swung open and then back, toward the vehicle. Then it swung open again. Carson watched as two feet, duct taped together, appeared. Liza's face peeked out from the cab. Caron stared at her. With her busted lips and missing teeth he couldn't tell if she was smiling but her eyes shone with delight.

"Kee, kee, kee-less stard," she said.

"I love you babe," he responded. It took almost all his breath, to utter these words.

"Wuv you, wuv you too."

He watched as she slowly lowered herself to the ground. For someone trussed up like a steer at a rodeo she did very well. Using the side of the Mercedes she was able to stay upright until she almost reached Carson. He slid the knife under him and reached out for her. She fell into his arms. The impact almost made him pass out. He then used the knife to cut her bindings. *Finally, I get to use the knife, on something.* Carson thought.

"Can you walk?" Liza asked. The last word sounded more like wok.

"I can...for you." Carson wheezed. It wouldn't be easy, but he knew he would do it. But it would have to be now. His vision was starting to get fuzzy. *Is this a sign of oxygen deprivation?*

"Lez go," she said as she helped him to his feet. Remnants of duct tape hung from her wrists, but she didn't pay them any attention. With grit, determination and maybe even some heavenly intervention they moved the 12 feet to Fred's truck. She opened the passenger door and then pushed Carson up against the seat. He was spent and it would have been easier to climb Mt Everest than the three feet into the cab. Liza wouldn't quit though. She lifted his right foot off the ground and rested his knee on the frame of the cab. She then tried the same with the opposite leg. But every time she tried to lift it off the ground, he felt like he would fall backward. Both hands were slick with blood and there was no purchase on the leather seats. Every time he tried to grip the the seat his hands failed to work. They struggled like this for what seemed to be hours but was probably only minutes. Liza begged and pleaded with him to work with her. But her voice sounded far off, like in a tunnel.

"Say here, say here," Liza commanded, and she left him. *Did she mean stay here?* Carson wondered. He wasn't going anywhere.

He wasn't sure how much time had passed but he saw the driver's door open and Liza climbed into the cab. As she did so she grabbed the driver's seatbelt and thrust it at Carson. As she moved across the seat, she pushed the cigar box onto the floor. The Mauser flew out and landed under the brake pedal. "Gab hole, gab hole, gab hole. She waved the seatbelt in his face. *Grab hold*, his brain registered. And he did. He looped the webbing around his wrist started to pull himself into the cab. Hand over hand, hand over hand, an inch, then two inches, then four inches. Liza, pulled on his jacket, another four inches. As he grabbed for the steering wheel, they saw it. They couldn't help but see it because the trucks lights were pointed right at it.

Weber was still alive and wiggling out from between the Mercedes and the tree. Carson and Liza could not have been more vulnerable. Carson was laying on the front seat with the mobility of a wounded caterpillar. Liza was kneeling on the front seat and pulling for all her worth. She couldn't repeat her last trick. This truck didn't have state-of-the-art keyless start. Carson had the keys in his pocket. Force of habit.

"Knife, knife, gif me your knife," she pleaded.

"Can't, it's outside. I dropped it on the ground, after I cut your tape. It's outside. There, there". He was pointing with his right hand but not outside. He was pointing to Nana's gun.

"Woaded?" she asked.

"Yes."

Before he finished this word, she was reaching for it. Weber was less than five feet from the truck and had his knife. But he was in rough shape. His left foot was turned the wrong way and he dragged it like an anchor. At four feet, Liza opened up on him. The gun bucked wildly as all ten rounds exited the barrel. She pulled the trigger so fast it seemed like it was an automatic. An almost continuous flame shot from the barrel, like a highway flare. Even after the slide locked open, she kept pulling on the trigger. When the flame died away, she realized the gun was empty. Four of the rounds found their mark and did what they were designed to. He lie dead just a foot in front of the truck; eyes wide open and staring at nothing.

Liza drew on the last reserves of her adrenaline and walked to the body. She picked up the knife and continued to the opposite side of the truck. She slid the blade into Carson's pocket and pulled down. The truck coins and truck keys spilled out. "Moo, moo, moof, gahd damm id, gahd damm-id." With both hands Carson grabbed the steering wheel and hoisted himself into the truck. He pulled his legs into a fetal position as Liza slammed the door. Before Carson could do anything else, she jumped into the driver's seat and pushed him against the opposite door. He wrapped the passenger seat belt around his right forearm to remain upright.

Liza started the truck, threw the gearshift into D and stomped on the gas. The seat wasn't set to her small frame and it was all she could do to see over the dash. Through the patchy ground fog, they raced across the field, with the truck bucking wildly. It was anyone's guess how many of the four tires were on the ground at any given time. The clock on the dash read 3:47 a.m.

Had it really only been an hour since he pulled into this field? Carson asked himself. His vision got fuzzy again. No matter, Liza was in control, they would make it. He was certain they would make it. The speedometer read 52. Yes, they would make it. She would get them to a hospital and all would be good. This thought warmed him. He didn't realize he had been cold, but the thought of rescue warmed him.

Twenty feet from the highway he saw a pair of headlights barrel out of the fog. He then watched mutely as Liza yanked the steering wheel to the right. Self-preservation took

348

over and he shut his eyes. He felt the truck lurched to the right. The impact was bone-jarring. Carson's world went black when the airbags deployed.

EPILOGUE
Ilha da Queimada Grande, Brazil
September 10, 2001

During the flight Carson scanned the horizon from a side window of the Bell 430. They were about 1,000 feet above the waves and their destination was in sight. The island, not much over 100 acres in size, was home to one of the most unique ecosystems in the world.

He then scanned the interior. Every time he was inside a Bell, of any type, he was reminded of the time his father took him on a tour of their factory; when Bells were assembled in Buffalo.

That was about 35 years ago, and now they were built somewhere in Texas. Carson's fascination with helicopters began on this day with his father, and even though he had a piece of one in his leg it, didn't dampen his enthusiasm for rotor wing flight.

Carson took another look at their cargo. A hooded man sat in a jump seat, opposite him. The man wore a pair of dress slacks, a button-down shirt and a one Gucci loafer. *I wonder what happened to the other shoe.* It didn't really matter in the scheme of things. When the clothes were new, they probably cost more than Carson's Subaru. But you wouldn't know that now. Saturated with blood, sweat and other fluids, the pants had been soiled in a very personal way. This man had probably not shit himself since he was a toddler.

As tasteful accessories, the man also sported handcuffs and leg irons.

The man's hands rested uncomfortably in his lap. All the fingernails were missing, and heavy scabs covered the once protected flesh. Some of the fingers were bent at odd angles and the right pinky had been pounded flat. Red and black streaks raced up the arm from this digit. The cabin reeked of gangrene.

The interrogation had been thorough. So thorough the man had volunteered all sorts of info. He had surrendered

350

everything associated with the Galcoes; names, addresses, phone numbers. But he also provided the interrogators with other info. Banks account numbers, hidden assets and even stock tips had poured forth in an attempt to stop the pain.

King of the Galcoes. *Oh how the mighty have fallen!* Carson thought.

Although the face was not visible Carson knew what he looked like, or at least had looked like. Carson was certain the face had received rough treatment. Through the combined efforts of the Interpol, the Agency as well as Carson's contribution it was learned he was the lead dog, so to speak of the Galcos. This was news to everyone outside of his immediate clique. But this man, Dolph Bauer, was well known in other circles. Circles that read Forbes magazine and The Financial Times. Senor Bauer, of Argentina, was a self-made billionaire, and often referred to as The Warren Buffett of South America. Carson wondered why a man like this would bother with the pittance the Galcos earned him. Maybe it was a philosophical thing? Or maybe he got his jollies from sending forth hitmen armed with poison-tainted knives like they were jungle savages. In a few minutes it wouldn't matter anymore. *Let's see how he survives in the real jungle.* The odds weren't in his favor.

The pilot called to Carson on his headset. "Go to channel six. I'm gonna hover over that meadow. I'm not putting down, but I'll get you within 3-4 feet. I don't wanna to pick up any hitchhikers."

"Copy that," Carson responded. He flipped the selector switch to channel six and listened to the automated warning. It was in three languages, but he only understood the English version. He listened to the warnings four times. His smile grew larger each time he heard it. He knew Mr. Bauer would understand every word, regardless of the language. Carson plugged in a spare set of headphones and put them on the prisoner's head. Bauer started bucking and squirming immediately.

When Carson was sure the message was received, he gave the pilot a thumbs up.

As promised the pilot hovered over some short grass. The height was closer to five feet than four, but it didn't matter. The crew chief slid open the door, as Carson wrangled Senor Bauer to his feet. Carson removed the headphones and gave Bauer a push.

"Cargo away," he heard the crew chief yell to the pilot. The aircraft shot for the clouds as the door was slid closed. Carson put the headphones back on and smiled as he listened to the entire message again.

"Atenção! Por ordem da Marinha. Você entrou em uma área restrita. A Ilha da Queimada Grande, também conhecida como Ilha da Serpente, abriga uma das maiores concentrações de cobras venenosas do mundo. Esta área é administrada pela Marinha e nenhum acesso não autorizado é permitido. Repetimos que nenhum acesso não autorizado é permitido."

"Advertencia! Por orden de la Armada. Usted ha ingresado a un área restringida. Ilha da Queimada Grande, también conocida como Isla de las Serpientes, es el hogar de una de las concentraciones más altas de serpientes venenosas del mundo. Esta área esta administrada por la Marina y no se permite el acceso no autorizado. Repetimos que no se permite el acceso no autorizado."

"Warning! By order of the Navy. You have entered a restricted area. Ilha da Queimada Grande, also known as Snake Island, is home to one of the highest concentrations of venomous snakes in the world. This area is administered by the Navy and no unauthorized access is permitted. We repeat no unauthorized access is permitted."

Senor Bauer was not long for this world. He'd been given a death sentence that would be measured in minutes. His means of execution was fitting. *God doesn't like ugly*, Carson thought as he picked a satellite phone. The phone rang four times before it was picked up on the other end. "Lo." said the voice.

"Babe, it's me," Carson paused before adding "Breakfast has been served." The message was coded but the meaning was clear.

"Copy that. Wuv you," Liza replied groggily.

"Love you too. Get some rest. I'll be home soon."

*** THE END ***

Please turn to the next page for the first installment of:
DEPLOYED – THE PARABELLUM PROJECT
And look for the completed project in 2020.

<u>DEPLOYED – THE PARABELLUM PROJECT</u>
By: Jack Nanuq

Chapter 1
Albany, NY
May 2, 2002

Liza Carbon sat on the park bench and looked at her soulmate. He was absentmindedly rubbing a thumb over her left ring finger. Her bare ring finger. "Carson, you're staring again". The thumb stopped.

"Guilty as charged," he responded. Carson Nowak and Liza Carbon had been an item for less than two years, but they had already shared a lifetime of experiences.

"What are you thinking about?" she asked.

"I was just thinking your scars are healing well and should be gone in a year."

"Damnit!" she said. Most women are self-conscious about their imperfections but not Liza. These were battle wounds and she wore them proudly. Sometimes she had even joked "You should see the other guy." The other guy had not fared as well. She hit him with a car and then shot him. She had vanquished evil and, in the process, not only saved her life but Carson's as well.

"I was also wondering how you're fixed for money?" Carson asked.

"I'm okay. I've decided to sell my place in Boca Raton. I'm only there a couple times a year."

"Don't do that, let me help."

"You've helped enough. You've covered all the medical bills. Really...I should have sold it a while ago."

"But the boys love it there."

"The boys are old enough...they can buy their own place. They'll understand or will when I tell them."

"They're gonna blame me."

"Maybe… but it's not your fault. They'll come around. I'm sure I would have sold it even if the incident hadn't happened." She playfully bumped her left hip against his right hip. She felt the familiar Glock sitting there .

The "Incident". That's how they always referred to that night almost year ago. A simple word. That simple word told a story; a story that cemented their futures together. Prior to the "Incident" she had two part-time jobs. She taught math at a community college and also did on-call work, for a government contractor. Liza hadn't been able to work since. She'd been living off savings ever since.

"Let's get married," Carson said.

"No," she said for the hundredth time "we've been through this…it's too soon. Someday…someday…I promise, but not now."

"You're not making sense," Carson said with frustration.

"I know…just bear with me."

"I will, I will…I love you. Don't forget."

"Roger that," she replied.

Carson's cell phone rang and he moved away. Years of clandestine work had instilled this habit. He pulled it from its holster and looked at the display. "I got to take this…its Fred."

"Roger that," she repeated. She then turned toward the activity in the Park. A myriad of contractors, vendors and DPW employees scurried about getting the area ready for the Albany Tulip Festival. The festival had started as a celebration of Albany's roots and its Dutch founders. In recent years it had morphed into more of a carnival; food booths, interspersed with games of chance, interspersed with art vendors.

Tomorrow was the big day. The day a plaque was dedicated to Carson's great-grandmother, Nana. Nana, AKA: Mary Nowak, had been the unofficial Grand Dame of the festival. She was gone now, passing at age 101, shortly after last year's festivities. Over the decades she had donated

355

thousands of bulbs, hours and dollars to the Festival. The flowers were only one of many contributions she had made to the City and its inhabitants. And even though she had devoted so many resources to the Festival it barely registered on her charity barometer. Her true passion had been helping refugees. Refugees like herself who had come to this country with next to nothing.

Nana had arrived in Albany at the tail end of World War Two. She had the clothes on her back, a few French francs, her son and a murder weapon. Liza knew this because she had spent the past 18 months researching Nana's history. The gun had been stored for most of those years and had never again been used in anger, until the night of the Incident.

Liza was pulled from her reverie when Carson stood and said "He's gonna meet us for lunch at 20-Pho-7". Carson then did a couple of deep knee bends to help stretch the muscles in his legs. Both thighs bore signs the knife wounds. And the left hip was held together with titanium pins, but that was from a helicopter crash almost 10 years earlier.

"Sounds great, but I want to take a walk around the Park," she replied.

"Me too. Maybe I can find a velvet Elvis painting?" he joked.

***

As they moved through the light crowd of workers and lookie-loos Carson sensed a nervous anxiety in the air. He knew the sensation would be stronger tomorrow. It had been less than eight months since the attacks on the World Trade Center and the Pentagon. All Americans had been shaken to their core on that day. Now most people behaved with a bi-polar personality. They refused to give in to the terrorists but were certain another attack was just around the corner. This was especially apparent in large groups. It was almost as if everyone had an eye on the ground and an eye toward the sky. There existed an almost collective consensus, "We're going to have a good time, even if it kills us."

A police horse ambled into view and caught their attention. The animal was huge, with a brown body and white socks. It resembled a Clydesdale you'd see on a Budweiser beer commercial. The officer wore a blue and white riding helmet and that appeared to be the extent of his safety gear. The cop appeared to be more ambassador that law enforcer as he deftly navigated the large draft horse through the crowd. He spoke softly to the many kids in the area and kept the animal in motion. Carson marveled at how the two acted as one. He wondered how that bond was formed. Horses were one of the few animals Carson could never connect with, and he had the scars to prove it.

"How do you feel about dogs?" Carson asked Liza. He knew how she felt about dogs, but it was as good a way as any to segue into what he wanted to talk about. Liza gave him an quizzical look and said "silly question. I want one."

"Thought so. Fred…just got a call from Martinez." Alicia Martinez was a former MP, and canine handler. "She's got a mixed breed pup, that might be just what the doctor ordered."

"Yes!" Liza yelled triumphantly.

"She's not sure of its pedigree. It looks to be part Border Collie and part German Shepherd. It's seven months old, really good around women, is housebroken and knows a few commands. She says its sharp as a whip."

"What do you mean she doesn't know its pedigree? Does it have a name?"

"Well, it came from a friend of a friend, and it looks like its daddy was a fence jumper. Of course, it's got a name. You're gonna love it…Mauser."

"You mean like Nana's gun?"

"Exactly."

"Yes," she yelled again, even more excited than the first time. Wow, yeah, I want it."

"Slow down Skippy, maybe you should talk to her first? Besides we can't leave until after tomorrow."

"Party pooper." Liza emphasized this with an exaggerated pouty face. The scar that ran from the left side of her mouth, down to her jaw line, was now pronounced.

Carson brushed a finger along the raised skin. "You'll survive."

"Damn right I will. I got you, I got this..." She slid her hand to the Walther PPK, at the small of her back, "and now I'm getting a dog."

The police horse was drifting in their direction and Carson gently turned Liza away from the animal. He asked, "Can we go to lunch?"

Liza looked to him and in a childlike voice teased him with "Are you afraid of the big bad horsey, are you?"

"Truth be told. Yeah. Can we go now?"

"Okay".

***

Twenty minutes later they were seated across from Fred Hutchinson.

The interior of the small restaurant was festooned with both American and Vietnamese memorabilia. Photos and knickknacks were arranged in a chronology that told the story of the Nguyen family. The patriarch, Nguyen Quang Dong, and his wife were from in rural villages. These photos were in black and white. Then Polaroids of him in his ARVN (the Army of the Republic Viet Nam) uniform. One showed him standing with a group of Green Berets; his dress uniform festooned with medals. Then photos of US Navy warships crammed with refugees. The family and countless others were briefly known as Boat People. Thousands were forced to flee, as the Communists took control of their homeland.

One photo seemed out of place but wasn't. The photo showed Nana and the owner cutting a large ribbon over the front door of this same restaurant. Since 1975 Nana had done much to help the Nguyen family; including providing the financing for this restaurant.

Fred pointed a menu at Carson and asked, "What do you suggest?"

"Everything," Liza and Carson said in unison.

Fred was wearing his everyday uniform. A frayed flannel shirt, sun-bleached Carhartt pants and scuffed work boots. At first glance the average person would think he worked in the trades, maybe a carpenter or electrician. He did work in a trade, but not one most would understand. He was the number two man in a local CIA shop. His office was in a nondescript industrial building. The employees referred to it as, "The Cube."

"I take it from the smile on her face you told her," Fred said to Carson.

"Yeah, it's a done deal. Or it will be when we get to Buffalo."

Martinez had moved there shortly after she left the Army. Her last posting had been Fort Drum, near Watertown, NY. She now ran a kennel and K-9 training center. Her bread and butter was teaching family pets not to pee indoors. But she also trained working dogs.

"Can you tell me anything more?" Liza said with excitement. "And how's she doing?"

"What did Carson tell you?"

"Not much, typical male, treats words like they're expensive."

"That's not fair," Carson said in protest "I told you everything Fred told me."

"Not much to tell really. Martinez has a pup that needs a home and she thought about you. She called me first because she wanted to know if you were up to it. Wait...that came out wrong. What I meant, or what she meant was that with all your surgeries you've had she wasn't sure if it was too much of a burden. She was afraid if she called you direct you would say yes, without considering all the ramifications and responsibilities. Sorry if that sounds harsh but you know her. She couldn't talk long. She had two calls waiting. Says her' phone's been ringing nonstop since 9-11. Somebody heard about her service in Kosovo, and now everyone wants her to train their rescue dogs, or their bomb-sniffing dogs, or their attack dogs. She draws the line at attack dogs. Can't stand the thought of using dogs as weapons."

"Dogs mean a lot to her. And I understand her not calling me direct...and wouldn't expect any less," Liza said in a contemplative tone.

The restaurant's proprietor came to their table. He was dressed in his standard uniform; polished oxfords, pressed gray slacks, a short–sleeved white dress shirt and a thin black tie. This uniform only varied on cooler days, with the addition of a long-sleeved shirt. He walked with a slight limp because half of one foot was left in a rice paddy, near a Viet Cong booby trap.

In a singsong voice Mr. Nguyen announced "Missus gone now, so you pay. I take you money, so order food, not just coffee. I no owe debt to you, like I owe to Madame. You eat today and then I take money." This announcement was directed at Carson. When Nana was alive Mr. Nguyen would never take his money. So Carson never ordered anything but coffee.

The small plain looking man that greeted them was a millionaire, many times over. The owner of numerous restaurants, car washes and apartment buildings. He didn't need Carson's money, but it was his way to make Carson feel more comfortable and more welcome. "I miss her much, she nummer one cussamah, and nummer one friend. How doing you?"

"I miss her too, thank you. Will you join us?"

"You shuu? This no private party? You shuu?"

"Please," Liza chimed in.

"Okay." Mr. Nguyen then barked something in his native tongue, as he took a chair.

A teenager ran out form the kitchen with a tray of spring rolls and a bottle of Johnnie Walker Red. Nguyen slapped Carson on the back and shouted. "Today you spend much money, after today you be nummer one cussamah, and nummer one friend."

PARABELLUM: When you live in Peace, prepare for War

Jack Nanuq

Oh Christ! Carson thought as the proprietor broke the seal on the bottle of whiskey...

ACKNOWLEDGEMENTS:

This project took about five years to complete. During that time a number of people provided invaluable support and assistance.

First, I would like to thank Dr. Peter Arquin. Your stories provided the inspiration and catalyst for this novel. Please forgive my artistic license.

Next, I would like to acknowledge my Beta readers. Your contributions did so much to help polish all the rough edges. You all did so much that I can't single out any one person, so I am listing you alphabetically, not by importance.

> Mary Babb
> Chris Keifer
> Pat Mirza
> Suzanne Morlang
> Mary Mullins
> Ben Stedge

Third, I would like to recognize all those who operate, or have operated, in a clandestine capacity. Thank you for your secret service.

I wish I could list everyone, but alas that's not possible. For those who are not mentioned I will acknowledge your contribution in another way. Thank you all.

PARABELLUM: When you live in Peace, prepare for War
Jack Nanuq

AUTHOR'S NOTE:
This novel is a work of fiction. Names, characters, businesses, places, events, locales, and incidents are either the products of the author's imagination or used in a fictitious manner. Any resemblance to actual persons, living or dead, or actual events is purely coincidental.

ABOUT THE AUTHOR:

Jack Nanuq currently makes his living as a Private Investigator; hence the nom de guere (and no profile photo). Prior this occupation he lived the nine lives of a cat. He has been a teacher, police officer, park ranger, equipment operator, freight handler and even a ranch hand.

He has lived and worked in Egypt, Alaska, Oregon and New York (the State, not the City). He has snorkeled in the Red Sea. Slept on the Nile River and under the Northern Lights (but not at the same time). Walked among grizzlies, bathed in the light of the midnight sun, climbed Mt St Helens, and even jumped out of a perfectly good airplane.

He and his wife live on a small farm near Albany, NY. They share this property with three dogs, three cats, a handful of chickens and two peacocks. He enjoys, outdoor activities, writing, Tae Kwon Do and teaching self-defense.

His favorite mantra is:

Think, Dream, Write, Repeat!

Feel free to drop him a line at:

JackNanuq@aol.com